PENALIZED LOVE

THE CRESTWOOD UNIVERSITY SERIES
BOOK 2

EMERY PAIGE

EMERY PAIGE PUBLISHING

Cover Illustrator and Designer: Andra Murarasu

Editor: Chrisandra's Corrections

Proofreader: EAL Editing Services

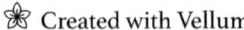 Created with Vellum

For all those who've had to suffer in silence because your illness wasn't visible.
May you always find the strength to keep fighting, even when the world doesn't see your struggle.
Never let anyone make you feel less than you are.

AUTHOR'S NOTE

Thank you so much for taking the time to pick up Penalized Love. This story is so close to my heart because I too suffer from the same illness Isla has and got diagnosed while writing this book. A lot of what she experiences mirrors what has happened to me and I hope I did a good job of representing those that also have this illness.

I did want to take the time to also give you a list of content warnings.

This book isn't dark, but your mental health is important and I want you to make the best choice for you.

Content Warnings:
Mentions of invisible illness related to women's
reproductive health (Polycystic Ovary Syndrome)
Mentions of family abandonment (not on the page)

PLAYLIST

Rush - Troye Sivan

Adore You - Harry Styles

The End - Halsey

golden hour - JVKE

we can't be friends (wait for your love) - Ariana Grande

I Can Do It With A Broken Heart - Taylor Swift

Forget About Us - Perrie

Titanium - David Guetta, Sia

The One That You Call - Mackenzy Mackay

Back to December (Taylor's Version) - Taylor Swift

Expresso - Sabrina Carpenter

Rewrite The Stars - Zac Efron, Zendaya

Don't Stop Believin' - Journey

Die For You - The Weeknd, Ariana Grande

You can check out the playlist on Spotify

1

ISLA

THREE YEARS AGO

We're going to get into so much fucking trouble.

It's the only thought going through my head as I watch my best friend, Selene, check out her reflection in the mirror. She appears incredibly confident, as if this is her moment, while I wonder if I'm on the verge of throwing up. I tug at the hem of my crop top as if that will make the fabric grow longer. I should be vibing along to the playlist that Selene created for us to get ready, but I can't. I swear my stomach is twisting up like a pretzel, leading me to whisper, "I don't know about this. Are you sure this is a good idea?"

"It's going to be fine for the fifty-millionth time," Selene says with a dramatic sigh that almost makes me want to roll my eyes. "You are always worrying. We're going to have the best time ever. Just trust me."

I force my hands to land in my lap, but before I can blink, my fingers fidget with my blonde hair, picking at my ends nervously. There is much more at stake for me than for her.

I glance around Selene's bedroom, trying to distract myself. I take in the delicate fairy lights strung along the walls. They cast a warm, calming glow over her room, contrasting sharply with the unease growing inside me.

Or it could be that I'm starting to get what I know are signs that my period is coming. After complaining to my doctors over the years about my irregular periods and painful cramps, I can't help but feel frustrated that there's still no clear answer as to why. I just have to deal with this, apparently, even though sometimes it leaves me curled up in a ball, unable to do anything but cry.

Instead of that, I choose to focus on the art and pictures on her wall, many of them taken by me. Several of them feature both of us, smiling and carefree. Eventually, my eyes land on the mirror she is standing in front of once more.

Although I haven't uttered another word, Selene stares at me through the mirror, probably sensing the doubt that is still within me.

"Relax," Selene says, turning to face me. Her dark eyes lock with mine. "We're going to blend right in. No one will even know we're still in high school."

"That's not what I'm worried about," I mutter, even though that's definitely part of it. Getting caught underage at a college party would be bad enough. But if word got back to my dad that his daughter was there, he would ground me until graduation. And if I'm being honest with myself, that's if I'm lucky.

"Then what?" Selene crosses her arms, her perfectly arched brow raised in question. "What's up?"

"It's just... if we get caught, you know shit is going to hit the fan. And with my dad being the hockey coach and all..." I trail off, not wanting to voice the rest of my fears aloud.

It will be an embarrassment to him. How could he keep the hockey team in line when his underage child was partying and drinking? His reputation will take a hit. I'll prove I'm not the perfect, responsible daughter he thinks I am. The weight of those expectations feels heavier than ever.

Selene's expression softens, and she sits beside me on her bed, bumping my shoulder with hers. "Hey. I get it, okay? But, Isla, we aren't going to get caught. I promise."

I chew my bottom lip as I consider her words. Selene is right—we've been planning on doing something like this for well over a year before the opportunity presented itself through my older sister, Grace. If we're careful, we can pull it off and return to her bedroom before her parents are any wiser.

I think about the lie I told my parents. The words easily fell from my lips. I told them the only thing Selene and I would do tonight was stay at her place and watch movies. Yet here I am, sitting on her bed, waiting for her to finish so we can sneak out.

With a big, deep breath, I push the guilt that I'm feeling down to the pits of my stomach. It's just one night, I tell myself. One night of freedom before senior year starts and the pressure of everything that comes along with that comes crashing down.

"Fine," I say, finally meeting Selene's gaze. "Everything is going to be fine." I don't believe those words, but she doesn't need to know that.

A grin spreads across her face as she grabs my hand and stands up, pulling me with her. "Yes! We are going to have so much fun tonight," she says as she squeezes my hand.

I force a smile, trying to match her enthusiasm as we grab our purses. I run through a mental checklist to ensure I have everything I need for the night. Selene glances at me before she turns and leaves the room, giving me two choices: follow her or throw myself back down on her bed and toss the covers over my body.

I choose the former.

"Wait, I have another idea," she says before walking over to her closet. She rummages around in her closet for a moment before emerging with a triumphant grin, clutching a large bottle of vodka in her hand.

"I swiped this from the liquor cabinet!" she announces. "This will help you loosen up."

My stomach drops because it might have the opposite effect. "Um, I don't know..." my voice trails off.

"Oh, come on, don't be lame," Selene says, rolling her eyes. "It's just one shot."

I bite the corner of my lip. The guilt is creeping up again. Then again, it's not like it went anywhere. My best friend looks at me like she's daring me to back down.

"Okay, fine. A shot won't kill me," I say, hoping I don't end up regretting those words later.

Selene holds out the bottle for me. "I forgot to bring up cups for us to drink out of... or any chasers. Just take a swig from the bottle."

How sanitary of her.

I eye the bottle warily as the clear liquid gently sloshes inside. This is another bad idea to add to the tally of bad ideas for the night.

"Well, let's fucking chug this thing," I say with a false sense of bravado. I take the bottle from her and raise it to my lips. The smell makes me wince. Squeezing my eyes shut, I take a quick swig, trying not to taste it.

The vodka sears a fiery trail down my throat, and I burst into a fit of coughing. Selene laughs and hits me on the back.

"Wow, that stuff is strong," I rasp out, my eyes watering. I pass her back the bottle while shaking my head. It takes a couple of seconds for me to open my eyes, but I witness her take a long pull without flinching.

"Alright, it's go time!" she announces, tucking the

vodka back into her closet. Taking my hand, she leads me out of her room and into the hallway. My head is already feeling fuzzy from the liquor.

Selene and I tiptoe down the stairs, careful not to make a sound. The coolness of the hardwood floor beneath my bare feet sends a slight shiver shooting through my body. I'm hyperaware of every tiny creak and groan her house makes. Selene's parents announced they were heading to bed about two hours ago, so we are assuming they are fast asleep. Even though their bedroom door is closed at the end of the hall, my heart still races at the thought of it swinging open and us getting caught.

We make it to the bottom of the stairs, and I sigh. Step one is complete.

Selene slips on her sneakers first and heads for the front door. A loud bang comes from upstairs as I reach for my shoes. We both freeze, eyes wide as we stare at each other in the dim light shining in the window from the streetlamp outside.

"What was that?" I whisper, my mind unable to figure out which emotion to feel.

Selene replies, "I'm not sure. Maybe something fell over in my room."

My heart is pounding so loud I swear it will wake up the entire neighborhood. I strain my ears, listening for other sounds or indications that Selene's parents are awake. But the house remains still and quiet.

"Let's just get out of here," I mutter, grabbing my

sneakers and jamming my feet into them. The sooner we leave, the better. This isn't what I signed up for.

Selene nods in agreement, carefully unlocks the door, and turns the doorknob. The door opens with a soft click that sounds much louder than it should. We both cringe as we stand there, almost as still as statues, but no other noises follow.

I step outside into the warm summer air, feeling slightly relieved. Selene gently closes the door behind us, and we exchange a look. Phase two is complete. Now we just have to get to the party without anything else happening.

"See, I told you it would be fine," Selene whispers with a grin as we make our way down the porch steps.

"But we haven't gotten there yet," I remind her, glancing over my shoulder at her house. When she walks away, creating distance between us, I move because I don't want to be left behind.

The streets are relatively quiet as we walk, lit only by the occasional streetlamp. I keep expecting to see a light flick on in one of the houses we pass or to find someone peeking out their window and have them see us. But the neighborhood remains dark, and the only thing that surrounds us is the sound of nature in the summer.

"How much further?" I ask after a minute of silence.

"Just a couple more blocks," Selene replies.

Envy rises in my mind as she pulls out her phone, most likely to confirm the address. Judging by how she looks, she's completely at ease, while I'm convinced I'm about to have a heart attack because of panic surging through my body.

"Didn't Grace mention that the party is at some dude named Tyler's house?"

I nod as she talks about the conversation we overheard my sister having, but I'm only half-listening because I'm scanning our surroundings. We're getting closer to Crestwood University's campus now. I can hear the distant thump of bass growing louder as we cross another street and get closer to a set of homes that I assume are off-campus housing. It would make sense, given that Crestwood's semester hasn't started yet. I don't think students are allowed into the dorms yet unless they have special permission. My stomach twists into another knot. This is really happening. We're about to crash a college party.

2

ISLA

"There it is," Selene says, pointing ahead.

My eyes follow her gaze to see a large, two-story house with several cars parked haphazardly in the driveway. Colorful lights flash in the windows, and I can see shadows of people moving inside. The music is so loud now that I can feel the vibrations in my chest.

We walk up the walkway, dodging red Solo cups and empty beer cans that were carelessly discarded. A group of guys are playing beer pong on a folding table near the garage. Their eyes are on me as we pass. I keep my eyes forward, trying to act like I belong here.

"Hey!" one of them shouts. "Wanna play a round?"

Selene flips her red hair over her shoulder and smiles. "Maybe later!"

I just nod and give a tight-lipped smile, not trusting

myself to say a word. I consider myself lucky that Selene has no issue with pretending that we belong here when it's clear that we don't. At least, it feels that way to me.

We make our way up the front stairs, the pulsating music growing louder with each step. I hesitate at the front door, suddenly feeling more unsure.

It is no surprise that Selene notices. "Come on, let's go in," she says as she hooks her arm with mine. Before I can protest, she swings the door open and practically drags me inside.

The house is packed with more people than I expected, most of them older college guys. They're holding drinks, talking loudly over the music. A few turn to look at us as we enter, and I feel my cheeks grow warm, convinced they know we shouldn't be here.

I barely have time to process it all before I spot my older sister, Grace, standing near a makeshift bar. She radiates confidence while dressed in fitted jeans and a t-shirt. Although we look similar, down to both of us wearing our blonde hair down, she looks as if she belongs here, while I'm sure I look as if my stomach just dropped to my toes.

Why hadn't we thought about her being here, especially since she was talking about the party?

Her eyes widen as soon as they land on me, and I can see her mouth my name. She makes her way over, her expression shifting between confusion and concern. The first thing she asks is, "What are you two doing here?" Her voice is just loud enough for me and Selene to hear over the music.

"Uh... just hanging out." We are so screwed.

"Do Mom and Dad know you're here?" Grace crosses her arms and stares me down.

"No... they don't. And please don't tell them," I plead, glancing toward Selene.

"Come on, it's just one night," Selene says, trying to keep things light.

Grace lets out a sigh, shaking her head. "You know this isn't a good idea, right? If Dad finds out..."

"I know, I know," I interrupt, my nerves already frayed since we came up with this plan. I don't need her to confirm what I already know. "We just... we wanted one night of fun before senior year starts. Please, Grace. I promise we'll be careful."

Grace studies me for a moment before her expression softens. "Alright, but you better be careful. And if anything happens, you call me. I mean it. I'll check on you guys in a bit, and if you leave before I do, text me."

Relief washes over me. "Thanks, Grace. I will."

She gives us a tight-lipped smile, still unsure but willing to let us have this moment. "I'm serious, Isla. Don't do anything stupid."

"I won't," I assure her.

Grace finally steps back, giving me one last warning glance before turning and disappearing into the crowd.

"Well, that was a close one."

I glare at Selene out of the corner of my eye. "But, Isla, we aren't going to get caught. I promise," I say, mocking her because what would she call that?

"It was just Grace, and everything is still fine. Now let's chill and..." her voice trails off for a second. "There's the keg, let's get a drink!"

It's apparent that she still doesn't trust that I will stay, so she grabs my wrist and drags me behind her. We make our way through the crowd, trying not to bump into anyone. I can feel the stares of a few guys as we pass by. My face burns, and the thought of blending into the wall and disappearing becomes more appealing after this and our run-in with my sister.

We reach the keg, and it is just my luck that a group of athletic-looking guys are standing around it and filling their cups. Selene grabs two empty red Solos and hands me one with a grin.

"Ladies first," one guy says with a wink, holding the tap out toward me. I freeze, not sure what to do. Selene nudges me from behind.

"Go on, it's easy. Just pull the tap toward you," she instructs.

I can't help but wonder how she knows what to do, but I don't question her. With shaky hands, I take the plastic tap, fumbling to get it into my cup. Foamy beer splashes over the sides as I fill it. The guys around me chuckle. I pass the tap to Selene while my face heats up in embarrassment.

She fills her cup in one smooth motion. We step out of the way, and Selene turns to look at me. "Cheers," she says, bumping her cup to mine. I take a wary sip of the bitter liquid. It's not great, but I have something to cling to now, so I don't look so out of place.

Selene and I make our way through the crowded living room to find a place to stand and not be in the way. Even with the alcohol flowing through my body, I still feel out of place.

I take a big gulp of my beer and let my eyes dance around the room. Eventually, they land on a guy who is staring in our direction. He's tall, with shaggy brown hair and light-colored eyes. The slight haziness I'm feeling because of the liquid in this cup is making me more brave. I hold his gaze for a moment, admiring the seconds of courage I had before turning my attention back to Selene.

"That guy in the blue shirt wants to fuck you," Selene says, having noticed our silent exchange.

"Selene!" I reply with wide eyes, my actions slightly delayed due to what I'm consuming.

"What? I'm just saying what we're both thinking."

I hadn't been thinking about that, but that isn't the point. Should I say what I've been thinking? All it takes is a millisecond before it slips out of my mouth. "He's cute," I admit.

"Excellent. Maybe I can get him to come over."

Before I can process what is happening, Selene's already waving over the cute stranger across the room.

The all-too-familiar sensation crashes over me like a wave I can't escape. I can't help but wish for the floor to open and swallow me whole.

The guy with the dark blue shirt and jeans makes his way over as I turn and look in the opposite direction. My heart rate picks up, and I take another big swig of beer to gain some more liquid courage. I hate that I can still see him out of the corner of my eye. When he's finally standing in front of me, it's hard to not notice how attractive he is up close. His strong jawline, bright green eyes, and the smirk on his face all make me want to fold like a lawn chair.

"Hey," he says, his eyes locked on mine. "I'm Asher."

"Hi," I squeak out. Smooth. "I'm Isla."

"And I'm Selene," my *former* best friend and now mortal enemy chimes in. "Nice to meet you, Asher. Are you a student here?"

"Yeah, well, I will be in a couple of weeks," he replies. "How about you two?"

I freeze, unsure of how to respond.

"We're starting here this fall too," Selene lies effortlessly. "Just moved into our dorm yesterday."

I nod along, trying to look casual as I take another sip of beer. I can't stand still because of the alcohol and because Asher might find out we are lying.

"Cool," Asher says with a smile. "Which dorm are you going to be living in?"

Crap. Although my father has been a coach here for as

long as I can remember, and I know parts of this campus like the back of my hand, my brain stops once more.

Luckily, Selene saves us again. "Oh, we're going to be in Thompson Hall. How about you?"

I try not to react to her lie. Thompson Hall is the co-ed freshman dorm on the east side of campus. I know this because my dad has complained about the rowdy freshmen living there for years. I bet if I'm admitted to Crestwood, Dad will do everything in his power to make sure I'm not placed there.

"Nice. I'll be in Clarkson once the school year starts," Asher replies. "So what are you planning to study?"

"Photography," I blurt out before I can stop myself. It's not a total lie because I do love taking photos. However, right now, it's more of a hobby than anything. I have my first big gig in a couple of days.

Asher's eyes light up, surprising me slightly. "That's awesome. I'd love to see some of your work sometime."

It takes everything within me to keep my mouth from falling open. He wants to see my work? I force myself to clear my head so I can reply. "Oh, um, maybe. I'm still learning."

"I'm sure you're great," he says with a warm smile that makes my stomach flutter. Or maybe that's the alcohol.

Selene clears her throat. "Well, I'm going to go mingle. You two chat!" She winks at me before disappearing into the crowd.

Great. Now I'm alone with this cute guy who thinks

I'm an incoming freshman. What could possibly go wrong?

"So," Asher says, leaning in closer so I can hear him over the music. "What made you choose Crestwood?"

I take a big gulp of beer to buy myself time as I try to calm the loud thumping of my heart. Or maybe it's the bass from the music. "Oh, you know. Good programs that fit my interests. Nice campus." I'm rambling now, praying he doesn't ask for more details because I can already see where this is going.

Asher nods. "Same here. Plus, the hockey team is awesome. Do you follow hockey at all?"

My heart skips a beat. Of all the topics he could bring up, it had to be this one. "A little," I say carefully. "My dad's kind of into it." That is an understatement.

"Cool. Maybe we can catch a game together sometime this season," Asher suggests.

Did he just ask me out? I take a split second to stop my mind from overanalyzing the situation. Chances are, this is nothing more than a friendly conversation. "Yeah, maybe," I reply. Part of me wants to come clean and tell him why I follow college hockey. But a bigger part is enjoying this fantasy, pretending to be someone else for one night.

We continue chatting, the conversation flowing easily. Asher tells me about growing up in a small town a couple of hours away and a bit about what he's looking forward to as a freshman. I share vague details about my life, carefully avoiding anything too specific. However, I find myself relaxing more. Maybe it's the beer, or perhaps it's just how easy Asher is to talk to.

"Hey, want to get some air?" Asher asks, gesturing toward the back door. "It's getting pretty stuffy in here."

I hesitate for a moment, glancing around for Selene. She's nowhere to be found. "Sure," I reply, surprising myself with how quickly I agree.

Asher leads the way through the crowded living room, holding my hand so we don't get separated. The contact sends a shiver up my spine. We step out onto the back porch, and the cool breeze helps soothe my skin.

While there are a few people nearby, it's much quieter out here. Asher leans against the railing, looking out at the backyard. I stand beside him, aware of how close we are, but pretending I'm not.

"You know," he pauses for a second before he continues. "I'm glad I came to this party tonight."

I turn to look at him. "Yeah?"

He nods, his eyes meeting mine. "Yeah. I got to be introduced to some pretty chill people, but most importantly, I got to meet you."

Before I can overthink it, Asher leans in and kisses me. His lips are soft and warm against mine. For a moment, I'm too stunned to react. The awkwardness fades, and I allow my eyes to close as I melt into the kiss.

Everything about this feels like heaven, and I'm convinced it has nothing to do with the alcohol coursing through my veins. I can taste the beer on Asher's breath, but it doesn't bother me one bit. The world around us drifts into the background until it's just us in this moment.

When we break apart, I'm breathless. Asher looks at me, the intensity of his green eyes forcing me to keep his stare before a small smile appears on his lips. "Wow," he whispers.

"Yeah," I agree, my voice barely above a whisper. My head is spinning, and I don't know if I ever want it to stop. Well, without the beverages I consumed tonight, it probably wouldn't feel this carefree, but right now, I don't care. I want this moment to last forever.

Asher tucks a strand of my blonde hair behind my ear, his fingers brushing against my cheek. "That was really something, Isla," he murmurs.

I feel a pang of guilt in my chest. He thinks I'm a college freshman, not some high school girl sneaking into a party. But how he's looking at me makes it hard to care about the lie.

"I have to agree," I manage to say, trying to sound confident despite the butterflies in my stomach.

Asher grins and leans in for another kiss. This time, I'm ready for it. I wrap my arms around his neck, pulling him closer. His hands find my waist, and I'm forced to stand on my tiptoes.

Suddenly, a loud crash from inside the house breaks the moment we shared. We jump apart, startled by the noise.

"What was that?" I ask, my heart pounding for a different reason now.

Asher shrugs. "Probably just someone dropping something. It happens."

But I can't shake the feeling that something's wrong as my thoughts wander to Selene and the fact that I left her in there. I scan the backyard, half-expecting to see my dad. "Maybe we should go check," I suggest.

Before either of us can react, Selene runs out of the back door, her face pale. We stare at each other for a split second, her eyes jerking to Asher before reaching mine once more. She mouths one word that makes my blood run cold: "Cops."

I swear my heart stops. Cops. Here. Now.

Everything moves in slow motion as panic takes over. I look at Asher, his face filled with confusion. Then my attention turns back to Selene.

"We have to go," I blurt out, grabbing Selene's arm. While hanging out with the boy standing next to me was fun, Selene's my main priority now.

"What's going on?" Asher asks as concern crosses his face.

I can't explain because it will only waste more time. "Cops are here! I'm sorry," are the only words I toss out before Selene and I take off running.

We sprint across the backyard, ducking under a gap in the fence. My legs feel like jelly, and I know it's a mix of adrenaline and alcohol. But we refuse to stop because we can't. If we get caught, my parents will ground me for the rest of the school year.

Behind us, I can hear shouting and the sound of breaking glass. I glance over my shoulder, and I'm met with blue and red lights flashing in the distance. The only option we have is to run faster.

We don't slow down until we're several blocks away, gasping for air in someone's front yard.

"Holy shit," Selene wheezes, doubling over with her hands on her knees. "That was close."

I nod, unable to speak as I try to catch my breath. My mind is reeling, replaying the last couple of minutes when I would rather relive the kiss I just had.

"We should keep moving," I finally say, glancing nervously over my shoulder. "Just in case we're being followed."

Selene nods in agreement, and we start speed walking down the sidewalk, hoping we don't look suspicious. Any buzz I had from the alcohol is fading away more quickly than I would have liked, but it is for the best.

"Well, that didn't go how I thought it would," Selene says after a few minutes of silence.

"Yeah, and it's something we're never doing again," I mutter, almost daring her to respond. When she doesn't, I let out a deep breath because the last thing we need is for us to get into a fight over this mess.

As we turn the corner onto Selene's street, some of the

tension in my body leaves. We've almost made it, and there's not a police officer in sight.

I jump when my phone buzzes in my pocket, and I find a text message from my sister.

Grace: Where are you? Are you okay?

Me: Selene and I are fine. I think we're almost back to her house.

Grace: Good. Text me when you get there.

I make a mental note to contact her when I get back to Selene's room, but as the adrenaline fades, the guilty feeling I'm experiencing only increases. Guilt over lying to Asher. Guilt over sneaking out and disappointing my dad, even if he may never find out about what I've done.

"Hey," Selene says as we approach her front yard. "Are you okay?"

I force a smile. "Yeah, I'm fine. Just glad we didn't get caught by anyone other than Grace. That was way too close."

She nods, but I can tell she doesn't quite believe me. We sneak back into her house as quietly as we left, tiptoeing up the stairs to her room, and she softly shuts the door behind us.

This is a night I won't forget.

3

ASHER

"Are you ready, Bennett?"

I stop tying my skates to glance up at Levi Jamison's big grin. He's already suited up and raring to go, but none of that surprises me. In the short time I've known him, I've learned that Levi's always the first one ready for anything. If all goes well, I wouldn't be surprised if he becomes the captain of the team in a couple years.

"Almost," I reply, finishing up with my laces. "Just need to make sure these are tight enough."

Levi chuckles, leaning against the locker diagonally behind me. "Man, you're wound tighter than those laces on your skates. Relax a little. Everything is going to go fine."

I wish I had his confidence, but there are a multitude of reasons I don't. He seems nice, but his nonchalant attitude about certain things annoys me. The weight of everything riding on my performance here feels like it's fucking me, and not in a good way. But I can't let it show. I force a smile and nod. "Yeah, you're right. I need to shake off the nerves, I guess."

I stand up and stretch, and it feels so good. It is time to get my head into the game and focus on what is about to happen. I had two days to enjoy myself on campus before things got messy, but now it is time to get to work.

My jaw clenches without me realizing it as I get caught up in my thoughts. An excellent performance here means I'm showing the school their decision to give me a full ride isn't in vain. It's my family's ticket out of our financial mess. My mom and little sister are counting on me.

Hell, I'm not even worried about the fact that I will have to sleep in my car tonight because the dorm room I'm supposed to be staying in during the duration of the clinic flooded. The dorms won't be ready for a few days, and I don't have anywhere else to stay.

But nothing is going to stop me from attending this clinic. There is too much riding on me having a successful start to my collegiate career, and I refuse to let it go to waste.

Then why can't I get Isla out of my mind?

It doesn't make any sense. I only met her briefly a couple of nights ago, but I replay the moments we shared on repeat in my mind. And this isn't the time for that.

I shake my head, trying to force the thoughts of her

soft lips and bright blue eyes from my mind. I can't get distracted by a girl, especially someone I barely know. The likelihood that I will see her again, given that we are both going to be freshmen at Crestwood, is high, so I can think about her when that time comes.

I look over toward the locker room exit when I hear loud chatter coming from that direction. Coach Johnson and his staff stroll into the room, and, as expected, all eyes land on them and talking ceases to exist.

Coach Johnson's eyes scan the room before he speaks. "Alright, gentlemen. Thank you for cutting your summer vacations short to spend this time with us. This wasn't a required camp, but being here shows your commitment. This is your moment to show us what you've got. Remember, we're not just looking for skill on the ice. We want to see heart, determination, and the makings of what it will look like once you start working together as a team."

I nod along to his words as if he and I are talking together one-on-one. I take a second to glance around the room and notice that everyone else is also focused on our coach. We're all here for the same reason: to prove ourselves worthy of wearing the Crestwood hockey jersey.

"Alright, let's hit the ice!" Coach Johnson's booming voice sets us all in motion.

Levi ends up next to me as we file out of the locker room with our gear, but this time he doesn't say a word. I wonder if the nerves are getting to him now too.

I feel at home when my skates touch the ice, although this arena is still unfamiliar. This is where I belong. I belong here because I've been working toward this for most of my life. I have to show my family that all the sacrifices that we've made aren't in vain.

Coach Johnson's whistle pierces the air, and all eyes are on him once more. He starts barking out drills, and suddenly, we're in motion, following his directions in order to not make today's session even more brutal than it needs to be.

I push myself harder with each drill, feeling the burn in my muscles and the weight of Coach Johnson's stare on me. Sweat trickles down my back, but it doesn't matter. I'm here to prove to myself and everyone else that I deserve to be here.

We move into scrimmage drills, and I find myself matched up against Knox Sanchez. I haven't spoken to him much since we arrived, but based on the stern look on his face, it's like he hates everything about me. Good. I always enjoy having a challenge.

We face-off, and I win the puck, driving it down the ice. I can practically feel Knox on my ass, but I outmaneuver him, faking left before cutting right. I line up my shot and send the puck flying into the top corner of the net.

"Nice one, Bennett!" Coach Johnson calls out.

A small thrill runs through me at his praise, filling me with another burst of adrenaline. However, I know that one wonderful play means nothing. I need to keep this up.

As the scrimmage continues, I push myself harder, even though my lungs feel like they are on fire. Knox is relentless, and I'm growing to respect him on the ice. We clash again and again, neither of us willing to give an inch to the other. The stress of all of this disappears, and now it's becoming exhilarating and fun. That is, until the whistle blows.

"Switch it up!" Coach Johnson says. "Bennett, you're with Jamison. Sanchez, take the other side with Dalton."

I skate over to Levi, who's grinning despite the sweat pouring down his face. "I told you everything was going to be just fine. Ready to do this?" he asks, bumping his shoulder against mine.

"Let's do it."

Before long, we fall into an easy rhythm. This leads to us beginning to anticipate each other's moves. We're vibing, and I know that with time, it'll seem as if we've been playing together for years.

I spot an opening and call out, "Jamison, cross!"

Without hesitation, he sends the puck sliding across the ice. I catch it on my stick, spin past Sanchez, and fire it into the net. The satisfying swoosh of the puck hitting the back of the net is music to my ears.

"Now that's what I'm talking about!" Coach Johnson's approval echoes through the arena. "That's the kind of teamwork we need!"

As we skate back to position, I catch a glimpse of movement in the stands. I do a double take when I spot a familiar face in the crowd. Isla. And she's holding a camera in her hands. Isla. She's here, capturing every moment of our clinic.

For a split second, our eyes meet. I see a flash of recognition as her eyes widen, and every emotion I can think of crosses her features. Her face becomes pale, and I wonder if she's about to faint before she ducks back behind her camera. The memory of our kiss floods back, threatening to derail my focus.

"Bennett!" Coach Johnson's comment snaps me back to reality.

I shake off the distraction, forcing myself to concentrate on everything but her. But as the practice wears on, I can't help but feel hyperaware of Isla being here and what it could mean.

By the time Coach Johnson blows the final whistle, my body has been drained all of its energy. However, I'm still happy because of a job well done. Or so I think. We gather around him to listen to what he needs to say before dismissing us.

"Good work today, gentlemen," he says as he looks at each one of us. "Hit the showers. We'll review the footage tomorrow morning."

As we head off the ice, I catch up with Levi and whisper, "Think we all made a good impression?"

He turns his head to look back at Coach Johnson. I

glance behind me and find the man in question, deep in conversation with his assistant coaches. "We should have, but I have nothing to base that on. The feedback he gave was constructive criticism, but it still felt pretty positive."

I agree, but I don't say anything as we head into the locker room. The hot shower helps ease some of the tension in my muscles, but my mind is still on the whirlwind I just experienced. As I'm drying off and putting on my boxers, I hear someone shout my name.

"Bennett, a word when you're dressed."

My stomach drops as I recognize Coach Johnson's voice. Did I mess up somehow? I throw on my clothes, ignoring the curious glances from the other guys. When I step out of the locker room, Coach Johnson is waiting with a woman I assume is his wife and... Isla. My heart rate kicks up again, but for an entirely different reason.

"Asher, I'd like you to meet my wife, Molly, and my younger daughter, Isla," Coach Johnson says, gesturing to each of them.

I force a smile and pretend like I'm seeing Isla for the first time. "Nice to meet you both."

Isla avoids all eye contact, and I don't blame her. "Hi," she mumbles.

I watch as she briefly closes her eyes and holds her stomach before she looks at her father. Asking her what is wrong seems inappropriate, so I don't.

"Isla's somewhat shy at times, but she's here taking photos for the team," Coach Johnson explains, oblivious to the tension between us. "She'll be a senior in high school this year."

"Dad. Stop."

Wait, what? Did he just say high school? I thought she was an incoming freshman like me. Oh God, I kissed Coach Johnson's high school daughter. I'm fucked.

"That's... great," I stammer, trying to keep my face neutral.

Mrs. Johnson smiles warmly. "We hear you're having some housing issues on campus. We'd be happy to have you stay with us until it's sorted out."

I blink long and hard because I'm shocked. "Oh, uh, that's really kind of you. Are you sure it's not an inconvenience?"

"Not at all." Coach Johnson's words leave no room for argument. "Consider it done. Grab your things, and we'll head home."

As I turn to walk back into the locker room to get my gear, I catch Isla's wide-eyed look of panic. It mirrors how I feel. How the hell are we going to survive the next few days under the same roof with everything that has happened?

As I grab my things, Levi shoots me a questioning look.

"Everything okay?" he asks.

"Yeah," I mutter. "Coach is letting me crash at his place for a few days until the dorms are ready."

Levi's eyebrows shoot up. "Seriously? That's cool of him. You could have also stayed with me at my house."

"Yeah," I say, unsure how I should feel instead of being thankful. "It'll be fine. Thanks for the offer. I'll see you tomorrow."

I sling my bag over my shoulder and walk back out to where the Johnsons are waiting. Coach pulls me to the side before I can reach his family and says, "Ready to go?" he asks.

"Yes, sir," I reply. "I'll follow you in my car if that's alright."

"That's fine, but I want to speak to you about something first."

I swallow hard and nod because forming words right now isn't possible.

"Since you'll be living under my roof for some time, I'm going to tell you this once. Stay away from my daughters or there will be consequences. Understood?"

My heart pounds against my ribs as Coach's words sink in. "Of course, sir," I say, and my voice sounds strained even to my own ears. "I understand completely."

Coach's eyes stay on mine, daring me to break eye contact. I assume he's also trying to determine whether I'm lying to his face or not. In my head, I'm praying he can't see the guilt written all over my face. Because I've already kissed Isla, although that was before I knew she was his daughter. After what feels like an eternity, he gives a curt nod.

"Good," Coach says. "See you at my house."

As we walk toward the parking lot, I can't help stealing glances at Isla. She's still doing everything she can to not look at me, and I should be doing the same. However, I am fighting the urge to say something, anything, to break the tension, but I know this isn't the time or place. Especially after Coach's warning.

Next thing I know, I'm in my old Honda, following the Johnsons' SUV out of the parking lot. I can't help but wonder what the hell I have gotten myself into and how interesting the next few days are going to be.

4

ISLA
PRESENT DAY

"Home sweet home," I mutter to myself as I pause the true crime podcast I'm listening to. I thank the flight attendants and pilots just before I step off the airplane. I adjust my bookbag as quickly as possible to better manage the weight on my back, walk past the gate, and head toward baggage claim. The faster I got out of here, the better.

How fast I can get out of here depends on how much my body is willing to cooperate with me. That's why I'm standing in this airport, anyway.

The trek to baggage claim doesn't take long, and I find my parents standing there just as quickly. I'm somewhat surprised to see Dad there at all, given his busy schedule coaching hockey, but it's the one tiny bit of happiness I have given the situation. Having both of my parents here means the world to me. I put a smile on my face and wave, bracing myself for our reunion.

"Isla!" Mom rushes forward, pulling me in a hug that threatens to squeeze the life out of me. "How are you feeling? Was the flight okay? Do you need to sit down?"

I resist the urge to roll my eyes, although I understand her overreaction. "I'm fine, Mom. Just tired."

Dad gives me a knowing look and rescues me from Mom's embrace. "Let's get your bags and head home. You look like you could use a nap."

He's not wrong about that. Although I'd dozed off somewhat on the plane, there's nothing like a warm bath and lying in my bed to make me feel better. Or so I hope.

As we wait for my luggage, I can't help but feel sad and disappointed with myself. I thought my return to Crestwood would go differently. Hell, I planned to fly home in December, and yet here I am, back stateside a few months early with a body that feels like it's betraying me.

Dad moves forward to grab my bags as they appear on the carousel. As I reach out to help, Mom's hand on my arm stops me.

"Let your father handle it, sweetie," she says softly, "You shouldn't strain yourself. In fact, hand me your bookbag, so you don't have to carry that either."

I bite my tongue, holding back the response that I want to make because I know what she's saying is coming from a place of love. However, that doesn't stop my frustration, which continues to build. I can pick up a suitcase, for crying out loud. But as I watch Dad snatch my over-stuffed suitcases off the belt, I admit that maybe she has a point.

I hand over my bookbag, and my parents and I make our way through the airport and out to where they parked the SUV they bought several years ago. Dad pops the trunk while Mom makes her way to the back passenger-side door.

"I brought a blanket, pillow, and some snacks in case you wanted something for the ride home," she says as she places my bookbag on the seat.

I walk around to the other back door and open it so I can stare at her. "Mom, the airport is, like, twenty-five minutes from our house."

"You might need something in that time."

I shake my head and take my time getting into the vehicle. For now, I feel okay, but who knows how quickly that will change.

As we pull out of the airport parking lot, I lean against the window, watching the familiar scenery that showcases we're on our way home. The fatigue is already settling in, but I don't want to fall asleep because we'll be home soon enough. I try to focus on what's outside my window instead of the dull ache in my lower abdomen.

"How are you feeling?" Mom asks for what feels like the hundredth time since we left the airport.

"I'm fine, Mom," I reply, trying to keep my voice neutral. "Just tired." That buys me some time before she asks again.

As we ride along, I spot the familiar sign for Crestwood University. All I can do is sigh as my stomach does a little flip because of the strange turn of events that has led me back here.

A few months into my high school senior year, I decided I wouldn't attend Crestwood University the following fall and instead went to NYU. This funny thing called life has shifted my plans entirely, forcing me to come back to Virginia during the middle of the school year so that I can be close to home while figuring out what is wrong with me.

As we pass the campus, I think about all the what-ifs and could-have-beens. What if I'd just stayed here in the first place? Would things be different now? Would I still be dealing with my body deciding that now is the time to fight against me?

I shake my head because the thoughts are ridiculous. There is no use in dwelling on the past now, and whatever is going on with my body could have happened at any time or anywhere. I'm here, whether I like it or not, and I'll have to make the best of it.

"Isla, I got your room ready," Mom says, twisting in her seat to look back at me. "I thought you might want to rest when we get home, so I made sure everything was all set up for you."

"Thanks," I mutter. I'm not in the mood for conversation, but I don't want to appear ungrateful. My parents don't have to do any of this for me, and I'm grateful for my support system.

"Grace also asked how you were doing." I know Mom is trying to keep the conversation going to help with the awkwardness of everything.

"I know. She sent me a text last night." And that is all I offer because there is nothing else I want to say.

Surprisingly, the rest of the ride back to my childhood home is quiet. Once Dad pulls into our driveway and cuts the engine, Mom is out of the car and opening my door before I can unbuckle my seatbelt.

"Careful," she says as she lingers nearby while I climb out of the SUV. "Don't overexert yourself."

I bite back a sarcastic retort. "Mom, I'm okay. Seriously."

"We'll get you settled in, and then your mom and I will leave you alone for a while," Dad chimes in.

That sounds all right to me. We go to the front door together, and we are immediately greeted by Bella, our golden retriever. Her golden coat shines in the light, her tail wagging so fast it's almost a blur. As if sensing that I need the most attention, or perhaps because it's been a while since she's seen me, Bella comes to me first, nudging my hand with her nose. Her boundless energy is something I truly missed while I was abroad.

"Hello, old girl," I say as I slowly bend down to greet

her. She gives me several kisses, and I can't help but laugh. She knows exactly what I need.

Once we finish our greeting, I stand up and notice the familiar scent that can only be described as home greets me. Mom or Dad must have put dinner in the slow cooker, and whatever it is smells amazing. It reminds me of all the times as a kid when Mom would fix dinner this way because we were always on the go between my dad's schedule and the activities Grace and I took part in.

"We'll bring your bags up in a bit," Mom says, already heading for the kitchen. "Why don't you go lie down? I'll bring you something warm to drink. Maybe tea?"

"Actually, I think I'm going to take a bath first. Is that okay?" I answer.

"Of course." Mom pauses for a second. "Do you need any help?"

I shake my head, already heading for the stairs. "No, I've got it. Thanks."

I make my way upstairs to my room, fighting the urge to collapse onto my bed. It's almost like a time capsule from when I was in high school. Posters of my favorite bands and photography awards still cover the walls. A picture frame sits on the nightstand with a photo of Selene and me, both of us smiling without a care in the world. Behind it is a secret I've been keeping. It's an older photo of Asher and me, from when we were happy and in love.

At first, I had placed it there as a symbol of our relationship hiding in plain sight. Now, it's just something I never had the courage to get rid of because it was such a cute photo. Not that any of that matters now.

Overall, I can't help but feel a strange mix of nostalgia and discomfort, as if I've stepped back into a version of myself I thought I had moved on from.

Instead, I walk toward my bathroom and am thrilled to see that Mom also restocked everything there. With a heavy breath, I lock the door behind me and turn the faucet on.

As I wait for the water to fill up, I catch my reflection in the mirror. Dark circles under my eyes, skin paler than usual. The messy ponytail I put my hair in before I left Italy is still intact. I look as exhausted as I feel.

I rub a hand across my chin and feel the stubble. The more pronounced hair on my face makes me want to cry. I do my best to hide it, but having to shave so often just to not feel self-conscious sometimes feels like a job in itself. Sure, it only takes a minute, but it's another checkmark on the list of things that make me feel broken. I open the brand-new razor Mom left me and get to work removing the hair as a tear slides down my face.

I watch myself in the mirror and think about the first time I noticed it. I was twelve, maybe thirteen, and I wondered why my face didn't look as smooth as the other girls'. Back then, I tried to pretend it didn't bother me, but it did. It still does.

Once I'm done, my skin feels smooth, but it doesn't

bring me much comfort. It's a temporary fix for something I wish I didn't have to deal with at all.

I toss a rose-scented bath bomb into the water. Once the water is at my desired depth, I peel off my travel-worn clothes and sink into the warm water, hoping it will soothe the aches and pains coursing through my body.

I close my eyes, trying to focus on relaxing and smelling the scent of roses. But my mind keeps drifting back to the whirlwind of the past few days. The sudden, intense pain that had me doubled over in my room in Rome. The frantic calls to my parents and being taken to the hospital. And then, before I knew it, I was on a plane back home.

A sharp cramp in my lower abdomen makes me wince. I take a deep breath, willing the pain to go away. This isn't how I pictured starting my junior year of college. I was supposed to be exploring Europe, learning more about its art and culture. Instead, I'm back in my childhood bathroom, trying to calm the war going on within me.

After soaking until the water turns lukewarm, I dry off and change into my comfiest pajamas. When I open the bathroom door, the smell of chicken noodle soup greets me. That must be what is in the slow cooker. My stomach growls, reminding me I didn't eat on the plane.

I spy my suitcases sitting near the end of my bed, informing me that my parents brought my things up for me. I debate whether I want to go downstairs to eat at the dining room table or stay here to eat in bed. Eating in bed sounds too good to resist, so I find my phone in my book-bag. I turn off airplane mode and quickly text my mom to let her know my decision before crawling under the covers.

I've barely settled in when there's a soft knock at my door. "Come in," I call out, wincing at the slight tremor in my voice.

Mom and Bella enter my room. Bella hops on my bed and gets comfortable near my feet while Mom is balancing a tray with what looks like a steaming bowl of soup, a mug of what smells like chamomile tea, a small plate of crackers, and some medicine. "Here's dinner," she says, setting the tray on my nightstand.

"Thanks for bringing it up for me," I say, genuinely grateful. The aroma of the soup makes my stomach growl again.

She hovers for a moment, clearly wanting to say more. "No problem. Do you need anything else? Extra pillows? Another blanket?"

I shake my head. "No, I'm good. Really."

She nods but doesn't move. "Okay. I'll let you rest. Let me know if you need anything else."

I force a smile. "I will, Mom. Thanks."

Finally, she leaves, closing the door behind her. I let out a long breath, reaching for the soup to get something in my stomach before I take the medication. As I eat, I scroll through my phone, seeing messages from my friends who are still in Rome, asking how I'm doing. I swallow a heavy lump in my throat as I realize what my leaving caused. My eyes fill with tears as I think about the fact that I won't be returning.

I set my phone aside, unable to muster up enough energy to reply. The soup is soothing but doesn't stop the dark thoughts surrounding me. I cannot express enough how grateful I am for my parents' care, but being back in my childhood room feels like a step in the wrong direction.

My phone buzzes again as I finish my meal and take the medication. This time, it's a text from Selene.

> Selene: Are you home yet? I hope you had a good flight.

I hesitate, my thumb hovering over the keyboard. Part of me wants to put the phone down and ignore her message for now until I feel more like myself.

I stare at it for a while, debating if or how to respond. Finally, I find the words.

> Me: Just got home. Exhausted. Talk tomorrow?

> Selene: Of course! Get some rest. Call me when you're up for it. 🖤🖤

I smile faintly at her response. Selene has always been good at reading my moods, even through text, and since she knows as much as I do about my condition, I knew she would understand. I set my phone aside and sink deeper into my pillows, letting out a long sigh.

I close my eyes, willing sleep to come, and when it finally does, the only thing I dream of is finding answers to the medical questions that are burning a hole in my soul.

5

ISLA

My hand flies to my chest as I'm jolted awake. It takes me a second to calm my racing heart. All I can hear is the blaring sound of my phone alarm coming from my nightstand. I've been sleeping in later since I returned from Italy, but I need to get up early today. It's the day I've been waiting for—one I've "affectionately" referred to as D-day, short for Diagnosis Day.

I groan as I stretch my arm out to stop the loud noise. As I sit up, a wave of nausea hits me, forcing me to stop my movements and take deep breaths.

Slowly, I swing my legs over the side of the bed and stand up. The room spins for a moment, but I close my eyes and hold myself up against the wall. A few more measured breaths do the trick, and I make my way out of my room.

I walk into my bathroom and splash some cold water on my face, hoping it'll wake me up and calm me down. It doesn't work, but at least I feel more human.

Or something like that.

With a sigh, I start getting ready for the day. Every movement feels like a chore, but I force myself through the motions because I've been waiting for this moment. I need answers. As I'm pulling on one of my favorite sweaters, I hear my mom's voice coming from what I assume is downstairs.

"Isla? Are you ready?"

"Coming," I reply quickly. I'm so ready to get this over with.

I grab my phone and take one last look in the mirror to make sure I look presentable. Even though I've been up for at least twenty minutes, I still look exhausted. The happiness I experienced living in Italy for the short time I was there is long gone. In its place are tired eyes that wish I could be anywhere but here.

You can do this.

The words do little to psych me up, but it is better than nothing.

I head toward the stairs and see my mom and Bella waiting near the front door. Mom has her purse and car keys already in hand. "There you are. Ready to go?"

I nod, not trusting my voice. There are a lot of thoughts coursing through my mind, but I don't trust myself enough to voice them appropriately. All of this is a lot to take in and deal with, and if I'm being honest with myself, I haven't begun to process most of what has happened.

"I stuck a couple of granola bars in my bag in case you get hungry, and I grabbed your wallet off the counter," Mom says as she opens the front door. Thank goodness one of us is thinking straight. I pat Bella on the head, telling her goodbye just before we leave the house.

The car ride to my new doctor's office is mostly silent, save for the low hum of the radio. After having several tests run and an ultrasound done already, I'm not all that enthusiastic about going back for the results. While my last couple of visits have gone fine, I don't have much hope. This isn't my first rodeo with doctors trying to figure out exactly what is wrong with me, so I have to say my expectations are pretty low. Thankfully, Mom doesn't try to engage in small talk because there is nothing she can say that will distract or make me feel better. Instead, I stare out the window, watching my hometown fly by. Being left to my own thoughts is all I want right now.

We pull into the medical center's parking lot, and Mom turns off the car. For a moment, we both sit there, neither of us making a move to get out.

"You ready?" Mom asks softly.

I glance at her and see her hand hovering over the door handle. "As ready as I'll ever be," I reply. That is such a lie. My stomach is tied in so many knots, and I can't tell if it's from the news I'm going to get or from the illness that has been plaguing me.

We step out of the car and walk into my OB/GYN's office. After checking in, I notice that the waiting area is quiet, with just a few other patients sitting in the room. I sink into a surprisingly soft chair while Mom sits beside me on a couch. I now more than ever appreciate that my doctor is trying to make her practice a relaxing and calming space because I'm anything but. My leg bounces as I wait and try to think about the results and how my doctor might deliver them.

"Isla Johnson?" a nurse calls, and I stand up faster than I should have.

Mom squeezes my hand, and I look down at her. "Want me to come with you?"

I hesitate for a moment, wondering which option to take. "I... I want you to come in with me."

Mom nods, and soon, we're following the nurse down a long hallway. As we reach a door marked "Exam Room 3," she gestures for us to enter. We take our seats, me in the examining chair and my mom in a regular chair nearby. The nurse takes my vitals before announcing that Dr. Patel will be in a few minutes. I pull my phone out to give myself something to do while we wait.

A few minutes later, Dr. Eva Patel enters, her kind smile doing little to ease the knot in my stomach that has only grown in size. "Hello, Isla. How are you feeling today?"

I force a weak smile. "A little nauseous, but I guess I'm more nervous than anything."

She nods, and I can feel the sympathy in her gaze. How bad are my results, or am I just overthinking everything? I watch as she takes a seat before pulling up my file on her tablet.

Dr. Patel clears her throat and says, "I understand. Let's review your test results, shall we?"

I choose to stare at the woman who is about to reveal my fate. Dr. Patel reviews the results on her tablet. Her expression gives nothing away, and I'm unsure of what to think. Mom reaches over and squeezes my hand, silently offering her support. The seconds that it takes Dr. Patel to speak feel like hours.

"Isla," Dr. Patel begins, her voice gentle yet unwavering, "your blood test results and your ultrasound show that you have Polycystic Ovary Syndrome or PCOS."

The words hit me like a ton of bricks. It feels as if my world is crashing down around me, though all the while, relief floods my veins. We have an answer? It's PCOS? I've heard of it before but never gave it more than a passing thought. This isn't supposed to happen to me. My mind races with questions as I struggle to keep myself from breaking apart.

A single teardrop falls from my eye. "Wait. You're actually able to diagnose me? We know what's wrong with me?"

Dr. Patel reaches over and takes my hand. "Yes, we are. Based on what you've shared with us in your intake chart, I'm so sorry it took this long for you to find the answer that you were searching for."

Another tear falls and it is quickly followed by more. "You believe me."

"Of course I do," Dr. Patel says as Mom comes over to hug me.

Thankfully, Mom is able to talk for me because I've started sobbing into her sweater. "We've been to appointment after appointment trying to figure out what was going on with her body, and now we finally know. You don't know how much of a relief it is. We now know what we are fighting against."

I know there is no way I could have said it better myself.

"I'm glad that I've helped," Dr. Patel says.

"You really have. What... what does it mean?" I ask after I finally pull myself together. My voice is so quiet that it is barely above a whisper, and I wonder if she even heard me.

Mom has moved back to where she was before but grabs my hand once more to squeeze it tighter. I'm so thankful I told her I wanted her to come back here with me.

I still am trying to process that I was believed and that

we now have an answer about why I feel the way I do sometimes.

Dr. Patel explains the condition, but her words blur together as I process the news. She mentions irregular periods, hormone imbalances, and potential fertility issues down the line. My fertility isn't something I've focused on, and now I'm being forced to. I can feel the tears welling up in my eyes again as she continues to talk to us.

I look over at Mom and see she's on the verge of crying too. She's trying to be strong for me, but she can't mask the concern on her face.

"Is there a cure?" I ask, my voice trembling.

Dr. Patel shakes her head. "Unfortunately, there is no cure for PCOS, but there are treatments available to manage the symptoms and reduce the risk of complications."

She discusses various options, from lifestyle changes to medication, but my mind is reeling. Nothing is making sense, yet in a way, it all does.

As the appointment comes to a close, Dr. Patel gives me her recommendations for dietary changes and some medication that I'm nervous to take but will try if it can help me feel better. We can pick up the prescription on the way home, and I can see Mom already making notes about what I should and shouldn't eat.

I leave the doctor's office with Mom in what can only be described as a daze. We walk back to the car, and once we fasten our seatbelts, Mom doesn't bother turning on the engine. Instead, we sit there in silence, both of us lost in our thoughts. The reality of my diagnosis is slowly sinking in now that I'm away from prying eyes, and it's filling me with fear.

"Mom," I whisper, my voice cracking, "I'm scared."

She reaches across the console and pulls me into a tight hug. "I know, baby. I know. But we'll get through this together, I promise."

I lean into my mom's embrace, letting the tears I've held back finally fall. Her arms give me a smidge of comfort after the news I've just received, and I don't take it for granted for a second.

After a few minutes, I pull back, wiping my eyes with the sleeve of my sweater.

Mom starts the car and thankfully turns on the radio to fill the silence I know will be present during our drive. I watch as she navigates the vehicle out of the parking lot before I speak up. "Where are we going?"

"I was thinking of the pharmacy, and then I can drop you off while I go grocery shopping."

That is silly. She'd have to go past the grocery store to drop me off at home and then go back. "I'll go with you. I should probably get out of the house, anyway."

Mom glances over at me and gives me a small smile. "Great. And we can take it as slow or as fast as you want to."

Thankfully, our adventure out and about doesn't last

long, and soon, I'm helping Mom bring in the food she bought. Tucked inside one bag is the medication that I've decided to start taking, though it's been weighing down on me the more I thought about it.

Everything is going to be fine.

I repeat the words to myself over and over, like a mantra that needs repeating. It will be okay because we have a path forward, and we will sort everything out in time.

"Isla, honey, why don't you go rest for a bit?" Mom suggests, her voice laced with concern. "I can finish up here and then get some breakfast ready."

That sounds good to me. "Thanks, Mom."

I grab the prescription bag and head upstairs to my room. As soon as I close the door, I sit on the edge of my bed and stare at the bag in my hands.

With a deep sigh, I open it and pull out the medication. I read the label repeatedly as I'm trying to figure out when I should take the first pill.

A soft knock on the door pulls me from my thoughts. "Come in," I call out.

Dad enters my room, and I'm confused by his appearance. What is he doing here? He hands me what looks to be a Greek yogurt parfait with berries and nuts before he sits down beside me.

I clear my throat. "Not that I mind you being here, but why are you home?"

"Came home to check on you under the guise of grabbing lunch."

I can't help but chuckle. It's way too early for lunch.

"Thanks, Dad," I say softly, taking the parfait from his hands. "You didn't have to come all the way home, though."

He shakes his head, a gentle smile on his face. "Nonsense. You're my daughter, and I want to be here for you. Plus, there's something else I wanted to talk to you about."

"Oh?" I bring the spoon up to my mouth. I'm ready to devour this whole parfait and then relax in bed.

"Have you thought about what this means for school?" Dad asks.

I drag my eyes up to meet his. Of course I have because I hate being behind. I want to graduate on time, but I'm not sure how much I'll be able to do until my health improves.

"I don't know what I'm going to do about it. The semester has already started, and I'm supposed to be in Italy right now."

Dad clears his throat, a hint of a smile tugging at the corners of his mouth. "Well, I pulled some strings, and if you want to, you can transfer to Crestwood University for the semester to continue your studies. I know it's not NYU but it allows you to be closer to home as you get better."

Those words are the last thing I expected him to say. "You're kidding."

"I'm not. Given the circumstances, it would be a good

option for you, but we can look into other options if that isn't what you want."

My mind races as I think of what my life would be like if I attended Crestwood. After all, at one point, it was my dream school. Some people would hate to attend the school where their father works, but it was always my dream to go there. At least, it was until my senior year of high school. That change was due to a certain someone who plays on the hockey team here. I had started to imagine being here with that someone, cheering him on at every game. Then that person broke my heart when he said our relationship wasn't working out for him and he thought I deserved someone better.

This same someone I've been trying hard not to think about since I got back. Hell, that's a lie. I've been trying not to think about him for the last three years.

Asher Bennett.

Fuck.

"I don't know, Dad," I say as I set the parfait on my nightstand. "I'm not sure if I'm ready to jump back into school just yet."

Dad places a comforting hand on my shoulder. "That makes sense. It's a big decision, and you don't have to make it right away. Just know that the option is there if you want it. I've also got special permission for you to begin your classes virtually at first if that would make things easier as well."

It doesn't make things easier for me. The extra tidbit

complicates things because of how accommodating Crestwood is. "Thanks, Dad. I'll think about it."

I find those words meaningless because, in my mind, I have already made the decision. If Crestwood will help me get back on my feet and bring some normalcy to my life, I would be foolish not to take the opportunity.

Even if it means seeing Asher again.

6

ASHER

I can't fight the yawn that slides out of my mouth as I run a hand down my face. Shaking my head to clear the sleep fog does little to help my current state. I'm trying to wake up after not getting enough sleep the night before, and it's proving to be a bigger challenge than I thought.

I blink my eyes once and then twice as I focus on forcing myself out of bed. With a groan, I sit up and swing my legs over the side of the bed. The first thing I reach for is my phone on the nightstand.

6:23 a.m.

Of course I would wake up seven minutes before I had set my alarm to go off.

With a heavy sigh, I unlock my phone and find a missed call and two text messages from Mom. I swipe them open and see that she wanted to check on me because I haven't spoken to her in about a week, outside of a couple of text messages here and there.

I send her a quick message, letting her know I'm doing okay and that I'm just busy. It's not entirely true, but I don't have the energy to dive into anything more than that right now. I'll call her later when I'm more awake and can string together more than two sentences.

I set my phone back down and force myself to start getting ready for the day. My head needs to be in the game because I can't afford to let myself get distracted. Hockey is my ticket away from my past, allowing me a pathway to take care of my family the way they should be.

With that in mind, I stroll into the bathroom and turn on the shower. Once the water has warmed up, I strip off the boxers I wore to bed and hop in without a second thought.

The hot water flows down my shoulders, easing some of the tension built up there. Hopefully, I can knock the rest of this tension out because the last thing I need is to be tight on the ice. This early morning practice will also fix my bad mood.

I finish my shower and dry off. I throw on some clean clothes and grab my backpack and hockey bag, double-checking that I have everything I need for the day. My stomach grumbles, reminding me I'm hungry, but that will be solved soon.

As I step out of my room, I nearly collide with Knox, one of my roommates. He mumbles something, but I can't quite catch it as he stumbles toward the bathroom. Our eyes meet for a split second, and he glares at me. I'm chalking it up to both of us having had a long night. In fact, I'm surprised to see him up this early.

I walk downstairs, and silence greets me. That's not surprising. I normally wouldn't be down here at this time either, but I promised my best friend, Levi, I would go with him to one of our on-campus coffee shops, so here we are.

I use my phone to light the way as I make my way into the kitchen. Once in there, I grab the protein-packed smoothie I made the day before, shake it up, and gulp it down as fast as possible. Once I finish and rinse the cup out, I head toward the door because Levi will be here shortly.

The vibration of my phone in my hand causes me to jump as I head toward the front door. I step outside into the cool morning breeze as my screen lights up. It's Mom.

I swipe to answer the call.

"Hey, Mom," I say as I hold the phone to my ear, locking the front door behind me with my free hand. "Everything okay?"

"Asher, honey, I'm sorry to call so early," Mom's voice comes through the speaker. She sounds tired, but that's normal for her with everything going on. "I did see your message, but I just wanted to check in before my shift starts."

"No worries, I was already up," I assure her, walking down the porch steps. "I'm waiting for Levi to come by and pick me up. We have practice soon."

"Of course, so I won't keep you. How are you really doing, Ash? Is there anything I can do to help you?"

I let out a breath, buying some time before I need to answer. "I'm hanging in there. Just taking it one day at a time. It's a lot, with classes, hockey, and everything, but I'm managing. How are things with you?"

"Oh, you know, the usual," Mom says with a tired chuckle. "Working, paying bills, and making sure Avery gets to school on time. She misses you, by the way. Keeps asking when you'll visit or if we can come to you."

Guilt hits me square in the chest. It's been weeks since I've seen my mom and sister. "I miss her and you too." I pause for a second to think. "Let me see if I can come home for a weekend soon."

"I didn't mean to talk you into coming home. We know how busy and jam-packed your schedule is with it being your senior year."

"I understand, but I want to see you both. I'll figure something out, I promise." The headlights of an SUV distract me for a second, and I check the time. Chances are high that it's Levi. "Hey, I gotta run. Levi should be here in a second. I'll call you again later, okay?"

"Okay, honey. Have a good practice. I love you," Mom says.

"Love you too, Mom. Talk to you soon." I end the call just as Levi pulls up in front of my house, double-parking because there aren't any parking spots on the block.

Levi pops the trunk, and I put my bags there before strolling over to the passenger door and hopping in. "Thanks for the ride, man."

"No problem. Thanks for deciding to wake up early to come with me to Brewed Beginnings," Levi replies with a grin.

I can't help but shake my head. We aren't going to Brewed Beginnings for the coffee. In fact, it's not about what we'll get at all; it's who we'll see. Levi is all about Hailey, a barista who works there, and I have to admit it's pure entertainment watching them interact with one another. Plus, he promised to buy me a coffee and take me to practice, so who could say no to that?

The drive to Brewed Beginnings is quick, and when he's done parking the SUV, we hop out and walk toward the coffee shop. The building's exterior has a charming red brick facade and large, welcoming windows. I reach for the door handle and pull it open. After the bell above the door sounds, the first thing that hits me is the smell of freshly brewed coffee. In no time, the urge to have a hot cup of coffee grows more urgent with every breath I take. The interior is cozy and has a rustic charm because of its exposed wooden beams. The soft lighting casts a lovely glow over the entire space. Local art decorates the walls, adding splashes of color and character to the room.

There aren't many people here yet, making it easier for Levi to achieve his goal. We step up to the counter, and Levi leans his elbows on it, a grin stretching across his face as he catches sight of Hailey. She looks up when Levi clears his throat. I watch as her eyes bounce between Levi and me twice before they settle on him.

"Oh, it's you," she says as she sets down the rag she was using to wipe the counter. "What can I get for you?"

"Just your presence is enough to make my day," Levi replies, his grin widening.

Hailey rolls her eyes, but I can see the smile tugging on the corners of her lips. "Flattery will get you everywhere, Levi Jamison. But it won't get you free coffee."

Levi clutches at his chest in mock offense. "You wound me. And here I thought we had something special."

"In your dreams," she responds, but there's an underlying playfulness to it.

The first time I came to Brewed Beginnings with Levi, that playfulness wasn't there. In fact, it could be argued that she hated us, although she didn't know us personally. However, the shift in their relationship is apparent, and I can't help but chuckle under my breath at their banter.

"Alright, alright, enough flirting, you two," I interject, stepping up beside Levi. "I'll just have a large hot chocolate with some whipped cream, Hailey. Someone promised to buy it for me." I shoot Levi a pointed look, daring him to say something denying it or about my drink order in general. I will defend my love for whipped cream until my last breath.

He waves a dismissive hand. "Yeah, yeah, I got you. And I'll have my usual." He pauses for a moment and then says, "We'll also have two of those breakfast sandwiches."

She nods, tapping our order into the register. "Coming right up." In no time at all, she has our drinks ready. She slides them across the counter to us, and although she looks slightly irritated, I can see a hint of a smile on her lips.

"Enjoy, guys. And good luck at practice today."

"Thanks. I'll be thinking of you while I'm on the ice," Levi says.

She shakes her head but can't hide her grin. "Just focus on not getting your ass kicked by your coach."

"Impossible," I chime in, taking a sip of my steaming coffee. The rich, slightly bitter flavor wakes me up better than any alarm clock could.

Levi chuckles. "I wish that was a lie... Well, we better get going before we're late. See you later, Hailey."

She gives us a little wave as we head out, the door chiming behind us. The cool air hits me for the second time this morning, feeling more refreshing after the warmth of the coffee shop and the coffee. Levi and I walk side by side to his SUV in silence, and soon we're sitting in his vehicle on our way to the arena.

Thankfully, the ride to practice is even shorter than

the ride from my place to Brewed Beginnings. On the drive, though, we both finish our sandwiches and sip our coffees as we walk into the arena. A chill runs down my spine as I take everything in. This is my element, where I ignore the outside noise and do my part to help our team achieve the success that I know is within reach. I've left all my other stressors outside, and I only need to focus on how this practice will lead to my being the best teammate I can be during our next game.

Levi and I make our way to the locker room, where some of our teammates are putting on their gear. Due to how early in the morning it is, there's not much talking, but I prefer it that way because it helps me get my head on right.

I change into my practice gear quickly because I don't want to be the last person out on the ice. Before we can step out onto the ice, Coach Johnson walks into the locker room, forcing our attention to him without a word.

"Alright, boys, when you get out there, I want to see you hustling because I know you can do it," he says. He pauses for a moment as his eyes roam the room, assessing each one of us. "I know what you can do and what you're capable of, but I need to see it. Is that clear?"

We all say a chorus of, "Yes, Coach," before we make our way out of the locker room. I'm one of the first ones to step out onto the ice, and a few warm-up laps help loosen my muscles.

Practice is grueling, but it's what I expect now. Coach

Johnson is tough but fair, and it is one of the many aspects that makes him an excellent coach for our team. I pour a lot of my energy into the drills and scrimmages, keeping in mind that I do have two classes I need to have energy for later today. Thankfully, only one class is in the morning, giving me time to eat and nap in between.

"Bennett! Watch your positioning on defense. Don't leave any gaps for them to exploit!" Coach calls out after I miss a check.

I nod, adjusting my stance and doubling down on my focus. By the end of practice, my legs are burning, and my lungs are heaving, but there's a deep satisfaction in the exhaustion. I know I've given what I could out there. Coach gives us a few final pointers before dismissing us. After a quick shower and change, I say goodbye to Levi and the rest of my teammates and head out.

As I'm walking across campus to my first class, I snack on a protein bar and drink water to hold me over until this class is finished. I'm halfway to Carver Hall, Crestwood's health science building, when a flash of long, blonde hair catches my eye. I do a double take just before I whip my head around because something about the image I saw triggers a memory for me. For a split second, I swear it's her.

Isla.

But as quickly as the moment comes, it's gone. The girl disappears into the crowd, leaving me standing there like an idiot. There's no way that was her. She doesn't attend

Crestwood. I heard she went to NYU to pursue her dreams, and I don't blame her.

I shake my head, trying to clear my thoughts of her. Class starts in a few minutes, and I can't afford any distractions.

Especially by ghosts and shitty decisions I've made in the past.

7

ISLA

The early morning sun leaves a warm, golden glow across the campus as I adjust the settings on my camera. I frame the shot with a few quick tweaks and capture a piece of Crestwood University's beauty. I pull the camera away from my face when I'm done, and I can't help but smile as I review the image on the display.

There is something magical about this time of day. The light makes even the most mundane objects look extraordinary. I snap a few more shots when I spot someone walking toward me. I lower my camera and grin, although I'm surprised to see Selene on campus so early.

"Well, well. I didn't know when I'd officially run into you on campus, but it's about time it happened," Selene says with a smirk. "Of course, I should have known it would be at the crack of dawn."

I chuckle. "It's not that early. Speaking of, what are you doing here?"

Selene rolls her eyes. "Early class. I swear, the person who came up with the idea of 8 a.m. lectures must be in cahoots with the devil, because what the fuck?"

"Hey, at least you're getting it over with early, right? Plus, you'll have the rest of the day to do whatever you want...that is, if you don't have more classes or homework."

"Ugh, don't remind me." Selene groans. "I've got a lab this afternoon and a group project meeting later. How have you been adjusting?"

That's a loaded question. I shrug to not appear stressed, but I'm sure I fail. Selene will call me out on my bullshit, anyway. "It's been a change, for sure. But I'm managing. The photography helps." I gesture to my camera.

Selene raises an eyebrow as a more serious expression settles on her face. "Yeah, I can see that. But tell the truth. How are you holding up?"

I take a deep breath, letting my eyes wander over the campus bathed in the soft morning light. "It's... different. There's just been so much going on with me changing schools and dealing with my PCOS on top of it."

That's an understatement. Crestwood's campus is nothing like NYU's and not like what I was experiencing in Italy before my life blew up. Although I know where certain things are due to living nearby all my life, it's still different because I'm attending the school now. It's also been quite the shift with me starting here after the semester has begun, but I've quickly caught up, so at least there's that.

And I've been lucky. I haven't run into "he who shall not be named," and I'm not prepared for when that eventually happens.

"I can imagine," Selene says, breaking me from the spell my thoughts had taken me under. "Speaking of, how's the new treatment going? Are you feeling any better?"

I debate with myself how much I should share. "It's helping. The meds seem to work, and my symptoms aren't as bad. But I have my ups and downs like we all do."

"I'm glad. You look so much better than the last time I saw you."

I cut my eyes over at her. "Thanks?"

"It's the truth."

She's right. The last time I saw her in person was a few days after I got back from Italy, and I'd just gotten my official diagnosis. I'm willing to admit that I looked rough, but she was still there by my side.

"I know, but I do feel better."

"And it's showing. That makes me so happy." Selene clears her throat before she speaks again. "Have you seen anyone else from high school around? Or anyone else you might know..."

As her voice trails off, I debate how I should answer

this. Of course she went there. I know exactly who she's talking about, but I decide to play dumb. "Anyone else?"

"You know exactly who I'm talking about," Selene says, narrowing her eyes at me. "Have you seen him?"

I try to keep my face neutral, but I can feel the heat rising in my cheeks. "No, I haven't seen Asher. And I'd like to keep it that way."

"Understandable, and I'm glad you haven't. You don't know how hard it's been not to kick his face in every time I see him around."

That statement forces a laugh from me. I appreciate Selene's friendship, but there is no reason to get violent toward anyone about this. What happened occurred three years ago, and harming him won't do any good.

Even if he left me with a broken heart.

"I would have loved to have seen that a few years ago, but that's all in the past. After all, I have more important things to worry about now."

"I know, I know. You're right. Nevertheless, the offer stands if you ever change your mind."

"I'll keep that in mind. But seriously, I'm good. I've got too much going on to worry about anything related to Asher Bennett."

"I hear you," Selene says, her expression softening. "Just know I'm here for you, always. If you need to vent or just want someone to hang out with and forget about all the bullshit, I'm your girl."

I smile as she opens her arms to hug me. "I know, thanks. It means a lot."

"Anytime, girly. I hate to cut this short, but I've got to run, or I'll be late for class. Catch you later?" She gives me a quick hug.

"Definitely. Text me when you're done with everything. Maybe we can grab dinner or something."

"Sounds like a plan!" Selene waves as she speed-walks away.

I'm left staring in her wake for a moment before I turn to start packing my equipment. I grab my camera bag and sling it over my shoulder before walking back toward my dorm.

As I approach the building, I can't help but feel a distinct pain forming in the center of my forehead. My roommate situation has been... tense, to say the least. I take a deep breath before pushing, using my key card to enter the building, and walking up to our door.

The last thing I wanted to do was live at home, so when I heard a bed was available in one of the upper-classmen dorms on campus because someone transferred out at the beginning of the year, I told Dad that's where I wanted to be. With that, I didn't know who my roommate was going to be or if our personalities would mesh well together. Turns out we don't vibe with one another, and I say a small prayer as I stick my key into the lock, hoping she's not there.

"Oh, you're back," my roommate, Tessa, says with little emotion, barely glancing up from her laptop. "I hoped to have the room to myself for longer."

I bite my tongue, resisting the urge to snap back. "Sorry, I just needed to drop off my camera gear before my first class."

I don't have to explain myself, but I'm doing my best to keep the peace. I set my camera bag down on my side of the room. Her side of the room is immaculate. Everything is organized, and there is not a single item out of place. In contrast, my side is a bit more messy, with a few clothes draped over my desk chair and my photography equipment occupying a significant portion of my limited space.

"You know, maybe if you didn't have so much stuff, there would be more room in here for both of us," she remarks, her eyes still glued to her laptop screen.

Annoyance continues to grow inside of me, but I take a deep breath and try to let it go. It's not as if my stuff is encroaching on her space, but I'm trying to keep the peace. "I'll try to keep my things more contained."

Tessa just hums in response, clearly uninterested in continuing the conversation. That is fine by me. The less I have to talk to or engage with her, the better. From the moment we met, it was clear that she wished she could have kept the room to herself, and I don't blame her. Sharing a room with someone isn't high on my list of wants either, but I'm willing to put in the work so that we can coexist. Her actions tell me she doesn't care about that, so I like to be here only when she isn't or when we're both asleep.

"Can you be a little quieter? I'm trying to concentrate.... Some of us actually have work to do instead of just taking photos of random shit."

I've had enough. "What's your deal?"

My roommate turns slowly. "What. Is. My. Deal?" she says slowly, as if she doesn't understand what I'm asking her.

"Why do you hate me? I haven't done a thing to you." I hate that I'm starting to sound desperate.

Tessa raises an eyebrow, her gaze cold. "Hate you? Don't flatter yourself. I just don't get why I have to pretend we're friends when we're not. You're just... here. Taking up space."

Her words sting more than I'd like to admit, but I refuse to back down. "I'm just trying to coexist. We don't have to be friends, but we don't have to make each other miserable either."

"Coexist? Sure. Just keep your stuff out of my way, and we'll be fine." She turns back to her laptop, dismissing me as if the conversation never happened.

I snatch my laptop off my desk and grab my backpack because I can't stay here a second longer than I have to. "Bye." Even though she was a prick to me, I can be nice.

Tessa barely acknowledges my presence, her eyes still glued to her screen. "Yeah, whatever."

Rolling my eyes, I slip out the door, letting out a sigh

of relief as it clicks shut behind me. I dash out of the building, happy to put my roommate and her bitchiness behind me.

Since my class isn't for another hour, I decide to go to the library to kill time. Unsurprisingly, it is quiet when I arrive, but there are only a handful of students around. It doesn't take long for me to find a secluded spot near the back on the main floor. Before I know it, I've plopped down and am ready to do some homework that isn't due for another week.

I pull out my laptop, turn it on, and open my school email. I scan the new messages that have accumulated in my inbox since I last checked. One catches my eye because it's from Dad, with the subject line, "Potential Opportunity For You."

I click on the message and read:

Hey,
I hope everything is going well.
I wanted to let you know about an opportunity that's come up.
The hockey team needs a new photographer, and I thought of you. I know you've got a lot on your plate right now, but I think this could be a wonderful chance for you to showcase your talent and get more involved on campus if you're selected.
Plus, it's a work-study opportunity. I've attached the announcement to this email for you to check out.
Let me know if you're interested, and we can discuss the details.

Love,

Dad

I stare at the screen, my heart racing as I reread the email. Working with the hockey team would mean being around Asher regularly, something I've been avoiding. And yet, the idea of being able to do something I love is so tempting.

If I get the job.

I click on the attachment and read through the job description. The position involves attending all home and select away games, capturing action shots of the players on the ice, and some behind-the-scenes moments in the locker room and during practices. It's a significant time commitment, but the pay is decent for a work-study gig.

And it's not like I don't have the experience.

I lean back in my chair, staring at the library ceiling as if it holds the answers I seek. Do I take a chance and apply for the position, knowing it means that I will come face-to-face with Asher at some point? Or do I look for another opportunity?

I stare at the screen before me, wondering what I should say. Before I can stop myself, my fingers begin moving across my keyboard.

Hey Dad,

Thanks for thinking of me for this opportunity. I'm definitely interested in applying. Can you send me more details on how to submit my application and portfolio?

Love,

Isla

I hit send before I can second-guess what the hell I'm doing.

8

ISLA

I clutch my portfolio to my chest as I pace outside the interview room. Was printing the photos that I submitted for the team photographer position overkill?

Yes.

Yes, because I submitted my application and pictures online. But did it make me feel better about what I'm about to do?

Debatable.

I'm a nervous wreck who is pacing a figurative hole in the floor outside of this closed door, all because I can't sit still. I tuck a stray strand of blonde hair behind my ear and smooth the creases in my blouse without missing a beat. At least I'm the last one out here waiting for my name to be called. Nobody can judge how ridiculous I look right now, and that's fine with me.

Deep breaths. In and out. You're a total boss at photography. They'd be lucky to have you.

Just then, the door I've walked past a million times at this point creaks open, and a woman with her dark hair in a high ponytail peers out. "Isla Johnson?"

I nearly jump out of my skin at the voice. "Yes, that's me," I blurt out.

"We're ready for you now. Please come in." The head disappears back into the room as the door opens.

With one last deep breath, I straighten my shoulders and march through the door like I own this place. That's the way boss babes do it, right? Or so I hope.

Inside, there are two people sitting there. They introduce themselves to me as Bailey, the Red Wolves team's PR manager, and Alice, her assistant. They are both sitting behind what I assume is Bailey's desk.

"Please, have a seat," Bailey says, gesturing to the only chair in front of their long table.

I do as instructed, clutching my portfolio that is now resting in my lap to give my hands something to do.

Bailey clears her throat and begins the interview. "So, Isla, tell us a bit about your experience with sports photography."

"Well, I've been photographing sports events since high school. I was the lead photographer for our yearbook and covered everything from football to volleyball."

I flip open my portfolio, pointing to a series of action shots. "At NYU, I photographed the basketball team's championship run last year." I'm very proud of those shots.

I continue with my well-rehearsed elevator speech about my work covering various NYU sports teams for the school paper and yearbook. Of course, I emphasize the long hours I've put in and the shots I've gotten. I even included some of the shots I took in Rome of a football match I attended with some of my classmates before I had to come home.

Alice speaks up this time. "How do you handle high-pressure situations?"

"Pressure is my middle name. I thrive on it, which leads to some of my best work." It sounds cheesy, but I think it gets the job done.

They both nod along, making notes on the papers before them. The questions continue, and the longer they go on, the more I feel at ease. They ask about my experience with different types of cameras, my editing process, and how I'd handle the demanding schedule. I answer as best I can and hope I'm saying the right things so they will consider me for the position. When Dad emailed me about the job several days ago, I didn't think I'd become this obsessed with getting it. I saw this as a way to keep me busy, so I don't have to think about all the other things I need to deal with.

But I want this.

I need this.

Bailey taps her pen on her desk, drawing my attention

to her. "This job requires the utmost professionalism. You'd be privy to many behind-the-scenes moments with the team, among other things. Having discretion is a huge quality involved with this job. Do you think you can handle that?"

Asher briefly enters my mind before I meet her gaze head-on. "Absolutely. When I'm behind the camera, I'm there to do a job. Document and create, nothing more. You can count on me to be professional above all else."

She makes another note on the pad in front of her, and I hate that her expression is unreadable. When she's done, she looks up and says, "Thank you, Isla. I think we have all we need. We'll be in touch."

I thank them for their time, shake their hands, and exit the room as quickly as I entered. The adrenaline is still pumping through my veins as I leave the room. I debate my next move as I begin to make my way toward the exit before I pivot and walk toward where I know Dad's office is.

I hate that I can't tell if the interview went well or not. Did I say the right things? Did I come across as confident and capable? Or did I just sound like a rambling hot mess?

I was both, but they didn't need to know about the latter if I could help it.

I make it to Dad's office and knock. When he says, "Come in," I push open the door.

"Hi, Dad. Sorry to disturb you, but I thought I would stop by since I was here."

Dad looks up from the papers on his desk, his reading glasses perched on his nose. His face breaks into a smile when his eyes meet mine. "There's my girl. How'd the interview go?"

I drop into the chair across from him with a heavy sigh. "Honestly? I have no idea. They were so hard to read."

He chuckles, leaning back in his chair. "I'm sure you did great. They'd be lucky to have you. Heck, you'd already have the job if I had any say."

"And that's why I'm glad you don't have a say. I want to get this on my own merit."

"I know you do, and you will. You're very talented, and they'd be fools not to hire you."

"That doesn't mean you're going to fire them if they don't, right?"

Dad laughs and shakes his head. "I can't fire everyone in the room with you, sweetheart."

I roll my eyes but can't help smiling at Dad's attempt at a joke. "You're hilarious. But seriously, no meddling, okay? Promise me."

"I promise. Scout's honor." He holds up his hand in a mock salute.

"You were never a Boy Scout," I point out with a smirk.

"Semantics." He waves a dismissive hand. "Point is, I

have full faith in you. And if they don't pick you, it's their loss."

"Thanks, Dad. Seriously, I needed to hear that." I stand up and put my bag on my shoulder. "I should get going because I have a paper to finish."

"Alright, and don't be a stranger. And let me know as soon as you hear anything about the job."

"Will do. Love you." I blow him a kiss as I head out the door.

"Love you too, Iz."

I grin because he uses a childhood nickname that I haven't heard in a while. It brings up this warm, fuzzy feeling that I haven't experienced in a while.

The smile stays on my face as I make my way toward the exit of the arena. I pull out my phone to see if I have any text messages or emails before I head back to my room. Maybe Selene is free so I can avoid my roommate for a while longer. I'm not paying as much attention as I should be, and that becomes apparent when I collide with a solid wall of muscle. I stumble back, an apology on my lips, when I look up into a familiar pair of striking green eyes.

"Whoa, sorry about that," a deep voice says, steadying me by placing his firm hands on my shoulders.

Asher Bennett.

I'm convinced I forget to breathe as Asher's hands linger on my shoulders for a beat too long. This is the first time he's had his hands on me in over three years. I swear

I can feel the warmth from his touch through my blouse. This simple thing is making me feel things I shouldn't.

I look down and shrug my shoulders, forcing him to drop his hands. "Um...sorry about that."

I've rehearsed repeatedly what I would say the moment I saw Asher again. If I ever saw him again. And now that the moment is here, those are the only words I can think of.

Asher takes a step back and shoves his hands into the pockets of his red hoodie with the words Crestwood Hockey written across the front. "It was you."

"Wait, what?"

"I mean, uh, I wasn't expecting to see you here."

"Well, I could say the same thing about you," I mutter, adjusting the strap of my bag because of nerves.

"I was just heading to see your dad. Coach wanted to talk to me about something."

"Right. Cool. I don't care, and I won't keep you." I step around him because I'm ready to escape this awkward encounter.

But Asher sidesteps and blocks my path on purpose. "Isla, wait. Can we talk for a second?"

I glance down at my phone, pretending to check the time. "I need to get going..."

"Please. It'll only take a minute."

I think about his request as I stare back into his green eyes. His eyes were one of the most entrancing things about him, and even now I find myself getting pulled into them. However, this moment reminds me too much of when he broke my heart.

"No, because I don't owe you a thing."

I step around Asher, and he doesn't try to block me this time. Without looking back, I make a beeline for the exit. I can't do this. I thought I might have been over all this, but seeing him again made me realize the wounds are still fresh, even after all this time.

"Isla, please," Asher calls after me. "I just want to talk."

I whirl around because the only emotion I have now is anger. "Talk? You want to talk now? Where was this desire to talk three years ago?"

Asher flinches at my words, his face falling. "I know I messed up and I should have explained myself better. I should have—"

"Save it," I snap, holding up a hand. "I don't want to hear your excuses. You made your choice, and I've moved on. That includes not hearing the shit that you're about to spew."

The lie falls off my tongue with ease. I haven't moved on, if my reaction to him is any indication. But Asher doesn't need to know that. He doesn't deserve to know the truth of how I feel or how much he hurt me.

Asher looks like he wants to say more, but he doesn't. Instead, his eyes search mine. For what, I'm not sure. Forgiveness? He's about to get an answer he won't like because he won't find that here. Not anymore.

"I'm sorry," he finally says. "That is what I should say

first. I'm sorry for everything and I never meant to hurt you."

A harsh laugh drips from my lips. "Well, you did a bang-up job of that, didn't you? Congratulations."

Why am I wasting my time talking to him? I have other things I could be doing. What's funny about this situation is that I'd rather be back in my dorm room with Tessa than have to deal with this.

I shake my head, clearing the fog in my head so I can address the man in front of me with a rational mind. "Your apology means nothing to me. You are a fucking coward and chose the easy way out. Nothing you can say or do will change what you did. So fuck you and get over it because I have."

With that, I turn on my heel, not giving Asher another chance to respond. I can't bear to hear another word from him. My heart is slamming around in my chest as I push through the doors labeled 'Exit.'

Of all the people to run into today, it had to be him. The universe must have it out for me. First the interview, and now this confrontation with my ex-boyfriend is the cherry on top.

I hop into my car and slam the door closed, shutting out the rest of the world. I take several deep breaths with my hands on the steering wheel because I'm barely holding on. Once I collect myself somewhat, I pull out my phone and shoot a text to Selene.

> Me: Hey, you free? I need to vent.

Her response comes almost immediately.

> Selene: For you, always. Want to grab lunch?

> Me: Perfect.

Thank goodness.

I start my car and pull out of my parking spot. I need something to go right today because there's no way I'm falling for whatever Asher is selling again.

9

ASHER

I'd entered the arena feeling confident about whatever Coach wanted to talk to me about. As I walk to his office now, I feel stressed out even more.

Seeing Isla tore through me like a sledgehammer. At first, I believed I was looking at a ghost because Isla had stated that she would never return to Crestwood University's campus as long as I was there.

Neither one of us can keep our promises, apparently.

However, I don't blame her on that front.

I can't figure out how I should feel or what to make of what just happened. It was almost like an out-of-body experience. Questions swirl through my mind as I focus on trying to comprehend the last few minutes of my life and how it feels like my entire world has shifted.

What the hell is she doing here? And why?

This isn't what I should be thinking about as I walk down the hallway to Coach's office.

Memories of the part of the summer we spent together when I stayed with the Johnson family flash through my mind with every step I take. Nostalgia can be an asshole because all I can think about is how we'd had the time of our lives until I fucked it up.

At least I've confirmed that I saw her on campus the other day. Part of me wishes she'd been a mirage because the churning in my gut wouldn't be as obnoxious.

As I approach Coach's door, I swear the air rushes out of my lungs as I try to push the images of Isla out of my mind. I pause with my fist poised to knock on the door when I hear the voice of Bailey, our PR manager.

"We think she's the perfect fit for the team photographer position. Isla's portfolio is impressive, and her passion and love for photography is obvious."

Then I recognize Alice's voice. "Agreed. This has nothing to do with her being your daughter, either. We looked at each candidate, and Isla blew us away."

That sledgehammer to the gut feeling makes its presence known again. Isla might be working for the team? I'll see her more often if she takes the job. I will get distracted, which means this will become a problem.

Fuck.

I shouldn't be eavesdropping on Coach. Swallowing hard, I rap my knuckles against the door, pushing down the anxiety that wants to wreak havoc in my body.

"Come in," Coach calls out.

I twist the doorknob and step into the office. Coach Johnson sits behind his desk, his expression unreadable as he motions for me to take a seat. Assistant Coach Daryl nods at me before he, Bailey, Alice, and a person I don't recognize leave the room.

"Asher," Coach begins, leaning forward and clasping his hands together on the desk. This must be serious if he isn't referring to me by my last name. "I wanted to check in with you. How are you feeling so far this season?"

I clear my throat, attempting to focus on the conversation at hand and not the thoughts my mind wants to drift back to. "I'm feeling good, Coach." I'm not sure what else to say because I have no idea what he's talking about. What has he noticed?

Coach Johnson studies me intently, and I don't like it. "You've still been doing well on the ice, but your focus has been slightly off. Is there anything you want to discuss? Is there anything I can help you with?"

I grip the armrest of the chair I'm sitting in. The last thing I want is for Coach to think I'm not giving my all to the team.

"No, Coach. I'm committed to the team and our goals this season."

Coach leans back in his chair. "I know you are, Asher. You're one of our most dedicated players. But it's easy to see when something else is on your mind. Is everything going well at home?"

He knows a lot about my home life because not only is Coach there for every single player on the hockey team, but he stepped up for me when I needed him most. If it hadn't been for him and his family, I would have been sleeping in my car until my first semester at Crestwood started.

And I betrayed him when I got into a relationship with his daughter.

I swallow hard, knowing I can't lie to Coach. Well, not about this, at least. Not after everything he's done for me. "Things are... complicated at home, but it's nothing new. I promise it won't affect my performance on the ice. I'll make sure of it."

"If it's not anything at home, is it your classes?"

I shake my head, trying to maintain a neutral expression. "No, my classes are going well. I'm on top of everything, and my grades are good."

Coach Johnson nods, but his eyes remain fixed on me as if he's trying to read between the lines. "Asher, you're in your senior year. This is a crucial time for you, both on and off the ice. I expect you to be focused and dedicated to the team and your studies. If anything is distracting you, it's important to address it."

His words hit a little too close to home, but I refuse to show how they've affected me. "I understand, but there's nothing to address."

"I hope so. You have a bright future ahead of you, and

I'd hate to see anything jeopardize that. If you ever need to talk, my door is always open."

I nod, thankful that it seems as if this talk is coming to an end. "Thank you, Coach. I appreciate that."

As I stand up to leave, Coach Johnson speaks again. "Remember, Asher, the team is counting on you. Don't let them down."

"I won't," I promise, hoping I can keep my word despite everything that is going on.

I exit his office, happy to get away from the line of fire, but nothing feels resolved. In fact, things have gotten more complicated, and it is only getting worse by the minute. As I make my way down the hallway, I grab my phone and find a text from my mom.

> Mom: Asher, we need to talk. It's about the bills. Call me when you can.

I stop walking and close my eyes for a moment, feeling a headache forming. Between Isla's return, my conversation with Coach, and now more financial issues with Mom, it feels like my whole life might break at any moment. I text Mom that I'll call her later before stuffing my phone in my pocket.

I need to clear my head before I talk to Mom. A load of homework is calling my name, but my ability to focus on it is nonexistent. As I spot my car, I make a decision to go to the gym and burn off this energy I'm feeling. Plus, that's helping to support my conditioning for hockey. Luckily, I keep a gym bag in my car just in case I want to go to there.

I drive almost on autopilot, and soon, I'm entering the gym with my bag swung over my shoulder. I spot Knox and Levi standing near one of the benches. They give me a small nod as I approach.

"Hey," Levi greets me, sitting up and wiping the sweat from his forehead. "What's up?"

"Nothing much. Decided to spend some time in the gym before heading back to the house."

Knox rolls his eyes. "You look like you need it. You look like shit."

I raise an eyebrow at him. It's not just what he said, but it's also the first thing he's said to me outside of the rink in days. "Well, I also feel like it, so that works."

Levi smirks. "Knox is trying to say that you've got that 'I need to punch something' look on your face. And it's something I'm only used to seeing from Blaise."

I shake my head, setting my bag down. He's not wrong. "Just got a lot on my mind."

Knox stands up and pats the bench. "Nothing like a workout to clear shit up. Iron therapy, if you will."

If I'm being honest, I need to see a therapist. The gym can help for now, however.

I sit on the bench and grab one of the fifty-pound barbells that Knox and Levi hadn't had a chance to put back on the rack. I start with bicep curls as I shut out the noise, crowding my brain between thoughts of my past with Isla, Coach's words, and Mom's worries. There is a time and place for that, and right now, I need to focus on one thing: myself.

I grab the other barbell and switch to shoulder presses. I can feel sweat forming on my forehead as I grit my teeth, trying to drown out my thoughts with physical exertion. The familiar burn yet euphoria that comes with pushing my muscles to their limits is a welcome distraction. I move on to lat pull-downs while Knox and Levi have moved on to complete their own routines. I'm locked in on this workout because it's the only thing that matters now.

If I wasn't, then what I did to Isla would take a front-row seat in my mind.

I should have known better. I should have been more careful with her heart. Hell, with my own heart.

And there she is again, penetrating my thoughts, even though I'm doing everything to distract myself. I finish my last set, and sit up, panting. Sweat drips down my face, and I grab my towel to wipe it away. Levi glances over at me with an eyebrow raised.

"You good, man?" he asks.

I nod, but it's a lie. I'm not good, not even close, but I don't want to announce it to the world. Instead, I stand up, my legs feeling slightly unsteady beneath me, but I can manage. I've pushed myself harder than usual, but it's still not enough to quiet the chaos in my head.

"I'll be right back," I say before I head back to the other side of the gym.

There is only one thing I can do to solve the problem I can control. I find an empty bench and pull out my phone. It's time for me to do something that I should have done years ago.

> Me: Hey, Isla. I'm not sure if this is still your number, but I thought it was worth a shot. Can we meet to talk?

I hit send and stare at the screen for who knows how long before returning to my workout. Now, all I can do is wait.

10

ISLA

Telling myself that I can't vomit because it will ruin my clothes is the only thing that is somewhat keeping me sane as I put my car into park. It will be even more embarrassing for me because today is my first day at my new job.

I'm the newest team photographer for the Crestwood Red Wolves hockey team. It is one of the best jobs I can have as a college student, and here I am, wondering if I made a big mistake.

I take a deep breath and leave my car while grabbing my camera bag from the passenger seat. The cool morning air brushes against my face, cooling my skin, but my anxiety is unwavering. I know I can do this. This is my dream job, and I refuse to let my anxiety get the best of me.

After I double-check that I've locked my car doors, I

walk toward the arena's entrance. I pull open the door and walk straight into the rink, where I find Dad and Bailey. Now that I think about it, I don't know how I'm supposed to address him while we are on the clock, and that adds to my anxiousness. Should I call him Dad or Coach? I'm still debating what I should call him as I walk toward the rink and feel adrenaline rush through my veins. This is where I belong.

Dad spots me first from across the rink and waves me over to where he's standing near the doors that lead into the men's locker room. As I walk toward him, he gives me a warm smile. "Isla, you're right on time. The team is just about to hit the ice for warm-ups."

"Thanks, Coach." The word feels foreign to my tongue, but I know I need to be professional while we're at the rink.

Dad places a reassuring hand on my shoulder while Bailey speaks up this time. "You might be nervous, with this being your first day and all, but you've got this. Just focus on getting some great shots and let the rest fall into place. Plus, Coach said you know a few of the guys anyway, so it'll be like taking pictures of friends. Or something like that."

Her confidence in me helps settle my nerves a bit. But then she adds the part about me being friends with some of the team and ruins it. However, I can't let her in on that secret. So, I take another deep breath and square my shoulders. "I'm ready."

Dad and Bailey lead me toward the locker room doors, and he knocks before we enter. "Is everyone decent?" A chorus of, "Yeses," rings out before he and I enter the room.

The locker room doesn't have the most pleasant smell, but that's to be expected. Thankfully, no one lied because everyone is dressed. However, it doesn't stop the warmth from growing in my cheeks. I try not to let my eyes linger on any one player for too long, mainly because I know he who shall not be named is here.

Dad clears his throat, getting everyone's attention. "Listen up, boys. I want to introduce you to our new team photographer, Isla."

He doesn't mention that I am his daughter, but I assume everyone will figure that out soon enough. I give a small wave, feeling the weight of their stares. "Hi, everyone. I'm excited to be here, to get to know you all, and capture some great moments for the rest of the season."

If it wouldn't be weird, I would give myself a pat on the back for getting those words out without stuttering.

A few of the guys nod and offer friendly smiles, but most just go back to lacing up their skates or taping their sticks. I try not to take it personally. They're focused on getting ready for practice.

As I scan the room, my eyes inevitably land on him, and I hate myself for it. Asher is sitting outside his stall, and his eyes are on me. A lump forms in my throat, and I quickly look away because this is the last thing I need.

"Alright, boys, let's hit the ice! Isla, head out to the stands, set up, and start snapping some pics."

"Awesome. Thanks," I reply, grateful for the excuse to escape the tension and anxiousness that results from being in the same space as Asher. I need to get out of here.

Bailey gives me a few more pointers about what she's hoping for me to do today. Then, I wait for the guys to head out before I follow, kicking myself that I wasn't prepared to take any shots of them as they make their way to the ice. It's a rookie mistake I promise I won't make again.

I make my way out to the rink and find one of the photo holes in the plexiglass, which allows photographers to capture clear, unobstructed shots of the action on the ice.

I adjust my camera settings while the team is doing warm-up laps. Levi and Wilder are the first to skate by me as I set my lens in the hole. Levi gives me a small wave while Wilder decides to put on a small show.

"Yo, Isla!" Wilder calls out with a goofy grin. "Make sure you get my good side!" He turns and wiggles his butt comically.

"Hate to break it to you, bud, but you don't have a good side," Levi says while shoving Wilder playfully.

I can't help but laugh at their antics, giving me something else to think about instead of my nerves. At least those two seem determined to make me feel welcome. I take a few test shots to make sure that I've got the settings where I want them. The sounds coming from the rink are as familiar to me as it is to breathe because this is what my family has known most, if not all, of my life.

As I adjust my lens, I observe Knox Sanchez completely engrossed in watching one of his teammates skate around a set of cones that the assistant coach has laid out. He barely acknowledges my presence, here or when we were all in the locker room. That's how I prefer it to be. When he throws a glance my way, it's brief and indifferent, as if I'm just another part of the rink's background.

My gaze shifts to Blaise Dalton, who is standing slightly apart from the team. He catches my eye and offers a warm smile and a nod. Unlike Knox, Blaise seems more approachable. As he watches the same scene as me, I can see a hint of amusement on his face.

I return Blaise's smile before refocusing my attention through the viewfinder of my camera. As I snap a few shots of the team performing their drills, I can't help but feel a surge of confidence.

However, that only lasts so long as my confidence wavers slightly when Asher skates into my frame. He's executing a series of quick, precise turns, his movements fluid and powerful. I take a few photos, trying to ignore how my nerves reach a feverish pace at seeing him.

As the team transitions into a new drill, I move to a different spot along the boards to get a better angle. My laser-like focus on my camera stops me from realizing that

Asher is skating toward me until he's in my personal space.

"Isla," he says, his voice low, as if anyone could hear us based on where we were standing. "Can I ask you a question?"

I glance up at him, taken aback. Is that desperation I hear in his voice? Nonetheless, if answering his question will get him back on the ice faster, I need to do it. I want to avoid drawing more attention to myself, especially on my first day. "What?"

"Did you change your phone number?"

"Uh, no?" Honesty is my greatest strength. Or so I'm telling myself.

He stands there momentarily, studying me before he skates away just as quickly as he came over. I'm left reeling from the interaction for a few seconds until it clicks why he asked the question.

Asher wants to know because I ignored the text message he sent me the other day.

Should I have responded to him? The answer is debatable, depending on how you look at our situation. On one hand, ignoring him feels like the safest option. Our history is complicated, including a breakup that left my heart shattered. The last thing I need is to reopen those wounds as I'm trying to find my place here.

On the other hand, I wonder if talking to him could provide the closure I've been craving. Maybe it would help me move on and put the past behind me. But every time I think about facing him, all the hurt and confusion from three years ago comes rushing back. I'm not sure I'm ready for it, and deep down, I know that's okay, even though the tension between us is bothering me.

Even then, who knows if that tension will ever dissipate...

For now, it's easier to pretend that his message never came. I can't afford to spend my time thinking about him. So, I shove those thoughts aside, determined to stay professional and keep my emotions in check. Today is about making a good impression and showing that I belong here, not dealing with the emotional baggage he left me with.

As the drills continue, I start moving around the rink, snapping photos from different angles and capturing the intensity of the practice. But something else draws my attention entirely.

Asher and Knox are engaged in a heated exchange, but given how far away I am from them, I'm not sure what is being said. Although I can't make out the words, their body language speaks volumes. Is this about to come to blows?

I raise my camera, zooming in to capture the moment. Just as I snap the shot, Coach blows the whistle, breaking up the argument. The two players skate away from each other, but I know this isn't over.

Not by a long shot.

I make a mental note to monitor what is going on

between them. The last thing I want to do is pay more attention to Asher, but I'm drawn to doing so in this instance. As the team photographer, it's my job to capture the highlights and the raw moments that tell the team's story. Whether or not these photos are made public isn't my decision, but at least we have them.

As practice winds down, I review my shots so far. Despite the rocky start and the unexpected run-in with Asher, I'm pleased with my work. The photos look great, and I can't wait to see what Bailey thinks of them.

Dad calls the team over for a final huddle on the ice while I gather my equipment. As I'm doing so, I can hear Dad giving some last words of encouragement before dismissing everyone but Asher and Knox. I decide to check in with Bailey in her office before I head out too. I'll talk to Dad later or grab dinner with him and Mom at home sometime this week.

To avoid running into any of the players, I dash out of the arena. Once I'm in my car with the doors locked, I take out my phone and ignore all the other notifications. I pull up my text messages and find the one that has been weighing on my mind since it appeared in my inbox.

> Asher: Hey, Isla. Not sure if this is still your number, but thought it was worth a shot. Can we meet to talk?

I stare at Asher's message, my thumb hovering over the screen. The temptation to delete it is there, but I know that won't solve anything. Ignoring the problem won't make it go away, no matter how much I wish it would.

With a sigh, I toss my phone into the passenger seat and start the engine. Everything else can wait because I have a million and a half things to do.

Not to mention that today wasn't just a practice run for the guys, but it was also one for me. After all, tomorrow is game day.

11

ISLA

I will go to my grave saying that there is nothing like game day. And if you disagree with me, you're just wrong.

The energy in this arena crackles around me as I take another shot with my camera. I swear I can feel the adrenaline coming from the ice flowing through my veins, even though I'm not one of the players going after the puck. The crowd's roars echo off the walls, but they fade into the background as I zero in on the action in the rink. My nerves are on high alert, being that this is the first game of the season that I am capturing, but I think I'm handling it well.

The other reason I'm slightly freaking out? Because of Asher Bennett.

I fix my gaze on him as he races down the ice. I pan my

camera, tracking his movements while keeping my finger over the shutter button.

There's a grace to his aggression, and I want to get it in all of its beauty.

Click. Click. Click.

I capture the moment his stick connects with the puck, sending it flying past the goalie's outstretched glove. The red light behind the net flashes, and the crowd erupts into a deafening roar. Asher briefly throws a fish up in triumph, and I can spy the smile that appears on his face.

Not only have I captured the image on my camera, but it's also seared in my memory for life. There's something so raw and unfiltered about this that I can't even bring myself to hate Asher at this moment. What he did will help our team win, and that's the bigger picture here.

Our team. I'm already referring to it as our team.

Not to mention, if I hadn't taken photos of the scene before, I wouldn't have been doing my job properly.

Several of the Red Wolves players swarm Asher as they celebrate the goal. I snap a few quick shots of their celebration, knowing these will be some of the most impactful images of the night.

As the team gets ready for the next face-off, I find Asher looking in my direction. I glance to my left and to my right to see if there is anyone next to me he might be watching, but when I look back at him, his gaze is still on me. He gives a quick nod of acknowledgment before turning away, and I'm left momentarily stunned.

What the hell was that all about?

I swallow hard and dig into my pocket for the Skittles I've stashed in there for emergencies such as this. Or just when I need a jolt of sugar. I toss a couple in my mouth and get back to the task at hand.

The game resumes, and I push any thoughts about Asher to the back of my mind. I readjust my stance and put my lens back through the photo hole to take more shots of the game.

A few more minutes pass before the buzzer signals the end of the second period, and the players skate off the ice. I lower my camera and take a deep breath before I grab a seat to review the photos I've taken so far. The screen on my camera lights up as I scroll through the images. I find myself analyzing each shot's composition, lighting, and emotions.

One image was taken just seconds before he scored the goal. I study the image that shows his stick connecting with the puck and the goalie from the opposing team diving to make a save. The red light behind the net glows in the background, adding a dramatic flair to the shot.

I can't stop smiling as I admire the beautiful photos I've captured. Sure, I might have been freaking out before I stepped foot in the arena today, but after working out some of the technical issues I had during practice, I have a clearer mind and more confidence in myself.

I check the scoreboard and realize we only have a few minutes before the third period starts. I quickly pop another Skittle in my mouth and head back to my position at the photo hole. Deep down, I know that eating this isn't the best thing for my PCOS, but I'm choosing today to give myself a break.

As I get my camera ready, I can't help but glance over at the Red Wolves' bench. I can see the players huddled together, no doubt discussing strategy for the next period. And there's Asher, his helmet off now, his dark hair damp with sweat. He has this intense look of concentration on his face as he listens to what my father tells the team.

The buzzer sounds, and the players take to the ice again. I refocus my attention on the game, determined to do my job. The third period kicks off with a bang, and I swear the noise from the crowd fuels me. I can't get enough of the energy and vibes, let alone the action on the ice.

It takes everything within me to contain my excitement as I witness how relentless the Red Wolves are. I can't wait to tell Selene all about this once the night is over. I know she doesn't give two shits about hockey, but there's no doubt in my mind that she'll listen to me ramble.

"Come on, boys! Let's go!" I can hear my dad's voice when there's a slight lull in the noise from the crowd. I shoot him a quick glance and can't help but grin at the enthusiasm coming from him. He's been coaching for years, but watching him lead this group of guys feels different—it feels much more personal.

But I'm not sure if that will be enough because the opposing team seems to have other ideas. The Red Wolves are up by one, and as the time ticks down, the pressure is on to prevent the opposing team from scoring. It appears as if the players are focused on defense, doing everything they can to maintain their lead. I know the game is almost over, but it feels like every second drags on forever.

The tension in the arena only intensifies as the players take their positions for the closing minutes. This game wasn't supposed to be this intense, and I can't help but feel both excitement and a twinge of panic at the thought of the Red Wolves losing their lead. How did it come to this?

As soon as the puck drops, chaos ensues on the ice. I click away, focusing on every movement, not knowing who will come out on top. Part of me wishes I could just be another fan in the stands, cheering without this being about work, but standing this close to the action is indescribable.

The crowd is on their feet, chanting and cheering as the last seconds tick away. Even though I can't take my eyes off the game because of my job, I almost wish I could shut them because I am nervous. I reach up to touch the white bow in my hair before rubbing a hand down the front of my Red Wolves hoodie. This isn't good for my heart.

My heart pounds as I watch Levi snag the puck and weave through the opposing team's defense. I snap a series of shots, capturing the determination etched on his face.

Levi intercepts a pass, but the opposing team quickly regroups, and the puck ends up back in their possession. Asher skates back, helping Levi as they track the puck while the opposing team moves toward their goal. Blaise is right there with them, adding extra coverage. Levi goes in for the block, Blaise positions himself to guard against any loose pucks, and Asher supports by cutting off the passing lane, ready to deflect any rebound. Levi blocks the shot, and I swear I stop breathing as Asher scrambles to his feet and clears the puck out of the danger zone. I let out a shaky breath while hoping they can hold the lead.

The final buzzer sounds just as the puck clears the Red Wolves' defensive zone. The arena erupts in a deafening roar as Red Wolves fans leap to their feet in celebration. I lower my camera, a wide grin spreading across my face as I watch the team swarm Levi, Asher, and Blaise, congratulating them for the game-saving play.

Although Asher and I are not on good terms, I'm still thrilled for the team. Although I've only been part of this organization and this school for a couple of days, I feel an enormous sense of pride. Then again, I've been part of this community since Dad took the head coaching job here over a decade ago.

I snap a few more photos of the team's celebration before lowering my camera. The adrenaline rush from the game is wearing off, and I can feel the exhaustion seeping into my bones. I pack up my equipment and consider the edits I need to make before sending the photos to Bailey.

Once I have my things slung over my shoulder, I leave the ice rink and walk to the tunnel. I find Bailey in her office. I make my way over to her with a small grin on my face.

"Hey, Bailey!" I say as I approach her. Was that too enthusiastic? "I'm all done for the evening. I'll have the edited photos sent over to you by tomorrow afternoon."

Bailey smiles warmly. "Excellent. I can't wait to see the shots."

Before parting ways, we chat briefly about the team's victory and the upcoming schedule. I'm ready to head home, take a hot shower, and collapse into bed. But as I walk out of the office, I hear someone call my name.

"Isla!"

I don't have to turn around to know it's Asher. I consider pretending not to hear him and making a quick escape, but something in his tone makes me pause for too long. As I make a move to walk away, I feel him touch my arm. Against my better judgment, I stop and turn to face him. "Yes?"

He jogs over to me, his hair still damp from sweat, I assume. "Can we talk sometime soon? Privately?"

I stare at him, momentarily taken aback by his request. A rush of conflicting emotions hits me like a ton of bricks—surprise, confusion, and what-the-fuck-ism. The last thing I want to be right now is alone with

Asher, especially after everything that's happened between us.

"What's the point? What's done is done, and it's been years."

"But now we're both working for the same team, in different capacities, obviously. I thought maybe talking things through could make things less awkward for both of us."

I cross my arms over my chest, feeling a mix of annoyance and exhaustion. Part of me wants to tell Asher to kiss my ass. However, I'm intrigued by what he could want to say after all this time. That doesn't include the short conversation we had when we ran into each other after my job interview. I chew on my lower lip, weighing my options.

"Fine," I finally say, my tone clipped. "We can talk. But not now because I'm busy." I was only going to go back to my dorm room and work on these photos and pass out, but he didn't need to know any details.

Asher nods as his expression relaxes. It's as if he's relieved by my statement. "Of course. Whenever you're ready. Just let me know. My number hasn't changed."

I raise an eyebrow at his last comment. "Oh, so you assume I still have your number saved after all this time?"

Asher rubs the back of his neck. "I mean, uh..."

Is it wrong that I can't contain my happiness at the thought of him feeling uneasy? "Don't worry about it. I'll text you when I'm ready to talk." I adjust my camera bag strap on my shoulder, eager to end this conversation and get out of here.

However, the intensity in his eyes has drawn me to him like a magnet. I'm not sure if I can walk away from him.

Like he walked away from me.

"I have to go," I say, stepping back. "I'll be in touch... or something."

Before he can respond, I turn on my heel and walk away, my heart pounding in my chest. I can feel his eyes on my back as I leave, but I refuse to look back.

It takes some time because the guests who came to tonight's game are still trying to leave the arena. When I reach the exit, I step out into the crisp night air, grateful to be out in the cool breeze. I take a deep breath as I try to calm my nerves after the events that took place tonight. I spot my car and make a beeline for it, eager to put some distance between myself and Asher. What I need to do is stop running from him, but that will have to be saved for another day.

Everyone loves a self-aware queen.

I unlock the vehicle and place my camera bag in the passenger's seat. Once I'm inside with the doors locked behind me, I lean my head back against the headrest and close my eyes. I'm not ready to deal with this, but what he said makes sense. We're going to see each other a lot more now, and it will be awkward if we don't clear the air. That doesn't mean I want to do that, however.

I grab my phone to type a quick message to Selene.

> Me: You're never going to believe what happened to me today…

Instead of getting a text message back, my phone rings. "Hey, Selene, can you hold on a second? I need to get on the road first, and then I can tell you what's up."

"No problem. I could tell by the vibes from your text that this was going to be good, and I only have a couple of minutes, so talking is easier."

I laugh out loud, harder than I should have because I needed it. After the conversation with Asher and deciding to talk to him about our past at some point, I want all of the unicorns, butterflies, and rainbows in my life.

Once I'm on the road, I tell Selene everything that happened. When I'm finished, I wait for her reply, but she's silent, which isn't like her.

"Did I make you speechless?"

"Not really. I'm trying to decide whether I should actually tell you what I'm thinking."

I glance at the phone before returning my focus to the road. "Why wouldn't you just tell me? What is that supposed to mean?"

"After you talk things out, I think you should fuck him."

My eyes widen as I tighten my grip on the steering wheel. It's a miracle I didn't drive off the side of the road. "Can you warn me before you say something like that?"

"Sorry."

No, she isn't.

"Didn't you tell me at one point it took all of your control to stop you from wanting to beat him up? Now you want me to fuck him?"

"There's a thin line between love and hate." I can see her shrugging even though I can't actually see her. "I'm glad you're going to talk to him, but I don't think it will be enough. You've been thinking about him a lot, and I think the best way to get him out of your system is to hate fuck him."

"This might be one of the worst ideas you've ever had, including when you convinced me to sneak out and go to a college party where we ran into my sister, met Asher, and almost met the cops."

"It wasn't a bad idea, and you know it. We had fun, just like you're going to have fun when you have sex with him again."

I can't believe the words coming out of her mouth, but I'm not surprised she's saying them. "This is pure madness."

"And you love it and me. I have to go, but I'll talk to you later. Think about what I said because I doubt he'd turn you down, anyway."

"Bye," I say, not bothering to explain to her why what she said made no sense. I'm left wondering why we are best friends again and what that was all about.

12

ASHER

The sigh that falls from my lips as I walk into my place is well-earned. Tonight was a hell of a night and one I will not forget anytime soon. I stroll into the kitchen after tossing my gear near the stairs. The post-game adrenaline is still flying through my veins, which is normal, especially after a hard-fought win. I wasn't expecting to see Knox leaning against the counter, chugging a Gatorade. He nods at me as I grab a bottle of water and a can of whipped cream from the fridge.

Is it the healthiest thing I could be eating? No, but here we are.

I pop the top and squirt the whipped cream into my mouth, enjoying each and every bit of this sweetness in my mouth. After I finish up with the whipped cream, I put it back in the fridge and turn to face Knox.

"Hell of a game today, Bennett," Knox says, wiping his

mouth with the back of his hand. There's some sarcasm there, dripping off every word, but I refuse to take the bait.

"Thanks," I reply, twisting off the cap of the water bottle this time and taking a long swig. The cool water soothes my somewhat dry throat. Knox's drink looks very appetizing, but I thought I would start with this first.

Knox smirks just before he says, "So, I saw you talking to Isla in the tunnel after the game. She's still hot, huh?"

I nearly choke on my water but manage to swallow what's left in my mouth. "What? Uh...yeah, I was just talking to her."

Knox raises an eyebrow, not buying my nonchalant response. "Just talking, huh? C'mon, man. You made a beeline for her and were almost late to address the media. You're lucky Coach didn't hand you your ass."

My grip tightens on my water bottle because I'm irritated that he's right. "Back off. It's not like that. Isla and I... we have history, alright? So just drop it."

Knox's smirk only grows wider. "History, eh? Now we're getting somewhere. What, did you two used to date or something?"

He knows we in fact did date, so I know he's full of it. To hell with not taking the bait. "I said drop it," I snap, slamming the water bottle on the counter.

Knox's eyes widen in surprise at my outburst. "Whoa, easy there, Bennett. What's your problem? It's not like she's your girl anymore."

I clench my jaw, feeling the muscle twitch as I glare at

Knox. He knows some of what went down back then. What I wish we still had, if I'm being honest with myself.

"You don't know what you're talking about," I growl, stepping toward him.

Knox straightens up from his casual lean against the counter as his eyes narrow. "Then enlighten me," he replies sarcastically. "Because from where I'm standing, you're acting like a possessive asshole over a girl you claim isn't even yours."

My irritation turns into anger as I take another step toward Knox. I flex my fists, which are resting at my sides, but I'm ready to fight if it comes to that. "I said back the hell off. Don't make me repeat myself because I won't say it as nicely the next time I remind you."

Things have been brewing between us for a while, but I can't remember the last time Knox and I got into a fight. However, I'm not afraid to have one right now. The rational part of me knows that this doesn't have to be and that, in reality, he's only teasing me. But that side of me isn't winning the war tearing through me.

Knox rolls his eyes at me. "Seriously, Bennett? You want to throw down over some chick? I thought you were better than that."

I take another step forward, and I'm right in his face. Every blaring signal about how bad this looks sounds in my head. I know this is so out of character for me, and if this comes to blows, I might be fucking up my college career, but none of that matters. I can't seem to talk myself down from this ledge. "She's not just some chick. You have no idea what you're talking about."

Just as Knox opens his mouth to respond, Blaise and Wilder walk into the kitchen. I can't see their facial expressions, but I assume they must have heard us from the living room.

"Whoa, what's going on here?" Blaise speaks first.

"Nothing," I reply. "Just a misunderstanding."

Wilder raises an eyebrow. "Looks like more than a misunderstanding to me. You two are about to throw hands."

Normally I would have chuckled at Wilder's observation, but I'm too pissed off to show any amusement. I let out a deep breath as I take a step back from Knox. "It's fine. We're fine. I'm just gonna head up to my room."

As I turn to leave, Knox calls out, "Running away from your problems, as usual?"

I stop in my tracks, my back still to him. The urge to turn around and deck him is at an all-time high. I know he's egging me on, much like he does to our opponents on the ice. However, I'm well versed in his shit. He will not have the last word.

I look over my shoulder and say, "I can say the same thing about you, can't I?"

Knox's eyes narrow at me, and I'm ready for him to say something else. But someone else speaks up before he has a chance to.

"Asher, man, just let it go," Blaise says calmly. "Whatever this is about, it's not worth fighting over."

"Yeah, seriously," Wilder chimes in. "Usually, I'm game for a couple of rounds and will let you two go at it, but I'm fucking tired. The last thing I want to do is break up a fight."

I appreciate their attempts to defuse the situation, but right now, I just need to get out of here before I do something I'll regret. Without another word, I head for the stairs, taking them two at a time until I reach my room. I slam the door shut behind me, happy to take out my aggression on something.

I need to find something to do, and fast.

Instead, I pace around my room like a caged animal as my thoughts race even more than they did during the game. Who the hell does Knox think he is? I know his mind drifts toward hookups at this point in his life, but that's not how I would characterize my relationship with Isla at all. His even hinting at it made me see fucking red.

My steps stop when I hear a knock on the door. Part of me wants to ignore it, but it's useless because whoever it is knows I'm in here. I walk over and open the door to find Blaise standing in front of me.

"Can we talk?" He phrased it as a question, but I know he won't take no for an answer.

I hesitate, but then step aside to let him in. Blaise, like me, has always been level-headed, which is probably why he came up to talk to me. He knows this isn't usually how I handle things.

He takes a seat on my desk chair as I plop down onto the edge of my bed.

"You want to tell me what that was all about?" Blaise prompts gently.

I exhale heavily, staring at the floor. "Knox was running his mouth about Isla. Acting like she's just some piece of ass."

Blaise nods slowly. "Coach's daughter? And that bothers you because...?"

"Because she's not," I snap, looking over at him. I don't feel like going through this line of questioning again.

Blaise holds up his hands as if he isn't trying to be offensive. "I'm not saying she is, man. But you've got to admit, your reaction was intense as fuck. What's the deal with you two, anyway?"

I run a hand through my hair. "We used to date, okay? It started just before our freshmen year and lasted a few months into the school year. It was serious." I almost mention how I fucked it all up, but I'm not sure if that is necessary.

Blaise's eyebrows shoot up before his facial expression becomes neutral once again. "Shit, I had no idea. No wonder you got so pissed at Knox."

"Yeah, well, it's not something I like to advertise," I mutter. "We kept things quiet because of Coach. The breakup was horrible, and I still regret it."

Blaise leans back in the chair, studying me carefully. "Do you still have feelings for her?"

I want to deny it, but what's the point? My reaction downstairs said it all. "I'm not sure. I don't know her anymore. When she joined the team, it was the first time we'd spoken in three years."

"Wow. I can't imagine how it must feel to have her back in your life after all this time."

I nod slowly. "It's fucking with my head, Blaise. Seeing her again has led to all these old feelings rushing back. But I know we can't go back to how things were before and that we are very different people than we were back then."

"Did you love her?"

Blaise's question makes my entire world stop turning. If you were to ask me if time has halted completely, I would say yes because that is how much of an impact his words have on me. For a moment, I can't move, think, or process the significance of the question. The silence in the room continues as I try to find the words to say to voice my opinion.

I rub a hand across my face before I respond, "I did." And on some level, I still do, but once again, admitting that out loud isn't something I'm ready to do.

While Blaise and I have a good relationship, I rarely share things like this with people outside of Levi. Blaise is the kind of guy you can count on, but our conversations typically stay surface-level—hockey, school, etc. Levi, on the other hand, knows all my shit. He's the one who's seen me at my lowest and still stuck around.

"That's heavy, man. I can see why you're so torn up about this."

I let out a humorless chuckle. "Yeah, well, it's not like I have much of a choice. We'll see each other a lot now that she's working with the team. That's why I was talking to her after the game."

"Oh?"

"I wanted to talk to her to see if we could chat privately at some point. To clear the air, so to speak."

"That makes sense." Blaise pauses for a second before he continues. "Sounds like a good idea and a way to move forward because there'll be no way either of you can escape one another unless the other quits. Plus, it could be an opportunity to open the door for something else."

My gaze narrows at him. "What, like try to be friends or something?"

Blaise shrugs. "Maybe. Or just find some closure. It could remove some of the guilt that you're obviously still carrying."

He hit the nail on the head. "That's an understatement." I stand up and start pacing again, unable to sit still any longer. "There's so much I would change regarding what I did and didn't do. But I think there isn't much I can do besides apologize. I tried on the fly when I saw her again for the first time in years, but it didn't go well."

"Yeah, that sounds rough, and I know you're trying to

make amends, but Isla also doesn't have to forgive you. Knox was being an ass, and you know how he gets when he sees he can press someone's buttons to get a reaction out of them."

"I know, and he's been more focused on me for whatever reason."

"He needs to get laid," he offers.

I scoff. "Maybe. Regardless, I should have been more in control, and it won't happen again." It's a lie because if it involves Isla, all bets are off.

Blaise stands up from the chair. "Cool. Well, I'll head back to my room because even with all the excitement tonight, I'm beat."

"Thanks, Blaise. I appreciate you coming to talk." I give him a half-smile.

"Anytime, bro. That's what friends are for." He claps me on the shoulder before heading for the door. "Try to get some rest, alright?"

"I will. Night, man."

With a wave, Blaise leaves, closing the door behind him. I flop back onto my bed and stare at the ceiling. My mind is still reeling from everything, and I hate that. I know I need to apologize to Knox tomorrow. As much as he pissed me off, Blaise was right that I overreacted.

Suddenly, my phone vibrates in my pocket, and my mouth drops open when I see a text from Isla.

Isla: We could meet after the team meeting tomorrow if you're available.

I read the message three times before I stop questioning what I read. It's straight to the point and sounds a little harsh, but I deserve that. After everything that happened, she has every right to be distant. The important thing is she's given me an opening, and that's more than I could have hoped for. I think of a response, and soon, my fingers fly across the screen.

> Me: That should be fine, and I'll meet you anywhere. Thanks for reaching out.

I hit send and set my phone down on my nightstand. I don't expect an immediate response from Isla. Playing this cool is key, even though by the end of this, I'll be opening up a gaping wound that I thought I'd healed years ago.

Good luck to me.

13

ISLA

As I open the door to Brewed Beginnings, the rich aroma of freshly ground coffee beans and the light jingle of the bell above the door greets me. I'm not a huge coffee drinker, but there's something about this place that feels like a warm hug, which I desperately need right now.

Because I'm freaking the fuck out.

I grip the strap of my book bag as I make my way to a corner table. It's tucked away from where most of the patrons are sitting, giving us some privacy in a very public space.

Part of me wishes I had asked to have this discussion before a team meeting or practice. That way, we would have a set end time, and I could escape. However, past me wasn't as smart as present me.

I slide into the chair, and my leg immediately bounces

under the table. I check my phone for the tenth time in the last five minutes. However, it's the first time I've checked it here, so I'm not being obsessive.

Girl math.

Asher isn't late, but I'm impatient, and my brain is jumping between wanting to get this over with or bolting out of here before he shows up.

I'm being ridiculous. It's just a conversation. A much-needed conversation, sure, but still. I've faced tougher challenges than this, including the one I'm battling with my PCOS. There's no doubt in my mind that I can do this.

As I wait for Asher to arrive, I check my phone and notice I have two emails. The first one is from my dad, reminding me about the team get-together at our house for hockey bonding this Sunday. The second one is from Bailey, asking if I can take photos at the volunteer event on the same day.

I can go to both things, just like I can have this conversation with Asher like an adult.

I'm so lost in my thoughts that I don't notice someone approaching my table until they're right in front of me. I look up, expecting to see Asher, but I find a girl with brown hair in a messy bun. She's wearing a Brewed Beginnings apron, leading me to believe that she works here.

"Hey there," the barista says with a small smile. "You're the new team photographer, right? I saw you at the game last night."

I blink up at her, surprised that she recognizes me. "Yeah, that was me. I'm Isla."

"Nice to meet you, Isla. I'm Hailey, Levi Jamison's girl-friend." She extends her hand, and I shake it as it clicks into place about how she recognizes me. "I was just about to clock out, but I can grab you something quick."

"Oh, that's so nice of you to offer," I say, my voice trem-bling slightly but enough that I want to roll my eyes at myself. The unexpected act of kindness has thrown me for a loop. I clear my throat before I continue. "But if you're about to leave, I don't want you to be waiting here on me."

"It's not an issue. I wouldn't have come over if it was."

"Uh, okay. I'd love a.... hot chocolate."

Hailey gives a small nod at my request. "One hot chocolate, coming right up." With that, she heads back behind the counter to make my drink.

While she's busy making my drink, I return to checking my phone. No new messages, but the time indi-cates that Asher should be here any minute now. And that doesn't do a thing to calm me down.

"Here you go, one hot chocolate." Hailey sets the steaming mug down in front of me a few minutes later. "Can I get you anything else?"

I hesitate, touched by her offer, but not wanting to drag her into what is about to happen. "Thanks, but that's it. Let me pay you."

Hailey raises a hand and shakes her head. "No need, it's on the house. And if you want to grab coffee or lunch sometime, let me know. It'd be nice to have another friend around who gets the whole hockey world thing."

"Really? That would be great," I say, surprised by the offer. "I'd like that a lot."

"Perfect. Let me give you my number," she says as she pulls out her phone from her back pocket. "Just shoot me a text whenever you're free."

"Oh, how about this Sunday?" I blurt out. How eager of me.

"That would be great."

We exchange numbers, and Hailey gives me a small wave before heading back behind the counter to clock out. I wrap my hands around the warm mug, letting the heat seep into my skin as I take a hesitant sip. The rich, velvety chocolate coats my tongue, providing a momentary distraction from the thoughts clouding my mind.

Just as I set the mug back down, the bell above the door jingles again, signaling that someone is walking in or out of the coffee shop. My heart leaps into my throat as I look up to see Asher walking in, his hands shoved deep into the pockets of his hockey hoodie. Our eyes meet across the room, and for a moment, everything else fades away. A quick glance down at my phone confirms he is right on time.

He makes his way over to my table, and as he pulls out the chair across from me and sits down, I can't help but notice the dark circles under his eyes. I don't remember seeing them the last time we saw each other. It makes me wonder if he didn't sleep well the night before.

Join the club.

Not that his sleeping habits are any of my business...

"Hey," he says. His voice is a little lower than normal. "Thanks for meeting me."

I nod, my fingers tightening around the mug. "Of course. You are right in that we need to talk, especially since we'll see a lot of each other now that I'm back."

His gaze lands on the cup in my hand as I take another sip, allowing the warmth from the drink to soothe me. He studies me as I finish taking another sip, causing me to raise an eyebrow. "Do you want something to drink?"

"No, I'm good. I have my water bottle."

Makes sense. "Hailey, Levi's girlfriend, actually served me. She seems nice."

Asher chuckles, and I hate that I'm transported back to a time when we used to laugh with one another. "She can be. Levi and she are 'couples goals' or something like that."

I smile at his words. It's a small, involuntary reaction that I quickly regret. Why am I sharing any of this with him? It's because I used to tell him anything and everything before he broke my heart. Old habits die hard, I guess.

Instead of saying something else, I take another sip of my hot chocolate. As much as I want to act like things are like they used to be, I know I can't. Too much has changed between us.

He ruined us.

Asher clears his throat, drawing my attention back to him. "So, about what happened when we broke up..." He trails off, his eyes searching mine for a reaction.

I set my mug down because it is nothing but a distraction, anyway. "We didn't break up. You broke up with me and gave a bullshit excuse." The words don't come out quite the way I planned, but here they are.

Asher's jaw tics at my words, but I can see he's trying to control his emotions. "It wasn't a bullshit excuse, Isla. I had my reasons."

"And what were those, exactly? Because from where I was standing, it seemed like you just decided one day that you were done with me. With us."

"It wasn't like that. I didn't just wake up and decide to end things on a whim."

"Then explain it to me," I challenge, leaning back in my chair and crossing my arms over my chest. "Because I think I deserve an explanation after all these years."

Asher drums his fingers against the table, and I can see the wheels turning in his head. "You're right. You deserve an explanation." He pauses, his gaze dropping to the table before he looks back up at me. "The truth is, I was struggling. With balancing hockey, academics, and things going on with my family. It was a lot of pressure, and I felt like I was drowning."

I frown, trying to process his words. "But why didn't you talk to me about it? We could have figured it out together."

He shakes his head. "I didn't want to burden you with my problems. We were just kids, and you had your whole life and college career ahead of you."

I grip the edge of the table to stop myself from slamming my hand down on the table. Thoughts about whether people are watching our interaction cross my mind, but I've given up caring. "That's bullshit, and you know it, Asher. We were supposed to be a team.... we talked about our future and what we were going to do when I came to Crestwood the following year. We were supposed to be in love!"

Maybe Brewed Beginnings isn't the best place to have this conversation, but I'm doing my best to keep my voice low. The sounds coming from the espresso machines and the soft chatter of other patrons create a background noise that makes me think few people are paying attention to us. I don't want the tide to shift, and we become a spectacle.

Asher's gaze narrows at me. "I loved you more than anything. Don't ever think I didn't. Even with all the things that happened, never for a second doubt my love for you."

His words hit me like a punch to the gut, and for a moment, it feels like I can't breathe. I didn't expect to hear the conviction in his voice or the raw emotion. The feelings I thought I did a good job of burying over the years rise to the surface, and I'm trying to hold back tears. I'm not sure if he is waiting for me to say something else, but I can't find the words right away.

My hands reach for the mug again because it's become a safety blanket for me. I take a minute to decide what I'm going to say, and while I'm worried about whether my voice will hold, I know it needs to be said. "How could you love someone and break their heart?"

Asher's face falls, and I can see my words have hit their mark. "I thought I was doing the right thing," he says quietly. "In my mind and heart, I was protecting you. The last thing I wanted was for you to be dragged into the chaos of my life, among other things."

I shake my head as I tighten my grip around the mug. Chances are I can't break it, but given the emotions surging through me, I might develop super strength. "You didn't protect me, Asher. You left me with no explanation, no closure. Do you know how many nights I stayed up wondering what I did wrong to deserve this?"

"You did nothing wrong, Isla. It was all on me. I was the one who messed up."

I laugh without a hint of humor in my tone. "You're damn right, you messed up. But that still doesn't explain why you did it. If you loved me as much as you claim, why would you just cut me out of your life like that?"

He takes a deep breath. "It is because of all the things I

listed and because you're Coach Johnson's daughter. I was afraid that if he found out about us, my collegiate hockey career would be on the line. I couldn't risk losing my scholarship, the potential at NIL deals, and my spot on the team."

My mouth drops open and closed, probably making me look like a fish. I reel back, and my mouth falls open again because I'm in shock. "Are you serious right now? You broke up with me because of my dad? Because you were afraid of what he might do?"

"Yes, I was worried about what your dad might do if he found out about us. He's always been protective of you, and I didn't want to jeopardize my future. Hockey is everything to me, Isla. It's my ticket to a better life. Hell, he helped me when I didn't have housing when I first got here, and I repay him by dating his daughter behind his back?"

I stare at Asher as I think about his words. Part of me understands where he's coming from. My dad can be intimidating, especially when it comes to Grace and me. But the other part of me is furious that Asher let his fear dictate our relationship without consulting me.

"So instead of talking to me and trusting in what we had, you just ended things? Without even giving me a chance to have a say?" My voice is rising as the hurt and anger I've had for years is making its presence known.

Asher runs a hand through his hair. "I know I handled

it poorly. I was young and stupid, and I thought I was doing the right thing. But I've regretted it every day since."

"I appreciate you telling me the truth, but you can't just say that and expect it to fix everything," I finally manage, my voice barely above a whisper. "You hurt me, Asher. More than I ever thought possible. And now you expect me to just forgive and forget?"

He shakes his head, his eyes pleading. "No, of course not, but I hope this is the first step for us to at least build a professional relationship."

I agree with him. As much as I want to hold on to the anger and hurt, I know that since we're working together, we must move forward.

"I appreciate your honesty, Asher. It doesn't erase what happened, but it helps to know your reasons, even if I disagree with how you handled things. You're right. We need to figure out how to work together professionally. But that's all this is."

"I get it, and I wasn't expecting us to go back to how things were. I just want us to coexist without all the tension and awkwardness."

"It's going to take time," I warn him. "I can't just flip a switch and pretend like nothing happened. But I'm willing to try for the sake of the team and our jobs."

"That's all I can ask for." He offers me a small smile. "Thank you for hearing me out, Isla."

I return his smile as a mixture of emotions swirl inside me: relief that we had this conversation, anger that it took so long, and bittersweet nostalgia for what we once had and will never have again. "Thanks for explaining things."

Asher nods, his shoulders relaxing slightly. "I should have done it a long time ago."

"Well, better late than never, I suppose." I finish my now lukewarm hot chocolate. "I guess we both had some growing up to do."

"Definitely." He chuckles softly. "Look at us, being all mature and shit."

"Yeah, who would have thought?" I say with a small smile. The tension between us has eased a bit but is still very much present.

Asher's gaze lingers on me for a moment before he speaks. "Now that we've mostly gotten that out of the way...how have you been? Besides the whole photographer gig."

I shrug, tracing my finger along the rim of my mug. "Oh, you know, just living the glamorous life of a college student. Classes, homework, existential crises. The usual."

He laughs at that, a genuine sound that brings back memories. "Sounds about right."

I chuckle along with him. Relief is the only emotion I feel as we shift the conversation to something lighter after... that. "And what about you? How's the life of a hockey superstar treating you?"

Asher shakes his head. "I don't know about superstar, but it's been good. Busy, but good. The team's coming together this year."

"I can tell. You guys looked great out there last night."

Asher's eyes light up at the mention of the game. "Thanks. It felt good to get that win, and hopefully, it's a sign of good things to come this season."

"I have a feeling it will be. You guys have a lot of talent, obviously. Made it easy to get some excellent shots."

"I saw the ones posted on our social media pages. You did an excellent job."

I shake my head, willing myself not to blush. "Only a few of those were mine."

"My point still stands."

"Well, I appreciate the compliment," I say, trying to keep my tone casual. "I'm just happy to be a part of the team."

"Do you still love Skittles? I know you used to eat them sometimes when you were shooting."

My head jerks back. "You remember that?"

"Of course I do." His gaze softens. "I remember a lot of things about you, Isla."

The way he says my name makes my heart ache. I take a long breath before trying to steer the conversation back to safer ground. "Well, that was a long time ago. Things change."

"Some things, maybe. But not everything."

There's an intensity to his gaze that makes me want to look away, but I force myself to hold steady. "Asher, don't. We can't go down that road again."

He sighs, leaning back in his chair. "I know, and I'm sorry. I didn't mean to make this weird."

"It's okay." I manage a small smile. "We're both still figuring out how to navigate this new...thing."

"That we are, sunshine. That we are."

I look back up at him, startled by the words he's just said. However, it's as if he doesn't realize he's said them. The nickname he gave me years ago rolls off his tongue as if he's been saying it all of this time.

I debate whether I want to point out what he's done, but quickly decide against it. I have to put an end to this. "Listen, I need to go, but it was great to get all of this out in the open." I gesture to the two of us.

As I stand up from the table, Asher does the same. "Thanks again for meeting with me. I know it wasn't easy."

I nod, adjusting my book bag on my shoulder. "It needed to happen. For both of us."

"Agreed." He hesitates a moment before adding, "I really am sorry, Isla. For everything."

"Thank you. Hopefully, this will be a step forward and go in the right direction."

Asher gives me a quick nod. "It is, and maybe if you're okay with it, we can be friends again someday."

Friends. The word feels strange in terms of Asher and me, but I guess it's a start. "Maybe someday," I repeat, not wanting to make any promises I'm not sure I can keep.

"Anyway, I should get going."

"Right, of course." Asher steps back, shoving his hands into his pockets. "I'll see you later?"

"You will." With that, I leave Asher standing in Brewed Beginnings, happy he doesn't try to walk me out or to my car. The quicker I put distance between us for me to process what just happened, the better.

14

ASHER

The crispness of the morning air swipes at my face, but I ignore it as I keep up with the pace Levi has set. I groaned when Levi suggested that we go for a run last night. It is one of the few weekends we don't have a hockey game, and while we have a volunteering event tomorrow, I'd been hoping to sleep in today. However, now I don't think this run is such a bad idea. It's helping to clear my mind, especially after my conversation with Isla last night.

As my feet pound the pavement, I can't shake the memory of how Isla looked when I explained my reasoning for doing what I did. I'd been expecting her to stand up and leave Brewed Beginnings pissed off, and I know I'm fortunate that didn't happen. With a deep breath, I push myself to run faster, as if I can outrun the emotions that she displayed that have been running on repeat in my mind.

"You're quiet this morning," Levi says as he glances at me as we round a corner. "Still thinking about Isla?"

"Yep. Can't get her out of my head. I thought talking through what happened years ago would make me feel... more at peace with what occurred, but it didn't. Seeing the look on her face..."

I trail off, unable to find the right words to describe the expression on her face. It'll take a long time for me to forget it, that's for sure.

Levi nods, his breath coming out in steady puffs. "It's a start, though. You've taken the first step in mending things with her. That's not easy."

"I know, but I can't help feeling like I should do more. I want to prove to her I'm not the same guy I was back then. That I've grown and changed."

"And you will," Levi assures me, his tone confident. "Just give it time."

I grunt in response, my thoughts circling around my next move. It would be easy to just avoid her when I can and keep things professional when I can't. But I know that's not the right approach. I can't let this opportunity slip through my fingers, not when Isla and I are in the same place at the same time.

None of this is a coincidence. I know she's the one that got away, and now I have the opportunity to right my wrongs.

"Well, I'm thinking of doing something to show her I'm serious about fixing things between us," I say, breaking the silence between us.

I look over at Levi and see that he's raised an eyebrow at me. "Oh yeah? What did you have in mind?"

"I'm not sure yet. But something is telling me to do this because just having the talk isn't enough."

"What are you trying to get at?"

The tone of his voice almost makes me pause. "What do you mean?"

"Answering my question with a question. Interesting."

I let out a sigh, my pace slowing so I can think. "I just... I want to do something that shows Isla I'm sincere. That I'm not just saying empty words."

Levi matches my stride, thankfully. "I get that, but you gotta be careful. You don't want to come on too strong and push her away."

"I know, I know." I run a hand through my hair, which is getting damp. "It's just... funny. I feel like I was giving you advice about Hailey not too long ago."

"You were, and now I'm returning the favor, even though I'm still not exactly sure I understand your motives."

I don't understand my reasoning either, so at least we're both on the same page. The headache that is starting to form becomes more pronounced as I try to make sense of all of it. That forces us into another round of silence. The only thing I can hear is the sound of our sneakers hitting the pavement.

"Look, man," Levi says. "I know you care about Isla. And I respect you for wanting to make things right. But you gotta be honest with yourself about your intentions."

I let out a heavy sigh, knowing he is right. The truth is, my feelings for Isla have always been more complicated than I've been willing to admit. Even after all these years, the connection between us is still there. In fact, it might have grown stronger because of us being apart.

"I don't know what I want," I confess for the first time out loud.

"Are you sure about that, or are you trying to bullshit me and yourself?"

He got me again. "Fine. I want Isla back in my life and in my bed."

"Makes sense, given that she's causing you to snap on some of our teammates."

"Of course you know about that," I say as I think about Knox. We'd been doing our best to avoid each other since things hit the fan in our kitchen and have been doing a good job at it. I wonder who ratted, but it doesn't matter in the grand scheme of things. "By the way, he started it."

"I'm not surprised. And I'm talking to you not only as your best friend but also as the captain of the team. We can't have you and Knox on the outs and expect to continue winning games."

"I get it, but you know how Knox can be. He just gets under my skin sometimes."

"I know, but usually, you're good about avoiding his shit. We need you to find a way to work together, regardless of your personal issues."

The team has to come first above everything, even if that means swallowing my pride and making nice with Knox. And I can do that if he keeps Isla's name out of his mouth.

"I'll try to smooth things over with him," I promise, already dreading the conversation. "But I can't guarantee anything."

"Just do what you can. We don't want this to raise to the level where Coach needs to get involved."

Fuck. That's the last thing I want to happen.

The mention of Coach getting involved sends a chill down my spine. That's a complication I don't need right now, especially with everything else happening.

"I'll handle it," I assure Levi. "I'll talk to Knox and smooth things over. We'll figure it out."

Levi nods, satisfied with my response. "Good. The team needs you focused and on your game."

We alternate between silence and small talk for the rest of our run, and before I know it, I run up the front stairs of my house and unlock the front door. The heat from inside is a welcome relief from the crisp morning chill. I kick off my running shoes and head upstairs, straight for the shower, because I need it.

I wrap up my shower and spend the next few hours working on some assignments I need to get done. Just as I'm about to close my laptop, my phone's ringtone plays because of an incoming call. I glance at the screen and see that it's my mom.

"Hey, Mom. What's up?"

"Nothing much, just wanted to check in on you and see how things were going."

"Things are...okay. Are you sure everything is fine?" I hate questioning her reasoning, but I can tell something is up.

"Just tired, you know, the usual. By the way, thank you for sending the money for the bills. I...really appreciate it, Ash."

I can hear the embarrassment in her voice, so I change the subject quickly. "No problem. What are you doing today?"

"I'm running around trying to make sure your sister has everything she needs for her basketball game today." She finishes her sentence with a yawn.

"When is her game?" An idea is forming in my head as I wait for her to respond. I stand up from my desk and stretch as I grab my bookbag.

"It starts at 2 p.m."

"Why don't you do what you can, and I'll come there to pick her up and take her to her game? That way, you can stay home and rest on your day off. It can be a surprise."

"I couldn't ask you to do that."

"You're not asking. I'm telling you, this is what I'm doing."

There's a pause on the other end of the line before Mom replies. "Oh, Asher, that would be wonderful. Are you sure you have the time?"

"Absolutely," I assure her, already rearranging what I thought I would do today in my mind. "I don't have any pressing commitments, and it's been too long since I've seen you all. I'll head out soon and be there in plenty of time to get Avery to her game."

"Thank you, sweetheart. That means more than you know." The weariness in her tone is evident, and it tugs at my heart. I know how hard she works to keep our family afloat, and this is something I can do to help her.

"Anytime, Mom. I'll see you soon."

After we hang up, I quickly throw a few essentials into a backpack and head out to my car. I check on a few things before I pull out of the parking spot in front of my house and start driving to Hill Haven.

The ride is quiet, and I get there in record time. As I pull up to my childhood home, Avery is already waiting on the front porch, her basketball bag at her feet. A grin appears on her face when she sees me. It takes a split second before she's running down the steps as I exit my car.

"Asher! I didn't know you were coming home today!"

She flings her arms around me as soon as I close the car door.

I wrap my arms around her in return, lifting her off the ground before setting her back down. "Surprise. Thought I'd come to cheer you on at your game. Maybe show you a few pointers."

Avery rolls her eyes, but she's still smiling. "Please, I could probably beat you on the court these days."

"Oh, is that so?" I raise an eyebrow. "Guess we'll have to put that to the test sometime. Can't have my favorite little sister beating me."

"Whatever. I'm your only sister."

We both laugh, and I give her another side hug. It feels so good to trade barbs with her in person versus via text message. Our relationship is pretty solid, given everything we've experienced. We have our arguments here and there, but for the most part, we get along well. I've watched her grow from a shy little kid into a confident teenager with aspirations bigger than I could ever dream.

I look up as Mom appears in the doorway then, looking tired but happy to see me. With a grin, I jog up the steps to give her a warm hug.

"Thanks for coming, Ash," she says softly. "I really appreciate you taking Avery to her game today to give me a bit of a break."

"I'm happy to do it." I pull back to look at her, noticing the dark circles under her eyes makeup can't quite hide.

"You're working too hard, Mom. I wish you'd let me help more."

She pats my cheek, her eyes glistening a bit. "You're already doing so much, sweetheart. And I want you to enjoy your college years."

Her words are a much-needed reminder of how much is riding on my ability to turn hockey into a career. I need to take care of my family someday.

We chat for a few minutes, catching up, before I check the time and realize we need to get a move on it or else we'll be late.

"Ready to go?" I ask, and Avery nods eagerly.

"Bye, Mom!" she calls out as we head for my car. "I'll see you after the game!"

As I pull out of the driveway, I glance at her and ask, "So how's school going?"

Avery nods, her ponytail bobbing. "Yeah, I'm doing pretty well. Math is still kicking my butt, but I'm getting extra help from a tutor after school."

"That's great, Avery. Education is so important."

"I know, I know. You sound like Mom."

She's not wrong. "It's where I got it from." I chuckle, but my tone turns serious. "Seriously though, keep at it. I know it's not always easy, but it'll pay off in the long run."

"I will because I want to make you and Mom proud."

Moments like this are where I feel she should be able to include Dad, but things didn't work out that way.

Instead, I glance at her before returning my attention to the road. "You already do, Aves. Every single day."

15

ISLA

Today has been an exciting day, to say the least. First, I got up late and almost didn't arrive on time. Second, volunteers wearing matching t-shirts are hauling all types of materials to help with this project. Not that any of this is surprising, however.

Today is Sunday, an off day for hockey and Crestwood University's Volunteer Day. The organizers told the hockey team they would assist in the construction of a house for a family in Crestwood. Because this is a big event all around, it means that I also need to be here to capture some shots of the team making their mark in the community. I've taken part in the past with Mom and Dad because of his job with the university, but this felt different.

So here I am. A little after the crack of dawn, listening to the sounds of power tools whizzing around me. Not to mention, it's a very cool morning, and I'm left wishing I would have thought twice about wearing more than just a hoodie and jeans. But I'm here, taking photos of the guys doing their thing. On any other day, I would have been okay with being up this early, but everything becomes a struggle when you get only a little sleep the night before.

This is becoming a trend, and I don't like it.

It didn't help that I spent most of the night tossing and turning because I couldn't stop thinking about Asher. Then, when I finally fell asleep, I had a dream about him too. The whole point of the conversation we had the other day was to help us move forward, not for me to think about him constantly even while I'm sleeping.

And what a wicked, wet dream it was.

Maybe Selene had a point. Dammit.

Regardless, I'd pay to be back in bed right now rather than to be paid to be at this event. However, I can't, so I might as well do what I'm supposed to do and take some photos.

"Hey, Isla!" Wilder calls out. It looks like he's the first one to notice me. "Glad you're here to get my good side, the ladies will be disappointed if you don't!"

I roll my eyes but can't help smiling as I snap a few shots of him posing dramatically with a hammer. Leave it to Wilder to be this happy this early in the damn morning.

I make my way around the construction site, snapping photos of Crestwood's hockey team as they work. I can't help but wonder how many medical waivers needed to be signed to get the team here, but it was the right choice. Their progress this morning is impressive, and I'm growing more tired looking at it. The day is only supposed to last a few hours, and soon, I'll be back in my bed, hopefully without any commentary from Tessa.

As I round one of the corners of the house, I freeze. Asher is there, working side by side with Knox. Based on what I've noticed during their interactions, I can't help but wonder if they did this on purpose or not. If I'm able to figure out these two are at odds right now, the other guys have to know too.

I lift my camera, zooming in to capture their faces as their focus is on the task at hand. As if he's heard me over the construction noise, Asher looks up, his gaze locking with mine. For a moment, the world seems to stop. The sounds of construction fade away, and it's just us staring at each other across the distance.

Everything in me tells me to look away, but I can't. I'm determined to decipher every emotion that I see flash across his face. Surprise is the main one I am able to pinpoint, but it doesn't last long. What appears next is anyone's guess, and the only one who could confirm it is Asher.

Out of the corner of my eye, I see Knox glance up and start watching us. Having someone intrude on whatever moment this is, is enough to make me shift my attention. I look over at Knox, and it's like he's trying to piece together what is going on, but I'm not sure. I can't help but wonder what conclusions he's drawing.

Knox leans over and says something to Asher, who rolls his eyes at whatever is said. But it's enough to get Asher back to work on the house and me back to taking the photographs I'm supposed to take. I continue moving around the site, focusing on capturing the day's spirit because it will help the community and provide good social media content. Levi talks with some of the other volunteers while he works, and I see Wilder standing nearby, joking around with another group of people.

Blaise catches my eye as he works on his own, unfazed by the chaos around him. He's off to the side, focusing on securing a section of siding. Or so I think it's called. I snap a few shots of him before I feel like I'm intruding and decide to walk away.

The project continues, and I move around, photographing what everyone is doing so that we have a ton of shots to choose from for socials. The fact that I'm moving around helps bring some warmth to my body, but I'm still mentally kicking myself for not bringing some warmer outerwear. That's what I get for rushing out of my room and deciding that not waking up my roommate is a priority.

After taking a few more photos, I step to the side to take a small break. I look around to make sure that I'm not in anyone's way before I pull up the last photo that I just took on my camera. While reviewing some of my shots, I nearly jump out of my skin when I feel a hand on my shoulder. I whirl around to find Asher standing behind me.

"Hey, you okay?" His voice is barely audible over the construction noise.

I nod as the fear leaves my body. Being this close to him and feeling the weight of his hand through my hoodie is too much. Now I'm thinking about him touching me in places I vowed he never would again.

It's crazy that you can both hate someone and want to fuck them at the same time. I take a step back to create some distance between us.

Asher's hand falls to his side, and I can see the hurt flash across his face before he masks it with a neutral expression. "I just wanted to check on you. Saw you standing over here alone."

I force a smile, trying to ignore the way my body reacts whenever we are alone together at this point. "Yeah, I'm good. I'm just taking a quick break to review some photos I've taken so far."

Asher nods, his gaze drifting to my camera. "How are they turning out?"

"They're looking good," I reply, turning the camera so he can see the display. "Everyone seems to like this project. It's nice to see the team coming together for a good cause."

He leans in closer, squinting slightly as he studies the photos. His expression softens, and I hate myself for noticing the change. It's something I would have picked up on when we were dating. Apparently, it's still a skill I have when it comes to him.

"You always had a great eye for catching the perfect photo," he murmurs before sucking in a deep breath. "Looks like that hasn't changed."

I swallow hard, trying to ignore the way his words make my stomach want to flip upside down. "You're way too kind. I'm sure I've gotten better over the years, though."

"I don't doubt that for a second. There's one more reason why I came over here." Before I can blink, Asher takes off his black coat and tosses it over my shoulders.

"W-what are you doing?" I ask. I hate that I'm stuttering because of him.

"Keeping you warm," he says, as if it's the most normal thing in the world. This would be the norm in a different lifetime, but it makes little sense here. However, I'm cold, so I'd be silly not to take him up on it.

I slip my arms through the sleeves, instantly feeling the warmth from Asher's body heat and coat. I hate that the coat smells like him, a cologne that I'm very familiar with. It smells like a sea breeze with hints of citrus that I remember from years ago.

"How did you even know I was cold?" I ask, trying to keep the emotions that are surging through me in check. Why does he still use the same cologne that I used to love?

Asher shrugs, a hint of a smile playing at the corner of his lips. "I've known you long enough to pick up on the little things, and I saw you shivering. You didn't seem to be wearing many layers, so I made an educated guess."

I hate that he's right. I hate that he still knows me well enough to pick up on these little things. It's been years since we were together, yet he can still read me like an open book. It's unsettling and comforting all at once.

"Well, thanks," I mumble, pulling the coat tighter around me. "I appreciate it."

Asher's smile widens, and my traitorous heart skips a beat. "Anytime, Isla."

Before I can respond, I hear Levi's voice from across the construction site. "Hey, Ash! We need your help over here!"

Asher glances over his shoulder, acknowledging Levi with a nod. He turns back to me, his expression apologetic mixed with something else. "Duty calls. I'll catch up with you later, yeah?"

All I do is nod, because I'm unsure what else to say. Asher holds my gaze for a moment longer, searching for something in my eyes. Whatever he finds seems to satisfy him, and he turns to jog over to where Levi is waiting.

I watch him go, my fingers curling into the sleeves of his coat. His warmth and scent linger, and I fight the urge to bury my nose in the fabric.

I love this cologne, and the memories it resurrects are

from happy times—not when my heart was breaking into a million pieces.

I shove those thoughts to the side and take a few more pictures before taking another small break. My hands are getting cold, and I want to give them a chance to warm up.

When I place my right hand in the coat pocket, I gasp. I pull out a regular-sized bag of the original Skittles. I flip the candy around in my hand, stunned that I'm holding this item. Is this a peace offering of sorts?

Despite the complicated emotions swirling inside me, I tear open the corner of the bag and pop a few Skittles into my mouth.

Pure bliss spreads through each one of my taste buds. The burst of fruity flavors on my tongue is heaven, and I know I shouldn't be eating candy this early or basking in the joy this small gesture has given me. But dammit, it's a bag of Skittles.

My eyes land on him, and as if he can feel me looking at him, he turns his head, so his gaze is on me. It only takes a second for me to find the answer to the question that has been burning in my mind for the last few minutes.

This had been his plan the entire time.

16

ISLA

I cross my feet as I lean back against a wall in the campus center. I'm wasting time listening to the latest episode of *You're In Danger, Girl* while waiting for Hailey to arrive.

The campus center is quieter than normal because it is the weekend, and most students are probably hungover from partying the night before. This is why this was the perfect time to meet up with Hailey for lunch.

Speaking of, I find Hailey before she sees me. She's standing by the smoothie counter, looking around to, I assume, find me. I wave my arm, and she gives me a small nod.

As I approach, she gives me a look. "There you are. I was starting to think you ghosted me."

I laugh because I know she's being sarcastic. "Now, I wouldn't do that... not on purpose, anyway."

Hailey smirks. "Well, if you did, just know I'd haunt you for the rest of your life. Let's go grab a table."

We make our way to a small table by the window. By placing our things down before ordering food, we show that the table by the window is taken. We both end up with sandwiches and she also gets a smoothie, while I decide to just drink water with lunch.

I'm glad she breaks the ice first when we sit down at our table.

"You know, I'm so glad you didn't say you wanted to meet at Brewed Beginnings," Hailey says as she takes out a reusable straw from her bag.

I shrug. "I figured you were already in there so often, why would you want to spend more time there on your day off?"

That causes her to chuckle for a second. "Not to mention, I'm also the chess club president, and we meet there as well. Sometimes, it feels as if I sleep there too."

So far, things aren't awkward between us. I wasn't sure what to expect when we made plans to meet up, but now I'm glad we did. "Sounds like you're super busy."

"That's an understatement. My best friend, Jade, always tries to convince me to let loose and go out to parties with her, but I have a packed schedule between Levi, school, work, and chess club. I assume yours is too with the hockey team?"

Since I'm in the middle of chewing a piece of my sandwich, I wait until I'm done to respond. "I'm in a similar boat with the business and having a best friend who also tries to cause chaos in my life. But between classes, the team, and everything else... it's been nonstop."

She raises an eyebrow. "Everything else? Care to elaborate?"

"It's not as interesting as it sounds. I have some health issues I'm trying to get a handle on. Dad's got the hockey team over tonight for some bonding thing, and I'm helping out and attending."

Hailey nods along as if this isn't a surprise to her. "Levi mentioned it to me. He'll be there tonight. Sounds like a good time to observe all their drama up close. The stories I hear from Levi sometimes are just...wild. I swear, some guys get into situations I could never dream of."

I laugh to cover up the fact that I'm thinking about the tension between Asher and me and the issues that Asher is having with Knox. Asher seems to be the common denominator here. "I doubt there's that much drama. But you never know. I just hope it doesn't turn into a mess."

"With all those guys in one place? It's bound to be."

"And I assume Asher is going to be there? That could also cause a mess."

I jerk my head as my eyes land on her. "Wait. What are you talking about?"

"I saw you two having a pretty intense conversation after one of their games."

Fuck. "That wasn't even a good segue."

"And you're avoiding the question."

Touché. "Things are...complicated, to say the least. We used to date, but I went away to another college, and now I'm back." That's the condensed, clean version, at least. I don't mention how he broke my heart or how he can still set my body ablaze when his green eyes meet mine. Or how his presence sets my nerves on fire.

She studies me for a moment. "There's more to it than that, isn't there? I can see it in your eyes, Isla."

I shift in my seat because she nailed it. This is why I'll never excel at poker... or become a serial killer. My eyes will betray me each and every time. "It's been awkward, but we're making it work because we see each other so often now."

"Awkward how? Like, you want to rip each other's clothes off awkward, or you want to rip each other's throats out awkward?"

I can't help but laugh at her bluntness. It helps relieve the tension this questioning has been creating within me. The truth is, it's a bit of both, but I am not sure if I want to admit it to her.

"You sound like my best friend, Selene, now."

"It sounds like we need to get you, me, Jade, and Selene together at some point."

I like that idea. "That sounds like a plan. But in terms of Asher, it's complicated," I repeat. "We have a lot of history."

See? Simple diplomatic answer.

"But you'll figure it out, I'm sure."

I'm glad she has more faith in that than I do.

The rest of our lunch goes well as we take our time getting to know each other. Once we wrap things up and say goodbye, I decide to head to my car and drive home versus running the risk of having to see Tessa by going to our dorm room. I replay my conversation with Hailey in my mind as I'm trying to wrap my head around what tonight will be like if Asher shows up. As I pull into my driveway, I see Bella at the window. As I walk up the front porch stairs, Bella's excited barking greets me even before I open the door. She is all over me as soon as I step inside.

"Hey, old girl," I say, bending down to give her a few scratches behind the ears. She licks my hand in response, her whole body practically vibrating with excitement. "You ready for a house full of people?"

She tilts her head at me as if she's never heard such a preposterous thing. I laugh and give her one last pat before heading into the living room, where my mom is wiping down the coffee table.

"Hey, Mom. Need some help?" I ask, and she looks up, smiling.

"Perfect timing, sweetheart. You can help me with the drinks and then make sure everything is ready in the living room," she says.

"Where's Dad?"

"He's out back, double-checking the grill. Why don't you go say hello?"

"I will, and then I'll come back in and help where I can."

I walk to the back of the house and find Dad outside, rocking his 'King of the Grill' apron that Grace and I got him on his birthday years ago.

"Looking good, Dad," I say, gesturing to his apron as I step out onto the back patio.

He glances up from the grill and pushes his glasses so that they sit on top of his head. "This old thing has seen its fair share of team barbecues."

"That's true. Looks like you're almost done setting up."

Dad confirms that with a nod. "Yeah, we should be ready to go before everyone arrives. I have called in reinforcements to help, and they should be here to set up within the hour."

It's fantastic because my parents can relax and not have to spend their entire evening working to ensure this event goes well. "You know, it's been a while since I've been here for one of these."

"It has. I think the last one you went to was your senior year of high school."

That was when Asher and I were still together. We spent the night stealing glances at one another to avoid letting anyone know the true nature of our relationship. I remember being so hopeful about everything between us, but it all crashed down around me weeks later.

"Are you excited about tonight?"

Dad's question brings me back to the present day. "I

guess, but I'm more focused on how I can help you prepare. If you don't have anything for me to do, I'll go back in and check with Mom."

"I don't, so please go help your mother. I'll come in when I'm done and help too."

With that plan in place, I walk back inside and get more marching orders from Mom. Bella follows me around as I move through the house, setting things up. She sniffs at everything I put down, as if giving her own little seal of approval. Her carefree energy makes me smile, although it takes a little longer for me to get things done due to her investigation.

I spend the next hour or two helping my mom, dad, and the team they hired to help cater the event with foods and beverages they won't be making. When it is go time, Bella runs around the house excitedly and greets our guests as they arrive.

Despite all the preparation, I'm still feeling overwhelmed.

Many of the players and staff have arrived, and this is the most people I've seen in our backyard in years. I spot Levi chatting with my dad while others gather around the snack table, helping themselves to chips and dip. I walk into the kitchen and share a smile with my mom, where she's putting the finishing touches on a platter for the sliders.

"Is there anything else I can do to help?" I want to stay

busy, so I don't have to think about the elephant in the room.

"Sweetheart, you've already done enough."

"I want to help, though."

She leans in to tell me, "You're also supposed to be enjoying this party too. After all, you're a member of the team."

Although I've told myself and others I am, it still feels weird. But it's true, I might not be on the ice, but I am a member of the Red Wolves' organization.

I make it a point to greet and chat with Bailey and Alice. I want to get to know them better outside of work. As the conversation reaches a comfortable lull, I bring the soda I'd been nursing to my lips, and just before I can take a sip, my eyes land on the man who has a starring role in my mind.

Asher.

He's standing with a group of teammates, one hand in his pocket, the other holding his drink. As if sensing that he is being stared at, he looks up, and our eyes clash across the backyard.

If the heat lamps weren't already keeping me warm, I know the look in his eyes would. It makes me think of every dirty thought known in history, and I think I can thank Selene and Hailey for that.

I need to get out of here.

I chug the rest of my soda and then turn to Bailey and

Alice. "If you'll excuse me, I need to head inside and check in with my mom."

They give me small smiles as I leave them in my backyard. As I walk into the kitchen, I don't see my mom, but I find her in the living room talking with one of the college administrators. She gives me a small wave, and I plaster on a fake smile as I continue walking toward the stairs and up to the next level of our house.

Am I being absolutely ridiculous for running away from someone in my house? Probably, but I want to put as much distance between us as I can. Because if anyone notices, I know they'll be able to pick up on what's going on within seconds.

I debate whether I want to go into my room or bathroom to get a breather and then make the snap decision to walk into my bathroom. There, I can at least throw water on my face and try to cool my skin, which now feels like it's scorching hot.

I close the bathroom door behind me and put my hands on the vanity. I study my reflection in the mirror, confirming that my cheeks are flushed. Damnit. I hate that Asher still has this effect on me, even after all these years.

Turning on the faucet, I cup my hands under the stream of cold water and splash it on my face. The shock helps clear my head, but it does little to calm anything else. I hear a soft knock on the door as I reach for a towel and pat my skin dry.

"I'll be out in a second."

"Take your time. I'm just checking up on you."

Recognizing the voice, I freeze with the towel still pressed to my face. There's no way that this could be happening to me. There's no way that Asher is standing right outside that door.

And he wants to see how I'm doing?

All rational thought flies out the window as I toss the towel over my shoulder and scramble to the door. I unlock it within a second, yank the door open, and pull him inside, not caring that anyone might have witnessed what happened.

Asher stumbles into the bathroom because of my aggressive move. While I usually would have taken the time to dissect how I managed to move this giant hockey player like I did, I don't. Instead, I shut the door behind him and lock it before I face him.

Is this considered kidnapping? It might be.

"Isla, what are you—" he starts, but I cut him off, pressing a finger to his lips.

"I'm about to do something crazy and don't want to give it much thought. If you don't want to kiss me right now, please say so," I whisper, my voice trembling as I do.

It takes a second for it to click in his head, but then he pushes forward and kisses me. Everything about this is oh so wrong, yet it feels so right. So, instead of worrying about what I'm doing right now, I focus on what I'm feeling.

Everything about this kiss is hot, and Asher is so demanding. I can taste the sweetness of the juice he was drinking on his tongue as it tangles with mine. It's like no time has passed at all, and we're right back where we left off. Alarm bells are ringing in my head about this turn of events, but I'm ignoring them all.

Asher's hands slide under my sweater, and his fingertips touch my lower back. I shiver just before I arch into him, deepening the kiss. Despite being locked away in my bathroom, a distant part of my brain continues to remind me that anyone could come up the stairs and catch us. But I can't bring myself to care with Asher's body pressed against mine.

I moan into his mouth, my hips rolling shamelessly against his. It's like my body has a mind of its own, desperate for anything and everything he is willing to give.

Asher tears his mouth from mine, trailing hot, open-mouthed kisses along my jaw and down the column of my throat. I tilt my head back, giving him better access as my fingers move from his shoulders to his hair.

"Fuck, I've missed this," he groans against my skin. "I've missed you, sunshine."

His words make me melt even further into him, my body molding to his as if no time has passed. The familiarity of his touch, his scent, the way he feels against me. All of it is intoxicating.

Asher's actions grow bolder, hands sliding up my

ribcage and brushing the underside of my breasts. I gasp, and the words fall out of my mouth before I can stop them. "That's not where I want you."

"Then where do you want me, baby? You know I love when you tell me what you want."

I bite my lip for a second, but I've already decided. Fuck it. This is what I want, and this is what I need to take the edge off. "I want you to fuck me. With your tongue."

Asher's eyes darken because of my words, and a wicked grin spreads across his face. He looks as if he's just won the jackpot. Without warning, he hooks his hands under my thighs and lifts me up. He spins us around and carries me to the vanity.

He sets me down, and we both fumble to get the button on my jeans undone. I lift my hips to help him slide them off, along with my panties. None of this is romantic, and I don't care. This is about pure lust, and I want to get him out of my system. The cold counter against my bare ass makes me shiver, but it's quickly forgotten as Asher drops to his knees before me.

He presses hot, open-mouthed kisses along the inside of my thigh, and the feel of his stubble against my skin creates goosebumps. My fingers are in his hair because I want him to be locked in on where I need him.

"Before I begin, you'll have to be quiet, sunshine. We don't want Coach to hear what I'm doing to his daughter, right?"

The only thing I can do is nod my head like a bobble-head doll, and he takes that as confirmation that I'm all in. He hooks my legs over his shoulders and puts his hands on my hips just before burying his face between my thighs.

The first swipe of his tongue has me seeing stars. I swear I lose all control of my body as my head falls back against the mirror with a soft thud. He groans as if this is bringing as much pleasure to him as it is to me. He looks into my eyes as he fucks me with his mouth, driving me closer and closer to the edge.

He stops what he's doing and says, "Keep quiet or I'm going to stop. Got it?"

I nod and wonder where this side of him came from, but I don't ask any questions. Instead, when he gets back to licking me again, I grab his hair with one hand while the other flies over my mouth. It's all I can do to try to keep quiet the moans and screams that are threatening to be unleashed.

All that does is encourage him to double his efforts. His tongue moves faster as he alternates between every motion known to man and then some in order to get me off. His fingers are digging into my hips now as if to keep me steady because he can sense that I'm about to lose it.

I'm so close.

My thighs begin to shake, and my breaths come in short, sharp pants in between the animalistic noises I'm making. He doesn't let up, and soon, I'm flying off the deep end as my orgasm crashes over me.

He works me through it, his tongue only slowing down as I come down from my high. When I finally catch my breath, he presses a soft kiss to my inner thigh before standing up.

"If you ever need my services again, you know how to contact me." He kisses me with such passion that I not only taste myself, but I feel lightheaded. That could also be the result of the mind-blowing orgasm he just gave me. When he pulls away, he walks over to the door and says, "I plan on making up for lost time."

With that, he leaves me in my childhood bathroom with more than just a physical mess to clean up.

17

ISLA

I mentally replay the interactions I've had with Asher over the past week.

On the one hand, I can't help but smile every time I think about him giving me his coat and the Skittles on Saturday. Deep down, I know I shouldn't be feeling this way. He's my ex, the one who broke my heart and made me build these walls around myself. Nevertheless, I can't deny that I appreciated the gesture—or that I swooned a little when he made sure I was warm, even though he didn't have to.

And I can't even think about what we did in my parents' house during the team bonding event. The way he looked up at me with his head between my legs almost made me have another orgasm. It made me forget, just for a moment, all the reasons why we shouldn't have been doing it. I have no regrets outside of wanting more of him, not less.

Damnit, Selene and Hailey. More so Selene, but that's beside the point.

I sigh as I use my key to unlock my dorm room. Thoughts of Asher evaporate as soon as I'm greeted by the icy glare of my roommate. She barely acknowledges my presence before turning back to her laptop, choosing to type loudly on her keyboard.

"Oh, you're back," she says a few seconds later as I put my bookbag down near my desk.

"That I am," I reply, taking off my coat. "Hope you had a good day."

I don't want to be nice to her, but I can't help but be polite because I don't want things to get worse between us.

She snorts, and I can feel her rolling her eyes even though I can't see her face. "As if you care."

I bite my tongue, holding back what I really want to say. It's not worth it to engage. With a sigh, I run a hand across my face and realize it's been a while since I shaved the hair that grows on my chin. It's one of the many perks of PCOS—unwanted hair in all the wrong places. I try not to let it bother me, but sometimes it feels like one more thing I have to deal with, as if everything else isn't enough.

I've asked Dr. Patel about some remedies for that and will be trying a medication soon.

Making a mental note to do that the next time I shower, I sit at my desk and pull out my laptop. I brush it off, focusing instead on the pile of homework waiting for me. I have a couple of papers that are due in the next couple of weeks, and I want to at least start them, so I'm not rushing at the last minute. At least that's the hope, because who knows how much I'll actually procrastinate.

I settle in at my desk, open my laptop, and try to concentrate on the assignment in front of me. But my mind keeps wandering, and the tension in the room makes it hard to focus. The clickety-clack of my room-mate's furious typing is getting on every last one of my nerves. Instead of pouring gasoline on an already burning fire, I dig into my bookbag, find my Bluetooth head-phones, and try to enter my own world. Once I put the headphones in my ears, I find my go-to homework/study playlist and press play.

I take a deep breath, attempting to center myself. I can't let her get to me because I have work to do. She will not be a distraction.

The music I listen to time and time again does some-thing to my brain. It is helping to drown out the bitchy vibes that are attempting to slap me in the face, thanks to my roommate. I open up the syllabus for my media and society class and download the PDF I'm supposed to read for class, which will help with the paper I need to write.

I force myself to focus on the words before me, trying to absorb the information about social media's impact on modern society. It's an interesting topic, one that I can relate to as a college student and as a photographer who shares my work online. But even as I read, my mind keeps drifting back to Asher and what has happened between us.

No, I can't think about that. What I have to do is stay focused on my studies. I highlight a relevant passage in the PDF, wishing I had printed it out at the library so I could write some notes in the margins. I force my attention back to reading because I need to make progress on this assignment. The words blur together as I try to concentrate; my mind still wanders to thoughts of anything but the document in front of me.

After what feels like hours but is probably only thirty minutes, I can't take it anymore. Although I haven't been back in my room for long, I need to get out of here. I know I need to find another place to study and do homework because I can feel Tessa's negative energy from here.

I save my work and close my laptop, stuffing it into my backpack along with the rest of the work I need to do. I grab my coat and head for the door, not bothering to acknowledge my roommate as I leave. The cool evening air hits my face as I step outside, and I take a deep breath, feeling some of the tension leave my body.

I start walking, not really sure where I'm going, but I need to move. The campus is quiet at this time of night, which I don't mind at all. The library is a great place to go, where I can get some work done and find the quietness I'm craving.

I pull out my phone to check the time. Selene sometimes works the late-night shift at the library, and it would be nice to catch up with her, but it's not late enough. Then again, if there's a chance she'll be there tonight, maybe I'll stay there until she's done with her shift and take the couch in her room. The idea continues forming in my head as I text Selene.

> **Me:** Hey, are you working at the library tonight?

Selene: I am. What's up?

> **Me:** I needed to get out of my room because of you-know-who and could hang out there through your shift.

Selene: Ah. That's fine, and then you can come back to my place.

> **Me:** Thanks so much. I'm so grateful for you. 🤍🤍

Selene: As you should be.

Selene: Just kidding. I love you, too. See you soon.

I smile at my phone before stuffing it back into my pocket. She's absolutely ridiculous, but I love her, so I guess that's why I keep her around. Plus, we can talk about the latest that has happened between Asher and me because I haven't filled her in. I wanted to wait until I processed it. However, at this point who knows when that will be?

As I approach the library, my phone buzzes with another notification. Expecting it to be Selene, I glance at the screen, only to see that I have a new email. It's from Bailey, and I'm left confused by the subject of the message.

The subject line of Bailey's email reads, "Meet Tomorrow?" Confusion floods my brain. I stare at my screen for a moment before tapping on the message to open it.

Hey Isla,

If you have time, I'd like to meet with you tomorrow to discuss your work and a few other things. Would 10 a.m. work? If not, let me know what times work.

Best,

Bailey

I frown at my phone screen, trying to decipher the cryptic message. Discuss my work? A few other things? What could it be about? I can't figure out what I might have done wrong. Should my mind have gone straight to me thinking I fucked up? Probably not, but that's where it goes.

Could it be about Asher? Not too many people know about our history, and they shouldn't know what has gone down in the last week.

Did Asher tell anyone?

But that doesn't make sense either. I would also expect to hear from my dad if it was about Asher.

My mind races with possibilities as I stare at Bailey's

email, my feet carrying me on autopilot toward the library. Could it be about my photography work for the team? Did I somehow mess up an assignment without realizing it? Or... is it about Asher? The thought sends a jolt of anxiety through my body.

I take a deep breath, trying to calm my nerves as I type out a reply.

Hi Bailey,
10 a.m. works for me. I'll see you then.
Sincerely,
Isla

I hit send before I can second-guess myself. I shove my phone back into my pocket because my anxiety is climbing. Now I have something else that's going to screw with my brain until after 10 a.m. tomorrow. But I have to focus on the work I need to complete right now.

The entrance to Ramsey Library is finally only feet away. I say finally because it feels as if so much has happened in the last hour. Warm light spills out of the enormous windows, and I can see rows and rows of bookshelves from across the street.

I walk through the automated doors and stop. Selene will be working at the circulation desk soon, so it makes sense for me to stay on the main floor so that she will see me when she comes in. I scan the room, searching for an empty table where I can set up my stuff for the next few hours.

Spotting a somewhat secluded area near the computer lab, I make my way over to the table in question. I settle into a computer chair with wheels and pull out my laptop, binders, and highlighters for the second time this evening. I arrange them neatly on the small table in front of me and open my laptop.

The first thing I do is print out all the papers I need to read about media and society. If I'm going to the library, I'm going to read and digest the information the way I want to, which just so happens to be by highlighting things and taking notes the old-fashioned way.

Once I collect my printouts, I put my headphones on, press play on my playlist, and get to work. The change in scenery and being able to mark up the documents does wonders for my focus because I find myself getting things done. The words flow more easily now as I highlight passages and write down key points that I'm taking from the reading. Time seems to slip away as I work. The outside world has faded into the background, and I'm finally getting things done.

A gentle tap on my shoulder startles me back to reality. I look up to see Selene standing beside me with a soft smile. I take my headphones out so that she can speak to me. "Hey, best friend. How's it going?"

I lean back in my chair, stretching my arms above my head. "Better now that I'm here, if I'm being honest."

She glances at my things scattered across the table. "Looks like you've been productive."

"Yeah, I feel like I'm killing it for the first time in a while. There's so much we need to catch up on. Plus, something else happened that has me kind of freaking out." I pull out my phone and show her the email from Bailey. "I got this message asking to meet tomorrow morning. She wants to discuss my work and 'a few other things'. Whatever that means."

Selene reads the email before she looks up at me. "Huh. That is a bit cryptic. What do you think it's about?"

I shrug. "No clue. I've been racking my brain trying to figure out if I did something wrong, but I can't think of anything."

"I'm sure it's nothing bad," Selene reassures me. "You're an amazing photographer, Isla. The team is lucky to have you."

"Thanks, Selene." I give her a small smile. It is what I need.

"Would it be weird for you to ask your dad if he knows anything?"

I sigh. "I thought about it and even double-checked that Bailey hadn't CCed him on the email. Wouldn't they have included him if it was something serious?" I say, trying to convince myself more than Selene.

She nods. "That's a good point. Honestly, if it was something awful, I doubt Bailey would wait until tomorrow to talk to you. She'd probably want to discuss it ASAP, even if it's late on a Monday."

Her logic makes sense. "You're right. I'm just over-thinking it. As usual." I shake my head at myself.

"That's why I'm here. To bring you back down to Earth. Now I have to go and start my shift."

I glance at the clock on my screen. Had that much time really passed? "Okay, I'll be here, and thanks for letting me stay with you tonight."

"It's not a problem." She flips her red hair over her shoulder dramatically. "Now, if you need to check out any books, I'm your girl."

"Duly noted." I roll my eyes at her as she walks away. A few seconds later, I snatch my phone from its resting place on the table. I immediately set an alarm to make sure that I'll wake up with enough time to make it back to my dorm room.

The last thing I want is to be late for this meeting with Bailey.

18

ISLA

"About time you came to my humble abode."

I can't help but chuckle as Selene moves out of the way to let me into her apartment. Also, it's not like she's wrong.

In the time that I've been back home and enrolled at Crestwood, I haven't had a chance to stop by Selene's place on campus. Now that I've finally made it here, I'm struck by how much the place is ... just her.

Video chatting hasn't given me the full scope of her room that it deserves. Selene lives in a single dorm room in one of the older, yet recently renovated, buildings on campus. Although the space is small, she's made it her own. The room is filled with a warm glow from the string of fairy lights draped across the walls, reminding me of how she decorated her childhood bedroom.

A twin bed is pushed against one wall, made and

covered with what looks to be a soft quilt in shades of blue and green. There are a few clothes scattered on the bed, but it doesn't look too messy. Near the window hangs a dreamcatcher gently swaying in the breeze from the air vent. There's a small television resting on a TV stand on one part of the wall facing the bed. The other part has a small desk that is cluttered with textbooks, notebooks, and a laptop. My eye catches a framed photo of us at our high school graduation, and I can't help but smile at the memory.

Despite the limited space, Selene has created a welcoming and comfortable environment for herself. Her room is a reflection of her, and it makes me wish I had a space on campus to do the same.

Technically, I do, but having to deal with Tessa makes me not even want to bother.

Selene plops down on her bed and pats the space beside her. "Come, sit. Tell me everything."

I follow her lead and ask, "Where do I start?" I sigh, leaning back against the wall.

"From the beginning. Duh."

I tell her about the conversation Asher and I had, where things ended up, and what happened at the volunteering site. However, I save the best for last.

"But that's not all."

I try to make the thoughts in my head make sense enough so I can voice them out loud. Never mind. It's time to rip the Band-Aid off. "Well, I took your advice."

Selene stares at me for several seconds, as if she has no idea what I'm talking about. Then, the realization hits. "YOU. DID. WHAT?"

All I can do is nod and bite my lip.

"THAT'S ALL YOU'RE GOING TO SAY?"

"Selene, stop yelling."

She looks around as if she doesn't realize she's doing it. "Oops. When I suggested it, I didn't expect you to actually do it. You usually blow me off."

"Well... he blew me off in my childhood bathroom. During the team bonding thing at my house."

"I'm so... proud of you. Was it worth it?"

I roll my eyes at her praise. I've already proved that I suck at lying, so here goes nothing. "It was fantastic. The only issue is that our playtime session didn't result in me not wanting him anymore. I didn't fuck him out of my system."

"This is such a—"

"A mind fuck? Yep, that's pretty much the way I would describe it," I finish for her. "It's surreal, and I can't believe I did it. However, I have no regrets, so there's that."

"Have you talked to him since?"

I shake my head. "Nope. I've seen him at the rink this week, but haven't spoken to him. Mostly because I've been running from him every chance I get. What's funny about all of this is that he said he wants to try and rebuild some sort of professional relationship, given that I now work for the hockey team, and we'll be seeing each other frequently. And look what I did. Made things more complicated, apparently."

"And how do you feel about all of it now?"

I let out a humorless laugh. "Honestly? I don't know. It's a hot mess, and a large part of me wants to avoid him like my life depends on it."

"Yes, but you work for the hockey team."

I sigh. "Yes, Captain Obvious, I know. And it is a dream gig for me. You know I did something similar at NYU, and I wanted to continue it here...to help me feel like everything is returning to normal."

"True, and you shouldn't have to give that up just because of Asher," Selene says. "This is your chance to do what you love on your own terms."

I nod slowly because she's right. But it's easier said than done. "I know, I know. It's just... hard. Being around him again stirs up all these old feelings. Feelings I thought I'd buried a long time ago. Between being in love with him and growing to hate him, it's just hard. As was he when we did what we did in my bathroom."

That makes Selene burst out laughing, and it takes her a second to catch her breath and be serious again. "That's understandable. It's difficult facing your past, especially when it's wrapped up in someone you used to love who betrayed you. I remember how crushed you were when he took you out on that date, only to tell you he didn't think things would work out."

And here come the painful memories that I tried so

hard to forget. Selene was there for me almost immediately after, when I called to let her know what Asher had said to me. She'd been there to wipe away the tears that hadn't stopped flowing, no matter how hard I tried, because I'd had my heart broken for the first time in my life. She was also there when I declared that there was no way in hell I was going to Crestwood University because he was going to be there.

"I remember it like it was yesterday," I say, rubbing my index finger across my lips. "How he looked at me after we enjoyed your standard dinner and a movie was so cold. His words made me question whether I was hallucinating or not. I truly thought I was going to spend the rest of my life with him, and then he just... ended it. Just like that." I punctuate the end of my sentence with a snap of my fingers.

"And yet, you didn't let him break you."

"Oh, he broke me. I just didn't let him keep me from putting myself back together."

Selene smiles at me. "And that's what matters most. You picked yourself up, dusted yourself off, and kept moving forward. It wasn't easy, but you did it. And now, here you are, back at Crestwood, ready to chase your dream and get drunk."

This time, my laughter is genuine. "I don't know about the drinking part, but thanks. I don't know what I'd do without you."

"Probably be an even bigger hot mess," she teases,

nudging me with her elbow. "But I'm proud of you for handling this situation with much more grace than most people would."

"I don't know about that," I say, shaking my head. "I still feel like I'm barely keeping it together sometimes."

"Who doesn't feel that way?"

"Good point."

Selene reaches over and grabs her phone. "Enough talking about Asher for now. Let's focus on more important matters, like what we're going to eat tonight. My treat."

"We can just go to one of the dining halls."

She glares at me, but I can see she doesn't mean it. "I already said I was treating you, and I don't want to leave my room, so..." Her voice trails off as she looks down at her phone again.

I can't help but grin at her. "You always know how to cheer me up."

"It's a gift," she says with a wink. "Now, what are you in the mood for? Chinese? Pizza? Thai?"

I pretend to think about the options. "Hmm, I could go for some greasy, cheesy goodness right about now."

"Pizza it is!" Selene says and hands me her phone. You pick the toppings, and I'll place the order."

"Okay, I'm thinking pepperoni, sausage, and extra cheese," I say, handing the phone back to Selene. "With a side of garlic bread, because why not?"

Selene taps the screen to finalize our order. She then

walks over to her desk and grabs her laptop. "Now, while we wait, why don't we watch a movie? *The Princess Bride* or *10 Things I Hate About You*?"

"You know me so well. Let's go with *10 Things I Hate About You*. I could use a good dose of '90s rom-com magic right about now."

"Excellent. Let me hook this up so we can watch it on the bigger screen."

As the opening credits of *10 Things I Hate About You* start to roll, I lean back against Selene's pillows. There are a million things I should be doing right now related to school, but I'm not. This is what I needed after the emotional rollercoaster of a week—some quality time with my best friend, getting ready to eat some comfort food, and watching a movie.

About thirty-five minutes into the movie, our food order arrives, and after Selene walks back into her room with it, my stomach growls at the sight.

The aroma of melted cheese and garlic fills the room as Selene sets the pizza box down on the bed between us. She hands me a paper plate and a can of soda before settling back into her spot. I let her grab a slice first since she bought it, but once she's done, I dig in and almost moan when I take my first bite. The combination of cheese, pepperoni, and sausage is heavenly. While I might regret it later, depending on how my body reacts, it's the least of my concerns right now.

"Mmm, this is exactly what I needed," I mumble with

a mouthful of pizza. My manners have flown out the window, apparently.

Selene laughs at my lack of decorum. "Same, and I didn't realize it until it got here. I'm glad you went through emotional turmoil for us to get this."

I swallow my bite and stick my tongue out at her playfully. "You're an asshole."

"Clearly," she says with a smirk.

As we watch the movie and continue enjoying our food, we fall into a most comfortable silence. The only noises that can be heard are our eating, drinking, or the sounds of the movie we're watching.

Once the ending credits roll, I stretch my arms above my head, the movement almost causing what's left of my soda to fall over. I snatch the can from its resting place on the bed and make Selene laugh in the process.

"Nice save," Selene comments, still chuckling at my fumbling attempt to prevent a spill. "Can't have you ruining my precious quilt now, can we?"

I roll my eyes. "I wouldn't dream of it."

"Well, I appreciate you looking out for my stuff." Selene stretches her body too, then hops off the bed to clean up our empty plates and napkins.

As Selene tidies up, I find myself lost in thought, drifting back to my meeting with Asher. Ending the day with Selene sort of cancels out those feelings, leaving me feeling drained yet content.

"Earth to Isla," Selene says, waving a hand in front of my face.

I blink, snapping out of wherever my mind traveled to. "Yeah, sorry. Just... thinking."

Selene nods, understanding in her eyes. "It's been a hell of a day for you. I get it."

"That's an understatement," I mutter, flipping my ponytail over my shoulder. "But thanks for being here for me. I don't know what I'd do without you."

She grins, plopping back down on the bed beside me. "I stand by what I said earlier. You'll probably be a hot mess. But seriously, I've got your back. Always."

I lean my head on her shoulder. "I know. And I've got yours."

We sit like that for a moment before Selene breaks the silence. "So what's your game plan for dealing with Asher? Sure, the conversation was a good start, and you lit the house on fire by letting him eat you out, but what now?"

I sigh, lifting my head from her shoulder. "I know, and I'll just have to take it one day at a time. We should probably talk at some point, but for now, I'm going to keep it professional. I can't let him get under my skin again."

Which sounds hilarious because he's already there.

"Damn right. You're stronger than that. And if he tries anything you don't like, I'll kick his ass myself."

I can't help but laugh at the image of Selene taking on Asher. "I'll keep that in mind."

"You better." Selene glances at her phone, checking the time. "It's getting late. Are you staying here tonight or heading back to your place?"

I consider taking Selene up on her offer. The thought of returning to my dorm room doesn't give me warm fuzzy feelings, but there's a chance that Tessa will either be out or asleep.

"I'll stay here. I don't want to cut our hangout, now slumber party, short."

Selene claps her hands together and says, "That's my girl! Now let's get back to talking about everything Asher did to you, because I want more details."

19

ISLA

The sound of my name being called jolts me awake. "Isla, wake up! You're going to be late!"

Nothing makes sense, however. Who is that? It's not Tessa. She wouldn't spit on me if I was on fire. I open my eyes to see Selene standing by the side of the bed, already dressed and holding out a cup of coffee.

It takes a second for me to sit upright. I swear, my heart skips a beat as I scramble to grab my phone. I glance at the clock time shining on my phone. 9:00 a.m. Crap, I'm supposed to be meeting with Bailey at ten.

I'm late.

"Here," Selene says, pushing the mug into my hands. "You need to go now!"

"Yeah, I'm up!" I reply, jumping out of bed. I try to calculate how much time I have. Fifteen minutes to walk back to my dorm, another twenty minutes to shower and change, and then I have to drive over to Bailey's office. It's not ideal, but it's doable.

"Thanks for waking me," I mumble, taking a sip of the coffee as I try to shake off the sleepiness. The warmth of it does little to calm the anxiety growing by the second. "I can't believe I overslept."

"It happens, but you're fine. You'll get there in time."

I nod, but my mind is already elsewhere. I grab my things in a rush, thankful that I'd packed most of my stuff last night. On the bright side, I slept in the sweatpants and t-shirt I wore here, so at least I don't have to change.

I grab my bookbag and hug Selene before running out the door. The crisp morning air hits me like a slap in the face as I power-walk across campus. This is the last thing I need, but I can't deny that my brain is firing on all cylinders bright and early this morning.

By the time I reach my dorm, I'm slightly out of breath. My nerves are frayed. I burst through the door, relieved to find the room empty. Tessa must have already left for class.

Thank fuck.

I drop my things, pick up the items I need to shower, and hurry to the bathroom. If there was a timer, I am confident I could prove I took the quickest shower on record. I even remember to shave. As I dry myself off, I catch a glimpse of myself in the mirror. My blonde hair is a tangled mess, and some dark circles are under my eyes.

Great. Just great.

I rush back to my room, throw on a clean pair of jeans and a sweater, and put my coat over it. I run my brush through my hair to make it somewhat presentable. With one last glance at the time on my phone, I grab my camera bag, bookbag, and keys and head out to my car.

The drive to Bailey's office is a blur. I barely register anything outside of obeying traffic laws as I clutch the steering wheel. Since there aren't many people there, it's easy to find a parking spot near the entrance of the arena and make it to her office with just minutes to spare.

I take a deep breath, trying to calm my racing heart as I knock on Bailey's door. When I hear her call out, "Come in," I push open the door and step inside.

"Isla, good morning! I'm glad you could make it," Bailey greets me with a warm smile, gesturing for me to take a seat across from her desk.

"Morning, Bailey. Sorry, I'm a hot mess. It's been a... hectic start to the day," I admit, setting my bags down and sinking into the chair.

"No worries, we've all been there," she says, assuring me slightly. "Now, let's get down to business. First, I want to thank you for all of your hard work so far this season. You've far exceeded my expectations."

This makes this meeting sound as if it won't be my worst nightmare come to life. My cheeks grow warm because of Bailey's praise, momentarily pushing aside the lingering anxiety from my frantic morning and the stress I had about this meeting. "Thank you, that means a lot," I reply sincerely. "I've really enjoyed working for the team so far."

Bailey's smile widens at my response. "I'm glad to hear that, Isla. It is the reason why I asked to meet with you today. I have a new project I'd like you to take on if you want to."

I tuck my hair behind my ear and lean forward in my seat. Maybe this won't be such a bad idea. "A new project?"

Bailey nods. "We want you to create a video series focusing on one of our hockey players. The goal is to showcase their life off the ice—their community involvement, personal interests, and the like. It's a chance to give fans a glimpse into who they are outside of hockey. If it's successful like we think it will be, we'll do more."

I run a hand through my hair as I digest the information. "That sounds incredible! I'd love to take this on. Who's the player?"

"I'm not sure yet, actually. We are still waiting for Coach to ask who is interested, and we'll go from there. We should have an answer later this week."

It takes everything in me to keep my mouth from dropping open. The uncertainty of not knowing who I'll be working with sends my anxiety spiraling once again. I try to keep my composure because the last thing I want her to think is that I don't want to do it or that I can't handle it.

"Okay, that makes sense," I say, chewing on my lip for

a second. "What's the timeline for the project? And how many videos are we looking to produce?"

"We're aiming for a series of eight to ten videos over the next few weeks. Think more short-form content than something like a fifteen-minute vlog. Ideally, we'd like to release two videos per week."

"Got it. And in terms of access, will the player be available for regular filming sessions? I know their schedules are crazy, and I don't want to disrupt them too much."

"Absolutely. We'll work closely with the player and you to find a balance that works for everyone involved. Your primary focus will be on capturing their story in a compelling way, but we don't want your or their grades or schoolwork to suffer in any way."

To say I'm excited is an understatement. The creative possibilities are endless, but the looming question of who I'll be working with continues to nag at the back of my mind. Particularly when one player could be in the mix.

Bailey and I spend the next half hour discussing more details of the project. At some point, I take out my phone and begin taking notes on the things she expects me to capture. She emphasizes the importance of filming genuine moments that showcase their personality and avoid scripted moments because they might come across as fake.

By the time our meeting wraps up, my head is spinning with ideas. I thank Bailey profusely before gathering my things and heading out of her office. As I walk back to my car, I'm still thinking about the opportunity that I've earned. I need to tell Selene, Mom, and Dad about it. My parents might already know since Dad is presenting this idea to the team at some point.

Still, they should hear it from me.

As I climb into my car and turn it on, I decide to call Mom on the way to my first class of the day. I pull out of my parking spot, hit the call button on my steering wheel, and wait for Mom to pick up. After a few rings, her voice fills the car.

"Hi, sweetie! This is a nice surprise. How are you doing?"

"Hey, Mom, I'm doing alright. Just heading back from a meeting with Bailey, my boss," I reply.

"Oh, that's great! How did it go?"

I take a deep breath before I begin. "Actually, that's why I'm calling. Bailey offered me the chance to lead a new video project. It's a series profiling one of the hockey players, showing their life off the ice and community involvement."

"Isla, that's incredible! I'm so proud of you," Mom says, and I can practically hear her beaming through the phone. "You've worked so hard, and it's paying off."

"Thanks, Mom. I'm excited but also a bit nervous," I admit, biting my lip. "The thing is, I don't know which player I'll be working with yet. What if they're a dick?"

Mom doesn't know anything about Asher and the heartbreak he caused me. I didn't want to put her in an awkward position with Dad because he absolutely couldn't know. On one hand, I shouldn't have really cared about what happened to Asher after what he did to me. But something still makes me want to protect him from my father's wrath even after all these years.

Mom is quiet for a moment before responding. "Honey, I understand your concerns, and don't blame you for being anxious. But much like when you decided to apply for this position, try to focus on the amazing opportunity this is for your career. I know you'll handle it well, regardless of who you're paired with. And your dad and I will support you every step of the way. Does he know about this?"

I shrug, even though Mom can't see me. "I assume he does because it would directly affect the team, and he's not really one to like many distractions. So he must...and the logical choice would have been for me to produce and film at least some of the content. But maybe he was waiting for me to accept and announce the news?"

"Could be... Regardless, I'm so excited for you. How about you stop by the house sometime soon, and I'll make you your favorite dinner? Maybe Dad will be free too, and we can have dinner as a family for the first time in what feels like forever?"

"That's a great idea. I'm sad Grace won't be there." And I mean every word. It would be nice to get off campus for a bit. In fact, I might stay the night because at least that means I don't have to deal with Tessa for a bit.

"Yeah, she needs to come visit. I'll text you, and we'll figure out a day that works for all of us," Mom says warmly. "In the meantime, try not to stress too much about the project. You're going to do an amazing job."

"Thanks, Mom. I really needed to hear that," I reply, feeling a weight lift off my shoulders. "I'll let you know as soon as I find out more details."

We say our goodbyes, and I end the call, pulling into the parking lot near my first class of the day. I gather my things and head inside. At least this time, I'm on time and don't have to worry about rushing.

Because there is some time before class starts and there are still people sitting in the classroom I'll be entering. I pull my phone out and text Selene.

> Me: I finished the meeting with Bailey. She wants me to work on short-form/vlog-style content for the team, which will provide new and different content for their social media channels.

It doesn't take long for her to reply.

> Selene: That's awesome…I think? What does that require you to do?

I lean against the wall, sparing a glance at the classroom door as students file out.

> Me: I have to shadow a player and get footage of their lives beyond hockey.

Selene: Huh. Who will you be following?

Me: No clue. I won't find out until later this week.

Selene: So it could be Asher.

I knew I wouldn't have to spell it out for her. She knows me well enough to read between the lines.

Me: And that's why I'm freaking the fuck out.

The last few students trickle out of the classroom, and I stroll toward the door, still focused on my phone.

Selene: I get it. But the chances of it being him are lower than it not being him.

Me: You're right.

Selene: You can repeat that anytime, haha.

I roll my eyes as I walk into the classroom.

Me: Haha, very funny. Well, all I can do is hope for the best.

Selene: How true that is. We should meet up for lunch. I'll text you after I'm done with class.

Me: Sounds good.

I slip my phone into my pocket as I reach the desk I usually sit at. I settle into my seat, pulling out my notebook and pen, and in a few minutes, my professor begins her lecture. Despite my best efforts to focus, my mind keeps drifting back to the video project and the possibility of working with Asher.

There's no way my luck can be that bad.

20

ASHER

No one can ever say that I don't go after what I want. After all, it's the reason why I'm up earlier than usual to talk to Isla before my early morning practice.

Convincing Coach Johnson that I should be the star of the new video series that Isla will help put together was almost too easy. None of the other guys were eager to have their lives taped; honestly, I'm not either. But this opportunity allows Isla and me to spend more time together, something I've wanted to do since I thought I saw her on campus weeks ago.

Before the incident at her house.

As I'm headed to my car, I glance at my phone, double-checking the time to make sure that I'm not late. I know I'm not, but checking to confirm I'm not provides some reassurance. Instead of riding over with one of the other guys, I drive myself because I want to talk to Isla alone.

I assume she wasn't too pleased to learn that I would be the subject of her series, but she didn't decline the job, nor did she have an issue with meeting me at the arena early this morning. We are meeting to iron out some last-minute details before we start this whole experiment.

The campus is quiet as I drive to the arena, and when I pull into the parking lot, I spot Isla's car already there. However, I also spot Coach's and a few other vehicles. It makes sense he would be here because he's always here before the rest of us, but now I'm almost wishing we agreed to meet elsewhere. But there's nothing I can do about that now.

You need to remain calm, Bennett. I repeat the mantra as I turn my ignition off and exit the vehicle. I need to control how I act around her with Coach nearby, because he'll pick up on something wrong if the interaction between Isla and me is weird. Yes, we're practically strangers at this point, but we spent a significant portion of the summer together when Coach and Mrs. Johnson allowed me to stay with them for hockey camp just before starting my freshman year.

And then we fell in love, and I fucked it all up.

However, I've recently had my tongue in her pussy, which tells me she's not disgusted by the sight of me.

I take a deep breath and enter the arena, my eyes scanning the hallway for any sign of Isla. Since I don't see her, I approach the locker room. Just as I enter the tunnel, I spot her leaning against the wall, her eyes on her phone. I notice that she has her blonde hair tied back in a ponytail and has placed her camera bag on the floor beside her. She doesn't realize that I am walking toward her because she is engrossed in whatever is on her phone.

"Hey," I say, trying to keep my voice casual despite feeling anything but. "Thanks for meeting me early."

Isla looks up from her phone, her eyes meeting mine. "No problem. I think you're right and that it is a good idea for us to talk before we start this whole thing."

I nod, shoving my hands in my pockets. "Yeah, I figured it would be good for us to set our expectations for this project. Make sure we're on the same page."

Isla tucks her phone into the back pocket of her jeans, her focus on me never wavering. "Okay, so let's talk. How do you want to handle this? What are you okay with me filming? What should I avoid doing?"

I pause for a moment, considering her questions carefully. "Well, I want to keep it real, you know? I don't want anything to appear rehearsed. But," I run a hand through my hair, "there are some parts of my life I'd rather keep private. My family, for example. They're not part of this, and I'd like to keep it that way."

"I can respect that. This project is about you, and although your family is a part of that, I get not wanting to drag them into it. I'll focus on your day-to-day as an

athlete, routines, interactions with the team, the fans...
that kind of thing."

"Yeah, that sounds good," I reply, happy that we've
come to that agreement. "And as for the rest...just let me
know if something feels off or you're uncomfortable
filming something. We can always work around it."

She nods. "Likewise."

This almost feels too easy. I thought the conversation
we needed to have would have been longer, but now I'm
left standing here with her, trying to figure out what
should happen next. Bringing up the bathroom incident is
risky, given where we are, but I'm not sure when I'll have
an opening next.

I'm about to say something else when I hear footsteps
down the tunnel. I turn to see Coach Johnson approaching, his eyes narrowing as he takes in the scene
before him.

"Asher, Isla," he greets us, his tone giving nothing
away about what he's thinking. "Everything alright here?"

"Yeah, Coach," I respond quickly. "Just going over
some last-minute details for the video project that Isla will
be filming."

"Ah," Coach says, as if he just remembered what this
could be about. "Good. Remember, Asher, this is a great
opportunity, but hockey comes first. Don't let this distract
you from what's important."

"Of course, Coach," I reply, hoping my words don't

give away my true feelings about this. "Hockey is always the priority."

As if he is satisfied with my answer, Coach Johnson gives me a curt nod before his attention shifts to Isla. His stern expression softens instantly, and a warm smile spreads across his face.

"Hey, kiddo," he says, opening his arms. Isla steps forward, and he pulls her into a hug. "It was great having you over for dinner the other night. Mom has been talking about it ever since."

Isla laughs softly. "I know. She already texted me a couple of recipes she wants to try next time."

"You know how she gets when she's excited about something. Speaking of excited," Coach states. "I also know how you get when you're focused on something challenging that brings you joy. Remember to take care of yourself too. I know this project will be time-consuming, and you have a bunch of other responsibilities."

"I will, Dad."

The two share another hug before Coach's gaze shifts back to me. "Go on ahead and suit up. The other boys should be here any minute."

With that, Coach Johnson walks away, leaving Isla and me standing alone once more.

"Well," Isla says, breaking the silence, "I guess we should get started."

"Yeah," I agree, rubbing the back of my neck. "I need

to get ready for practice. Meet me outside the locker room in ten?"

She nods, picking up her camera bag. "I'll be here."

I give Isla a quick nod before heading into the locker room. As I change into my practice gear, I find myself thinking about Isla instead of focusing on what drills we'll be doing during today's practice session. I'm doing the exact thing I promised Coach I wouldn't do, but what he doesn't know won't hurt him.

I finish suiting up just as the rest of the team trickles into the locker room. Knox, who I've barely talked to outside of what went down with us in the kitchen, gives me a curious look as he sets his things down in his stall, which just so happens to be next to mine.

"You're here early," he comments, pulling his practice jersey over his head. "Trying to get in some extra practice to keep up with me?"

I roll my eyes, tying up my skates. "Just had some things to take care of before practice."

Knox smirks. "Things like chatting up Coach's daughter? You seemed overly eager to be the star of America's Next Top Hockey Star."

My head snaps up, and I shoot him a warning glare. I really don't want to deal with his shit this morning. "Fuck off."

"Hey, you two," Levi says as he's sitting next to me. "We're not dealing with this bull shit today. It's too fucking early. Got it?"

Knox holds up his hands, his smirk never leaving his face. "Relax, dude. Just making an observation."

Levi shakes his head, muttering something under his breath as he finishes getting ready. I don't know what has snuck up Knox's ass and died, but I'm tempted to punch him so hard that it falls out.

While repeating a mantra to keep my emotions in check, I finish tying my skates and grab my stick, heading out of the locker room without another word. I spot Isla waiting near the entrance to the rink, her camera already in hand. She gives me a small smile as I approach.

"Ready?" she asks, lifting the camera.

"Mmm hmmm," is the only thing I say. I'm still heated from Knox's bullshit in the locker room. I don't want to take it out on her, so it's best that I keep my responses short and to the point.

We walk to the rink in silence, and as I step onto the ice, I feel the familiar rush of adrenaline coursing through my veins. This is where I belong, where everything else fades away, and it's just me, my stick, and the puck. I take a few laps around the rink, feeling the cold air whip against my face as I pick up speed.

I glance over my shoulder and see Isla standing at the boards, her camera trained on me. For a moment, I feel self-conscious, which is silly. I'm used to being filmed on the ice. But knowing that my every move is being captured on video by her causes me to feel some type of way. Then I remind myself that this is what I signed up for, and I need to push through the discomfort if I want to spend more time with her in this manner.

As the rest of the team joins me on the ice, Coach blows his whistle, signaling the start of practice. We run through a series of drills, focusing on puck handling and shooting. I throw myself into the exercises, finding that although I'm focusing on hockey, Isla isn't too far from my mind.

As practice winds down, Coach calls us over to the boards for a final pep talk. "Good work out there today, boys," he says, his eyes sweeping over the group. "Keep this up, and we'll be in good shape for our next game."

When we break from the huddle, I can't help but glance over at Isla, who's still filming. She catches my eye and gives me a subtle nod, and I find myself licking my lips in response.

Once the entire team is back in the locker room, the next few minutes pass in a blur. None of the guys talk to one another, as we're all busy getting ready for the rest of the day.

After I'm dressed, I grab my things and head out of the locker room to find Isla waiting for me. She's fiddling with her camera; I assume she's reviewing the footage from practice.

"Hey," I say, approaching her. "How'd it look out there?"

She glances up, a small smile on her face. "Great. I got some excellent footage."

"Glad to hear it," I reply, shifting my hockey bag on my shoulder. "So, what's next on the agenda?"

Isla consults her phone. "Well, according to your schedule, you've got class in about thirty minutes. I was thinking I could film you walking to class, maybe get some shots of you on campus, and then I'll head to my class, and we'll meet up later. If that's okay with you, of course."

"You know my schedule?" I don't remember sharing that information with her.

She raises an eyebrow at me. "Yes. Because it's now a part of my job to follow you."

"Who told you?"

Isla gives me a little shrug. "I'm resourceful." I stare at her until she responds. "Fine, Dad gave it to me."

I can't help but smirk. "Pulling rank to get your way. Okay, but yeah, that works. Let's do it."

Isla rolls her eyes, and together, we head out of the arena. Isla walks slightly ahead of me to get some footage of me in motion. It feels a bit strange having her film moments like this, but I remind myself that this is all part of the process.

We wrap up filming and agree to meet on campus near my first class. As I'm driving to the building, I can't help but be thankful that we both drove to the arena this morning because it gives me an opportunity to take a breather from being around her. My thoughts have been drifting between wanting to reestablish our friendship and wanting to bend her over and fuck her until we're both satisfied.

Thinking about the bathroom incident doesn't help matters. The last thing I needed her to see was the hard-on I was sporting just being in her presence.

We both pull up to campus, and I grab my bookbag as I step out of the car. Isla follows suit and locks her car behind her.

"Ready to film some more b-footage?"

"Is that what it's called?" I ask, not sure if I've heard the term before.

Isla nods. "Yeah, we should probably make it quick so we can both make it to class on time."

Just as we're about to film again, my phone rings, and I glance at the screen. It's my mom. I pause for a second, then look at Isla.

"Give me a minute?" I say, already stepping away to take the call. I don't wait for a response from Isla as I answer the call. "Hey, Mom. What's up?"

There's a brief pause on the other end, and when she speaks, I can hear the strain in her voice. "Hey, sweetheart. How are you doing?"

I can tell she's trying to put off what she wants to say to me, which means it's not good. "Pretty good. I'm about to go to class. How are things there?"

"Not good. I hate to bother you with this, but we've got a serious problem with the roof. There's a leak, and it's pretty bad. The contractor said it's going to cost more than I can afford to get it fixed."

I exhale what feels like all the air out of my lungs. "How bad is it?"

"It's bad, honey. Water's been getting into Avery's room. We've tried to patch it up temporarily, but no dice. The contractor says we should just replace the entire roof. I knew I would have to do it because of its age, but it deteriorated quicker than we thought."

I close my eyes and shake my head. "Did he give you an estimate?"

"Yeah... It's going to be around nine grand, Asher. I... I don't know how we're going to swing it."

I run a hand through my hair, pulling on it as if it will lead to us finding money to pay for it. I have some funds available, but throwing this much down will make things tight for us. "And this isn't something that we can charge to...I don't know, like insurance or something?"

Mom sighs on the other end of the line. "No, our insurance won't cover it. They say it's normal wear and tear, not damage from a specific event. I've been trying to figure out a way, but..." Her voice trails off as if she doesn't know what else to say.

I glance over at Isla, who's trying to look occupied with her camera, but I wonder if she can hear what I'm saying. She meets my gaze, then quickly looks away, pretending to adjust the settings on her camera.

"Listen, Mom," I say, keeping my voice low. "I've saved some money from those NIL deals I did. It's not a ton, but it should be enough to cover the roof repairs. I'll transfer it to you tonight, okay?"

"Oh, Asher, I hate to ask you for this. You work so hard for that money, and—"

"Mom, it's fine," I cut her off gently. "This is what the money is for. You and Avery need the money more than I do right now. Take it."

There's a moment of silence, and I can practically hear her fighting with herself to accept the help. Finally, she speaks. "Thank you, sweetheart. I don't know what we'd do without you."

"We both know you'd figure out some way to make it work. But you don't have to. I'm happy to help."

"Thank you. Thank you so much. You know how much I hate asking you—"

I stop her before she starts crying because I can already hear the emotion in her voice. "I love you, Mom," I say, my voice softening. "Everything's going to be okay."

"I love you too, Asher. More than you know."

We say our goodbyes, and I hang up the phone. I turn back to Isla, who's watching me. She's put the camera away, and I'm grateful for her discretion.

"Everything alright?" she asks gently.

"Yeah, just some family stuff. Nothing to worry about."

Isla doesn't push, but the look she gives me tells me she knows I'm not telling the full truth. "Okay. If you ever need to talk, though, I'm here."

Her words catch me off guard. Why would she want to lend an ear to my shit after everything I've done to her? "Thanks, Isla. I appreciate that."

And I mean every word.

"No worries."

I glance at my phone, realizing we're both going to be late for class if we don't get moving. "We should probably get going."

"Right, of course," Isla agrees, bending down to put her camera back in her bag. "I'll catch up with you later for more filming?"

"Sounds good. Text me when you finish classes, and we'll figure something out."

With that, we part ways. As I walk into the building, I still think about the conversation I had with my mom. I know I did the right thing, but I can't help feeling pissed off. Maybe resentment is the better word for it. Not toward my family, who have made more than their fair share of sacrifices for me, but toward the situation. Toward the fact that no matter how hard I work, it never seems to be enough to get us ahead.

At least for now.

I shake my head, determined to silence the inner voice that tells me I'll never be good enough. It's crucial that I stay focused right now and not let anything distract me. I need to focus on my classes and on hockey. I sit in the back of the classroom and pull out my notebook. It is time to force myself to tune into the lecture versus my personal life.

21

ISLA

The cursor on my laptop blinks at me like it's mocking my attempt to stay on top of things. I have my precalculus notes scattered around me, along with half-finished problem sets and some I haven't even started yet. On my monitor are photos I've been staring at for an hour.

How does anyone make sense of this?

I'm at the point where I want to take my brain out of my head and bash both of them against the wall. The tension in my shoulders is almost becoming painful, and I can feel the headache forming. I rub my temples in an attempt to stop it from coming on, but to no avail.

This doesn't include the things I need to get done for one of my photography classes and the hockey team. I hate to admit that I'm falling behind, and I might have to pull a couple of all-nighters to catch up.

Maybe I'm foolish for trying to do two things at once. Focusing on just one is going to be hard, but that might be the way forward. Photography might be a reward for getting my math homework done.

As I'm about to try to accomplish something, I move my mouse, and the cursor doesn't move. I pause and move my Bluetooth mouse again, and I get the same result.

What. The. Hell?

My laptop is frozen.

No, no, no. Not now.

I frantically press the keys, trying to get any sort of response, but nothing happens. I resist the urge to slam my head against the desk, knowing it will only make my headache worse. At this point, the universe is laughing at me.

"Having a rough day?"

The voice startles me out of my frustration. I look up to see Asher standing there with what looks to be two cups of coffee in his hands. He places one cup in front of me, along with a couple of sandwiches from Brewed Beginnings. I forgot we agreed to meet at the library this evening.

"You could say that," I mutter, eyeing the coffee in his hand. "Thanks for this. You're a lifesaver."

Asher pulls out a chair next to me and sits down. "I figured we both could use a pick-me-up." He looks over at my textbook before he responds. "Pre-calc kicking your ass?"

I let out a humorless laugh. "That's an understatement. I swear, I can't understand these equations. They're written in another language. Not to mention my laptop has decided to be a proper dick."

That makes Asher laugh. "Want me to take a look?"

I stare at him for a moment and slide the textbook and binder over to him. "Be my guest. But I warn you, it's a mess."

Asher flips through the pages and sighs several times as he scans the equations. After a moment, he looks up at me with a sympathetic smile. "I can see why you're struggling. This stuff is no joke."

"Tell me about it." I take a sip of the coffee he brought. I can't believe he actually remembers how I like my coffee. The warmth and caffeine are more than welcome. "I feel like I'm drowning."

"Well, let's see if we can make some sense of it together." Asher scoots his chair closer to mine, and the next thing I know, our shoulders are touching as he leans over the textbook to get a closer look.

At that moment, I realize that his cologne, the scent that feels like a warm hug, surrounds me. I'm ready to swoon over this coffee and the smell of his cologne, but I can't.

I do my best to focus on the work in front of me. Asher starts explaining the problem, but my mind keeps drifting to how close he is to me and his cologne.

"Isla? Are you following?" Asher's question snaps me

back to reality. He takes a sip of his coffee as his green eyes land on me.

"Sorry, I zoned out for a second there." I lick my lips to cover up my nervousness. "Can you run that by me again?"

Asher chuckles. "Sure thing. So, for this equation, you need to..."

As he continues his explanation, I force myself to concentrate on his words rather than on anything else. Slowly but surely, the numbers and symbols start making sense. Asher's guidance and the caffeine from the coffee work their magic, and I nod along as the terms start to make sense.

"I think I'm starting to get it now," I play with my ponytail because I don't want to look him in the eye. "Thanks. I'm now convinced you're a better teacher than my actual professor."

Asher grins, and it takes me back to happier times when we were a couple. He still looks like the boy I fell in love with, with slightly more scruff at the moment. "Happy to help. Let's see if we can get your laptop sorted out."

He reaches for my laptop and his fingers brush against mine as he pulls it toward him. The brief contact sends a jolt through my entire body, and I hope he doesn't notice how my breath catches in my throat. My thoughts circle back to how he used to use those fingers on me. Time after time, from the moment I gave him my virginity until the very end, it had been absolutely magical, and it's something I don't regret, even with how we turned out.

I just realized he didn't use his fingers on me the last time we were together.

Am I ovulating? I must be ovulating. I have to keep laughing in order to keep from crying about my diagnosis.

"Let's see what we're dealing with here," he says as he examines the frozen screen. He taps a few keys, tries the trackpad, then the mouse, but nothing happens. "Hmm, looks like it's really stuck."

"Yeah, I was in the middle of editing some photos when it just froze up on me." I sigh, leaning back in my chair. "It's been a day."

"I get that completely. Okay, let's try a hard reset. That will do the trick."

He presses and holds the power button until the screen goes dark. I could have just done that myself, but I felt more comfortable bitching and moaning to myself. We both wait as he powers it back on, hoping for a miracle.

As the laptop comes back to life, I hold my breath, praying that it hasn't lost my work. The familiar startup sound plays and the screen lands on my desktop background. I let out a sigh of relief when Asher wiggles the mouse and the cursor moves.

"Thank fuck," I say out loud with thinking. "You're a hero."

Asher chuckles in response. "You're welcome. Glad I could save the day."

"Seriously, what would I be doing without you?"

"Probably still be staring at a frozen screen and cursing the universe and everyone else out." He takes a longer drink from his coffee, looking far too pleased with himself.

I can't help but laugh. "You're probably right. But don't let it go to your head."

"Wouldn't dream of it." He grins, and it feels like old times for a moment. It's nice, even if it's temporary.

As we sit there, sipping our coffee and eating our sandwiches, the tension in my shoulders starts to ease. If I can remember the things he told me about math, I might have an actual shot at passing this class. Editing my images will come, but I do feel some relief. Having this time where I don't have a camera in his face reminds me of the question I wanted to ask him several weeks ago at this point.

"This is random, but remember when you offered me your coat at the volunteer event a couple of weeks back?" I ask. "You left a bag of Skittles in one of your pockets."

"I know."

"Why? And had you planned to offer me your coat?"

"Honestly?"

I nod, waiting for him to respond.

"I was planning on giving you the candy, but I didn't have a master plan to give you my coat that day. It was just a spur-of-the-moment thing when I noticed you were cold."

I tilt my head, studying Asher's expression. "So the Skittles were just a random act of kindness?"

"I guess you could say that. I just thought they might cheer you up."

The conflicting emotions that are coursing through me are causing a war. I shouldn't be enjoying any of this, but I can't help but smile at that. It's such a small gesture, but it means more to me than he probably realizes. "Well, consider me cheered. Skittles are still my fav."

"I'm glad. I figured they would be a safe bet. And I have a question for you."

Oh no. The way he says the words sends a chill down my spine. This isn't good. "What is it?"

"Was the bathroom incident planned?"

My face falls into my hands because I can feel myself turning red. I had a feeling this would be his question, but I was also hoping that we could just not talk about it— ever.

"No, it wasn't. I let Selene and Hailey get into my brain and let my intrusive thoughts win. I didn't even know you were going to follow me to the bathroom."

"Hailey? You've hung out with her?"

I roll my eyes. "Yes. We got lunch just before the team bonding night at my house and have texted a few times since then. I can have friends, you know."

"I didn't say you couldn't. Do you regret the bathroom incident?"

His reference to it again has me doing a slight double take, even though we haven't switched topics. "I love that you're calling it that."

Asher tucks a piece of my hair back behind my ear as if he has the right to do that. "Don't avoid the question, Isla."

His tone reminds me of the way he told me I needed to be quiet while he made me climax for the first time in three years. "I don't. Do you?"

"Absolutely not. That's why I said you can call me anytime if you want to redo or take things up a notch."

Good to know. "This isn't a date, by the way." It's childish, but I need to make that clear.

"Never said it was."

I don't know what else to say, so I take another bite of the sandwich Asher bought me. We enjoy a comfortable silence, and I'm struck by how we've fallen back into our old pattern of just enjoying each other's company. If I'm being honest, I'm not sure how good of an idea this is.

I clear my throat when I finish my last bite. "We should probably head out soon if we want to get some more filming done today."

Asher nods before checking the time. "Why don't we head up to the gym, and you can take some footage of my gym workout?"

"Sounds good to me," I reply, gathering up my things

and shoving them into my backpack. "Then I'll spend the evening finishing this math homework and editing photos and video footage."

Asher helps me pack up before grabbing his book bag. Once I'm done, we leave the library and go to the gym. As we walk, Asher fills me in on his workout routine, explaining the different exercises he'll be doing and how they help with his hockey performance. I make a note to ask him some questions related to the exercises he's performing to get him on camera talking about it.

When we arrive at the gym, I set up my camera while Asher changes and then warms up. I try to stop myself from staring at how his muscles flex and shift under his tight t-shirt as he stretches. It takes everything for me to focus on adjusting the settings on my camera.

Once Asher is ready, I film him as he begins his workout routine. I zoom in on his focused expression as he does a set of weighted squats. Despite the strain, he maintains perfect form—or so I think, because, if I'm being honest, I don't have the slightest clue.

"Today is leg day, so that's what we are going to focus on," he says as he walks over to get a set of dumbbells.

"Sounds good."

Between sets, I ask him a few questions about the specific exercises and how they translate to his performance on the ice. Asher's responses are thoughtful and insightful, giving me a glimpse into the mind of a serious athlete. Perfect for the audience that will be viewing this.

"Squats and lunges help build explosive power in my legs," he explains, wiping sweat from his brow. "That burst of speed can make all the difference when I'm chasing down the puck or trying to beat a defender."

I nod, impressed by his knowledge and the way he articulates it. I know it will come across perfectly on the Crestwood Red Wolves' social media channels.

As Asher continues his workout, I circle around him, capturing different angles and close-ups. I want to showcase not just the physical effort, but also the mental focus and determination that goes into his training. He has the look of someone who's driven to be the best, no matter the cost.

After a grueling set of deadlifts, Asher takes a break to hydrate. I lower my camera and hand him his water bottle.

"Thanks," he says, taking a long swig. "How's the footage looking so far?"

"Fantastic," I reply honestly. "You're a natural on camera. The fans are going to love seeing this side of you."

Asher grins, a hint of pride in his expression. "Well, I have a pretty brilliant photographer/videographer to thank for that."

I feel a blush creeping up my neck at the compliment. Is he flirting with me? "I'm just doing my job."

"Nah, it's more than that," Asher insists. "You have a way of making people feel comfortable in front of the lens. It's a gift, sunshine."

His use of my old nickname catches me off guard

again. I went from not hearing it in years to hearing it multiple times over the last couple of weeks, which has thrown me for a loop. And it does nothing to help the complex emotions I'm feeling.

I clear my throat, trying to steer the conversation back to safer territory. "Well, I think we've got some great material here. A few more shots of your cool-down stretches, and we should be ready to wrap this up."

He nods, grabbing his towel to wipe his forehead again. "Sounds good. Then I'll hit the showers, and maybe I can take you back to your dorm? I parked my car in the parking lot."

And I didn't bother driving today. Shit. "That's okay. I don't mind walking back to my dorm room."

Asher's gaze narrows at me. "It's late, and you shouldn't be walking around campus by yourself this late at night."

I do a double take and fold my arms across my chest. "Crestwood University is pretty safe, Asher. I've lived in this town for the majority of my life."

"I know Crestwood is safe, Isla. But humor me, okay?"

I hesitate for a moment, weighing my options. On one hand, accepting a ride from Asher feels like we might be crossing a line. It's blurring the boundaries I've tried to maintain between us. But on the other hand, he's right. It is late, and the thought of walking alone in the dark isn't exactly appealing. And it's just a car ride. Friends and coworkers ride in the same car as each other all the time.

Exes probably don't, though. And didn't I cross the line when I pulled him into my childhood bathroom?

Yes, Isla. You did.

"Okay, fine. I'll take you up on that ride. But only because I don't feel like arguing with you right now."

Asher chuckles, a victorious grin spreading across his face. "I'll take what I can get. Give me ten minutes to clean up and change, and I'll meet you out front."

I don't mention that I could probably be back at my dorm in the time that it would take for him to be ready. True to his word, Asher emerges from the gym's locker room ten minutes later, his hair damp from the shower and his book bag slung over his shoulder. We walk side by side to the parking lot, and neither one of us says a word.

As we reach his car, Asher opens the passenger door for me, ever the gentleman. I slide in, trying to ignore the flutter in my stomach as he closes the door and walks around the vehicle to the driver's side.

Once he pulls out of the parking lot, he glances at me before turning his attention back to the road. "Are you excited about our next game?"

At least he is keeping the conversation pretty neutral. "I am. This is the furthest away game you guys will be having, right?"

"Yeah, it's a pretty long drive. The game should be pretty good, though, because of the quality of their team."

"Y'all are going to do great. You've all been playing really well lately."

"Thanks, I agree. So far, this season has been pretty good."

"Stop being humble. You guys are a force to be reckoned with this season."

"And having you there to capture all the big moments definitely helps keep morale up." He punctuates his comment by sparing another glance at me.

I roll my eyes playfully. "Flattery will get you nowhere, Bennett."

"It was worth a shot." He chuckles as he pulls up in front of my dorm building. He puts the car in park and turns to face me. "Here we are, safe and sound as promised."

"My hero once again," I reply sarcastically. "Thanks for the ride. I really do appreciate it."

"Anytime, Isla. I'm always happy to help."

We just sit there for a moment, our eyes locked on each other. The air between us feels charged with sexual tension, and in the back of my mind, I can hear my brain telling me that I need to get out of his car. Finally, after some more nudging, I'm the first to break eye contact, reaching for the door handle.

"Well, I should head in. I have a bunch of work to finish and all that."

"Right, of course." Asher clears his throat. "I'll see you at practice, then?"

"Yep, I'll be there, camera in hand, as usual." I step out of the car, slinging my book and camera bags over my shoulder. Before I close the door, I lean down to catch his eye one more time. "Thanks again. For everything today—the coffee, the math and tech help, the ride. It means a lot."

He gives me that lopsided grin that was only reserved for me once upon a time. "That's what friends are for, right?"

Friends. Is that what we were? "Right. Friends. Night, Asher."

"Goodnight, sunshine. Sweet dreams."

I shut the car door and enter my dorm building, feeling his eyes on me until I disappear inside. As I climb the stairs to my floor, I can't help but replay our interactions over the last couple of hours. If I didn't know any better, it would feel like almost no time has passed at all.

And the thought of that is frightening. We're not the same people we were three years ago. Too much has happened. Too much has changed. Whatever this is between us now—this tentative friendship—it's fragile. And I'm not sure how to feel about any of it.

22

ISLA

Do you ever feel like déjà vu is slapping you in the face?

It's what I feel as I walk into a party, the bass pounding in my head as Selene and I enter the house. However, we are both attending this college this time, and we were invited to a party at the hockey team's off-campus house because of my connection to the team.

That does nothing to calm my nerves as I walk in behind Selene.

I can't even count the number of red Solo cups I've spotted as we enter the living room. Everyone is here to celebrate the Crestwood Red Wolves' latest win. Well, I'm sure some people are just here for the drinking, but that isn't uncommon on a college campus.

"Wow, the hockey team knows how to throw down,"

Selene remarks, her eyes wide as she takes in the chaotic scene in front of us.

"You're not lying," I reply.

My eyes scan the room, and I recognize most of the hockey team, but not anyone else. My gaze lands on Hailey, who is standing across the room. The last time I saw her, she was wearing her hair in a messy bun while we were eating lunch in the campus center. This time, her brown hair is in a neater bun, and she's wearing jeans and a sweater with chess club written across it. Standing next to her is someone who, I assume, is her friend. The two of them are standing between Levi and Wilder; the former has his arm wrapped around Hailey.

As soon as Hailey spots me, her face lights up and she waves us over. I don't want to be rude, so I grab Selene's hand and say, "Hey, there are some people I want you to meet."

We make our way through the crowd, dodging people and beer sloshing out of cups until we reach Hailey and her friend. Hailey speaks first. "Isla, how are you doing? Is life still crazy for you?"

"Unfortunately, yes. College life is so hectic."

"You can say that again." Hailey looks at her boyfriend before turning to her friend. "Since you already know these two guys... Jade, this is Isla, the hockey team's photographer. Isla, this is Jade, my best friend."

Jade sticks her hand out to shake mine before Wilder snatches her hand back. "Hey! She's my best friend too."

Jade pulls her hand from Wilder's grasp and rolls her eyes. "Ignore Wilder. It's nice to meet you, Isla."

I return the handshake before gesturing to Selene. "And this is my friend, Selene. We've been best friends since elementary school."

"That's true. She can't get rid of me no matter how hard she tries." Selene glances at me before a smirk appears.

"It's true. She is a pain in my ass," I say, and Selene elbows me in the gut. "Ow." The poke didn't actually hurt me, but I want to be a little dramatic.

Hailey laughs at our exchange. "Well, it's great to meet you. I can show you where the drinks are."

Hailey and Jade lead the way as we make our way through the crowd. Levi and Wilder trail behind us, and they get stopped multiple times by people who want to congratulate them on their win. I glance over at Selene, and she smiles at me, probably proud that I went out at all.

Hailey finds a cooler in the kitchen and hands us two cans of beer. Selene and I open our beers at the same time. I hold up my drink and say, "Cheers."

Selene responds in kind. "Cheers!"

As we clink our cans together, I feel somewhat at ease. Sure, parties are more Selene's thing than mine because I'm not too big on crowds. Despite the crowd in the kitchen, I don't feel panicky.

Well, that's not true. But the party environment isn't

causing me to feel that way. It's the man that I assume will also be here that I haven't had a chance to see outside of work in the last few days.

Levi and Wilder end up chatting with one another on the other side of the room, but I've already noticed that Levi has glanced at Hailey at least once.

"So, how long have you been into photography?" Jade asks.

I take a sip of my beer before answering. "Since elementary school, actually. It started as a hobby I got more serious about in high school, and now it has become so much more."

"That's awesome," Hailey chimes in. "I've seen some of your shots of the team on their social media pages. You've got a real talent."

I can't stop the grin from taking over my face. "Thanks. That means a lot." It feels good to be recognized for my passion. And it feels good to be friendly with other people, something I never thought I would say. I enjoy keeping my inner circle small, but I don't mind socializing every now and again.

"How long have you been working at Brewed Beginnings?" I ask the first question that comes to mind. I feel slightly awkward about doing so, but here we are.

"Oh, I've been there since freshman year. It's a job... you know. Not exactly thrilled about it, but at least I'm getting paid. Since my manager got transferred out of our store, things have gotten better."

Jade nods, picking up on Hailey's tone. "Retail jobs can be brutal. I used to work at a clothing store in Crestwood Mall. The stories I could tell you…"

Selene leans against the kitchen counter, nursing her beer. "Oh, do share. I'm always up for a good story."

Jade pauses for a second, trying to figure out how to start before launching into what happened when an irate customer walked in and had a meltdown because the store wasn't carrying a dress in the color that she wanted it in. The way she recounts it has us all laughing.

As the laughter dies down, I notice Selene's attention shift, her eyes narrowing as she looks past us. Following her gaze, I spot Knox standing across the room. Unsurprisingly, he stands out even in the crowded space. He's got that intense look on his face, like he's analyzing everything around him.

Hailey must have noticed what happened because she says, "See something interesting, Selene?"

Selene snaps her attention back to the group, and although she tries to play it cool, I know her well enough to know it's all an act. "Who's that guy over there?" she asks, nodding in Knox's direction.

I glance back at Knox, who's now chatting with a group of guys, including Levi, Wilder, and Blaise, on the other side of the room. There is no sign of Asher. "That's Knox Sanchez. He's also on the hockey team."

"Interesting," Selene murmurs, her eyes lingering on

Knox a moment longer before she turns back to the group. "Maybe I'll introduce myself later."

"That might not be the best idea," Jade says. All our eyes shift over to her as we wait for her to continue.

"Why not?" Selene asks for the rest of us.

Jade takes a sip of her drink before answering, her eyes darting between Selene and Knox across the room. "Let's just say Knox has a bit of a reputation. He's not exactly known for his long-term commitments, if you catch my drift."

Hailey nods in agreement. "She's right, at least based on what Levi told me once."

Selene raises an eyebrow. "That works for me because I'm not looking for anything serious."

Her words hang in the air for a moment, and I can't help but be concerned. I know my best friend can handle herself, but I also know that guys like Knox can be trouble. Before I can say anything, Selene downs the rest of her beer.

"Well, I think it's time for a refill. Anyone else need another drink?" she asks.

Hailey and Jade exchange a look before shaking their heads. "We're good for now," Hailey says, holding up her half-full cup.

As Selene makes her way back to the cooler, I turn to Hailey and Jade. "So what else do you know about Knox?" I ask.

Jade shrugs. "Not much. Just that he's kind of a player and doesn't seem interested in anything serious."

Hailey nods in agreement. "Yeah, that's it."

I chew on my bottom lip, still not entirely convinced. I'm impressed by Selene's honesty with people we've just met and vice versa. Hailey and Jade have more loyalty to Levi and Wilder and, by association, the hockey team, than to us, but they have no problem talking about Knox. It would be easy for them to just keep quiet, but I appreciate them telling the truth.

But I don't trust them enough to talk about Asher. Hopefully, Selene, who knows where all the proverbial bodies are buried, doesn't say anything.

Selene returns with her refilled cup. "So what did I miss?"

I'm the one that replies. "Nothing important. Just chatting."

Our conversation continues, and soon, we are back in the living room with the guys joining us. Levi and Hailey are together once again, chatting with Jade and Wilder. Knox stares me down for a moment before Selene takes the opportunity to talk with him. Of course, she's ignoring the warning Jade and Hailey gave her. What the hell was that look from him all about? Blaise didn't bother coming over, and I'm not sure where he went.

I will credit everyone for their efforts in trying to talk to me, but it still feels like everyone is paired off except for me. I turn to Selene, who's deep in conversation with

Knox. Is it bad that it wouldn't surprise me if she ended up going home with him tonight?

Wilder claps his hands together, and everyone looks at him. "Alright, who's up for some flip cup?" he announces, his voice loud enough to cut through the music. Everyone agrees, but I notice that the teams are uneven.

"Looks like we're short one player," I point out.

Just then, I see Asher making his way through the crowd to join us. I can feel my pulse pick up the second I lay eyes on him, but I force myself to not react.

"Hey, look who decided to show up," Levi says, slapping Asher on the back. "Thought you weren't going to make it tonight."

Asher grins, his gaze flicking to me for a split second before his eyes are back on Levi. "Nah, just needed a minute. Didn't want to miss the action."

Apparently, this is enough to draw Selene away from Knox for a second because she nudges me and throws a side-eye my way. I ignore it, taking a sip of my drink instead.

"Glad you're here, man," Wilder says, raising his drink. "We were just about to start a round of flip cup. You in?"

"Definitely," Asher says, then turns to me, his eyes meeting mine with a hint of a smile. "What about you, Isla? Are you ready?"

I raise an eyebrow because I can hear the challenge in his voice. "Oh, I'm always ready."

As the group sets up for the game, I catch Asher's gaze

again. He smiles at me, and I can't help but smile back despite not knowing what is happening between us. I hope that, at least for tonight, we can keep things casual. We are just two people having fun at a party.

Everyone walks down to the basement and gathers around the table. Knox stands there with his arms crossed as if he would rather be elsewhere. Selene leans over to talk to him, and it's only then that his mood slightly changes.

Since no one else says a word, I think I'm the only one who notices their interaction. Interesting.

As the group starts setting up for the game, Asher leans closer. "Hey, can we talk for a sec?"

I glance at him and nod. We step to the side, just out of earshot of the others.

"So, I've been thinking about the content we've been filming."

That got my attention. "Oh? What about it?"

He hesitates for a moment, then smiles. "I was thinking maybe we could film A Day in the Life—like, follow me through a game day or something. Give people a real behind-the-scenes look. I think it could be cool and show more of what it's like from my perspective."

I raise an eyebrow because it was something that was thrown around, but it wasn't what Asher had agreed to initially. "A Day in the Life, huh? I like it. It could add a more personal angle people would connect with. Plus, you're already getting used to the camera, so it wouldn't be too awkward."

He chuckles. "Yeah, I trust you to make me look good. And, you know, maybe it'd be fun to spend some more time together."

Ah, that's what all of this was about. "Asher—"

"Look, I know we've been through a lot. And I know there's still a lot we haven't figured out yet. But you can't deny that there's still something here." He gestures between us, his eyes searching mine. "I feel it. And I think you do too."

I bite my lip, but he's not wrong. "It's complicated, Asher."

He nods, his expression serious. "I know it is. But I'm willing to put in the work. I'm not the same guy I was back then. I've learned from my mistakes, and I'm willing to prove it to you, however long it takes, sunshine."

23

ASHER

lthough it's early in the morning, I have a smile on my face. Sure, I'm still tired, but I also feel rejuvenated. Not only did Isla agree to spend more time with me, but I also had a wonderful dream last night, and she was starring in the film. I would have been pissed if my alarm had gone off during it.

I check the time before getting out of bed. Coach will have my head if I'm late to practice. Plus, I can't tell him the reason I'm late is because I'm dreaming about banging his daughter.

But it's more than that.

Do I want to have sex with Isla? Yes, without a doubt, but it's so much more than that. I want to wake up next to her every morning, be the reason she smiles, support her dreams, and be her rock when life slaps her in the face. I caused one of those challenges she experienced, and I will never get over the look that appeared on her face when I told her I was done. However, I meant it when I told her I would prove she could trust me again.

With a heavy sigh, I throw on clothes for practice and grab my hockey bag. As I walk down the stairs, I hear my roommates getting ready, but I don't bother waiting for them because I want to be alone.

The drive to the rink is unremarkable, and when I get there, I notice that Coach Johnson and Levi are here before me. Levi didn't mention coming in early, so I'm curious about what that is all about. The locker room is quiet because most of the guys haven't arrived yet, but I see Levi standing there, half-dressed in his gear.

"Hey, man, you're early," I say as I drop my bag on the bench.

"I could say the same for you."

I shrug because he's not wrong. "Everything good?"

"Couldn't sleep. I figured I might as well come in and get some extra shots in."

"Hailey wasn't there to help knock you out?"

Levi chuckles. "She pulled an all-nighter last night to finish a paper. She was still awake when I left my place to come here."

"I know the feeling, man. Last night wasn't too bad, but my sleep has been screwed for a while because my mind's been all over the place."

Levi raises an eyebrow, and I already know where this

is going. "Does this have anything to do with a certain blonde photographer we both know?"

I'm not shocked that he picked up on it. "Is it that obvious?"

"Only to those who know you well," Levi says, sitting on the bench to lace up his skates. "Want to talk about it?"

I hesitate for a moment because I don't know if I'm ready to unleash my thoughts about what happened the night of the team bonding event. Or how that moment has lived rent-free in my mind ever since. I check the time and realize that our teammates will be coming in at any minute, so it makes sense not to discuss this here. Plus, if Coach or anyone else on staff hears me talking about Isla, I'm screwed.

"Not now, man. The guys will be here soon, and I don't want anyone to overhear. Especially not Coach."

"Got it. But hey, if you need to talk later, I'm here for you, okay?"

"Thanks, I appreciate that." I clap him on the shoulder before starting to gear up for practice.

As predicted, the locker room soon fills up as everyone tries to make sure they are on time for practice. I keep my head down, focusing on suiting up and trying to push thoughts of Isla from my mind. I need to focus.

But even though I'm happier than I've been in days, I know I'm off my A-game. My passes are sloppy, and my shots are wide of the net. Coach blows the whistle, his eyes narrowing as he watches me fuck up another play.

"Bennett! Get your head out of your ass and focus!" he barks.

I grit my teeth, frustrated with myself because I can't stop thinking about his daughter's ass. "Yes, Coach."

My gaze lands on Knox, who I figured would have a smirk on his lips, but his face is blank. I try to shake off Coach's words, but my mind keeps drifting back to Isla. However, I get it together enough that I don't experience the wrath of Coach anymore during practice.

As I'm unlacing my skates in the locker room after practice, Levi plops down beside me on the bench. "Okay, spill. What happened with Isla?"

I glance around to make sure no one's within earshot before turning to face him. I lean forward to whisper in his ear. "Our relationship, or whatever this is, is so chaotic that she goes from hating me one minute to wanting me to fuck her the next." I don't elaborate because I know I don't need to.

Levi's eyes widen. "Whoa. We've had some wild moments, but this might top it."

"It's like whiplash, but I'm not going to lie and say that the moments where things are great haven't been fantastic. Everything I've ever wanted and more." I run a hand through my sweat-dampened hair. "But then she pulls away, and then she's back. And I know it's because we're both working on our own stuff."

"Which we all are, but that doesn't mean it isn't rough."

"Tell me about it. I can't stop thinking about her, but I don't want to push too hard and scare her off for good. Plus, we're still filming content, so we have to be around each other."

"I hear you, and letting her take the lead so you can figure out where her headspace is and supporting her that way is the right way to go. Let her sort through her feelings without feeling pressured."

"But what if she decides she doesn't want anything to do with me?" I can't help but sound desperate because I am.

Levi rubs a towel over his face before looking at me again. "It's a risk, yeah. But you've got to trust that if it's meant to be, giving her space won't change that. Sometimes, you have to step back and let things unfold naturally."

I pull off my pads and jersey, tossing them into my locker. "I know you're right, but it's difficult, especially when I have to see her often."

Levi's about to respond when Wilder walks over to us, already dressed and ready to head out. He's got a grin plastered on his face, completely oblivious to the conversation Levi and I are having. "Are you guys planning on staying here all day, or what? Coach is gonna start wondering why you're holed up in the locker room."

Levi and I exchange a quick look, realizing we've been deep in conversation longer than we thought. Shit, had that much time passed? The last thing I need is for Coach to catch on to anything related to this.

"Yeah, I was just talking to Levi about something that I need to get done," I respond without hesitation. I'm proud of myself for thinking of a vague comment on the fly like that.

Levi gives me a look as he picks up what I'm putting down. Don't say shit. "Right, that thing... Well, I'm here to help if you need it."

"Appreciate it."

Wilder's eyes jump from me to Levi and back to me before he raises an eyebrow. "Alright, just don't take too long. Blaise and I are grabbing breakfast. You coming?"

"Yeah, I just need to shower first. I'll meet you guys there." I can guess which dining hall they'll eat at since they often go to it for breakfast.

Wilder shrugs, tossing his gear into his bag. "Cool. See you soon."

As Wilder heads out, I turn to Levi. "I'm going to hit the showers."

"Alright, dude. I'll see you later."

I grab my towel and head toward the showers. What should be a relaxing shower is anything but because I know that Levi's right. I need to give her space and let her sort through her feelings without me hovering over her. But the thought of losing her again fucking sucks.

I finish my shower and get dressed. I allow myself to have this one shitty practice, but I can't let this affect my game and, in return, affect my teammates. They're counting on me to be focused and to be there to help lead them to victory.

When I walk into the dining hall about fifteen minutes later, I spot Wilder and Blaise seated at their usual table. I grab a tray of food and join them, grunting a greeting.

"About time," Wilder says just before he stuffs his face with a mouthful of eggs. "We were starting to think you'd drowned in the shower."

I roll my eyes, stabbing at my food. "Yeah, yeah. I got into the showers late. It's fine."

Blaise raises an eyebrow at me as I start shoveling food into my mouth. "You good? You seemed a bit off at practice today."

"Just didn't sleep well last night. It's nothing. Need to finish so many assignments."

"Fucking tell me about it," Wilder mumbles.

I look up, and I swear he hasn't taken a second to breathe the way he's inhaling his food.

"Speaking of finishing things, when are you and Knox going to cut the bullshit?" he asks bluntly.

I glance at Blaise, who's stirring his coffee slowly, but his eyes are on me, waiting for my response. I let out a deep breath. "What?"

Wilder is not buying it. "Cut the crap. You can't keep pretending there's not something going on between you two. It's like walking on eggshells at practice sometimes."

Blaise nods as he sets his coffee cup down. "He's right.

The tension's bleeding into everything, including how we function in our house. You and Knox need to figure out how to work this out before it affects our games."

I toss my fork down, and it lands on my plate with a loud clack. Thankfully, the dining hall is loud enough that no one around us seems to notice. "It's not that simple. Knox... I'm not even sure why he keeps trying to press my buttons. And I'm allowed to defend myself."

Wilder's expression is serious for once. "Look, I get it. But we are all on the same team, fighting for the same goal. We need to be united, or it's gonna screw us all over. You don't have to be best friends, but you need to coexist."

Once again, I'm willing to admit that my teammates are right. I promised to figure it out, but other shit has come up, and I pushed it to the back burner. None of this is fair to the rest of the team. I know Wilder and Blaise are right. Whatever this is with Knox, it's not just affecting me, it's affecting the entire team. And that's not fair to any of them. They shouldn't have to deal with the fallout of whatever the hell is going on between us.

This is something else that I need to own up to. "I get it, and I'll figure it out. I'll talk to Knox."

Blaise nods, a small smile on his lips. "Good. That's all we're asking. We're a team, and we need to act like it. Especially as we get deeper into the season."

"Speaking of the team," Wilder chimes in, his mouth finally empty of food, "we should have a game night or something at our house. Maybe we can play video games, because I'm ready to kick your asses in every single one."

This is a good idea, but I should focus on working things out with Knox. However, I choose to concentrate on Wilder's cocky declaration for the sake of conversation. "You really think you can beat me at COD? In your dreams, maybe."

Wilder leans back in his chair, a smirk on his face. "Bring it on, Bennett."

Blaise chuckles, picking up his coffee again. "I'll believe it when I see it. You two are both so full of shit."

This feels good; it feels normal. It shifts my attention from the issues I have with Isla and Knox to the background, which is what I need for the time being. The trash talk continues as we finish our breakfast. It's a welcome distraction, but before we leave the table, I pull out my phone to send a text to Knox.

It's time to get this over with.

> Me: We need to talk. Let me know when you're available.

There. I've made the first move to squash whatever this beef is. Now, it's up to him to respond in kind.

24

ISLA

I need to get my life together. Today is supposed to be that day, however, my body isn't cooperating.

Right now, I'm curled into a tight ball as cramps rip through my lower abdomen. I try to shift positions, but it doesn't help the pain. Getting my heating pad might work, but I'm already a hot, sweaty mess, so all I would do is get hotter.

And not in a good way.

Thankfully, my professor canceled today's class, so I don't have to worry about that. Not to mention, Tessa hasn't been around in a couple of days. I don't know why, and I don't care.

The only other thing I had on my agenda today was to get more footage of Asher, but that is not happening. I don't want to be in the same vicinity as him right now. I'm

still fighting with myself about whether this mess of whatever is going on between us is all a bad idea.

One that I poured fuel on when I kissed him and let
him kiss me elsewhere.

Groaning, I fumble for my phone on the nightstand
and send a quick text to him. I swear that takes all of my
energy.

> Me: Hey, I'm not feeling well. We'll have
> to reschedule our recording session for
> tonight.

I don't give any details because, well, that would be
awkward as hell. I toss my phone aside and bury my face
in my pillow, wishing that the pain would subside. It's
been a while since I've had cramps this bad, not since I got
my PCOS diagnosis. Just my luck that they hit me full
force now when I'm already dealing with the emotional
fallout from everything else.

My phone vibrates with a response from Asher.
Should I read his message? Who am I kidding? I pick up
my phone and look at the text.

> Asher: I'm sorry to hear that. Do you
> need anything?

I stare at the words on the screen, half-tempted to
ignore them. But I know Asher, and he will only let this go
once he gets a response. With a sigh, I type back a reply.

> Me: I'm fine. Nothing I can't handle.
> Thanks though.

I set my phone aside again, not expecting any further response. Asher has a busy schedule, so I'm sure that'll be the end of it. I curl tighter into myself, wishing the pain meds I took earlier would kick in already.

But then my phone vibrates again. What the hell? I put the phone up to my face again to read Asher's message.

> Asher: What are your symptoms?

I blink at the phone screen because I'm surprised by Asher's follow-up question. Does he really want to know about my period symptoms? That seems a bit... personal. But then again, it's not like we haven't seen everything there is to see about each other, so what does it really matter?

But I'll give him an out first.

> Me: Don't worry about it.

> Asher: Tell me.

I debate how to respond. Part of me wants to brush it off and tell him it's nothing serious. His genuine concern is touching. Before I can overthink it further, another wave of cramps hits, and I wince. Screw it, might as well be honest.

> Me: Some horrible cramps amongst other things.

I hit send and close my eyes, focusing on my breathing to try to ride out the pain. A few minutes later, my phone buzzes again. Asher's response pops up.

> Asher: I'll be there in 20.

My eyes widen. He's coming over? Now? Why? A small thrill goes through me at the thought of seeing him, followed by panic. I'm a mess right now, sweaty and gross, and not in any state to entertain anyone.

> Me: You don't need to do that. I'll survive. Really.

I chew my lip as I wait for his reply, praying he listens. But that's foolish. If Asher can help someone, he'll do it, even when it means going out of his way.

> Asher: Too late, already omw. Be there soon.

There's no way this is real life. My ex-boyfriend, who I've been avoiding like the plague since the kiss that shouldn't have happened, is on his way over. Right now.

While I'm curled up in a ball of period-induced agony. Just perfect.

I drag myself out of bed with a groan, determined to at least make myself somewhat presentable before he arrives. Somehow, I replace my sweat-soaked sheets and change into a clean pair of leggings and an oversized hoodie. I manage to make it to the bathroom to brush my teeth and hair and splash some cold water on my face. It's not much, but it's the best I can do, given the circumstances.

I'm rushing around my room to the best of my ability. As I move around, my elbow knocks over a stack of papers on Tessa's desk.

Shit.

I take my time bending down to gather the things I dropped when something catches my eye.

It's a small black notebook. I know I shouldn't open it, but what the hell? She already hates me. When I do, I see a list of names written in Tessa's handwriting.

My heart skips a beat as I recognize some names. They are people from our dorm, classmates, and even a few professors. Next to each name are details about each person, and I'm only more confused by it all. Why would she take the time to do this?

On the bright side, as I'm skimming through the pages, I notice my name isn't among them.

Since I don't know why she's doing this, there isn't much I can do. So, I place the notebook back among

Tessa's papers. I carefully stack everything into a neat pile and set it back on her desk. As of now, what's on her desk doesn't concern me.

I walk over to my bed, and then there's a knock on the door. With a quick glance at the time, I can see Asher kept his word. He's here twenty minutes later. I take a deep breath before I open it to reveal Asher standing there with a grocery bag in hand. He looks amazing, as always, in a simple t-shirt and jeans. His hair is messy, as if he's been running his hands through it. I hate that it reminds me of how it looked when I ran my hands through it while he was fucking me with his tongue.

"Hey," he whispers. I can see that his green eyes are full of concern as they sweep over me. "How are you feeling?"

I step aside to let him in, shrugging one shoulder. "I've been better. You didn't have to come all the way over here."

Asher sets the bag down on my desk, unpacking it. "I know. But I wanted to. I got you some stuff that might help." He pulls out a bottle of extra-strength Tylenol, a large bag of Skittles, some chocolate, some tea, and some comfy socks.

I hold back tears at the thoughtful gesture. "Ash... Thank you. That's really sweet of you."

He shrugs, looking almost shy. I can't remember the last time I've seen him like that, if ever. "It's nothing. I just hate the thought of you suffering alone." He hesitates, then adds, "I wanted to see you. Even if it's not under the best circumstances."

I'll never admit that my heart does a little flip in my chest. It's taking everything within me to keep my expression neutral. "Well, um, thanks again. I appreciate it."

Asher nods, his gaze lingering on mine for a charged moment before he clears his throat and looks away. "You should lay back down. Can I get you anything else? Want me to make you some of that tea?"

I hesitate, torn between wanting his company and not wanting to be vulnerable around him right now. But the pain wins out, and I find myself nodding. "Sure, tea would be great. Thanks."

Asher makes me some tea while I gingerly lower myself back onto my bed, propping myself up with pillows. He returns a few minutes later, carefully handing me a steaming mug.

"Careful, it's hot," he murmurs, settling himself in my desk chair, keeping a bit of distance between us.

I blow on the tea and take a small sip. It's the perfect temperature, and he's even added a bit of honey, which is just how I like it. "It's perfect. Thank you."

We sit in semi-awkward silence for a few minutes as I drink the tea and the medicine I took starts to kick in. Finally, I can't take it anymore.

"You didn't have to do this. I would've been fine on my own."

"That's not the point. What matters is that you don't

need to be alone. I'm able to be here for you, and more importantly, I want to be here for you."

Silence passes between us as I try to figure out the words to say. He's almost stunned me into silence, and it takes a second for my brain to catch up. "Thanks. Again. I normally wouldn't admit this, but it means a lot that you're here." Damn, these hormones are making me more emotional than usual.

Asher's facial expression relaxes. "Anytime, sunshine. You know that."

This time, I can't take it anymore. The question slips past my lips before I can stop it. "Why are you calling me sunshine again?"

"I guess old habits die hard."

I shake my head. "Bullshit."

"Prove it."

I narrow my eyes at Asher, trying to read between the lines of his cryptic response. "What's that supposed to mean? Are you saying calling me sunshine is more than just an old habit?"

Asher leans back in the chair, studying me with an inscrutable expression. "I'm saying that you need to prove that this isn't more than me being stuck in a loop of calling you that name. Then again, maybe some things never really went away, even if we both tried to pretend they did."

I look down and play with the handle of the mug in my hands as I try to process Asher's words. Is he implying what I think he is? That his feelings for me never went away, despite everything that's happened between us?

The thought both thrills and terrifies me. I've worked so hard to move on, to convince myself that Asher and I are better off being acquaintances since I came to Crestwood. But if I'm honest with myself, my feelings for him never disappeared. I've only buried them because of the pain he inflicted on me.

Speaking of pain, I slam my eyes shut as another cramp rolls through my stomach. When the pain dulls, I hold my arm out, and Asher takes the mug.

"This sucks," I mutter, more to myself than to Asher. "Having a uterus is the worst sometimes."

To my surprise, Asher chuckles. "I can only imagine. Is it always this bad?"

I shrug one shoulder. "Not always, but often enough. A few weeks ago, my doctor diagnosed me with PCOS. It varies by person, but it can make everything worse."

Asher's eyes narrow, confusion filling his expression. "PCOS? What's that?"

"Oh, um. It stands for Polycystic Ovary Syndrome," I explain, shifting to sit up a bit more. "Basically, my hormones are all out of whack, which causes a bunch of lovely symptoms and can cause super painful periods, weight gain, acne, excess hair growth... the list goes on. It's a real treat."

"Shit, that sounds rough. I'm sorry you have to deal

with all of that." He rubs a hand across his face. "Is there anything that helps manage the symptoms?"

A snort leaves my lips. "Birth control pills, for one. It's ironic since PCOS can also make it harder to get pregnant. Not that I'm thinking about that anytime soon," I add quickly.

Why did I have to bring up pregnancy, of all things? That's awkward as hell. When Asher doesn't react, I'm intrigued and thankful. I clear my throat and continue. "Anyway, yeah, the pill helps regulate hormones. Losing weight can make a difference in some people, as can cutting back on sugar and carbs. Easier said than done when all you want is Skittles and chocolate, though."

"Speaking of..." Asher reaches for the things he unpacked from the grocery bag. He picks up the huge chocolate bar he bought. "For medicinal purposes, of course."

I can't help but laugh. "Oh, of course. Totally legit." I make grabby hands for the chocolate, and he hands it over with a grin.

As I tear into the wrapper, Asher speaks again. "For real, though, if there's ever anything I can do to help, even if it's just bringing you emergency candy, I'm here."

I glance up from the chocolate bar. "I... Thank you. That means a lot." I break off a piece of chocolate and pop it in my mouth, letting the sweetness melt on my tongue before I speak again. "I'm not used to having someone around who wants to take care of me like this. Outside of my parents and Selene. It's nice. Strange, but nice."

I don't bring up the fact that he did his best to take care of me when we were dating. It's pointless because we both know he seems to be slipping into that role again.

"Happy to be of service. You deserve it, Isla. More than you realize."

His words make my heart clench because, deep down, I know he's right. I take another bite of the chocolate as I wonder if I should switch it out for the Skittles that are next to Asher. Once I'm done with the piece of candy I'm eating, I say, "If you bring those Skittles over here, I'll let you stay and watch a movie with me."

Asher's eyes widen before a smirk appears on his face. He grabs the bag and stands up. "Sounds like a lot of work, but I think I can manage it."

He walks over and sits down on my bed. He's careful to maintain a bit of space between us. It is difficult, given how big he is and how small my bed is, but we figure it out. I grab my laptop and pull up Netflix. "Do you have any preferences?"

He shrugs. "Lady's choice. I'm just along for the ride."

I scroll through the options before settling on a light-hearted rom-com. As the opening credits roll, I find myself snuggling deeper into my pillows, and it just so happens that my head lands on his shoulder.

And neither one of us says a word.

25

ASHER

The silence between Knox and me feels like a ticking time bomb as we sit across from each other in our living room. I didn't expect the words to flow like we were on the best of terms, but this is painful.

With a sigh, I lean forward, my elbows land on my knees, and I say, "So..." I clear my throat, trying to find the right words. "I know things have been weird between us lately."

Knox snorts. "Weird? That's the understatement of the fucking year."

I open my mouth to respond, but Knox cuts me off before I can get a word out. "Look, about what I said the other day, about Isla—"

I cut him off this time. "I overreacted, and I know you

didn't mean anything by it. There's a bunch of stuff going on, and I don't know up from down half the time."

Knox's eyes zero in on me. It's the first time he's looked me in the eye in who knows how long. "I can see that. You've been playing well for the most part, but you've still been off your game."

The truth hurts, and I can't deny that he's right. "I'm doing the best I can right now," I say.

"Your best?" Knox's laugh is harsh. "Your best isn't good enough if this is it. We're all busting our asses out there, and you're dragging us down with whatever the hell's going on in your head."

I flinch at his words, feeling the weight of my own failures pressing down on me. "It's not like I'm doing this on purpose, Knox. I'm trying to keep it together."

"Trying?" Knox rubs a hand across his chin. "You think trying is enough? We're not just talking about you here. The whole team is feeling it. You used to be the guy we could count on. Now? You're a fucking liability."

His words slam into me like a sledgehammer, and for a moment, all I want to do is fight back, to tell him he doesn't know what he's talking about. But I can't because, deep down, I know he's right.

"I get it," I say, my voice barely above a whisper. "You're right. I've been off my game, and it's affecting everyone. But it's not just about Isla. There's a lot going on that I haven't talked about."

"So talk."

"It's also my family. My mom... she's been struggling... financially, I mean. We weren't rich by any means when I started here, but she's had blow after blow over the last few months. I've been trying to help where I can, but it's difficult."

"I get it. Family stuff is never easy. But you can't let it follow you onto the ice. You've got to compartmentalize and get help."

I nod, knowing he's right, but it's easier said than done. "I'm trying, but sometimes, it feels like everything is just too much. It feels like I'm being pulled in a million different directions and can't keep up."

"So ask for help. You've got a whole team behind you, Asher. We're here for you, but you've got to let us in. You can't keep shouldering all of this on your own."

I lean back, running a hand through my hair as I exhale. "I just don't want to be a burden and let anyone down."

"You're not a burden. But you are letting us down when you don't trust us enough to tell us what's going on." Knox's words are blunt, but I can hear the underlying concern in his voice.

He makes an excellent point that I agree with. "You're right. I'm sorry. I know I need to communicate better and ask for help when I need it."

"Damn right, you do. We're a team, Asher. On and off the ice. We've got your back, but you've got to let us in."

This conversation is helping more than I expected

because I do feel the tension leaving my shoulders. "Thanks, Knox. I mean it. I know I've got some work to do, but I'm going to try to be better about leaning on you guys when I need to."

"Good. Because we need you, Asher. The team needs you. But more importantly, we want to be there for you as a friend." Knox reaches out, clasping my shoulder.

I manage a small smile. "I know. And I'm going to do my best to be there for you guys, too."

"I think the guys will appreciate that. And I'm sorry for pushing your buttons the way I was." Knox asks as he drops his hand from my shoulder. "So what's the plan? What can we do to help?"

"...I'm not sure yet," I finally say.

It is the truth. None of this is easy, and I'm not sure which way to turn at this point. My schedule is pretty much what it is at this point. Having more money would be helpful, but I'm not ready to beg for handouts. My family and I are doing fine, but it could be better.

"I get it. And—"

Knox's words get cut off as heavy footsteps hit the stairs. If I didn't live here, I would assume the person is falling down the stairs. But I know it's Wilder trying to get... somewhere. As if conjured by my thoughts of him, Wilder pops his head in the room and says, "Is the coast clear?"

"The fuck..." Knox mumbles before I can comprehend what is going on.

"Are you two done? Are we all cool?"

Knox and I exchange a confused glance before I turn back to Wilder. "Uh, yeah, we're good. Why?"

Wilder's face splits into a grin. "Because the cavalry has arrived!"

He steps into the room, followed by Levi and Blaise, both of whom are carrying pizza boxes and a case of beer.

"Wilder was hungry and thought we could all use some bonding, so here we are."

I shake my head because I'm not at all surprised that this is Wilder's big idea. "You guys are something else. Thanks for this."

Levi sets the pizza on the coffee table and plops on the couch beside me. "Anytime. That's what friends are for, right?"

The feeling is mutual. I give him a slight nod and reach for a slice of pizza. The smell alone is enough to settle any tension in the room. It's not New York-style pizza, but as soon as I take a bite, it hits the spot.

Wilder flops onto the armchair across from us and takes a long drink from his beer. "So what else are we going to be up to tonight? Should we continue the deep feelings talk? More heart-to-heart conversations?"

I roll my eyes, but Blaise speaks first. "How about we just watch the game? Although there is a time and place for it, I'm not drunk enough for a feelings talk."

"Seconded," Knox agrees, reaching for another

slice. "I've had enough serious conversation for one night."

"I'm not going to disagree with that," I say before taking another bite of the pizza in my hand. The warm, cheesy euphoria is sitting in the top three of the best things ever, right behind hockey and sex. The order of importance for those things changes depending on the hour. Is it right? I'm not sure, but it's where things stand in my head.

Levi grabs the remote and flips through the channels until he finds the game we've all been waiting for. "Here we go. The San Diego Sharks versus the DC Titans. Perfect timing because the second period is just starting."

Our TV screen lights up with the packed arena, and I wish I was there. The DC Titans, in their bold red, white, and blue uniforms, are known for their excellent offense. On the other side, the San Diego Sharks, wearing deep navy and gold, have a reputation for their disciplined, hard-hitting defense. The clash of styles promises an exciting game, and because we are in Virginia, most people in our area will root for DC, including myself. However, I know that Isla's older sister works for the San Diego Sharks, so I'm curious about who they are rooting for.

Probably still the Titans.

I stretch my legs as the second period begins. My discussion with Knox fades into the background as we focus all of our attention on the game. The Sharks strike first, a quick wrist shot from their star forward sneaking past the Titans' goalie. Wilder lets out a groan, shaking his head.

"Come on, Titans. Get it together," he mutters, taking another swig of his beer.

But the Sharks keep the pressure on, their defense smothering the Titans' attempts to generate offense. By the end of the period, it's 2-0 Sharks, and the mood in the room has shifted from relaxed to slightly anxious.

"They've still got time to turn it around," I say. I don't know how my optimism is going to fly at the moment, but here we are. "One goal, and they're right back in it."

"They better," Knox grumbles. "I've got money on this game."

I raise an eyebrow at him. "Since when do you bet on hockey?"

He shrugs. "Since I had a good feeling about the Titans. Which they're currently making me regret."

This time, Blaise chimes in, "You don't bet on our games, right?"

Knox rolls his eyes. "I'm not gambling. Someone bet me that the Sharks would kick the Titans' ass. And I couldn't say no."

The third period starts, and I'm ready to lace up my skates and jump in there myself if they don't turn it around. Thankfully, it seems as if the Titans have gotten it together after the last period. They come out as if their asses are on fire, and I'm thrilled. They get rewarded for their efforts five minutes later when their captain, Hunter Callahan, scores on a deflection from the point. My living room erupts in cheers.

"There we go!" Wilder exclaims, pumping his fist. "That's what I'm talking about!"

The goal energizes the Titans, and they control the play. But the Sharks aren't going down without a fight. Their goalie makes a series of spectacular saves, if I say so myself. Because of that, it robs the Titans of what looked to be several goals. Fuck.

As the clock winds down on the last period, the tension in the room is almost back to where it was when Knox and I were talking, but for a different reason. With just two minutes left, the Titans pull their goalie for an extra attacker. It's a risky move, but they need a goal.

Everyone in the room is on the edge of their seats as the Titans swarm the Sharks' zone. Passes are flying, and shots are being fired from every angle. The Sharks' goalie is making save after save. If they weren't up against the Titans, I would be impressed, but how well they are playing only irritates me.

"Come on, come on," Levi mumbles under his breath, his eyes glued to the TV screen. I'm not sure if he realizes he said the words, but I agree with his sentiments.

With just thirty seconds left, the Titan's defenseman, Caleb Raine, winds up for a slap shot from the point. The puck rockets through a maze of bodies and finds its way into the back of the net.

"Yes!" I shout as I jump to my feet. "Fucking finally!"

The room feels like pure pandemonium. We all exchange high fives, and there might have been some beer spilled, but we can deal with that later. I swear it has been some time since we've felt this joy from our games.

The game isn't over yet because it heads into overtime with a tied score. My leg is bouncing up and down as it begins, and I'm not sure if I'm going to make it through this alive, given the anxiety that I'm feeling. My heart threatens to leave my body unassisted the longer this game goes on.

Although both teams have the opportunity to score, neither one of them can make a goal happen. I rub a hand across my face when it's becoming more apparent that we are heading for a shootout. I look to my left and find Knox pacing back and forth, clenching and unclenching his fist. A lot must be riding on this bet he took, and I can't help but wonder why. However, now that we are just back on good terms and with the high stakes of this game, this isn't the time to ask.

But then, with just over a minute left in the extra period, the Titans' forward, Luke Drake, picks up a loose puck in the neutral zone and makes it all the way to the goalie.

I swear the room holds its collective breath as Drake makes his move. Forehand, backhand, forehand again. The goalie bites, and Drake tucks the puck into the open net.

Game over.

Titans win!

"Oh my—" An explosion cuts my words off.

"Unbelievable!" Wilder yells, spilling his beer again. "What a finish!"

Knox lets out a triumphant shout, pumping his fist in the air. "Yes! That dude is going to pay up!"

I turn to him, grinning. "Looks like your bet paid off, huh?"

He nods, a smug smile on his face. "Never doubt the Titans, man. Never doubt them."

Levi leans back on the couch with a grin on his face. "That was one hell of a game. Reminds me why I love this sport so much."

"Couldn't agree more, brother," Blaise says as he reaches for another slice of pizza.

As the post-game analysis starts on the TV, I look around at my friends and teammates, happy to have them all here to experience this with me. "You know," I say, grabbing a slice of pizza myself, "this is exactly what I needed tonight."

Levi raises his drink in a mock toast. "To the Titans and to nights like this."

We all raise our cans in agreement, and for a moment, everything feels right. No stress, no pressure, just a bunch of guys enjoying the sport they love.

There isn't much better than that.

26

ISLA

I can't believe I'm doing this.

My fingers hover over my phone screen, my heart pounding as I debate whether to send the text. After two days of bottling up my emotions, I finally feel ready to face Asher after his help while I was dealing with a very heavy period. Not to mention, we need to get back to filming the short-form content that Bailey and our social media followers absolutely love.

When he was there for me, it was just like he used to be years ago.

It's stupid, really, how much I've overthought this moment. I keep replaying that afternoon in my mind— the way he showed up at my door with the goodies he purchased for me in hopes that it would make me feel better. It's not like I forgot how kind he could be. But feeling it again, so unexpectedly, cracked something open inside me.

I take another deep breath as I stare at the message I've typed, urging myself to press send. What if I'm being foolish about all of this? Could this be something that I've just drummed up in my head, and he's not thinking anything about it?

Honestly, I don't even know what "this" is.

> Me: Thanks for everything a couple of days ago. I was wondering if we could talk?

The words are lame, but I'm not sure what else to say. Before I can stare at the message for fifteen more hours, I hit send and toss my phone down on my bed. It's silly because I'm going to end up picking it back up in the next minute to see if he responded anyway.

I glance at Tessa's side of the room, thanking the universe that she has class right now and isn't here to watch me do this. The only one who can judge me as I pace back and forth is me. The likelihood of me getting a response anytime soon is low because of his busy schedule, and I know that. Even with that in mind, each second still feels like an eternity. Have I made a terrible mistake?

All of that changes, however, when I hear the tiny sound of my phone vibrating on my bed, stopping the spiraling that I've gone down and am about to get deeper into.

Asher: Of course. Are you feeling better?

I read his words once and then twice. The fact that he's still concerned about my well-being, even days later, makes the butterflies in my stomach flutter.

Me: Yes, much better. Thank you.

I press send quickly this time, so I don't stare at the text, and he responds in a flash.

Asher: I'm glad. How about you come over to my place? We can talk here.

Relief washes over me, followed by a fresh wave of nerves. Going to his house feels intimate, but it's better than meeting in public or here because Tessa might disturb us.

Me: Sure, that works. When do you want to meet?

Asher: I'll be free in an hour if you are. No practice today.

I stare at his response. In an hour? As in today? I knew there wasn't practice today, but the timing of this is throwing me for a loop. I glance down at my outfit—an oversized sweatshirt and leggings. At least I have time to change.

Me: An hour works. See you then.

I hit send before I can second-guess myself. Now, I have less than sixty minutes to get ready and go to Asher's place. My heart races as I rummage through my closet, trying to find something to wear that looks put together but not like I'm trying too hard.

Why am I even thinking this way?

I settle on a pair of dark-wash jeans and a soft, cream-colored sweater. It's casual, but still nice. I decide to shower and change, which takes up most of the time. I run a brush through my hair and apply a touch of mascara and lip gloss.

Asher sends me his address just before I leave my room. Although I was there for the hockey party, it was dark, and I was drinking. Once I hit the road, the drive to his place feels way too short, but it makes sense because his house is just off campus. When I pull up out front, I sit in the car for a moment, trying to gather my courage. The place is typical of what you'd expect for a group of college guys—rough around the edges, but I can still see the charm in it. The house itself is two stories, built decades ago, with weathered brick and white trim that could use a fresh coat of paint. Their front yard is small and unkempt, unlike the grounds of the university. But I have to admit, I'm surprised by how clean the outside is and wonder if it carries on into the inside of the home.

This is it. No turning back now.

I step out of the car and make my way up the front porch. I can feel myself slightly shaking as I make my way to the front door, but before I can even knock, it swings open.

Asher.

Has he been watching and waiting for me to arrive? I can't deny that the thought of that makes me happy.

"Hey," he says, stepping back to let me in. "Thanks for coming."

"Thanks for inviting me," I reply.

I step inside, taking in the surprisingly tidy hallway and living room. The furnishings are simple but comfortable, with a well-worn couch, a couple of armchairs, and a coffee table with a few textbooks. It feels lived in but not messy.

Asher closes the door behind me and gestures toward what I assume is the kitchen. "Make yourself at home. Can I get you anything to drink?"

I shake my head, feeling too nervous to even think about consuming anything. "No, I'm good. Thanks, though."

The war within me rages, screaming that this is a mistake and I'm being a boss by reaching out to meet. I should have thought more about what I was going to say before texting him, but here we are. It would have been easy just to text him and say thanks, but I wanted to meet with him in person.

Why am I lying to myself? I know exactly why I wanted to see him.

"Are your roommates here?" I ask, glancing around and breaking the silence at the same time. Go me.

He shakes his head. "No, they're gone, at least for now. It's just us."

"Ah." I'm not sure how to feel about that. I'm glad we're alone, but given what I'm feeling right now, I'm not sure if that's a blessing or a curse.

Asher leads me into the living room, and we both take a seat on the couch, which leaves a respectable distance between us. I exhale as my fingers make their way to the hem of my sweater. I'm struggling to find the right words to start this conversation.

"So," I begin, my voice sounding a little shaky, and I hate it. "I wanted to thank you again for coming over the other day. It meant a lot that you were there for me."

Asher's green eyes meet my blue ones, and I see a flicker of emotion in their depths. "You don't have to thank me, Isla. I'm just glad I could help. I couldn't do much to take the pain away, but—"

There he goes, being all sweet again. I shake my head and put my hand up to stop him from talking. "No, you did so much, and I appreciate it. Even though I wonder if it has made things awkward between us. Or maybe that's just me being caught up in my own head about all the things that are going on between us and I should—"

Asher's chuckle stops me. "Sunshine, you're rambling."

I feel my cheeks grow warm because of his words. He's right, I am rambling. I take a deep breath, trying to slow myself down. "Sorry. I guess I'm just a little nervous."

"Why?"

I bite my lip. "Because of everything that has happened since I moved back here. It's just... it's brought up a lot of old feelings."

Asher nods slowly. "I know what you mean. I'd be lying if I said I haven't been thinking about it too."

Relief washes over me, but I can still feel the heat on my cheeks. At least it's not just me. "Really? I wasn't sure if... I mean, after everything that happened between us..."

Asher leans forward, resting his elbows on his knees. "Isla, what happened back then... I was young and stupid. I made a mistake letting you go. And seeing you again, being around you, it's made me realize how much I've missed you."

My heart swells at his confession. "I've missed you too. More than I wanted to admit. But what about my PCOS diagnosis?" I blurt out the question without processing that I was going to ask it.

"What about it?"

"I experience some of the side effects that come along with it."

Asher tilts his head as if he's trying to understand

what I'm trying to say. "I don't understand how that would change how I feel about you."

"But I have difficult periods sometimes, as you saw the other day."

"And I wish I could take the pain away."

"I have excess hair growth that I sometimes shave off."

He shrugs. "So what? I'm hairy too."

That makes me laugh for a second. "And I told you about the weight gain and pregnancy—"

Asher touches my cheek, silencing me without saying a word. "I don't care about any of those things because all I want is you. All of you. I also did some research after you told me about it so I could educate myself. Like things you can eat that might help lessen the symptoms, medicines you might have to take...."

I close my eyes while leaning into his touch and trying my best not to cry. It feels so natural to me, and I refuse to fight against what seems to be instinct. I've missed his touch, and it's only now that it hit me.

"But that's not all." I open my eyes as he finishes speaking. He reaches into his back pocket and pulls out a slender, off-white box. "Glad I didn't smash that in my back pocket."

He hands me the box. I stare at it for a moment before opening it to reveal a delicate silver necklace with a small teal charm shaped like a lotus flower and a teal ribbon intertwined. "This is a reminder of how strong you are in your battle with PCOS. The teal lotus flower and ribbon represent your fight, resilience, and strength throughout all of this. You're a warrior."

My tears make their appearance as I look at the necklace. I touch the charm gently before looking back up at Asher. "It's beautiful," I whisper. "Thank you so much."

It takes a moment for him to put the necklace on me, and he helps me wipe away my tears. Once he does, I look up and find what I can only describe as doubt in his eyes. "What's wrong?"

He runs a hand through his hair. "I hope I'm not fucking all this up. We have a lot of history, and I don't want to mess it up again."

"Aren't we older and wiser and all that now?" I ask as I play with my new necklace and earn another chuckle from Asher.

"I suppose we are."

"But what are we doing?"

Asher's thumb gently caresses my cheek, sending shivers down my spine. He doesn't wait for me to respond to his question. "I think," he says, "we're giving ourselves a second chance."

I search his eyes, trying to read the true meaning behind his words within them. "Is that what you want?" I whisper. "A second chance?"

Asher nods, his gaze never leaving mine. "More than anything, sunshine. I know I hurt you before, and I'll never forgive myself for that. But if you're willing to give me another shot, I promise I'll do everything in my power to make it right this time."

"I want that too, but I'm terrified."

"Completely understandable. It was the same way for me the first time around, but not anymore. I'm not running away from this again. I'm not running away from whatever this is and what it could turn into."

"But what about my dad? He's still your coach." Apparently, blurting out questions today is the name of the game. I'm stating the obvious, but it's the truth. I still work with the team. Is that against any rules in the paperwork I signed?

Asher's gaze shifts for a moment, and I can see the cogs in his brain turning before his eyes meet mine again. "I know it's complicated with your dad being my coach and you working with the team. But I'm willing to face whatever challenges come our way. I'm not going to let that stop me from being with you. I did it once, but I'm not doing it again."

"But I don't want to be a distraction for you."

"You would never be a distraction for me. Hell, if anything, you'd be the reason I'm less distracted. Knox would be proud."

I tilt my head to the side, and Asher drops his hands from my face. I immediately miss his touch. "What does he have to do with this?"

A soft smile plays on Asher's lips. "It's a long story, but

Knox has been on my case about you since the moment he saw us together at the rink."

I raise an eyebrow, intrigued. "Oh really? And what has he been saying?"

Asher chuckles before leaning back against the couch. I might stare for a second longer than I should when his shirt rises, showing a hint of abs, but his words bring my attention back to his face. "He pretended like he was going to go after you to piss me off because I was denying what I knew to be true, even though it was the first time we'd been in each other's presence in years."

I can't help but laugh at the thought of Knox pushing Asher's buttons that way. It's oddly reassuring to know that Asher's feelings for me are so obvious that his teammates, who would know him best, have noticed.

"Well, I'm glad he could give you a little nudge in the right direction," I tease. Some of the nervousness I've been feeling since the moment I decided to text him leaves my body.

A smirk appears on Asher's face. "I agree, but it didn't take much. Now, enough about him. The last thing I want you to think about right now is another guy."

"Oh really?" The words sound more flirty than I anticipated, and I have to give myself a mental pat on the back.

Asher leans in closer, his face mere inches from mine. "Really," he murmurs as his hand cups my cheek once more. "Right now, I only want you thinking about me and what I'm about to do to you."

And then his lips are on mine.

27

ISLA

This kiss is so much different from the one we had at the team bonding event. The thought of getting caught fueled that one, and while there's a chance that Asher's roommates might walk in and find us, the idea of it is so far from my mind. The only thing that matters is getting as close to Asher as I can, and I don't want this to stop.

Ever.

Our kiss starts slowly, as if we're exploring each other for the first time all over again. Given how long we've been apart, it might as well be. However, the kiss grows in intensity, igniting something more fiery inside of me. The kiss becomes something that grows more urgent, and soon I'm desperate to have more. I can tell that Asher feels the same as his arms tighten around me, and my hands end up fisting his shirt.

I'm convinced that I can rip the fabric with my bare hands if I want to.

A soft moan escapes my throat as Asher deepens the kiss. When his tongue slips past my lips, it becomes tangled with mine, raising the temperature within my body. I can't get enough of him. All I can think about is the taste of his mouth, the feel of his body pressed against mine, and the scent of his cologne.

His hands slide down my back, gripping my hips and pulling me closer. My fingers end up tangled in his hair, tugging on his strands. Without breaking the kiss, Asher stands and lifts me up with him. A small squeal leaves my lips, which are still attached to his, as I wrap my legs around his waist. The kiss ends when he spins us and carries me up the stairs. Once we are on the second floor, he takes a few steps down a hallway and opens the second door on the left. Before I can blink, he closes the door behind us with his foot and tosses me on his bed.

His eyes never leave my body as he pulls his shirt over his head and tosses it aside. My breath catches at the sight of his abs, sculpted and defined from years of working out and hockey. His body was beautiful years ago, but it's something to behold now. I can't help but reach out and run my fingers along the rugged ridges of his stomach. Asher's eyes darken with desire as he watches me, his breath quickening under my touch.

I love having this effect on him.

He leans down, capturing my lips in another searing

kiss as his hands find the hem of my sweater. We break apart just long enough for him to pull it over my head, discarding it somewhere on the floor. His gaze rakes over my exposed skin, taking in the sight of me in my plain black bra. Now I wish I'd worn something sexier, but Asher doesn't seem to mind.

"Fuck. You're so beautiful."

His words send a shiver down my spine as he lowers his head and gives me another kiss on the lips, but he doesn't stay there long. He leaves a trail of kisses along my jaw and down my neck, and I swear he doesn't miss a single inch. I tilt my head back, giving him better access, and I'm rewarded when he finds a sensitive area just below my ear. He takes his time, nibbling, sucking, and licking the spot, and as a result, another moan forces itself from my lips. With how much attention he's giving to that spot, I wonder if I'm going to end up with a hickey.

As if he's only just realized there is more to explore, Asher shifts his body to continue his trail of kisses down to the tops of my breasts, which are spilling out of my bra. His stubble grazes my skin, and I sigh at the feeling. I arch my back, begging for more, but he doesn't give in.

Instead, Asher lifts his head and finds my eyes. I swear I lose my breath when our gazes connect. His hands slide around to my back, and I feel him unclasp my bra. The straps fall down my shoulders, and he tugs the garment away, exposing my breasts to his heated stare.

"Perfect," he murmurs, almost to himself, before cupping my breasts in his large hands.

I gasp at the contact, taking a few quick breaths as a result. He plays with them as if he's savoring every moment. And after over three years, I don't blame him one bit because I never want to forget this either. When his thumbs brush over my already hard nipples, I jump slightly. His touch sends a jolt of electricity straight to my pussy, and I can feel the dampness growing between my thighs.

"Asher." His name falls off my lips, and my voice sounds needy even to my ears.

He smirks, clearly pleased with the effect he's having on me.

And I'm not complaining.

Without warning, he dips his head and takes one of my nipples into his mouth. I cry out at the sudden contact of his mouth on me. He swirls his tongue around my nipple before gently grazing it with his teeth. My hands fly to his hair, threading through his strands as I hold him against me.

Asher's mouth continues to torture me, and I'm left dumbfounded. His alternating between sucking and nipping at my flesh leaves so much uncertainty. I can't figure out the rhythm he's using, and that makes it both frustrating and satisfying. My moans only grow louder as he continues, not caring that any of his roommates could come home and hear what we are doing. Soon, I am writhing beneath him because I'm so desperate for more. His hand travels down my torso, skimming over my ribs and across my stomach before toying with the waistband of my jeans. I whimper as his fingers dip just below the edge, teasing me with both his hands and his mouth.

"Please." The word falls out, and I'm not even sure what I'm begging for. The only thing I know is that I need him to keep going, to never stop.

As if reading my mind, Asher lifts his head and captures my lips in a searing kiss. His tongue slips into my mouth, tangling with mine as his hands make quick work of the button and zipper on my jeans. Before I can think of anything else, he yanks my pants down with my help. His eyes study me for another moment before his body takes over, and his hand reaches its destination.

A gasp escapes my lips as Asher's fingers brush against the damp fabric of my underwear. In any other circumstance, I might have felt embarrassed by what he discovered, but it's the furthest thing from my mind. Although the touch is light and teasing, it ignites a fire deep within me. I arch my back, pressing myself against his hand, begging him for more.

Asher chuckles, a low sound that vibrates through his chest. "Someone's eager," he murmurs against my lips before nipping at my lower lip. His fingers continue their exploration, tracing the outline of my clit through the thin cotton barrier.

I whimper, my hips rocking instinctively, seeking the

friction I crave. "Asher, don't make me beg again..." My voice is barely above a whisper.

Asher's eyes hold my gaze, his fingers still teasing me with featherlight touches. "But I like it when you beg," he says. "I like knowing how much you want me."

I feel the same way.

Slowly, deliberately, he slips his hand beneath the waistband of my underwear. I inhale sharply as his fingers make contact with my bare skin, skimming through the slick folds. He groans, and it's like music to my ears.

"You're so wet, sunshine," he rasps, his breath hot against my ear. "Is this all for me?"

"You know it is." I say it more as a confession to myself than to him. I'll have to unpack that later.

One of Asher's fingers slips into me, leaving me gasping for air. He knows exactly how to touch me, as if he memorized every moment we spent together years ago. I can't help but wonder if he's been dreaming of this moment as much as I have over the time we've been apart.

Shit. There's another confession I'll have to dwell on. But not right now.

"Ash... Ash..." His name sounds like a mantra as he slides another finger inside me, just before setting a slow rhythm that has my hips rolling to meet his every thrust. The sensation is both familiar and new, igniting memories of stolen moments in the backseat of his car and in my childhood bedroom when my parents were away. But there's more confidence in his touch now. I assume that has come with age and experience.

He sucks on my nipple again before letting it go with a loud pop. "You have no idea how much I've missed this. How much I've missed you."

His words play on repeat around me, echoing the same thoughts that have swirled through my mind. I've missed him too, with an intensity that both thrills and terrifies me.

"I want you to show me," I say. "Show me how much you missed me."

That is the only encouragement Asher needs. In one swift motion, his fingers leave my body just before he tears my underwear away, and my mouth drops open. I gasp at the sudden exposure because there is no way that has just happened. But then his mouth is on my pussy, and once again, every coherent thought evaporates from my mind.

"Oh god..." I moan as I throw my head back, so it falls against the pillow.

I swear he's stolen the breath from my lungs. When he looks up at me from where he is between my legs, sparks of pleasure start to simmer. It's as if he hasn't eaten in weeks, and he's starving for me. His groan of satisfaction vibrates throughout me as if he's reading my thoughts.

Every stroke of his tongue sends shockwaves through me. My hips buckle off the bed when he adds a finger to the mix. My hands end up tangled in his hair again. It's almost instinctual because I need something to anchor me as he drives me closer to the edge. The sensations are nearly too much, and I am lost in a haze of need. It's as if my world has narrowed down to where his mouth and fingers are holding me in a chokehold.

He adds a second finger, curling them both just right, and I cry out as the pleasure intensifies. My grip on his hair tightens, my nails scraping against his scalp, but he doesn't seem to mind. If anything, it only spurs him on. He flicks my clit with his tongue, drawing out the tension coiling inside me until it's wound so tight I feel like I might collapse.

"Fuck, oh fuck..." I'm not even sure if those are the words that fly out of my mouth, but that's what it sounds like.

His fingers thrust faster, more profound, hitting that perfect spot inside me again and again until I'm teetering on the brink, ready to fly apart at any second. It only takes one more well-timed curl of his fingers and one final flick of his tongue, and I'm ready to explode.

"That's it, sunshine," Asher murmurs against my skin, his voice a low rumble I swear I can feel in my bones. "Let go for me. I've got you."

And with those words, I'm gone.

My body shatters into a million pieces as ecstasy courses through my veins. I'm vaguely aware of the hoarse cry that tears from my throat as I come undone, my hips arching off the bed as wave after wave of intense pleasure crashes over me. Asher doesn't stop, his fingers and tongue working me through it. His actions prolong the experience until I'm left trembling and gasping for air.

When the last aftershock fades, I collapse back against the mattress. Asher places a final, gentle kiss on my lower stomach before crawling up my body. He settles over me, and I enjoy feeling his weight against me. He nuzzles into the crook of my neck, and his breath causes goosebumps to form along my skin.

"You're so beautiful when you come," he releases a low growl that sounds as if it came from deep within him. "I could watch you fall apart like that every day for the rest of my life and never get tired of it."

28

ISLA

I'm still trying to catch my breath because my heart is racing in my chest when Asher's words wash over me. Part of me wants to say bullshit as a coping mechanism, but I can't bring myself to because of the raw honesty in his voice.

Instead, I tilt my head to gaze into those mesmerizing green eyes I'm convinced are piercing through my soul. What greets me in return is the heat in Asher's eyes, showcasing his desire for me. Hell, that's not the only thing. I can very much feel his cock up against me, and it's obvious that he is ready to come out and play.

The intensity in his eyes grows as he slowly rolls his hips against me. The movement allows him to press his hard length right where I need him most. A moan catches in my throat at the delicious friction, and my body starts humming in anticipation.

"Tell me what you want, Isla," he commands, as his lips graze my ear. "I need to hear you say it."

I shudder as his teeth nip at my earlobe. "You," I gasp out. "I want... I want your cock, Asher." Thank fuck I can get the words out.

A low, approving hum rumbles through his chest. "Good girl," he praises.

The unexpected words send a thrill straight to my pussy, but that isn't all that shocking, to be honest.

Asher's lips claim mine once more. I arch into him, my body craving more of this and so much more. He seems to sense this because his hand trails down my side. When he reaches my hip, he grips it possessively, pulling me flush against him so I can feel every hard inch of him.

"I need to be inside you. Now."

"Then stop waiting and take me."

Asher's eyes flash with a mix of hunger and something else I can't quite decipher before he pulls away from me. I watch as he stands and removes his jeans and boxer briefs in one fluid motion. My breath catches at the sight of him, and there's no doubt he's not ready for what is coming next.

Not to mention, he's even more impressive than I remember.

Asher crawls back onto the bed, but then pauses before a frown lands on his face. "Shit, I need to grab a condom."

The words snap me out of my lust-filled haze, and I

nod; suddenly feeling awkward lying there naked while he rummages through his nightstand drawer. The momentary interruption allows some of my nerves to creep back in. It's been so long since I've been with anyone, let alone the man in front of me.

After what feels like an eternity but is probably only a few seconds, Asher finds what he's looking for and rolls the condom on. Then he's back on the bed, settling his hips between my thighs.

"Hey," he says while cupping my cheek and forcing me to meet his gaze. "You okay?"

I nod, leaning into his touch. "Yeah, I'm good. Just... it's been a while."

He pauses for a second before placing a tender kiss on my forehead. "We'll take it slow. If you need to stop at any point, just tell me, okay?"

His thoughtfulness makes my heart clench, and I pull him down for another sensual kiss. Asher groans into my mouth as I feel him reaching down to line himself up at my entrance.

With a slow, controlled thrust of his hips, he pushes inside me. I gasp at the intrusion just before my nails dig into his shoulders. I take a few deep breaths to adjust to the feeling of him stretching and filling me. It's overwhelming in the best possible way.

"Fuck, you feel incredible," Asher tosses out quickly as he stiffens up, likely doing everything he can to control his body right now. He presses his forehead against mine, allowing me time to get acclimated to him. "So tight and perfect."

I can only whimper in response because I am genuinely lost in the sensation of our bodies becoming one again after so many years apart. When the initial discomfort subsides, I experimentally roll my hips to urge him to move.

Asher takes the hint and thrusts, setting a steady, deep rhythm that has me seeing stars. This moment is both familiar and new as our bodies remember how to move together while also discovering uncharted territory. We aren't teenagers anymore, and the finesse with which we are moving now makes that very apparent. Each snap of his hips sends sparks of pleasure radiating through me.

"Oh god, Asher," I wrap my legs around his waist to take him even deeper. The new angle allows him to hit what I swear is the perfect spot, and I can't hold back the moans spilling from my lips.

Asher's pace quickens, spurred on by my obvious enjoyment. His lips find my neck once more, sucking and nipping at the sensitive skin there. I should be irritated if he leaves a mark there, but my mind is preoccupied. In fact, I tilt my head back, giving him better access to the area.

"You feel so good, sunshine," he groans against my throat. "I never want to stop."

"Then don't," I manage to get out. I give myself a mental high five. "Don't ever stop."

He captures my mouth in a searing kiss, swallowing the sounds that are desperate to fall from my lips. The longer we kiss, the more the tension within me grows once more. The feel of his skin against mine is too much but not enough at the same time. He breaks the kiss and pulls back, giving his hand the opportunity to slip between our bodies. My clit is his intended destination, and the added stimulation from his fingers has me on the verge of screaming in ecstasy.

"Come for me, Isla," he commands. "I want to feel you come all over my cock."

His words and the relentless onslaught of sensations send me flying over the edge again. My orgasm crashes over me in intense waves, and I can feel my inner walls clenching around him. Asher's rhythm falters as he chases his own moment of bliss, his hips snapping against mine erratically.

I watch as his eyes slam shut, and his mouth drops open. Soon, it's followed by a hoarse groan that sounds primal. Asher's body tenses above me, his muscles rippling under my fingertips as he finds his release. I can feel him pulsing inside me, his cock twitching with each wave of pleasure that crashes over him. He leans forward to bury his face in the crook of my neck, his breath coming in hot, ragged pants against my sweat-slicked skin.

For a moment, we stay like that, intertwined, our hearts racing in sync as we float down from the high we've both just reached. I run my fingers up and down his back, savoring the feel of his warm, damp skin beneath my touch.

Eventually, he lifts his head to gaze down at me, his green eyes much softer than they were just moments ago. A lazy smile tugs at the corners of his mouth. "That was..." He trails off, and I know he's at a loss for words.

"Amazing? Incredible? Mind-blowing?" I toss out with a smirk.

Asher chuckles, the sound low and rumbling in his chest. "All the above." He leans down to press a tender kiss to my lips. "You're amazing, Isla."

I feel a blush creeping onto my cheeks at his praise. "You're not so bad yourself, Bennett."

"Since when do you call me Bennett? This is the second or third time you've said it."

I shrug halfheartedly. "I guess the team is rubbing off on me."

Asher grins just before he drops this bomb. "Well, as long as I'm the only one rubbing off on you, I suppose I can live with that."

I can't fight the laugh that erupts from my lips. When I'm finished laughing, Asher gives me a quick peck on the nose before carefully pulling out and rolling off me. The sudden loss of his warmth and weight makes me want to pout, but I stop myself from doing so. I watch as he disposes of the condom and then settles back onto the bed, pulling me into his arms.

I rest my head on his chest, listening to the steady

thump of his heartbeat. His fingers comb through my hair, working out the tangles our activities caused. The tender gesture makes something in my chest tighten. It's been so long since I've experienced this with anyone, let alone him. I hadn't realized just how much I'd missed it until now.

"What are you thinking about?" Asher asks.

I hesitate, not sure if I'm ready to voice the tangled web of emotions swirling inside me. "Just... how right this moment feels," I say. "Being here with you like this. It's like no time has passed at all."

Asher is quiet for a moment, and I wonder if I've said too much. Of course, I did. I'm excellent at putting my foot in my mouth. But then he tightens his arm around me, pulling me even closer against his side. "I know what you mean," he says in a low voice, as if worried about how I might react to his words. "It's like we just picked up right where we left off, even though so much has changed."

I nod, tracing idle patterns on his chest with my fingertips. "Do you ever wonder what would have happened if you hadn't broken up with me?"

See? Foot. In. Mouth.

Asher's body tenses up beneath my touch because of my blunt question. Shit. I shouldn't have asked that. Everything was perfect, and I had to ruin it by bringing up the past. What is wrong with me?

"I'm sorry, I shouldn't have..." I backpedal, but Asher cuts me off.

"No, it's okay." He sighs, his chest rising and falling under my cheek. "I'd be lying if I said I haven't thought about it. Especially over these past few weeks after seeing you again."

I prop myself up on my elbow so I can see his face. I find him staring up at the ceiling as if it's the most exciting thing in the world.

"Asher, we don't have to talk about this now..."

"I think we do, though." He turns his head to meet my gaze. "I need you to know that breaking up with you was one of the hardest things I've ever had to do. And not a day has gone by when I haven't wondered if I made a mistake. Hell, I know I made a mistake."

I swallow hard when he stops speaking. I search his face, looking for any sign that he might not be being sincere. But nothing is shouting at me that he's lying right now.

"You mean that?" I ask softly. I'm almost afraid to believe him, afraid to let myself hope that maybe, just maybe, this could be our second chance and not just a quick fuck.

Granted, nothing about this has been quick, and I love that for me.

Asher reaches up to tuck a strand of hair behind my ear, his fingers lingering on my cheek. "I do. I was young and stupid, and I thought I was doing what was best for me at the time because Coach was your father. That was not the case."

His confession hangs in the air between us, neither one of us knowing what to say after that. A part of me wants to be angry with him for making that decision for both of us all those years ago. But another part, a bigger part, understands the pressure he must have felt, the fear of jeopardizing his hockey career and his relationship with my dad.

Not to mention the effect it could have had on his family.

"I get it," I say softly, leaning into his touch. "I totally get it."

But I'm not sure if Asher hears me. His eyes have a slight glaze, and his words do not directly correspond to what I said. "I was terrified of disappointing him and losing my spot on the team. But in the end, I lost something far more important—you."

Tears form in the corners of my eyes as the gravity of his words rests on my heart. There's no doubt in my mind that his focus is completely on me. His eyes bore into mine, and I feel a shiver. The intensity in his gaze reminds me of the stare down we shared just before we climaxed. I'm not sure what to say in response. However, Asher has no problem filling in the gap.

"And I refuse to make that same mistake again, sunshine."

29

ASHER

I'm at home on the ice because my head's exactly where it needs to be for the first time in a while.

I smirk as the cold air slaps my cheeks as I fly across the rink. This movement almost feels like a warm embrace, but it doesn't compare to how I feel when she wraps her arms around me.

Hell, her legs, either.

Speaking of, I can't ignore the prickling sensation at the back of my neck. It's because I'm aware that I'm being watched. I can feel the weight of eyes following my every move. I know without looking that it's her.

My sunshine.

Her presence is like a magnetic pull, drawing me in even as I try to focus on the task. I catch a glimpse of her out of the corner of my eye, her camera raised to capture the action in the rink. But I swear, for just a moment, her lens lingers on me a beat too long.

The thought of her watching me makes me giddy, but I will never admit it to the guys. It's a secret rush that I have to keep hidden because I know shit would hit the fan. I can't let it show on my face or in my body language, even as I'm dying to meet her gaze head-on.

I channel that energy into my movements, pushing myself harder and faster. Part of me wants to dare someone to say that my head isn't in the game, more so this practice, based on my performance. I am slightly distracted by Isla. However, knowing that I have back part of what we used to have is enough to make me keep my head down and get to work on the ice.

I'm aware of where she's standing with her camera in hand. I already have an image in my mind of the way her blonde hair cascades down her back and her eyes sparkle as she does her job.

With a slight shake of my head, I tear my focus away from Isla, determined to prove that I can keep my head in the game despite everything else that is going on. I skate harder because I'm determined to prove myself after a shitty couple of weeks. The wandering that's occurring in my mind needs to stop, especially with Coach's watchful gaze tracking what feels like my every move.

I've decided to talk to him once I know that Isla and I are on solid ground regarding rekindling our relationship, and I'll take whatever he throws at me.

Because I'm not going to lose her a second time. At least, not if I can help it.

But now isn't the time to think about that.

As I push myself through the drills, I swear every muscle in my body burns. Sweat drips down my face, stinging my eyes, but I barely notice. The thought of fucking all of this up has me on edge, even though I know there is nothing I can do about any of this now besides focusing on killing it at this practice and at our next game. I'm determined to show Coach that I'm back in control and that the last couple of weeks were just a fluke.

The puck flies across the ice, and my eyes are on it. Every movement I make is sharper, and my stick handling is clean. I catch Levi's eye as I pass the puck, and for the first time in a while, he gives me a nod of approval.

A quick glance toward the bench confirms Coach is still watching me, his arms crossed, and eyes narrowed. But I'm not slipping up this time. I'm laser-focused and do not give him any reason to question me today.

We move into one-on-one drills, and I'm up against Knox. He's quick as always, but today, I'm faster. I break toward the goal and fire it at the net with everything I've got. It sails past Wilder's outstretched glove and slams into the back of the net with a satisfying crack.

"Nice shot, Bennett!" Levi yells from the side, and even Knox gives me a small grin.

After several deep breaths to calm my heart, I realize I'm happy. Sure, there are things in my life that could be better, but at this moment, I'm content. And while it took my time on the ice to realize that, my gaze drifts back to the stands, finding Isla. She lowers her favorite piece of equipment, and our eyes lock.

But I shake it off before I'm caught staring for too long.

Thankfully, the rest of practice flies by in a blur, with no complaints from anyone about me. It takes everything in me to not look at Isla as I leave the ice and head into the locker room. I can hear the usual post-practice chatter and laughter, but my mind is elsewhere. As I pull off my sweat-soaked practice jersey, I can't stop thinking about Isla because now she has my full, undivided attention.

I'm jolted back to reality by a slap on my shoulder. It's Wilder, whose grin is taking up his entire face. "You were on fire out there today, man. Whatever's gotten into you, keep it up."

It's more what I've gotten into, but I digress. "Thanks, bro. Just trying to stay focused and help the team in any way I can."

The truth is, I've never felt this focused or more alive than I do right now, and I know it has everything to do with Isla being back in my life. It's like her presence ignites something within me, a fire that burns hotter and brighter every time she is near.

After showering and throwing on some fresh clothes, I grab my gear and head out. Most of the guys have left, meaning the tunnel is nearly empty, but I know she's nearby. I hope it doesn't make me sound like a creep, but it's almost as if I can sense that she's near. As if summoned by my thoughts, Isla appears from around the corner, her camera bag slung over her shoulder. The sight of her takes my breath away, and I can't help but smile. She returns my grin, her blue eyes sparkling as she approaches me.

"Hey there, hotshot," she teases. "Quite the performance out there today."

I chuckle, running a hand through my damp hair. "Well, I had some extra motivation today."

She arches an eyebrow, a playful smirk tugging at her lips. "Oh really? And what might that be?"

I glance around the empty hallway before taking a step toward her. "You know exactly what, or should I say who, that is." I punctuate my sentence with another step toward her.

"You're playing a dangerous game, Ash," she murmurs, her gaze flickering to my lips. "This is a high-traffic area, and anyone could see us."

"I know, but I can't seem to give a damn."

"We can't," Isla whispers. "Not here."

"Then let's head out of here so we can be alone. I don't care where; I just... I need to be with you."

Isla hesitates, her eyes darting down the hallway before they land back on me. "Okay. Meet me at my dorm room after we leave here. Tessa is hardly ever there lately, so we should be alone."

"What's going on here?"

The two of us jump apart like kids caught trying to sneak snacks out of a cookie jar. We both turn to face Coach, who's standing a few feet away. The suspicion in his eyes is hard to miss. "Nothing, Coach. Just chatting about some shots Isla got during practice."

Coach's gaze shifts between us before landing on his daughter. "Well, wrap it up. Isla, didn't you mention earlier that Bailey needs those photos edited and sent to her by tonight?"

"Yes, Dad," Isla replies. "And I'll get right on it."

With a final pointed look at me, Coach turns and walks away, leaving us alone once more. I let out a low whistle as the tension leaves my shoulders. That was too close for comfort.

Isla shoots me a glare. "See what I mean? We have to be more careful."

I nod because I know she's right. "Let me walk you to your car. After all, since Coach has already seen us talking, that shouldn't look too strange."

Not to mention that this was an evening practice, and there's no way I'm letting her walk out to her car by herself when it's dark outside.

Isla agrees with me. "Okay, let's go."

As we walk out of the arena, I notice the air has become significantly cooler than when I arrived. The parking lot is nearly empty, with only a few cars scattered under the dim streetlights. I keep a respectable distance from her, but my body is dying to close the gap by pulling her into my arms.

We reach her car, and she turns to face me. I fight the urge to tuck a strand of her hair behind her ear. "Thanks for walking me out. I'll see you in a few minutes?"

"I'll be there soon."

It takes me a few minutes to walk to my car and get settled before I head over to Isla's. The drive feels longer than it should, but I'm sure it's because I want to be with her right now.

After parking, I don't bother texting Isla to let her know I'm here. I just grab my phone, lock my car, and sprint up the stairs to the entrance because someone is holding the doors open, so I don't have to worry about calling Isla to let me in. As I'm about to knock on her door, I can hear muffled voices on the other side.

I hesitate for a split second, unsure if I should knock or wait. But before I can make up my mind, the door swings open, and I find myself face-to-face with a tall brunette. Her eyes widen as she takes me in, and a slow, appreciative smile spreads across her face.

"Well, hello there," she says, leaning against the door-frame. "Is Asher Bennett really standing outside my door?"

It clicks who she must be. I clear my throat, feeling slightly uncomfortable because of the look she's giving me. "Uh, yeah. Is Isla here?"

The girl's smile widens, and she steps aside, gesturing

for me to enter. "She sure is. I'm Tessa, by the way. Isla's roommate."

When I step into the room, my eyes land on Isla. She's standing near her desk, a tight smile on her face as she watches my interaction with Tessa. It's obvious that she's annoyed by all of this, and I get it—especially because she doesn't get along with Tessa and was expecting her to be gone.

"Thanks," I say to Tessa, trying to keep my tone polite but not overly friendly. "I just need to talk to Isla for a moment."

I watch as Tessa studies my face before her eyes drift down my body. "Of course," she purrs. "You're welcome here anytime, Asher."

I fight the urge to scoff at her comment. Isla clears her throat, and Tessa rolls her eyes before grabbing her purse from the nearby chair.

"Well, I was just heading out anyway," she says. "You two have fun." She brushes past me, and given that there is enough room for her to walk by without touching me, I know it's on purpose.

The door closes behind her with a click, leaving Isla and me alone. She lets out a heavy sigh, her shoulders sagging. "I'm so sorry. She's usually not around and—"

I cross the room to get to her, and my hands find her waist. I pull her closer to me. "Hey, it's okay. We're alone now."

Isla leans into my touch, her forehead resting against

my chest. I can feel the stress leave her body as I hold her. "That we are, and now I have to worry about her telling people about... whatever this is."

I tilt her chin up, making her meet my gaze. "You mean our relationship, sunshine?"

She raises an eyebrow at me. "Is that what this is? You're trying to lock me down already?"

I can't fight the chuckle that slips out. "Locking it down would be asking you to marry me, wouldn't it?"

I can feel Isla's body stiffen in my arms at the mention of marriage. "Wait, what—"

"I'm not there either... at least not yet." I give her a reassuring squeeze. "But I think what's going on between us is a relationship—unless you think differently?"

Isla bites her lip before she speaks. "No, I... I want this to be a relationship too."

"Good. Glad we agree on that."

"But this is complicated."

I stare at her for a moment, searching her eyes for where this might be leading. If it's where I think it's going, it's something we should talk about, even though I hoped that the time we're spending together could just be about us and not external factors. "Are you referring to your dad and the team?"

Isla nods. "Yes, because if what is going on between us gets out, it could cause problems for both of us."

I sigh, running a hand through my hair. "I know. Believe me, I've been thinking about it nonstop. But

Isla," I cup her face gently, "I don't want to lose you again. Not because of hockey, not because of your dad, not because of anything."

Isla leans into my touch. "I don't want to lose you either, but we have to be smart about this. We can't let anyone catch on, at least not until we figure out how to handle it. I would rather my father find out from us versus hearing about it through the grapevine."

"Well, would Tessa gossip about me coming here to see you?"

I watch as the realization hits Isla's face. "Oh fuck yes. And she would have no issue telling the world what she knows. You can't come back here until we figure out how to tell my dad. I'll tell my mom to get her feedback on how to approach Dad with the news."

"Then if we're only going to hang at my place, I need to tell the guys," I toss out there.

"Are you sure that's a good idea?"

I sigh, my thumb absently brushing along her cheekbone. "I think so. The guys are like my brothers. They'll have my back and can help cover for us if needed. Plus, if I'm being honest, they probably already suspect that something is happening, anyway."

Isla considers this for a moment. "I guess you're right. But can we trust them not to say anything?"

"Absolutely," I assure her. "They know how to keep a secret, and they'd never do anything to jeopardize the team or my relationship with you. And that includes Knox."

That forces a laugh out of her just before her hands slide up my chest to loop around my neck. "Okay. If you think it's best, then I trust you."

I'm not sure she understands how much hearing her say that is like a weight off my shoulders and a breath of fresh air. "Thank you," I murmur, kissing her forehead softly. "We'll figure this out together."

"Yes, we will. Together," she repeats.

30

ISLA

"You know, this wasn't such a bad idea," says Jade.

"I told you it wasn't." I glance over my shoulder at her and chuckle.

Since today is Friday and none of us have early morning classes, I managed to get Selene, Hailey, and Jade to come on a hike with me. It's something I've wanted to do since I got back, but adjusting to life in Crestwood and my health issues made that take a lot longer. Not that it matters though because at least I'm out on the trail now. Not to mention having this break with new and old friends will hopefully help settle my nerves about the upcoming trip I need to take with the hockey team.

I swear, I'm not mentally prepared for that at all, especially after the talk I had with Mom. I didn't tell her who, just that I was dating one of the players and asked how she thought Dad might react to that. She said I need to make sure we are serious before I do anything, because Dad could be harsh depending on who the player is, and we need to be careful and make sure we are prepared for whatever happens. So with that on my mind, I hoped this hike would calm my nerves. We'll see how it goes. I turn my attention back to capturing some shots with my camera.

"Earth to Isla," Selene's voice cuts through my concentration.

I look over at her, Jade, and Hailey and notice she's practically bouncing up the path ahead of me.

"Less photo taking, more walking!"

I lower my camera. "Some of us actually like to take in the view and keep a record of it."

"Yeah, well, some of us would like to keep moving along," Hailey chimes in from behind me.

I roll my eyes playfully and pick up my pace, catching up to the rest of my group. I take a moment to look at each of the women standing in front of me and wonder at how lucky I am to have them in my life. Selene has always been there practically as long as I can remember at this point, but to have Hailey and Jade welcome us in with open arms has been an amazing experience.

And now they are hiking with us and I'm getting emotional about it.

Maybe it's the fresh air getting to me.

I watch Selene bend down and start digging through

her backpack. When her face lights up, I know we're in trouble. Knowing her, it could be anything from confetti cannons to a portable karaoke machine. Asher would be thrilled with the latter.

"I know you didn't actually pack party supplies for a morning hike," I say because of the expression on Selene's face. I wouldn't put it past her.

"Bold of you to assume I didn't pack something like glow sticks," Selene shoots back, grinning. She's already pulled her phone out, probably queuing up a playlist called, "I conquered this hike, bitch."

"I swear to god, if you start blasting Sabrina Carpenter up here—" I say, but I'm quickly cut off.

"You'll what? Finally admit you secretly know all the words to 'Espresso'?" Selene challenges.

"But that's not a secret. I do know all the words," I throw back.

"Of course you do," Jade laughs. "From what I now know about her, I don't think anyone who's spent more than ten minutes with Selene can escape without learning at least one pop song by heart."

"I agree, and you can add Levi to the list too," Hailey adds.

A rustling in the brush ahead catches our attention, and it's immediately followed by rapid footsteps on the trail. A girl with her dark hair in a ponytail comes jogging around the bend, nearly colliding with our group. She's

wearing hiking boots and carrying some kind of
sketch pad.

"Oh! Sorry!" She comes to a stop, breathing rather
hard. "I was trying to catch up to—" She pauses, looking at
each of us. "Wait, you're in my Creative Writing seminar,
aren't you?" She points at me. "Isla, right?"

"Yeah," I nod, recognizing her now. "Willow, from
Professor Martinez's class?"

"That's me," she says, tucking a loose strand of hair
behind her ear. "I thought I was the only one crazy
enough to be up here sketching landscapes at this hour."

Selene's eyes light up once more, probably because
she has another potential person to corrupt with her
music choices. I'm not complaining about the corruption
either way. "Well, you're definitely not alone. Though
some of us—" she shoots me a pointed look, "—prefer to
capture the view through a camera lens."

"And some of us prefer to actually complete the hike,"
Hailey interjects, but she's smiling as she says it.

Willow looks at each of us before her eyes land on me
again. "Would you mind if I joined? I've been trying to
work up the courage to ask about your photography in
class. I use sketches as references for my writing, but I've
always wanted to learn about taking better photos."

"Of course you can join," I say, already reaching for my
camera to show her some of the shots I've taken. "Just be
warned though. If you're hiking with us, you might end up
starring in an impromptu music video."

"Please don't give Selene any ideas," Hailey adds with a laugh that's not meant to be funny.

"Hey!" Selene jumps in. "Don't judge me. The video might go viral or something."

"Getting back to the topic at hand, what brought you out here so early?" Jade asks Willow as we continue up the trail. Our pace is more leisurely now as I show Willow some basic camera techniques.

"I've been working on this story that takes place in the mountains, but something about the setting felt... off. My professor—well, our professor," she glances at me, "suggested I might benefit from experiencing it in the real world."

I adjust my camera strap as I try to think of how to properly word my answer. "I can see that. It's the same thing with photography. Getting out into the real world and taking photos of different subjects is one of the biggest ways to gain experience. It just clicks."

Selene suddenly gasps. "Oh my god, speaking of clicking—" She whips out her phone. "Group photo time!"

"Is this a regular thing?" Willow whispers to me as Selene herds us all together against a particularly scenic backdrop.

"Eh, it comes in waves. She's very hyper right now," I whisper back. "It could go either one of two ways; we'll take your basic photo, or she'll start coordinating our poses."

As if on cue, Selene starts telling us where to stand

and how to pose like a film director instead of someone who decided to take a selfie with her phone. "Okay, Isla, you stand here. Willow, next to her. Jade, can you crouch down a bit? Perfect! Now, Hailey, actually give me a smile!"

I can't help but laugh at the absurdity of it all. This is supposed to be just a regular hike and what it is turning into is something I both could and couldn't have seen coming.

Thanks, Selene.

Once we are done taking photos, we begin to head down the trail again until Willow stops walking abruptly. "Wait. Is that a red-tailed hawk?"

We all look up. I watch as a medium-sized bird flies around up above. There's no way I'm going to be able to positively identify what type of bird it is.

"It's a cooper's hawk, actually," Jade says.

Our attention shifts from the bird in the sky to the woman who just blew our minds. All she does is shrug.

"What? I took a zoology course last semester. There was a focus on ornithology during one of the sections."

I raise my camera, adjusting the zoom. Bird photography isn't a specialty of mine, but if I can snap a photo, I know it has the potential to be amazing.

The hawk circles overhead and I hold my breath with my finger poised over the shutter button. The world narrows to this moment as I tune everything else out.

Click. Click. Click.

The rapid-fire shots capture the hawk's graceful descent.

"Got it?" Willow asks, peering over my shoulder.

I lower the camera and check the display. The sequence shows the hawk diving through patches of sunlight, wings pulled tight against its body. It's not perfect because the last shot's a bit blurry. But I'm proud of the shots I got.

"Here, look at this one," I say, zooming in on the second shot. The hawk's silhouette is crisp against the morning sky. Its wings catch the light just right, making it look even more majestic.

"That's incredible," Willow says, already reaching for her journal. "The way the light hits the wings—"

"If you two are done with your artistic bonding," Selene cuts in, "some of us are starving."

My stomach growls in response, informing our group that Selene isn't wrong.

"Told you we should've eaten before we started climbing," Selene says, already shrugging off her backpack. I shake my head as she unzips her bookbag and digs through what she's dubbed her 'adventure preparedness kit.'

"You're the smart one here," Hailey admits, sitting down on a nearby rock. "I completely forgot breakfast."

"Which is exactly why I came prepared." Selene pulls out an impressive array of trail mix, protein bars, and fruit. "Hiking takes energy, and I've got us covered."

"Is she always this organized?" Willow asks, gratefully accepting an apple.

"You should have seen her during our last month of high school," I say. "Color-coded study guides, backup USB drives, emergency coffee supplies. She's basically the reason why I survived and made it to NYU alive."

I shove away the small pang of longing that I have for the life I had to leave behind. After putting my camera away, I grab some trail mix and lean against a tree trunk. After a few minutes of peaceful snacking, Selene starts fidgeting with her phone.

Uh oh.

"Okay, but seriously," Selene says, already queuing up another song on her phone. "Who's ready for the descent playlist?"

"No one," we all say in unison, but we're laughing, because of course she would say that. I swear we all continue laughing the entire way back down to where I parked my car.

And at least for this short period of time, I've forgotten how nervous I am for my first overnight away game with the Crestwood Red Wolves.

31

ISLA

With a small groan, I shift my body to get comfortable in this hard-ass seat. But nothing can calm the jittery nerves bouncing around in my stomach. This is my first time traveling with the team for an away game, and it's exciting but also nerve-wracking. I glance out the bus window as the sun sets in the sky. The longest I've ever spent with the team is a few hours. But now I'm trapped in close quarters with them for an entire weekend.

Not even the true-crime podcast I'm listening to right now can take my mind off this.

My eyes land on Asher, who is only sitting a few rows ahead. He's chatting with Levi, unaware I'm staring at him. Not wanting to draw attention to myself, I force myself to look away before anyone notices.

I dig into my camera bag and come up with the only

thing that can make me feel better: a bag of Skittles that Asher snuck into my bag at some point, and I only discovered about an hour ago.

I stare at the bright colors of the Skittles as I pour a few out, though they're somewhat dimmed because of the lack of light on the bus. This is all just another subtle reminder of Asher's thoughtfulness. I toss the candy in my mouth and let it melt on my tongue. The sweet flavors serve as a momentary distraction from my nerves as I listen to how a serial killer avoided being caught for the last twenty years.

When I look up again, I catch Asher's gaze as he's now turned in his seat, talking to Blaise. A smile appears on his face, and I know who it is for because his eyes haven't left me. I pull the bright red candy wrapper out of my camera bag and mouth 'thank you' to him. He winks at me before returning his attention to what Blaise is saying.

I tuck the wrapper back into my bag and turn away. There is another moment we've shared that is ours alone. Just how we need it to be, at least for now.

A few minutes later, laughter loud enough that I can hear it over the podcast I'm listening to pulls me from my thoughts, and I look toward the front of the bus. Levi is leaning over the back of his seat, showing Knox something on his phone. Wilder tosses a crumpled piece of paper toward the aisle, and his grin widens when it lands near Blaise's feet. I stop myself from checking to see what

Asher's doing, but the guys are relaxed. That's great, as they are preparing for a big game tomorrow.

A few rows ahead of Asher, my gaze lands on Dad, who is busy talking to Darryl. It wouldn't surprise me if they are going over game plans for tomorrow. I shrink a little lower in my seat, hoping he doesn't notice the quick glances I keep stealing at Asher.

The team continues talking and every so often, I catch a phrase or two—something about tomorrow's game or an inside joke or two—but it's not enough for me to be engaged in what they are talking about.

I delve back into focusing on the words flowing through my headphones, and soon, I watch as the bus carrying all of us pulls into the hotel parking lot. With that, a fresh wave of nerves washes over me. I gather my things and wait for the team to exit before I stand up. Dad is at the front, giving instructions about room assignments and curfew. I try to focus on his words, but my heart is pounding loudly in my ears.

We file off the bus and into the lobby, where a frazzled-looking receptionist is waiting with keycards. Dad steps forward to handle the check-in process, and I hover nearby, unsure of what to do with myself. Asher is standing a few feet away, engrossed in conversation with Levi, but I feel his gaze flicker to me every so often. The guys are handed their keycards one by one, but when Asher receives his, he glances over his shoulder at me before walking toward the elevator.

I check my phone as I wait for it to be my turn to get my room key.

"Isla," Dad calls out, waving me over. I snap to attention and hurry to his side. "There's been a mix-up with the rooms. You'll have to stay with me."

My stomach drops. Sharing a room with Dad? For the entire weekend? I force a smile and nod, trying to hide my disappointment. "Sure, no problem," I say. But I was looking forward to having a room to myself.

Not to mention, it feels as if this is shoving our father-daughter relationship down people's faces even more. I still have a chip on my shoulder about showing that I got this job because of my talent and hard work, not because I'm Coach Johnson's daughter.

With a sigh, I take the keycard from Dad's hand as I'm trying to think of anything positive related to this situation. I follow Dad to the elevator with my things. My irritation is at an all-time high as the doors slide shut.

At least I have a place to sleep.

"I know it's not ideal," Dad says. "But we'll make do."

"Yeah, it's not a problem. I'm flexible."

It's a lie, and Dad glances over at me out of the side of his eye to confirm he doesn't believe my shit either. Thankfully, neither of us says another word because the elevator dings, and the doors open, announcing we have made it to our destination. We step out onto our floor and make our way down the hallway. Dad swipes the keycard and pushes open the door, revealing a standard hotel room with two queen beds.

I set my bag down on the bed furthest from the door. I throw myself on the bed while Dad moves around, unpacking his things and hanging up his suit for tomorrow's game. The room feels cramped only because I don't want to be here.

I pull out my phone, desperate for a distraction, and see a text from Asher. My heart skips a beat as I open it.

> Asher: Room to myself tonight. 704. Wait
> till Coach falls asleep and come up.

I stare at the message, confused about what I'm seeing. What the hell is that all about? How did Asher get a room to himself?

I glance over at Dad, who is still moving around the room, oblivious to the fact that I'm potentially going to have a panic attack. I type out a quick reply to Asher.

> Me: How? What about your roommate?

> Asher: Carson stayed back because he
> is sick. Trey is taking his place and
> already has his own room booked.

The butterflies in my stomach flutter hard as I read his words. How did I miss this? A room to ourselves, even just for tonight, could have been magical. Sure, Asher should be focused on tomorrow's game, but I can't stop the possibilities swirling through my mind.

But then reality crashes back in. Dad is right there. How am I supposed to sneak out without him noticing?

I need to come up with a plan. I know Dad falls asleep early the night before a big game. If I can just wait him out...

"I'm going to grab a shower," Dad announces, interrupting my scheming. "You need the bathroom before I go in?"

I shake my head, and he disappears into the bathroom. As soon as I hear the water running, my brain goes into overdrive once more. Dad sleeps pretty hard and has been known to use the pair of sleep headphones I gifted him for Father's Day a couple of years ago. Hopefully, he brought them with him, and that will make this so much easier.

But if I go, I don't want to be a distraction to Asher.

> Me: But you need to rest ahead of your game.

Asher's reply comes through almost instantly.

> Asher: I'll rest better with you here, promise. I want to see you. No, it's a need.

I tap my phone on my forehead twice as I think about my options. The temptation is overwhelming, even as every part of my brain whispers that this is a bad idea. But this is an excellent opportunity for us to be together alone. As long as I don't get caught.

As. Long. As. I. Don't. Get. Caught.

> Me: Okay. I'll be there as soon as I can.

I hit send before I can second-guess myself. Selene is the one who is all in on sneaking out, not me. But this is an opportunity I can't sit back and not take. In order to pretend like I'm doing something, I grab my laptop from my bag and pull up Photoshop to edit some shots I'd taken a couple of days ago.

The sound of the water from the shower turning off makes the nerves in my gut spring up once more. It takes another few minutes before the bathroom door opens, and Dad emerges with some steam trailing behind him. Thankfully, he's already dressed in his pajamas.

"The bathroom is all yours," he says as he sits at the only desk in the room. He grabs his phone from where he was charging it and speaks again. "I'm going to give your mother a call before turning in. You should get some rest too. It's a big day tomorrow."

I nod, trying to look tired, but I'm anything but. "Yeah, I will soon. I'll shower once you get off the phone with Mom. I want to say hey."

Dad pulls up his glasses to get a better look at his device before he taps the phone screen to call my mother. After a couple of rings, she picks up, and I can see her face from where I am on my bed. "Hey honey," Dad greets her warmly. "How are things back home?"

"Oh, you know, just holding down the fort," Mom replies with a smile. "How's the trip going so far?"

"Good, good. We just got settled at the hotel." Dad angles the phone so Mom can see me. "Look who's here too."

"Hi, Mom." I wave.

"Isla! Excited for your first away game?" Mom asks.

I nod. "Definitely. It's been great so far." If only she knew just how great I'm hoping it will be, with Asher waiting for me just a few floors away. "There was a minor hiccup with the hotel room situation, but Dad and I are making it work."

Mom pauses before tilting her head slightly to the side. "Oh? What happened with the rooms?"

"Just a mix-up," I say quickly, not wanting to get into details. "I didn't have a room, so Dad and I are rooming together. It's fine."

"Well, as long as you're both comfortable," Mom says.

Dad waves a dismissive hand. "It's no big deal. It's just for a couple of nights, and we have our own beds. We'll be so busy with the game and everything, we'll hardly be in the room. And it's not like Isla hasn't snuck in the bed to sleep with us a time or two in the past."

"Dad, I was a kid!" I can't help but roll my eyes because seriously?

Mom just laughs and shakes her head while Dad

shrugs. Thankfully, the conversation shifts in a different direction, giving my face an opportunity to calm down. As they continue chatting, I find it increasingly difficult to focus on their conversation. My mind keeps drifting to thoughts of Asher, alone in his room, waiting for me. I try to look as if I'm paying attention, nodding, and smiling at the appropriate moments, but I'm barely processing their words.

After what feels like an eternity, Dad finally says, "Alright, well, we should probably get some rest. Big day tomorrow," he says, echoing his earlier sentiment.

"Definitely," I agree, perhaps a bit too eagerly. "I'm just going to hop in the shower real quick, and then it's lights out for me."

Mom smiles warmly through the screen. "Sounds good. Get some good rest, both of you. And, Isla, I'm so proud of you. You're going to do great tomorrow."

"Thanks, Mom," I say, genuinely touched by her words, despite my world being tilted on its axis. "Love you."

"Love you too, sweetie. And I love you, Aaron," she adds, blowing a kiss to Dad.

"Love you more," Dad replies with a grin before ending the call. He stretches and yawns before he turns to me. "Alright, I'm turning in. Don't stay up too late, okay?"

"I won't," I assure him, gathering my bag of toiletries and pajamas. "Just a quick shower."

I disappear into the bathroom, my heart pounding as I

turn on the water. The sound of the spray usually helps put me in a relaxed state, but that's not the case tonight. My mind is still on how the hell I am going to get out of this room without waking my dad up.

I go through the motions of my shower with my body on autopilot because my mind is elsewhere. The warm water cascades over my skin but does little to soothe my nerves. I can't stop thinking about Asher, about the opportunity that awaits me just a few floors up. But the fear of getting caught by Dad looms large, threatening to overshadow my desire.

I step out of the shower and dry off. You would think I would be running through my routine, but I'm hoping that the likelihood of Dad being asleep increases because I'm taking my time. I slip into my pajamas, which consist of a cami and shorts. I make a mental note to myself as I brush my teeth to grab the hoodie that I wore here because there's no way I'm walking through the hotel wearing just this. As I brush my teeth, I watch the steam evaporate from the mirror I'm staring into. I take deep breaths and repeat, 'I can do this,' until it's drilled into my head. Where the hell is Selene when I need her?

Selene.

That's it. Why didn't I text her before?

I grab my phone from the bathroom counter and text her.

> Me: HELP. Need your expert sneaking-out advice.

I stare at the screen, waiting for those three dots to appear. Selene may be wild and unpredictable at times, but she's always there when I need her. Her reply pops up after an eternity, but in reality, it's probably only a minute.

> Selene: Ooh, sneaking out for a secret rendezvous with a certain someone? Do tell!

I roll my eyes, but it doesn't stop the smile from appearing on my lips.

> Me: Asher has his own room tonight. He wants me to come up, but I'm stuck sharing with Dad. Do you have any ideas?

> Selene: Girl, this is too good. Okay, here's the plan...

She proceeds to outline a step-by-step guide to sneaking out undetected. Wait until Dad is snoring (she suggests taking a video for proof and future teasing purposes), arrange the pillows under the covers to look like my sleeping form, keep the lights off, and tiptoe out of here. This is basic stuff but hearing it from her raises my confidence.

> Me: You're a lifesaver. Wish me luck!

Selene: Oh honey, you won't need luck
for what I'm sure you and Asher have
planned, but go get your man! And I
want ALL the details later!

I cover my mouth to try to stop laughing, but it doesn't
help. However, the laughter does help release the tension
I've been holding in my body. This is just one reason why
Selene is the best. I take one more deep breath before
quietly opening the bathroom door.

The room is dark, only the glow from the parking lot
lights peeking through the curtains. I can hear the slow,
even breathing that indicates Dad is already asleep. I
tiptoe over to his bed just to confirm. Yep, dead to the
world, with his sleeping headphones on.

This might just work.

I tiptoe over to my bed and arrange the pillows like
Selene instructed. It looks convincing enough in the low
light. I grab the spare keycard off the end table, throw my
hoodie on quickly, and, after one more glance at Dad, I
ease open the door and slip out.

My heart is pounding so loudly that I swear it echoes
in the empty hallway. But I make it out, and that is the
hardest part. Now, the only thing standing between me
and Asher is if someone sees me roaming the halls.

I pull my hood up, as if that will be enough to disguise
myself, and make my way to the elevators. I can't help but
thank the universe that I haven't seen a soul so far because
I don't want to stand there and have to explain what I am

up to. The doors slide open with a soft ding, and I step inside, stabbing the button for the seventh floor as if my life depended on it.

The doors close, and the elevator begins to move. I lean against the back wall, trying to calm myself down. *Everything is going to be okay, so chill out.*

The elevator dings again, and the doors open on the seventh floor. I step out into the hallway, which is empty as well. Room 704... I scan the numbers on the doors as I walk. 702...703... there. 704.

I pause outside the door as uncertainty begins to creep up again. Is this really a good idea? It's too late since I'm already here. I raise my hand and knock softly.

The door opens immediately, and I'm left staring at the sight before me.

32

ASHER

She came.

Well, she hasn't in the way I want her to yet, but there's no doubt that she's standing outside my door right now. And I've made it my mission that she will come tonight.

Multiple times.

I toss the condom I've been holding in my hand on the bed as I make my way to the door. That will be very useful in a few minutes.

As I reach for the doorknob, I slide a hand through my hair and take a deep breath. Her arrival at my door has been all I could think about since I was told I'd have a room to myself.

I twist the handle and pull, and as the door swings open, it reveals Isla in all her breathtaking beauty. I swear it doesn't matter what she wears—the hoodie and shorts she's in before me or dressed to the nines—she's always stunning. Her blonde hair tumbles around her shoulders in soft waves, and her blue eyes sparkle with a hint of apprehension, probably related to this scenario.

I rush to pull her into my room, removing the risk of anyone seeing her. The moment the door clicks shut behind her and her hand lands on my chest because of my actions, I get a whiff of something that smells floral, and I can't help but wonder what she used and where. It's intoxicating.

"Hi," Isla says, her voice barely above a whisper.

"Hey yourself," I murmur back, reaching out to tuck a stray golden lock behind her ear. My fingertips linger for a moment to trace the shell of her ear, and she shivers at my touch. I fight the urge to pull her flush against me, which would then lead to me claiming her lips with my own.

But I hold back.

"Asher, you know we shouldn't be doing this. You have a big game tomorrow."

"I know, but this will help me relax ahead of the game."

She tilts her head to the side slightly. "What will?"

"Having you here. Giving you as many orgasms as possible before I get off."

Isla looks taken aback by my comment. Her eyes grow wide, and even in the dim light of my hotel room, the desire in her eyes is evident despite the shock still present on her face. I can almost hear the gears turning in her head as she weighs the pros and cons of giving in to what is happening between us. And I know which side is going to win.

I grab hold of her hand on my chest to keep it there just before I lean closer. My lips graze her ear as I whisper, "Let me take care of you tonight, sunshine."

I know my words hit their mark when her hand clenches my shirt, grasping the thin material like her life depends on it. "I can't believe I snuck into your room."

It's a deflection technique, but I let her have it. "I'm proud of you for taking a walk on the wild side."

She scoffs at my comment. "Selene had to give me a little pep talk before I finally did it."

I can't help but chuckle at the mental image of Selene giving Isla a motivational speech to convince her to come to my room. "Remind me to thank her later."

My hands find their way to Isla's hips, pulling her closer until our bodies are flush against each other.

"Is this okay?" I whisper, giving her one last chance to back out.

Isla's response comes as a kiss, surprising me, but I catch up. I deepen the kiss as my hands slide under her hoodie. I need to feel her bare skin under my fingertips now.

Once I do, Isla pushes me backward, causing us to stumble until the backs of my knees hit the edge of the bed. I sit down, pulling Isla onto my lap without breaking the kiss. Her fingers tangle in my hair, tugging as she grinds against me.

Fuck yes.

I break away from her to pull her hoodie off and am pleased to find her in fewer clothes than I thought. The shirt she has on barely leaves anything to the imagination, including the fact that her nipples are hard right now. The sight is too appetizing to me, so I act on my impulsive thought and start sucking and licking one of her nipples through her shirt.

"Oh my gosh," she gasps. Her voice causes me to glance up, and I watch as she throws her head back. Her blonde hair flies everywhere, and I couldn't be more proud of what I've done.

And to think that this is only the beginning.

My hands roam Isla's body, caressing every inch I can touch as if I'm trying to memorize her through touch alone. Her skin is heating up beneath my skin to where I'm wondering if her clothes are going to disintegrate. Not that I would mind that, because it would make my job even easier. Her fingers tighten in my hair, urging me on as I continue to focus most of my attention on her breasts. The sounds that are flying from her lips shift from gasps to soft moans, and I love every moment.

I'm convinced it's the sweetest sound I've ever heard.

I pull back just enough to meet her gaze because I've missed staring into her eyes. "How do you want this to go tonight?"

A puzzled look appears on her face. "What do you mean?"

"Do you want it hard and fast or nice and slow?"

A light blush grows on her face as she considers my question. To be honest, I'm not sure if she's even aware she's now biting her lower lip. "I want it hard and fast," she whispers. "I want you to fuck me, Asher."

The only thing I can do is groan in response. My hands slide down to her hips, gripping them tightly as I grind against her. The friction feels good, especially given the thin material that stands between us, but it's not enough. I need to feel her bare skin against mine and taste every part of her.

I flip us over so that Isla is beneath me, and I stare at her in amazement. She is really here with me. I mentally pinch myself because I'm questioning whether this is real or a fantasy.

But this is the real thing, and she looks so damn good underneath me.

"You don't know how long I've been waiting to get you back in this position."

Isla's bright blue eyes narrow at me. "We just had sex a few days ago."

I shrug. "Doesn't matter. I wanted you again as soon as you left my place. We're not even going to talk about how many times I jacked off to what we did while we were apart, either."

"Part of me is shocked, but the other part thinks it all makes sense."

"It's all a part of the dichotomy that makes me...me."

Isla bursts out laughing. "Have you been wanting to use that word all day?"

My lips twitch to hold back the smile that is threatening to take over my face. "Maybe."

We can discuss this all night, but I have more important matters to attend to. I dip my head down and start by trailing featherlight kisses along her jawline and down the column of her neck. The scent of her skin, a heady mix of floral notes and something uniquely her, fills my senses.

Isla's pulse grows more erratic beneath my lips as I press open-mouthed kisses against her throat. I can feel her body melt into the mattress as my hands glide along her sides. I'm trying to take my time with her, but when my fingers slip beneath the hem of her shirt, I have to check myself.

When she lifts her arms up, I take it as an opportunity to slip Isla's shirt off, revealing her perfect breasts. "You're so beautiful. I could worship your body all night long."

"Then do it," she whispers. "I want you to fuck me like you don't respect me, even though you know that I'm all yours."

Her words are the only confirmation I need. Without saying another word, I lean down and capture Isla's lips with my own, further fueling the desire running through my veins. It is as if I haven't kissed her in years instead of just a few short days ago. My mind wants to drift down memory lane to figure out just how I survived without her kiss for so long. My cock has a mind of its own and wants nothing short of reaching its goal.

It's a terrible pun that I don't even give myself time to recognize.

I snatch Isla's tiny, soft shorts and panties off next, discarding them somewhere on the hotel room floor. The gasp that leaves her lips as I do so only makes me smirk. I take a moment to drink in the sight of her naked beneath me. The way she looks at me almost makes me forget my name, but I know I still have to make this good for her.

"I seem to recall that I said I would give you multiple orgasms before I got off. Is that correct?"

She thinks for a second before she says, "I think the word you used was many, but that's tomato, to-mah-to."

The smirk on my face grows wider. "Well, let's see how many I can give you, then."

I trail my hands along her inner thighs, keeping my touch featherlight to tease her. Isla squirms beneath me, and I can't deny that I love the sight. Her breath becomes more labored as my fingers inch closer to where she wants me most. But instead of doing what she thinks I'm going to do, I decide to switch things up. My fingers don't make a move, but my mouth does.

I look up at her as my mouth is inches from her pussy, and the scent of her arousal does something to me. It's irresistible to me, and I want more of it. My hands grip her thighs, spreading them wider with a little more force than I typically would use. I want this to be pleasurable for her and not be the source of any discomfort or pain. As I lower my head, I make it a point that my eyes never leave hers.

"Asher," she says, sounding like a plea. Although she hasn't said another word, I know what she wants and needs. And I'm more than happy to oblige.

I answer with the first stroke of my tongue, a long, deliberate lick that has her arching off the bed. Her fingers tangle in my hair, tugging me closer, begging me for more in her own way. But that's not enough for me. I want to hear her screaming my name so loud that my teammates figure out who I'm fucking.

Does that make me a masochist? I'm not sure.

"I want more," she blurts out as if she fears the words will be lost.

More is what I give her. My mouth is relentless against her pussy, alternating between broad strokes and sucking. Isla's moans grow louder, and I know I'm getting closer to my goal. I can feel her thighs trembling on either side of my head as she gets closer to the edge.

"Oh god, Asher, don't stop," she gets out, her back lifting off the bed. Her fingers tug at my hair almost painfully, but there's too much pleasure coursing through my body as well. I'm the one causing her to react like this. Not to mention, I want to give her everything because I'm determined to make her feel things she's never felt before.

I shift my body back so that I can look down at her. She only gets a few seconds' reprieve before I slip two fingers inside her tight pussy, curling them somewhat before my mouth lands back in its happy place. Isla cries out as she tightens around my fingers. She's so fucking close, and I know I'm about to claim orgasm number one.

"Come for me, sunshine," I murmur against her skin. "Let it go."

As if waiting for my permission, Isla's body tenses and then shakes slightly as her orgasm welcomes her with open arms. I coax her through it, gentling my touch, but not letting up until she's a quivering mess beneath me.

"That's my girl. Keep fucking my fingers until you're done with this round, baby."

Isla's body trembles as she rides out her orgasm. Her hips rock against my fingers until she collapses back onto the bed. I withdraw my fingers, studying them just before I bring them to my mouth.

"You taste delicious. I could spend all night eating your pussy."

Isla's eyes meet mine, but the look in them makes me wonder if she's still sailing on cloud nine. "What's stopping you?"

I chuckle because I can't help it. "Oh, sunshine, you have no idea what you're in for. That's only number one."

My cock throbs almost painfully in my pants, begging for attention, but I ignore it for now. This night is all about Isla and giving her as much pleasure as humanly possible.

I watch as a lazy grin appears on Isla's face. "You won't ever hear me complaining about that. Ever."

"Noted. Now get on your hands and knees."

Isla's eyes widen at my command, but she moves without hesitation. The sight of her on all fours, her back arched, and her perfect ass on display, nearly undoes me. I need to recite hockey stats in my head to calm myself before continuing.

I trail my fingers along the curve of her spine and watch the way goosebumps appear on her skin because of my touch. When I reach her ass, I give it a light smack, just enough to make her gasp.

"I love seeing you like this," I say as I reach over for the condom I'd thrown on the bed earlier. "So open and ready for me."

I take off my clothes while keeping my attention on Isla's body. I roll the condom on, stroking myself a few times to take the edge off.

Positioning myself behind her, I run my hands along her back. "Are you ready for me, sunshine?"

"Yes," she says, pushing her hips toward my cock. "Please, Asher..."

That's all it takes for my self-control to snap. I grip her hips, steadying myself as I slowly push into her pussy. I will never get enough of feeling her surrounding me. We both moan at the sensation as I fill her inch by inch.

"Fuck, Isla," I groan, my fingers digging into her hips. "You feel incredible."

Once I'm fully seated inside her, I pause, giving her a moment to adjust. But Isla has other ideas. She rocks her hips back against me, urging me to move.

"What did I say about you needing to fuck me hard?"

I pull back almost entirely before slamming into her. The room fills with the sounds or our bodies coming together as one. I lean forward, pressing my chest against her back as I continue to thrust into her. One hand snakes around to find her pussy, and I begin rubbing tight circles around her clit. Isla cries out as I watch her hands clench the bedsheets between her fingers. Her arms shake so much that she is struggling to hold herself up.

Excellent.

"That's it, baby. I know you're close again. Let go because I've got you."

As if on command, Isla's orgasm crashes over her. Her pussy clenches around my cock, the sensation nearly sending me over the edge with her. But I grit my teeth because I'm determined to get at least one more orgasm out of her.

I slow my thrusts, guiding her through the aftershocks before pulling out and flipping her onto her back. Her blue eyes are hazy once more. Her cheeks are flushed, and her hair is a wild, golden halo around her head.

"You're so fucking beautiful," I whisper, trailing my fingers along her jawline. Have I already said that? Maybe, but I can never say it enough. "And that was number two. I'm not done, and neither are you."

Her breathing is coming out in harsh, short spurts. "Are you sure about that?"

"Positive because I want you to ride me now. It's your turn to be in control."

Isla blinks up at me, her gaze still unfocused from the intensity of her second release. But as my words sink in, she agrees. It takes her a second, but she pushes herself up, and her hands land on my chest. Then she guides me onto my back.

I go willingly, watching as she moves her body so that she can straddle my hips. Her fingers dance along my skin before she takes my cock in her hand. When she positions herself above me, I have to fight the urge to thrust up into her.

"You want me to ride you, Asher?" she asks, her voice lower than usual. "Do you want to watch me take control?"

"Fuck yes," I groan, my hands settling on her hips. "I want to see you using my cock to get yourself off for the third time."

Isla's lips curve into a wicked smile as she sinks down onto me. We both moan at the sensation. She takes a moment to adjust, her hands braced against my chest before she moves.

And holy shit, what a sight it is. As Isla uses my cock, I am transfixed on her breasts, bouncing up and down with each roll of her hips. My eyes drift up to see the look of pure bliss on her face. I'm determined to commit this moment to my memory forever.

My hands leave her lips and land on her breasts. I play with her hardened nipples to add yet another sensation to the mix. Isla's pace quickens, and I'm rewarded with more moans as she chases her own pleasure.

"That's it, baby," I toss out there. "Take what you need. Use me to make yourself come."

Isla's head falls back as if my words spur her on as she grinds against me. I'm convinced I can feel her getting close to hitting that big number three.

Her thighs tremble as she rides me, and her movements as she fucks me become more erratic. The sight of her climaxing is intoxicating, and I know I won't last much longer. But I'm going to make her come one more time before I let go.

My hands slide down her body, gripping her hips tightly as I thrust up into her. Isla cries out, and her nails dig into my chest as she meets each of my thrusts.

"Asher." Her voice is just above a whisper, but I'm so locked in on her it's as if she has a megaphone to her lips. "I'm so close..."

"I know, sunshine." I end my words with a grunt because I'm this close to losing it all. "Let go for me. I want to feel you come around my cock one more time."

Isla's body tenses as her back arches, and her head falls back once more as her orgasm crashes over her. The sensation of her pussy clenching around me is the straw that breaks everything inside of me, and with a final thrust, I follow her over the edge.

Isla collapses against my chest after a job well done. I wrap my arms around her, holding her close as we both come down from our highs.

"That was..." Isla mumbles against my skin. Her voice trails off, and I wonder if she's about to pass out right here and now.

"Incredible," I finish for her, pressing a kiss to the top of her head. "Absolutely fucking incredible. Plus, that was lucky number three."

33

ISLA

I feel myself waking up, although everything around me tells me I should still be asleep. When my eyes finally open, I'm greeted by darkness.

What time is it? Where the hell am I?

It's then that the memories of last night flood my senses. Then I realize my hand is resting on a very hard chest. There's an arm wrapped around my waist, as if the owner is afraid to let go.

All of this feels like I'm caught in a dream that I never want to wake up from, but the reality is that I need to move because I shouldn't be here.

My dad is just a few floors down, unaware that his daughter snuck out in the middle of the night to be with his right wing. The guilt is there, sure, but it's drowned out by how right this feels. Even though I'm panicking about how this could go wrong in the blink of an eye, I feel safe in Asher's arms, with him sleeping beside me.

I reluctantly lift my hand off Asher's chest and try to get myself out of his embrace, but I struggle a bit. The mattress dips and creaks beneath my movements, and I hold my breath, praying that I don't end up waking him up. After all, he needs his rest way more than I do, and I might get a few more hours of sleep once I'm back in Dad's room.

Although I have a hard time removing his arm, I'm closer to being free. I shiver a little due to how cool the room is because the covers have shifted enough that more of my naked body is exposed. Not to mention, Asher's body heat must have been doing an excellent job of keeping me warm. I reach over to grab my phone and check the time.

4:14 a.m.

Damn, it's early, but I'm grateful I woke up on my own. I forgot to set an alarm to wake up and go back to my room. Not to mention, there are no missed calls or text messages from Dad, leading me to assume that he doesn't know I'm gone.

As I take a deep breath because I think I might finally manage to escape, the arm around my waist tightens, pulling me back against a solid chest. Asher's breath is warm against my neck as he murmurs, voice rough with sleep, "Where do you think you're going?"

I shiver, but this time, it has nothing to do with the

chill in the room. "I need to get back before my dad wakes up and realizes I'm gone."

Asher's lips graze along the shell of my ear. The motion sends a tingle down my spine, and I can't help but wonder if he's doing this on purpose. "Not yet," he whispers. "Stay with me a little longer."

I melt into his embrace, but know I can't stay. "Asher, we can't..." My protest is halfhearted, but it still needs to be said.

"How about we go take a shower instead? I'll have you in and out of there in a few minutes, and it will be one less thing to do when you go back to your room."

"I took a shower last night, though..." I say, wondering where this is going.

"Yes, but it wasn't with me. I can help you reach those places that are hard to or that you might have missed."

The deepness of his voice first thing in the morning is doing something to my brain. Given what time it is, I'm not thinking straight, and I have a feeling that I know what he's thinking about doing if I decide to take a shower with him.

"Bennett, you know this isn't a good idea and—"

My words die on my lips because he shifts our bodies so he's hovering over me. A small groan leaves his lips before he says, "Let me take care of you, Isla. Just for a little while longer."

And that's all it takes. I nod along, even though he

can't see me. That's when it clicks that I need to say the words. "Yes, I'll stay for a little while longer."

Asher moves his body, and it takes a few seconds before the lamp on the bedside table provides some light for us to see. Asher's eyes narrow for a moment, as if they are trying to adjust. Once his eyes return to normal, Asher's lips curve into a smile. When he drops his head to give me what I assume is a kiss, I put my hand on his chest, stopping him.

"Morning breath?"

He just shrugs. "Do you think I give a shit about that? I just want to give you a good morning kiss."

I shake my head because I can't fight the grin that is ready to appear on my face. He makes me so happy that it almost feels sickening. Is this what I've been missing for years?

Asher takes that as his sign to make his move because his hands land on the sides of my face just before he kisses me again. All thoughts of feeling self-conscious about morning breath and how I need to get back to Dad's room fly out of the window.

As if he's suddenly realized how limited our time is, he breaks the kiss with a few more quick pecks on my lips. "Shower. Now."

We stumble out of bed, and Asher grabs my hand to hold. It's as if he isn't willing to let me go, even for a moment, and I'm not complaining.

We make it to the bathroom, and he turns on the

shower. I lean against the counter as the sound of the water fills the room. I catch a glimpse of us in the mirror and shake my head. My hair is a hot mess, and he barely looks awake, yet I can't help but grin. I'm happy from just being with him. However, I know he has something up his sleeve related to this shower. I can feel it.

Asher comes up behind me and wraps both arms around my waist. Without missing a beat, he presses a kiss on my shoulder. "You're beautiful, you know that?"

I roll my eyes. "You're just saying that because you want me to shower with you."

He laughs as I lean back into his embrace. "Maybe. But it doesn't make it any less true."

I turn my head to look at him. He takes it as an opportunity to give me another brief kiss on the lips before he grabs my hand and pulls me toward the shower. Being naked has many benefits, including not worrying about taking off clothes. I step into the bathtub first, and I can't help but sigh. The water is the perfect temperature and feels like heaven, not to mention it is helping to wake me up.

Asher pulls me toward him, my back to his chest, while his hands are resting on my hips. Every part of his body feels hard against me, including his dick, which is obviously ready for another round. To be honest, I am too.

Before I can say a word, his lips find the sensitive spot just below my ear, and I make a noise that is the mixture of a giggle and a sigh.

One of his hands slides around to my front until his fingers brush against my pussy. I gasp, my head falling back against his chest as he starts to circle my clit. "You're so responsive. I love how your body reacts to my touch."

I moan, pushing my hips forward into his hand and then back into his cock. The friction from our movements causes both of us to moan as he takes the hint, increasing the pressure and movement of his fingers. My breathing grows harsher, and just as I feel as if I'm about to reach my climax, he pulls his hand away.

Before I can protest, Asher spins me around to face him. His green eyes stare into mine with an intensity that steals my breath. He backs me up against the cool tile wall, his body caging me in. The difference between the coldness on my back and the heat at my front is causing my brain to short-circuit.

"I want to try something," he says, ripping me away from my thoughts. "Do you trust me?"

I nod without hesitation. "Yes, always."

Asher reaches up and grabs the handheld shower head. He makes some adjustments before he angles the spray so that it hits my body. First, the jets land on my breasts, making my nipples harder than they already were. The warm water rolls over my sensitive skin, causing me to gasp. I swear Asher's eyes darken as he watches my reaction. The way he is making me feel only encourages him further as he drags the shower head lower.

And then he reaches his destination.

"Oh my—" I moan as my hips jerk forward. The jets have made my pussy their playground, and the intense sensations make my legs shake. Everything becomes so much that I'm forced to reach out and grab Asher's shoulders for support. I feel bad about how deep my nails are digging into his skin, but he doesn't complain.

I don't know how long I'm going to last.

"When I walked into the bathroom after checking in, I knew I wanted to do this to you. I feel bad for Carson, but I swear the stars lined up for me tonight."

Asher's words barely register because of where he's pointing the showerhead. What stars is he talking about? I can see them the longer he keeps the jets from the showerhead directed at my pussy.

My orgasm builds rapidly, to where it's hard for me to breathe. The urge to close my eyes is there, but I can't with Asher's eyes locked on mine. His free hand grips my hip, holding me against the tile wall as my body trembles even more.

"That's it, Isla," he says, just above the noise of the water rushing out of the shower head. "Let go for me."

His words push me over the edge. I cry out as my orgasm crashes over me in waves. Asher keeps the showerhead in place, prolonging my climax until it borders on too much. Only then does he pull it away, setting it back in its holder.

I sag against the wall because my legs feel like jelly.

Asher's arms come around me, and he takes on all of my weight. I feel at ease in his arms.

"You're so fucking gorgeous when you come," he says. "I could watch you fall apart all day."

A small laugh slips out. "I don't think I'd survive that."

He chuckles as his hands skim down my sides. When he reaches my hips, I gasp as he lifts me effortlessly. I wrap my legs around his waist without thinking about it, erasing our height difference. If his cock being hard wasn't apparent to me before, it is now.

"Fuck, I don't have a condom. I left it in the bedroom."

Dejection slams into me before an idea clicks in my head. "I'm on birth control. For PCOS, but I'm on birth control, and I'm clean."

Relief floods Asher's features, although there is still a tightness there. I know that's because he wants to find his own release. "I'm clean too. Just got tested at the beginning of the season and haven't been with anyone besides you. Nor have I ever had sex without a condom. Are you sure about this?"

This is what I want. "I'm sure I want to feel you. All of you."

His eyes search mine for a long moment. "Tell me if you want to stop at any point, okay?"

"I will."

With that, he positions himself at my entrance. He eases himself into me, and we both gasp. As I feel one of his hands land on my hip, I can't help but think this is a different experience. Here is another first I've given him and something he's given me in return. This new level of intimacy is indescribable. And that's before he even begins to move.

His thrusts start off slow as we're both adjusting to how wet everything is and this brand-new feeling. Without the barrier of a condom between us, I swear the movement between us feels more intense. I take a deep breath as my hands reach for his shoulders to give me leverage as he fills me over and over again.

Asher's grip on my hips tightens as he increases his pace, driving into me with a passion that steals my breath. The sensation of his bare skin against mine, the way he stretches and fills me so completely, is almost too much to bear. I cling to him, nails digging into his shoulders as the pleasure builds within me once more.

"You feel so good," he groans. "So perfect. You were made for me."

I can only whimper in response because, in my current state of mind, words and thoughts don't exist. The water cascades over our bodies and is cooling down, but I don't care. Asher's movements grow more urgent, and I do my best to meet each one. Our moans and gasps bounce off the walls in this small space, reminding me how intimate this is.

When the intensity reaches what I swear is new heights, it takes everything within me to keep myself from screaming. "I'm so fucking close."

"I am too," he grits out, and I know the chances of us both reaching our climaxes together are extremely high. He leans forward and gives me a long kiss on the lips, and that's all it takes for my body to let everything go.

He swallows my cries with his kiss as my orgasm takes over my body. Those stars he mentioned earlier? I have no problem seeing them as he breaks our kiss because his thrusts have become more erratic. A groan tears from his throat as I feel the warmth of his cum filling me, and it feels as if he's marking me as his.

We stay like that for a minute or two, and I'm left wondering how he even has the stamina to hold us both up. Another thing I need to thank hockey for, I guess. The cooling water leaves small trails over our skin, but I barely feel it because I'm lost in his eyes. Asher presses his forehead against mine as we struggle to regain our composure.

Once we both catch our breath, I slowly move my legs so that I'm somewhat standing on my own. However, Asher moves his arms so that they are around my waist. I'm grateful for his support because I'm not sure my legs can hold me up on their own right now.

I look down and notice that his cum is dripping out of me, and I gasp. "Holy shit."

Asher follows my gaze, and a smirk tugs at his lips. "Damn, that's hot."

I blush, feeling a mixture of shyness and thrill at the sight. "We should actually shower, and I'll clean that up."

"I'll do it," he says.

"Are you sure?"

The smile is now gone. "One hundred percent. What about you?" he asks.

"I'm fine. Excellent even."

Asher reaches for a washcloth and soaks it under the lukewarm water. He cleans his cum from between my thighs before turning to wash my body with soap. I rinse under the showerhead while he washes himself, and before I know it, our shower together is over. He reaches behind me to turn off the water, and the sudden absence of the sound makes the bathroom feel eerily quiet, but it doesn't make me feel uncomfortable.

It's because I feel loved.

This love differs from what I felt three years ago. It's more powerful and more mature in so many ways. Everything is still new, but also old too. It doesn't feel like we've picked up from where we left off, but it's also not a new book. Maybe it's a new chapter, and I'm excited to turn the page to see what's in store for us. But first, we need to get out of this shower.

As if sensing my unsteadiness, Asher guides me out of the shower and grabs a fluffy towel from the rack. He wraps it around me with infinite care before taking another for himself. The soft terry cloth feels heavenly against my body, but it still feels as if it's in overdrive.

We step out onto the bathmat, and the cool air hits my damp skin, causing me to shiver. Asher notices and wraps his arms around me. I lean into him so that I can feel his muscular body against mine for a few moments before I have to get dressed and head back to my room.

"You okay?"

"More than okay," I whisper, tilting my head to look up at him. His green eyes are soft as they gaze down at me.

He reaches up to tuck a strand of wet hair behind my ear. "I wish we could stay like this forever."

"Me too." I kiss his lips, and he responds instantly. "But I have to get back ASAP."

"I know. Let's get you dried off and dressed."

We step out of the bathroom. Asher grabs my clothes from where we haphazardly discarded them and hands them to me. I drop my towel and pull on my panties and shorts. When I finish putting on my tank top, I find Asher holding my hoodie.

"I don't want you to go," he says.

I turn to look at him and grab my last article of clothing. "And I don't want to either. But we both know I have to." With a heavy sigh, I put the hoodie on. "But I'll see you when you hit the ice in a few hours. Speaking of, you need to go get some sleep ahead of that. It's too early for you to be up."

"I promise to go back to bed as soon as I walk you back to your room," he says as he puts on a new pair of boxer briefs.

I stare at him for a moment. "You can't walk me back."

"Watch me." This time, he's putting on a pair of

basketball shorts, and I see him reaching for a white t-shirt next.

"What if someone sees you?"

Asher shrugs, as if this isn't the craziest idea in the world. "The chances of someone seeing us this time of morning outside of some cameras that might be in the hallway are slim to none. I'll take those chances."

I want to argue with him, but I know it's pointless. Once Asher sets his mind to something, there's no changing it. And if I'm being honest, I also want to have a few more minutes with him, even if it's just walking down the hallway.

"Fine, but we have to be quick and quiet."

He flashes me a grin, happy that I agreed. "I can do that."

Asher grabs his sweatshirt and throws it on while I gather the rest of my things. Once he has his hotel room key in hand, he checks the peephole to make sure the coast is clear before opening the door. The hallway is empty and silent, which makes sense given the time of morning. We step out of the room, and Asher takes my hand, lacing our fingers as we approach the elevator.

The elevator ride down feels both agonizingly slow and far too quick. He holds my hand the entire time, allowing his thumb to caress my skin as if trying to soothe all of my worries. The simple touch does more to me than I will ever admit out loud. We walk out into another quiet hallway when the elevator doors slide open. The plush carpet muffles our footsteps as we make our way toward my dad's room.

As we approach the door, a sense of dread crawls up my spine. Not only do I not want to leave Asher's side, but I don't want to go back into the room and risk waking Dad up.

"I'm a couple of doors down," I tell Asher. "You might want to turn around now, just in case."

"I'm not going to leave you before I walk you to your door, but I will do this," he says as he pulls me to a stop. He puts his index finger under my chin, tilting my face up so that I can look directly into his eyes. I already know what he's about to do, and the fact that he's going to do this in public, albeit in an empty hallway, feels impulsive, but yet so right.

Asher's lips meet mine in a tender kiss that has me ready to melt into a puddle on this floor. I know this is our "goodbye for now" kiss, and I hate that things have to be this way. When he pulls back, I'm left feeling slightly dizzy.

"I'll see you in a few hours, okay?" he whispers before resting his forehead against mine.

"Yes, you will."

My boyfriend stares at me for a second more before grabbing my hand and walking me to my door. I pull out the keycard, and with one last squeeze of my hand, Asher turns and walks back down the hallway to the elevator. I watch him go until he disappears around the corner. It's then I realize that I already miss him.

I turn my attention back to the task at hand and hold my breath as I swipe my hotel key against the card reader. I pray that it doesn't make a sound. The lock disengages with a soft click, and I open the door. The room is dark and quiet, the only sound being my dad's steady breathing from his bed.

I tiptoe inside, shutting the door behind me. I use my phone's light to guide me as I reach my bed. Soon, I'm taking off my hoodie and shoes, and the next thing I know, I'm slipping under the covers. I curl onto my side, hugging a pillow to my chest as I try to calm myself down from the excitement of the last few hours.

Mission. Accomplished.

34

ASHER

My house is quieter than usual, a rarity in a place shared by four guys, let alone hockey players. There's still some clutter, like empty Gatorade bottles and textbooks we need for our classes, which shows that there are college students on the premises. However, the constant noise that is around is absent. The atmosphere feels different, but I could be projecting because no one is talking. The only sound in the room is the hockey game on TV.

I glance around at my teammates. My best friend, Levi, is lounging on one couch, his legs kicked up on the coffee table, focused on the television in front of him. Blaise is sitting cross-legged on the floor, staring at his phone, but he looks up at the game every once in a while to check on the score. Knox is leaning back with his arms crossed, and while his eyes are on the screen,

I'm not sure how much he's paying attention to it. Wilder is sprawled across the other couch with the remote in his hand, and I can't help but wonder if he's about to piss everyone off by switching the channel for a joke.

Then there's me, who has been sitting around plotting about this moment for days. Isla and I have talked about it many times, and I need the support of my brothers before I talk to Coach.

I wait until the game goes to commercial before I clear my throat. All eyes are on me. "Guys, there's something I need to tell you."

Levi sits up straighter, Blaise sets his phone down, and Wilder even stops fiddling with the remote. He does mute the television before turning toward me. Knox is the only one who doesn't move, his eyes still fixed on the TV screen. But I know he's listening. He always is.

"Isla and I... are dating. Again."

The silence stretches on for a moment before Wilder speaks. "In the wise words of Jade, no shit." He shares a look with Blaise before he points at Knox and says, "And you owe me fifty dollars."

Wait, they'd bet on Isla and I getting back together?

The first one to laugh is Levi. "You didn't actually think we didn't know? Come on, dude."

I blink, not sure how to take their reactions. "You... you all knew?"

Blaise shakes his head and sighs. "Bennett, man, you

weren't subtle. The way you two look at each other when you think no one's watching? Dead giveaway."

I'm a fucking idiot, and the amused looks on my team-mates' faces confirm that fact. My face is growing warmer as I try to keep cool. I thought Isla and I were being discreet, but clearly, that is a lie. It's like they've all been waiting for me to catch up to what they already knew. The realization makes me want to laugh at myself but also cringe because that is what this situation has become.

Cringe.

Wilder clears his throat and snaps me back to what's happening in front of me versus the internal dialogue happening in my head. "Plus, that's not even mentioning how you were ready to kill Knox over his teasing. It was a matter of when, not if."

I roll my eyes. "That was, what, weeks ago at this point? Come on now."

"So? We still knew then," Knox says, finally deciding to join in on the conversation. "But now you have to think about what Coach is going to do when he finds out."

Well, that stops us all dead in our tracks as all eyes turn to him. He seems surprised by our reaction. "What? I'm just saying," he continues just before he takes a deep breath, "when Coach finds out, it might not be pretty. You know how he is—he's not just Isla's dad. He's the guy that controls your ice time. Just... make sure you're ready for that conversation."

I know he's right, but I've been down this road

before. "I know," I say. "Believe me, I've thought about it. A lot."

Levi leans forward, resting his elbows on his knees. "How are you going to approach this?"

I run a hand through my hair and then shrug. "I don't know," I admit. "Well, I know I have to tell him. Well, Isla and I have to tell him. But..."

"But you're scared shitless," Wilder finishes for me.

He isn't wrong. I don't say a word because I know they all get it. They understand what this could mean—not just for me, but for all of us, especially as a team.

"Coach is tough, but he's not totally unreasonable," Blaise says. "If you're honest with him, if you make him see what Isla means to you..."

Sure, but the most significant factor in all of this is the fact that one of his daughters is involved. We all know there are no guarantees here because of that.

Hockey is everything to me and has been everything to me for years. And with this being my senior year, I'm closing in on the goals that I want to achieve and the milestones I want to hit. The thought of losing it—losing everything I've worked for—because of how much I love Isla... it's almost too much to handle. But then I think of her. Of her smile, her laugh, the way she looks at me like I could be better than I am. And I know that, without a doubt, she's worth it. Worth every risk and every fight to make all of this right in the end.

"I'm not giving her up," I say as I look each of my

teammates in the eye. "No matter what happens, no matter what Coach does... I'm not letting her go. Not again."

The guys exchange glances, talking without saying a word to each other. Then Levi stands up and holds out his hand to me to give a man hug. "I think I can speak for everyone here and say that we'll always have your back. No matter what."

The others nod, even Knox. I can't stop the feeling that swells in my chest. I'm so grateful to have these guys in my life. We're more than a team. We are a family.

Wilder holds the remote up and un-mutes the TV. "Now that you've gotten that off your chest, I want to get back to the game."

Typical.

Everyone turns their attention back to watching the game more enthusiastically than before I made my announcement. I try to focus on what's going on, but my mind is still stuck on our conversation. Although it's something that I've been thinking about for a while, having Knox warn me hit a different chord.

A few minutes later, the period ends, and the guys start to stretch. I catch Knox's eye, and he tilts his head toward the hallway. We both get up, and he follows me into the kitchen, where I lean against the counter.

I cross my arms over my chest and brace myself for what he's going to say. "What's up?"

Knox shifts his weight from one foot to the next before

he rests his body against the far wall. "Look, man... first, I want to say that even with our issues this year, I still want what's best for you. With that being said, I just wanted to make sure you really get what you're risking here. I know you love Isla and how painful it was for you when you broke up with her years ago. But are you sure this is the road you want to go down again?"

"Yeah, I know. Knox, I've thought about it a lot, and I'm serious about her. This isn't just some spur-of-the-moment thing I'm diving into headfirst without thinking about. She's it for me, and I'm ready to face whatever comes along with that."

He shakes his head, his eyes narrowing a little. "I know you think you are. But it's not just about you. It's about her, the team—hell, even Coach. If this blows up in your face, it can fuck up things for a lot of people. We need you on the ice, not sitting on the bench or off the team."

I study him for a second because I'm reading between the lines, or his words, for that matter. "This is about more than just me and Isla, isn't it? Because you know this is my senior year, and once the season's over, he won't be my coach anymore. Isla is forever, man."

Knox sighs and looks away for a moment before meeting my eyes again. "Back in high school, I was with someone. It got complicated, and it screwed everything up —my game, my head, the team. It got to me, and it almost cost me my future. I don't want that for you."

I'm surprised. Knox isn't the type to open up about

this kind of stuff or share much of his life outside of the basics. He hides behind sarcasm, and I don't blame him, but this feels like a new chapter I'm being let in on.

"Is that why you don't do serious relationships?" I ask.

He hesitates for a moment. "Yeah. I guess so. I learned the hard way that getting too close can fuck everything up. And I just... I don't want to go through that again."

The gravity of his confession hangs in the air as I try to wrap my head around it. I'm floored because he's opened up to me. Does anyone else on the team know about this? There's a new level of trust there that I never expected, especially given what we've been through with our relationship.

I push off the counter and take a step toward him. "Thank you for telling me. I know it couldn't have been easy."

Knox shrugs, trying to play it off, but I can see it's all a facade. "Yeah, well. I just don't want you making the same mistakes I did."

"I hear you, and I promise, I'm going into this with my eyes wide open. Isla and I are not rushing into anything, given our history. She and I know what's at stake."

He searches my face for a long moment before he says, "Alright. I've said my peace, and I hope everything works out for the best."

"Thanks. That means a lot."

Knox walks up to me and places a hand on my shoulder. "Anytime, Bennett. Let's get back in there before Wilder starts placing bets on what we're talking about."

I chuckle because there's a good chance that is next on Wilder's to-do list. We walk back into the living room, and sure enough, Wilder's attention is on us, and the smirk tells me everything I need to know before he says a word. "So, what was that all about?"

I roll my eyes and plop down on the couch. "It was nothing important." It's obviously a lie, but I hope it's enough to dissuade him from prying further.

Levi jumps in before Wilder can respond. "Not everything's got to be your business, anyway."

"Fair enough, fair enough," Wilder concludes, but the smile doesn't leave his face.

Levi shoots me a knowing look, and I nod in silent thanks. I appreciate that he jumped in to deflect because I already have enough shit on my mind. The conversation shifts back to the game on television, and things start to feel almost normal again.

Almost.

35

ISLA

"Thanks for coming over this way," I tell Selene as I drop my body on the worn-out couch with a dramatic sigh. This is one of the few times I didn't walk over to her place so we could hang. Instead, she came to me. Because of that, we are currently in one of the common areas of my dorm. I took a risk telling Selene that we could hang out here before her shift at the library. The living space is empty, thank goodness. It gives us the opportunity to chat, but I don't know how long it will stay empty, though it also allows me to get away from my asshole of a roommate.

Selene does her best to get comfy on the old couch, tucking her feet under her butt before she responds. "Um, you sounded like you were about to fall asleep from pure exhaustion. Of course, I needed to come over and see how you were doing."

She's not wrong. "It's been a long week trying to keep up with all the things, and I feel like I'm just sitting down to catch my breath. Classes are well... my classes and I've still been trying to keep up with work. Asher told the guys about us this week, which was nerve-wracking enough on its own. I was so anxious about how they would react, no matter how many times I told myself it was going to be fine. And on top of that, I've been worried that one of them might end up telling Dad before we are ready. It's been... a lot."

"I can only imagine..." Her voice trails off as if she's still trying to think of the right words to say given the situation. "Telling the team about your relationship with Asher, especially given your dad's position, is a bit diabolical, I must admit."

My lips twitch because of her usage of the word diabolical. People have been tossing it around more because of social media. I know she threw it out there to lighten the mood a bit. My face loses the war I've been fighting with myself, and I let out a humorless chuckle. "Diabolical is the perfect way to describe this, because what the hell?"

"Well, if it makes you feel any better, I think Asher going all out like this is super romantic. You're living the life in a forbidden love romance novel... I can list all of the tropes right now if you like."

I can't help but roll my eyes.

"I love romance novels just like everyone else, but I

think you've taken a deep dive into one. It's not as glamorous as you make it sound."

"It could be worse. You could be living in one of the true-crime podcast stories you love so much."

Selene - 2. Me - 0.

"Yeah, that's not even something I want to joke about. Some of those stories are... whew." I shake my head just thinking about it.

"That's valid, but let's go back to what's going on with you and Asher and telling his teammates. It went well, I assume?"

I tell her what Asher said about how his conversation with the guys went. "Knox took him aside to confirm that he was okay with all of this."

I tilt my head as I watch Selene's reaction when I mention Knox's name. Her eyes grow wide when I say his name, and now I'm curious. I know they've hung out before at one of the hockey parties we attended, but nothing came of it as far as I knew.

"What exactly did Knox say?" she asks.

Although this part of our conversation only takes a few seconds to occur, the wheels in my head are spinning faster and faster. I didn't expect this scenario when I asked if we could chat in person, but now I'm very intrigued. However, I can't let my eagerness show too much, or Selene might try to play it off.

I know her way too well.

"He just wanted to make sure Asher was certain about

going public with our relationship. If this explodes in our faces, it will hurt Asher and me and affect the team. He had some experience in that arena when he was in high school. But I don't have any more details." I watch for her reaction.

Selene's gaze drifts a bit as if there is something on her mind that she's not sharing with me. Then she lifts her eyes and tucks a piece of red hair behind her ear. "That's interesting. It's a lot of pressure, having your personal life out there for everyone to see and judge. I wonder what happened to Knox in high school, though."

There's the opening I want. "I'm not sure, and if he did tell Asher, Asher didn't share it with me, which I'm completely fine with. I don't tell him all the things we talk about. Why are you so interested?"

I keep my tone light and teasing because I don't want my best friend to think I'm grilling her. There's a time and place for that, but right now, isn't it. She pulls at some imaginary lint on her sweatshirt, and I know she's trying to think of a way to evade the question.

"Just curious," she shrugs, trying to play it off. "Knox seems like a private guy, so it's surprising he'd open up about his past like that."

That's true; I can confirm that from my interactions with him, but how would she know that, having only met him briefly at a party? It's time to push her more here. "How do you know all this when you've only met him once, when we went to the hockey party? I get that he gives off that vibe, but what are you hiding?"

She stares at me for a moment, and I see a mix of emotions cross her face. First surprise, and I assume it's because she's shocked. And Selene is never caught off guard. Then there's some nervousness as she refuses to look me in the eye. There's no doubt in my mind that she can feel the beginnings of a blush appearing on her face, and she has to know that I can see it, given her pale skin. Finally, a soft, nervous laugh leaves her lips as if, once again, she might try to play it off as if it's nothing serious.

"I don't know what you're talking about. I'm not hiding anything."

"Bullshit. I know you way too well for that, and you know it."

"Okay, fine," she says, giving in. "We may have talked a bit at the last party. And maybe texted a little since then."

My brows lift in surprise. "Texted? About what?"

"Nothing major. Just, you know, random stuff. Memes. Recipes he wanted to try."

My mouth opens and closes a few times before I can get the words I want to say. I wish I had a bag of Skittles with me because this is pure entertainment. "What in the actual fuck? Since when have you texted anyone recipes?"

"I've texted you recipes!" she exclaims.

Doth the lady protest too much and all that, I can't help but think. Thank you, high school English class, for my being able to recall Hamlet. "Yes, but I'm your best friend, not a hockey player that you met at a party."

Selene opens her mouth, then closes it again. "Fine. I might be a little into him. But it's not a big deal. I don't think he's that into me, anyway."

I narrow my eyes, and it only causes her face to become more red. "Not into you? Selene, when has a guy ever not been into you?"

She shifts her body so her feet are on the ground, and her leg bounces up and down. "I don't know, Isla. Maybe I'm just imagining it. He doesn't want anything serious, and neither do I."

This whole thing is new territory for us because, as I said before, what the fuck?

Before I can say anything more, the door leading from the living room common area upstairs to the first floor of dorm rooms swings open with a loud creak, startling both Selene and me. I look up to see Tessa standing there, her eyes narrowing at the sight of us.

Just my damn luck.

"Ah, there is my lovely roommate," she says, her voice dripping with sarcasm.

She is going to start something and has no issue doing it in front of Selene. I should take the polite approach, although the urge to snap at her is growing by the second. "Tessa, did you need something?"

Her eyes shift between Selene and me, and I can see the calculations she is making in her head. The corners of her lips flip up into a smirk, and I brace myself for what she is about to say. "Oh, don't mind me. I was just heading out. You should keep your side of the room cleaner, though, because it's rude to have to be stepping over your shit to get what I need to get done."

Although I'm glad she didn't hear what Selene and I were talking about, Tessa's comment raises every red flag in my body. While I'm not the neatest person, I know for a fact that I left my side of the room in decent shape before I came down to meet Selene. I take a slow, deep breath, trying to stop the anger that is rising in my chest. "I'm not sure what you're talking about, Tessa. My side is clean."

Tessa snorts. "Really? Because from what I saw, it looks like a tornado blew through. Clothes everywhere, makeup scattered across the floor. It's a pigsty."

Selene grabs my hand to stop me from lashing out, but it's too late. "Did you touch my things?"

"No, of course not. Why would I do a thing like that?"

Tessa is lying, even if she hasn't said another word. The smirk on her face is a telltale sign. And I've had enough. "Don't touch anything that belongs to me ever again."

She raises an eyebrow, and I can tell my warning did not faze her at all. "Or what? You'll tell your daddy what I did?"

Her mocking tone makes my blood boil. What are we, in high school? This is obscene, and I don't want to get school officials or anything like that involved because I don't want the drama surrounding that. Hell, I don't want the drama from Tessa anymore, either. This needs to be settled here and now.

I pull my hand out of Selene's grasp and stand up. "I can forgive and forget that you've done this, and we can stay out of each other's way for the rest of the year. But stop pushing me."

"Pushing you? Oh, girlie, I haven't even started yet." She takes a step closer, invading my personal space. The scent of her sickly sweet perfume slams into me like a boulder and makes my stomach churn. "You think you're so special, don't you? With your perfect little life and your secret hockey player boyfriend. Does Daddy know about that? Or does Asher know how often you have to shave to control how hairy you are?"

I freeze. How does she know about Asher? We've been so careful outside of when he came to my room that one time, and I didn't think she would be there. He could have been there for any reason, though, so she's just pulling shit out of her ass. However, her implying that she has no issue telling Dad about this and her mocking my illness has me seeing red.

"Isla—"

I cut off Selene's warning with a tirade of my own. "You know what, Tessa? Mind your own fucking business. I'm done with this petty game. You have hated me since the school assigned me to your room. I've done my best to be a good roommate and stay out of your way, but you've continued to push my buttons to get me to move out. But it's not going to work because I can be an asshole too. And I'm much better at it."

I tilt my head back and forth as if I'm preparing for battle and take another step toward her. "First, fuck you for making fun of an illness that I can't control. Second, my relationship with Asher and whether my dad knows has nothing to do with you, and it's, once again, none of your fucking business. I know things about you that you don't want to get out, including that little black book you keep. So I'm going to go upstairs and clean up the mess you made because I don't want you laying another finger on my shit. You can keep being bitter and jealous if you want, but I'm moving on. This is the end of whatever you think this is between us. Have the day you deserve."

Tessa blinks hard, clearly taken aback. For a moment, she looks like she wants to argue, but then something in her expression changes. It could be the realization that I'm serious and that I'm not backing down. She scoffs, rolling her eyes. "Whatever, Isla. You're not worth my time." With that, she turns and stalks out of our dorm building. I'm sure she would have slammed the door behind her if she could.

"Holy shit, I'm so proud of you," Selene says just over my right shoulder.

I hadn't even noticed she stood up from the couch. I assume she was preparing to fight Tessa too, if it had come to blows. Thankfully, it didn't, and we don't have to worry about the drama that would have caused.

Before I can turn to look at her, my phone buzzes in my pocket. I pull it out, my heart skipping a beat when I see Asher's name on the screen. I answer, my voice softening. "Hey, I thought you were busy for another hour or so?"

"Hey, I just took a quick break to step outside. But I think I should set up a meeting with Coach. You know, to talk about us. I think it's time."

It's almost as if he knows what just happened to me, but I know there's no way he does unless Tessa telepathically told him. But when a sign is staring you dead in the face, it's time to take that leap.

"Yeah, I think you're right. It's time."

36

ASHER

I glance at the stunning woman sitting beside me in my car as I drive toward Crestwood's hockey rink. Isla is almost rigid in the passenger seat as she stares out the window, her gaze focused on the gray skies above. Strands of her blonde hair whip in the wind from the cracked window she's currently looking out of. She's not paying attention to her surroundings as she chews on her thumbnail.

"Hey," I say softly, reaching over to squeeze her knee before placing my hand back on the steering wheel. "It's gonna be alright. We are ready for this."

I can see her turn to look at me before she speaks. "But I can't stop thinking about what if he benches you, Ash? What if this ruins your shot at the pros? I'd never forgive myself..."

"Stop," I cut her off gently. "Everything will be fine, and you can't let yourself spiral due to what-ifs. This isn't just about hockey. It's about you and me and about how much I love you."

I grimace slightly as the mood in the car shifts because of my confession. This isn't how I imagined telling her I loved her again for the first time in years, but here we are. Sometimes, the best moments are spontaneous, I guess.

Isla is silent for a few moments, and I wonder how much I messed this up. I hear her let out a gigantic sigh, but I can barely hear it because of what feels like the blood rushing in my ears. This happens when I'm on the ice, but I can't remember the last time it happened when I was in a private setting.

She reaches over and squeezes my knee in much the same manner that I did just a few seconds ago. "I love you too. So much. But I'm still scared of what you might lose because of this."

The panic in my head and heart stops immediately. I intertwine our fingers and bring her hand up to press a tender kiss against her knuckles.

"We're not going to lose a thing, and we won't lose each other. In fact, we have so much to gain after this meeting, sunshine.... And I never thought I would say those words."

That makes her laugh. I've accomplished my goal. If there is anything I can do to reduce the burden she's carrying, I will do so, even if I am nervous about how all of this is going to go.

I keep our fingers laced as I pull into the arena parking lot. What normally has a very calming effect on me because I know I will be hitting the ice is anything but as I throw my car into park.

"We're here," I say unnecessarily because we both know that.

She nods as she does deep breathing exercises to calm herself down. I place another kiss on the back of her hand as I check the clock.

Two minutes until I'm supposed to meet with her father, which means I should head in now. "Let's go, baby."

I step out of the car, the crisp air hitting my face as I round the front of my car to the passenger's side. Opening her door, I extend my hand to help her out. She takes it, her fingers trembling slightly in mine. I give them a reassuring squeeze.

"Hey," I whisper, tucking a strand of her windblown hair behind her ear. "It's going to be okay. We're in this together, remember?"

Isla nods, leaning into my touch for a moment before straightening her shoulders. "I know. Everything is going to be fine. I have to hold on to that thought."

"That's all we can do right now," I reply, agreeing with her. I kiss her on the forehead before I grab her hand again. Together, hand in hand, we walk toward the arena entrance. Is it the smartest thing to hold her hand so her father can see us before we have this conversation? No, but I need to touch and comfort her and myself.

Once we're in the building and make a turn for the tunnel, we make our way toward Coach Johnson's office. The walk down the hallway seems to take forever, but Isla's hand tightens around mine as we approach the door I need to walk through.

I pause a few feet away and turn to face her. I cup her face gently, and my thumbs brush lightly over her cheekbones. "No matter what happens in there, it doesn't change how I feel about you. About us. We'll figure it out, okay?"

"Okay," she whispers. "I love you."

Hearing her repeat those words blows my mind. "I love you too, Isla. More than anything." I press a soft kiss to her lips before pulling away.

Isla steps to the side, hiding herself from view as I walk the last few steps to Coach Johnson's office alone. Taking a deep breath, I raise my hand and knock firmly on the door. There's a beat of heavy silence, and then Coach's voice calls out, "Come in."

I glance at Isla one last time before I turn the doorknob and step into what feels like the lion's den. Coach looks up at me as I step into his domain. I close the door behind me, and I swear the clicking of it engaging with the doorframe sounds louder than usual.

"Asher," he says. "Take a seat."

I do as he says and sit in the chair across from him. Normally, I would look around to see what trophies, photos, and newspaper articles he might have added to his collection because of all the accolades he's won, but I can't bring myself to do so.

Coach Johnson leans back in his chair. "Bennett, why did you want to have this meeting?"

"I want to talk to you about...." my voice trails off just before I rip off the proverbial Band-Aid. "...about Isla."

Coach Johnson's jaw tightens when I mention his daughter. "What about her?"

I swallow hard because my mouth has gone dry. The glare that he is serving me is warranted, but I refuse to let it intimidate me.

"Isla and I are together," I say. "We are dating."

There's no expression on Coach Johnson's face, but I catch the subtle twitch of his jaw. It's obvious that he's not amused. "Is that so?" he asks, his tone deceptively calm. "And how long has this been going on?"

I debate how specific I should get on the timing of our relationship, and whether to include when we dated years ago, but decide that it's not worth getting into the details right now. Instead, I meet his gaze head-on because I'm not backing down.

"A while now. But that's not what matters. What matters is that we're serious about each other."

His piercing blue eyes, so like his daughter's, stare into

mine. "Serious," he repeats. "And what, pray tell, does serious mean to you, Asher?"

I swear my t-shirt is restricting my breathing, but I push through anyway. "It means that I love her, Coach. And she loves me. We want to be together and don't want to hide it anymore."

"I see. I'm unsure how I feel about this, but you are both adults. And I will respect the decision you've made."

"Thanks, Coach." Those are the only words I can say because my brain has short-circuited, and this is going better than I expected. Not that I expected him to be unreasonable, and I did, and still do, have a lot of positive vibes about all this. But this is going almost too well.

"I just hope you understand what you're risking, both on and off the ice." Coach pauses and then sighs. "Look, Asher, I will not pretend this is easy for me, but that's because I wasn't expecting it. Isla's my daughter, and I want what's best for her. And I do like you as a person on and off the ice and have from the moment you stepped into that rink and stayed with us for a couple of weeks years ago. But if you care about her, you need to prove it to her. I'm more than confident that she can handle herself."

I nod and stop myself before I look like a bobble-head. "She's amazing."

"Don't you think I know that?"

The look on his face and the tone of his voice say it all, and I feel foolish throwing those words out there. I clear my throat, trying to find the right words and not stick my foot in my mouth again. "Of course, Coach. I didn't mean to imply otherwise."

His gaze stays on me for a moment before drifting to the door and landing back on me. "Is she here with you?"

"She is. She didn't want me to do this without support."

"Open the door so that she can come in."

I jump up out of my seat and hurry to the door. With more enthusiasm than necessary, I yank the door open and say, "Hey, Isla, Coach wants to talk to you."

I hold the door open as Isla steps into the office. Coach Johnson rises from his seat, his eyes softening as they land on his daughter. "Isla, come in, sit down."

Isla glances at me with a raised eyebrow, and I give her a reassuring nod. We all sit down in our designated chairs, and I wait for him to speak.

Coach Johnson studies his daughter for a few seconds before he speaks again. "Isla, I want you to know that your happiness is my priority. It always has been and always will be. If dating Asher brings that to you, then I support it wholeheartedly."

The tension in the room lifts as the air in my lungs rushes out. Relief fills my veins, and I almost miss Coach referring to me by my first name instead of my last. Am I traveling through the Twilight Zone?

Isla's hand finds mine just before she replies to her father. "It does, Dad. Asher makes me incredibly happy."

Coach Johnson's eyes dance between us, assessing the

situation in front of him once more. "I can see that. And I respect it." He leans forward, and his gaze once again locks on mine. "But understand this, Bennett. If you hurt her, if you break her heart—"

"You don't need to say the words because I know, Coach. I would never intentionally hurt her because she means everything to me."

Isla squeezes my hand as her father responds. "Good. See that you remember that." He sits back in his leather chair before he continues. "Now, this better not affect your performance on the ice. I expect you to keep your focus and to give 110% at every practice and every game. No distractions."

"Of course, Coach. Hockey is still a top priority for me. I won't let you or our team down."

"Alright then." For a second, I wonder if he's going to say something else, but that thought leaves my head when he speaks up again. "Why don't you both come over for dinner one night next week? We can talk more then, and you can spend time with Molly and Grace."

I glance at Isla before turning back to look at Coach Johnson. "That sounds like a great idea if Isla is cool with it."

"I am," Isla responds.

Coach claps his hands together once and stands up. "Excellent. I'm sure Isla will let you know the details."

Coach Johnson gives us a curt nod and dismisses us from this meeting. As we exit the office, the door closes behind us with a click that sounds much softer than the one I experienced when I first walked in.

Isla speaks first. "That went better than I expected."

"You're telling me, but now we have to face dinner with your parents and sister."

"That'll be a breeze compared to this."

I hope she is right.

37

ISLA

I walk up the steps of my childhood home with Asher standing by my side. It has been days since the meeting with my dad, and I still don't feel mentally prepared for this. I'm not upset about Dad suggesting that we have this dinner, but this also isn't a relaxing experience for me, either.

I glance at Asher, who is putting on a better poker face than I am. He gives me a small smile as his hand finds mine. At least one of us can put up a front like we aren't nervous. "The plan is still to stay here for a while and then head back to your place for the party?"

"That's the plan," he says without hesitation.

"Okay, cool." I pull out my key and open the door. I'm immediately greeted by the smell of something delicious, and my stomach rumbles, confirming what my nose has already picked up on.

"Mom, Dad, we're here," I call out as I cross the threshold.

Asher follows me and shuts the door behind him. As we are taking off our coats, Dad appears from the kitchen, wiping his hands on a dish towel.

"Welcome. Molly is talking to someone on the phone in the living room, and I was just helping her finish dinner," Dad says, opening his arms to hug me.

I stay in his embrace for several seconds before I pull back. We share a small smile as I step out of the way for him to greet my boyfriend.

It's still taking some getting used to referring to Asher as such again.

Speaking of, Asher steps forward, extending his hand to my dad. "Coach Johnson, thank you for having us over."

Dad grasps his hand firmly, giving it a hearty shake. "It's my pleasure. We could all use a delicious home-cooked meal every once in a while. Let's hang up your coats, and then we can head into the dining room."

We quickly hang up our things, and together, we walk into the dining room with Dad leading the way. Asher places his hand on the small of my back, and I can't help but think that the last time we were dating, and he was in my house three years ago, he wouldn't have dared do such a thing.

Oh, how times have changed.

As we enter the dining room, the first thing I notice is that the table is already set. It's a bit more fancy than I was used to growing up, but I appreciate my parents making Asher feel more comfortable. "What are we having for dinner?"

Before Dad can answer, Grace walks in from the kitchen with a glass of wine. She looks at me for a second before her eyes drift to Asher. "Long time no see... to the both of you." She punctuates her comment by taking a sip of her drink.

"It's good to see you again," Asher says as he holds out his for her to shake.

She returns the gesture without hesitation, but before she can respond, I speak up. "You're ridiculous, you know that, right?" I say as Dad shakes his head with a small smile and slips past Grace to walk into the kitchen. Dad is used to how we act around each other, so I'm not surprised he took that as his opportunity to leave.

"I got it honestly if you check out the two people who are the reason why we both walk this planet."

I can't disagree with her there. "Touché."

Grace's lips curl into a smirk as she takes another sip of her wine, and the smell of deliciousness hits my nostrils again. Then, I remember that my question still hasn't been answered. "What are we having for dinner?"

"Lasagna and a salad," my sister says, putting me out of my misery. "Do you guys want anything to drink?" Grace puts her glass on the dining room table, and we follow her lead, selecting where we will also sit.

"I'm going to have water, but I can grab it. Asher, do you want anything?"

"Water works for me too."

I nod and start walking toward the kitchen. I pause for a split second before I turn to look back at my sister. "Don't say anything weird or embarrassing."

She waves me off. "I'm not going to do a thing but sit here and enjoy my wine."

I raise an eyebrow at her response but leave the room without another word. I give Dad a quick smile before he turns his back to me to pull what I now know to be lasagna out of the oven.

"You know, I feel like I should ask you how your classes are going, but we see each other and talk so often that I already know."

That makes me laugh. "That's true, but I appreciate the attempt at small talk."

While I'm getting the waters for Asher and me, I can't help but think that my sister is acting a little strange, not to mention that it's weird that she's even in town, anyway. Because of her work with the San Diego Sharks, an NHL team, her trips back have to be planned unless she's traveling with the team for a game out here.

I debate with myself for a few seconds about whether I'm going to open that can of worms before deciding that I should. "Why is Grace home, anyway?"

Dad glances over at me once the baking pan is resting on the stove. "She took a couple of vacation days and decided to come here to enjoy the long weekend." He turns back to the counter to slice the lasagna.

I stare at my father for a second, wondering if he's going to continue because there's no way that is the whole story. When he doesn't, I say, "There's no way that's the full story."

"She didn't give any more details, so I didn't press."

"And Mom didn't?"

Dad laughs at my quick response because he knows his wife. He understands how she is sometimes, especially when she senses that something is wrong with one of us. "As far as I know, Mom doesn't know anything more than I do. Grace has been super busy, so I'm not surprised that she came back home during her downtime to recharge."

Sounds reasonable enough, but I still don't think it's the full story. A voice draws my attention back to the doorway.

"Okay, but I need to get back to dinner. We can talk tomorrow. Bye," Mom says as she pulls the phone down from her ear. Her eyes land on me as soon as she walks into the kitchen. "Oh, honey, I didn't know you were here!"

"We haven't been here too long," I say as I walk over to give her a hug. She leaves a kiss on my cheek as we're breaking apart. "I was just telling Dad I'm shocked Grace is here."

Mom gives me a look before she responds. "I'm a bit

surprised too, but you know your sister. Regardless, having the whole family together for a meal is nice. It's been too long. How are things going with you?"

"Pretty good," I say, because I don't really have much to complain about at the moment. "Asher's in the dining room with Grace, and I fear I've left him in there for too long with her."

"For his sake or hers?"

"His," Dad and I announce at the same time.

I pick up the glasses of water that I should have brought back to the dining room eons ago, and as I get ready to walk, Mom grabs my elbow softly.

"And things with PCOS are still going well?"

Her concern makes me emotional because I'm grateful for her support through that and all the things she's stood in my corner and helped me take on. "Yes, no complaints."

"Thank goodness," Mom says as she lets my elbow go. "Okay, I'll help Dad bring the food out, and we can eat."

That serves as my dismissal, and I walk back into the dining room. I notice that Grace and Asher are chatting, and neither seems worse for wear.

As I set the glasses of water down on the table, Asher looks up at me and it's easy for me to pick up on what he's telling me. *About time you got back here.* I can only imagine what kind of conversation Grace has roped him into while I was preoccupied with trying to find out more information about her.

"Everything okay in there?" he asks, gesturing toward the kitchen with his head.

"Yeah, just catching up with Mom and Dad," I reply, sliding into the seat beside him. Beneath the table, his hand finds mine, and I squeeze his in response.

Mom and Dad take that opportunity to enter the dining room, carrying the dinner we are about to enjoy. Dad sets a baking dish with lasagna at the center of the table. Mom follows with a big bowl of salad. I'm not a huge fan of salads, but I'm convinced Mom makes some of the best ones ever.

As they take their seats, Dad clears his throat. "Well, it's wonderful to have everyone here tonight. Shall we dig in?"

We all nod and dig into what I know is going to be a delicious feast. Once I serve myself the portion I'm planning on eating, I take a bite, and my eyes shut involuntarily. The layers of flavor have thrown my brain for a loop. It's then I realize how much I've missed this dish—not just because of the nostalgia of us eating it, but because the taste of the tender pasta, the savory meat, and the creamy ricotta reminds me so much of home.

Beside me, Asher reaches for his water glass, and his arm brushes up against mine. I steal a glance at him as he takes a sip. Why is that one of the sexiest things he's done today?

I tear my attention away from him and find Grace pouring herself another glass of wine. I tilt my head and narrow my gaze, and she just gives me a quick shake of her head, as if telling me not to say a word about it.

Between her and Selene, I don't know who's hiding more things from me at this point. Then again, who am I to judge?

"So, Asher," Mom's voice breaks the silence in the room. "How are your mom and sister?"

Asher finishes chewing the food that is in his mouth before he responds. "They're doing well. Things have calmed down over the last couple of weeks, thankfully."

"I'm glad to hear that," Mom says with sincerity. I'm sure she's thinking of when she offered to let Asher stay here so that he had the opportunity to play in the clinic and get more time on the ice before his freshmen year. "Have they been out to see you play this year?"

Asher shakes his head. "No, but I really wish they could. Mom works a lot and Avery's high school schedule is pretty packed."

I glance over at him and stuff some more lasagna into my mouth. An idea is forming of how I might be able to get his family to attend one of the Red Wolves' games. I'll probably need to have my parents involved at least.

The conversation continues, and I'm impressed with Dad's ability to not say anything off the cuff. I don't know if it's because Grace and Mom are here, but if he has any hesitations about Asher being a more prominent feature in my life, he hasn't let those show. My gaze turns to him when he starts laughing, and I realize it's at something Asher said.

Is this a parallel universe? Why am I questioning things when it seems to be working out in my favor?

Instead, I choose to enjoy the fact that my family is getting along with the love of my life, and hopefully, their relationship continues to blossom. I focus on eating again once more, and it's not until I feel a slight stiffness in my legs from sitting too long that I decide to stand up and stretch.

"Do you all want anything else? Maybe dessert?" Mom asks as she watches me from her chair.

"I don't want to speak for Asher, but I'm good."

"Same. I'm so full, and dinner was delicious. Thank you," Asher chimes in as he looks up at me from his seat. I wonder if he's trying to figure out what I'm thinking about doing since dinner is over. "We have to get back to campus soon, anyway."

Because of all this, I almost forgot about the party. I reach for my plate before Mom's voice stops me.

"While I wish you two were staying longer, why don't you go on ahead? Your father and I can handle the cleanup."

"But you guys cooked."

Dad reaches over and grabs my plate so I can't take it into the kitchen. "We have enough people here that we'll have this cleaned up in no time. You kids have fun tonight.

But not too much fun, you hear?" When he says the last part, his eyes are firmly on Asher.

"Yes, Coach," Asher replies.

Grace walks over and hugs me before grabbing her plate and wine glass. Her eyes are slightly glazed over, and I can't help but wonder if she's about to cry. Mom notices immediately and says, "Sweetie, why don't I take those from you, and you head upstairs?"

"I can agree with that plan. I'll see everyone later." Grace gives everyone a quick wave before she jets out of the room.

Mom stares at the space my sister just vacated before she turns back to me. "I'll check on her soon. You guys go on and enjoy your night."

"We will," Asher says for us.

"And Mom, I'll text you and Dad later about something I need to get done."

That makes Mom smile. "I'll look out for it."

I make a note to also text my sister later as Asher and I make our way to the front hall closet to grab our coats. Once we're protected from the weather, we leave the comfort of my childhood home to go back to my car.

It is almost time to let loose.

The drive back to Asher's place is quick and quiet as we both choose to sit in silence versus reliving dinner with my family. I glance at the man sitting next to me and watch as his profile is illuminated by the streetlights we're flying by. The best way I can describe his expression is that he's at peace.

And I love it.

Soon Asher's parking the car and we stroll up to the front porch of his house. Before Asher can put his key into the lock, the door swings open.

"Well, well, look who finally decided to grace us with their presence," Wilder teases as Asher and I cross the threshold.

Asher shakes his head at his roommate. "Blame it on me being fashionably late. You know I like to make an entrance."

I can't help but chuckle at Asher's quick-witted response, all the while rolling my eyes. I place a hand on his chest before turning my head to speak to Wilder. "He couldn't wait to get back here to hop on the mic."

"Is he going to sing about his sorrows after Coach handed him his ass at dinner?" Wilder wiggles his eyebrows as if he's so proud that he came up with that on the fly.

Jade approaches us and pokes Wilder in the shoulder. "Really? Can you at least let them walk in before you start?"

I throw Jade a big smile before I lean over to give her a hug. As I pull back from Jade's embrace, I feel Asher's hand on the small of my back. I glance up at him and watch as the smile on his face grows.

"Come on, let's show them how karaoke should be

done." He takes my hand, intertwining our fingers as he leads me toward the karaoke setup.

We all walk into the living room and find the rest of our group there. Levi and Hailey are cuddled up on the couch laughing at Knox and Blaise, who are having a debate over song choices.

"Isla and I are going first."

I do a double-take and narrow my gaze at my boyfriend. "We are?"

Asher gives me a firm nod and intertwines his fingers with mine. "You're going to do great, and I know the perfect song for us."

He guides me up to the makeshift setup in the living room before selecting the song he wants us to sing. My stomach is threatening to leave my body as I wonder what song he has in mind for us. The debate between Knox and Blaise comes to a halt while Levi, Hailey, Wilder, and Jade all turn their attention to us.

I know what the song is as soon as the first notes play out. I don't need the lyrics that appear on their television screen or any help from our audience. "Rewrite The Stars" by Zac Efron and Zendaya holds a special place in my heart and reminds me of the journey that Asher and I have been on.

As the familiar melody fills the room, I meet Asher's gaze, and I swear the world around us fades away as he begins to sing. My emotions get the best of me as his eyes never stray from mine. I almost forget that he's finished the first verse and the chorus and that it is now time for me to join in.

My voice trembles slightly as I begin to sing. Although I cannot sing, you wouldn't be able to tell that by watching Asher. His gaze never leaves mine as I continue the song, and it's almost as if he's staring right into my soul. When we begin the chorus together, goosebumps appear on my skin because I can see and hear every ounce of love that he has for me in his eyes and in his voice.

As the final notes of the song fade away, applause breaks out around us. Asher pulls me close, his forehead resting against mine as we catch our breath. He gives me a kiss on the lips.

"I love you, Isla," he murmurs, his words a secret meant only for me.

"I love you too, Asher," I whisper back.

We take the moment for ourselves before Asher turns to everyone and says, "I'm not done. It's time for 'Don't Stop Believin''."

Wilder groans. "He's never going to let the rest of us get up there and sing. I'm grabbing another beer."

The whole room erupts into laughter, and I've never felt happier or more invincible. Asher has given me so much in the short period of time we've been back together. I know that whatever challenges lie ahead, we'll face them together.

Always.

For now though, I can't wait to share the surprise I'm planning for him.

38

ASHER

There are so many things that I'm grateful for, but I can't list them. However, being back on the ice is definitely one of those things.

The energy in the arena is on fire, and I swear I can hear the roar of the fans echoing on every surface of this building. This game has been insane, and while we are down by a goal, there's a sense of peace and calm that surrounds me even in the chaos.

I know we're going to score again. We're going to win.

And the most important thing of all? I'm happy. I'm so fucking happy, even in this stressful situation, that I could break out and dance on the ice in front of everyone.

This isn't the time for that, but it's something I'm willing to do. But for now, I need to focus on helping our team win this game even though, in my mind, we've already won.

As I'm waiting for the whistle to blow and the puck to drop, something catches my eye. I do a double take because right behind the bench, I see my mom and Avery. They are here. My sister's holding a homemade sign that says "Go Asher! You're #1 in Our Hearts!" Mom is smiling, her hands clasped in front of her as if she'd just finished clapping.

What in the world? Didn't Mom have to work? Avery probably has a basketball game this evening, right?

I turn my attention back to the job I need to do until this game is over, but I can't deny that I'm perplexed. I still might have a little time before there's any action on the ice, so I shoot them another quick glance and give them a small wave, acknowledging that I see them and know they are here. A grin crosses my face as my sister bounces up and down, waving back like her life depends on it. Apparently, even though she's a teenager, she's not too cool to do that. Mom sends me two thumbs-ups, which she used to do when she attended my games as a little kid.

I remember playing in a small-town hockey league, and during my first big game, I was nervous as hell. Just before I scored my first goal, Mom gave me a thumbs-up, a shot of reassurance that everything was going to be fine. I was going to do great. When the puck hit the net, I looked up into the stands and saw my mom and sister cheering for me as loud as they could.

The memory starts up another round of adrenaline that feels as if it's injected straight into my veins. If I wasn't determined moments ago, seeing them would have given me the extra push I needed to prepare for the battle about to ensue.

I take a deep breath and get back into position. Seconds later, the puck drops, and we're back in action.

There is some back and forth, but the instant my stick connects with the puck, everything in my world revolves around this black piece of rubber. The roar of the crowd fades because I'm dialed in on the task at hand. I dodge and fake out one of our opponents. I know Coach likes the move I just pulled.

As I approach the net, something in my peripheral vision draws my attention. I know the defenders are closing in on me, but all I can do is think smart and stick to the plan. I'm going to carry out the mission I accepted as soon as I laced up my skates.

Help the Red Wolves win this game.

The goalie crouches as I get within shooting range, and I can see the look in his eyes. He's ready to stop me from scoring at all costs. His eyes are locked on me, and I can see the calculations running through his mind. He's trying to predict my next move, but I won't let him. I've got a few tricks up my sleeve.

With a flick of my wrist, I send the puck flying. I watch as it sails toward the top corner of the net. The goalie lunges, his glove stretching out in a desperate attempt to catch it or knock it away. For a heart-stopping moment, I doubt whether what I've done is enough for us to add another point to the scoreboard.

But then, the puck slips past his glove and rattles the netting with a satisfying thud. For a split second, it feels as if everyone goes silent just before the crowd erupts into the loudest roar I might have ever heard. I throw my arms up, my heart slamming in my chest because I tied the game.

"Good fucking job, Bennett!" I hear, but the blood rushing in my ears makes it hard to tell who said it.

As we celebrate, my eyes land on the blonde beauty with her camera pulled up to her face, blocking some of the features I stare at when we are together. When she finishes getting her shots, she lowers the camera and gives me a small wave. I blow her a quick kiss, and then something clicks.

Did Isla make sure that Mom and Avery could be in attendance today? She and her family are the only ones I spoke to recently about them and how they haven't been to one of my games in a while, so that would make sense. Speaking of which, my gaze lands on them, and I find them on their feet once more, jumping up and down. I feel invincible, like I can take on the world, and no one can stop me.

But this is far from over. We still need to win.

As I line up for the face-off, I take several deep breaths, slowing my racing thoughts to regain my earlier calm. I remind myself of everything we've gone over in practice, and I'm confident that Levi and Knox know exactly what to do. We've got this, and we're going to finish what we started. I have to concentrate because the clock is running out and only a couple of minutes remain.

The puck drops, and it's a scramble. Levi fights for control, pushing against the opposing center, sticks clashing. The puck slips loose, and Knox is scooping it up. He maneuvers around a defender, moving it up the ice, and I follow close, my legs burning, adrenaline pushing me forward. The seconds are ticking down, and we need this. Right now.

Knox passes to Levi, who, as the center, skates up along the right boards, dodging an opponent who tries to pin him. Levi's agility makes him hard to catch, and he takes full advantage of it, weaving through the defense. He spots Blaise coming up on the other side and sends a hard pass across the ice.

I take the puck from Blaise and charge toward the net once more. When I see Knox is open, I pass the puck to him, hoping he can finish the play. He fakes a shot to throw the goalie off-balance. The goalie falls for it, lunging to the side. Knox wastes no time and sends the puck flying toward the opposite corner of the net.

The goalie stretches to recover, but it's too late. The puck hits the back of the net, and the red light flashes. And then, chaos erupts. The crowd roars louder than before, and I yell too. I throw my arms up as the team and

I rush toward Knox. I reach him first, slapping his helmet and screaming in his ear.

We did it. We actually did it.

But this feeling of winning is only part of it. As I look back toward the stands, I spot my family first before my eyes land on Isla. She keeps her camera focused on us, capturing this moment. Not even the camera can block the grin that's on her face.

And I can't wait to have her in my arms.

39

ISLA

Is this real life or a fantasy?

I repeat the question over and over again as I try my best to stay focused on my job. I'm still in shock that the Red Wolves won the game, but I shouldn't be. The team is amazing, and I'm so happy that I'm able to do my part as a member of this organization. In fact, I think I've cemented my place with the hockey team because the video project that Bailey gave me is a huge success and she wants me to do more of them, but I can't say I'm not elated that this one is all finished now.

But also, holy shit, what was that game?

I still can't process it, but I'm so happy I could capture the images I shot. Because seriously, this game feels like one for the history books.

After I lower my camera, I catch Asher's eye while he's still on the ice. I shout, "Congratulations!" but I'm pretty sure he can't hear me. I'm not sure I've ever heard the noise in the arena be this loud. That includes the times I used to come and watch the Red Wolves before college.

For a moment, it seems like Asher is just looking at me, but then he skates, putting one foot in front of the other. It takes a couple of seconds for me to realize he's skating toward me.

Before I can fully register what's happening, he steps off the ice through the open gate, his skates crunching slightly against the rubber mats as he approaches me. He stops in front of me, his eyes locking with mine.

Confusion and excitement swirl in my brain as I watch what's unfolding. Why is he coming here? He should be celebrating with his teammates, not coming my way.

His pace slows because he doesn't have blade guards on his skates as he walks across the rubber mats. When he reaches me, I put down my camera and manage to close my mouth. I lift my head, struggling more than usual because our height difference is even greater when he's in his skates.

He reaches out, his gloved hand brushing against my cheek. I go back to my musing about whether this moment is a dream I'm about to wake up from.

"Isla," he says, "I couldn't have done this without you."

I blink once and then twice. I swear my brain still hasn't caught up with everything that has happened. "Me? But I did nothing."

A smile tugs at the corner of his mouth. "Just having

you in my life again has changed everything for me in the most positive way. That is more than I could ever thank you for."

Tears form in the corners of my eyes, and I do my best to hold it together. "I could say the same about you."

"I love you more than anything else in this entire world."

"And I love you even more than that."

His stare holds mine, and there's no way I could look away even if I wanted to. There's an intensity in his green eyes that reminds me of the determination he showed throughout the whole game. The roar of the crowd fades into the background, and for a moment, it's just us, and the rest of the world ceases to exist.

I instinctively lean into his glove-covered hand because it's currently our only physical connection. But that doesn't last for long.

We close the remaining distance between us, and my eyes drift closed as his lips meet mine. As cliché as it sounds, I swear fireworks go off behind my eyelids. I melt into him and almost forget where we are as my hands land on his shoulder pads as he pulls me closer. In this moment, nothing else matters. Not the game nor the cheering crowd that now sounds like a murmur in the background. All that exists is the feel of his lips against mine and the unshakable knowledge that this is exactly where we're meant to be.

The crowd's reaction barely registers at first, but when

I hear more cheers, it triggers something in my brain that it might be toward us. When we break apart, I come back to reality, and I realize what just happened. Did we just kiss in public for everyone to see?

I glance toward the bench, catching Dad's expression. He looks shocked, leaning more toward stunned. But then he gives me a small smile. The last thing he probably wants to see is his daughter kissing one of his players, but it seems as if he's accepting of what he just witnessed.

I look back at Asher and say, "Well, that was a surprise."

He tosses a grin back at me. "Yeah, it was." He briefly looks over into the stands before looking back at me. "Speaking of surprises, did you invite my mom and Avery to the game?"

I nod because the jig is up, and I'm so happy that my plan worked out. "You wanted them here, and it's something I wanted to do for you. It took a little maneuvering, but we made it happen."

"Asher!"

Both he and I turn to see who called his name. We find his mom and sister making their way toward us. I glance up at Asher and watch his face light up. I can't help but smile because I know how much all of this means to him.

Once they reach us, Avery launches herself into Asher's arms, nearly knocking him off balance. He laughs as he catches her easily, but I'm slightly concerned they both might fall down, given that he's still in his skates.

"You were amazing out there!" Avery exclaims as she playfully hits him.

"Thanks," he replies as he puts her down. "I can't believe you're here."

Asher's mom, Clara, steps forward, and I can see the tears in her eyes. I'm convinced that she's going to be the one who makes me cry. She pulls Asher into her arms, and a tear slips from my eye at that beautiful moment.

"I'm so proud of you, sweetheart," she whispers. "You played your heart out."

Asher hugs her back and buries his face in her shoulder. I swear I can see the tension leaving his body, even if it is just for this moment.

When they pull apart, Clara's gaze falls on me. She smiles warmly and opens her arms to hug me too. I'm this close to full-on sobbing as I step into her arms, and she says in my ear, "Isla, thank you for making this happen and for being there for him. This means the world to us, and he's happier than I've ever seen him. I know it's because of you."

When we pull apart, I do my best to swallow the lump that has formed in my throat. "It was my pleasure. I know how much Asher wanted you both here, and I'm happy that we could make his wish a reality."

Asher reaches out to me and pulls me into his side. He bends down and says, "This is everything. Thank you, sunshine," before placing a quick kiss on my hair.

Avery's eyes dart between us, a knowing smile playing on her lips. "So, when's the wedding?"

Heat rushes to my cheeks as Asher chuckles softly beside me. "One step at a time, Avery," he says, his tone gentle but firm.

At least his reaction is calm, cool, and collected because it takes every ounce of control I have to keep my reaction down to just blushing.

"Why don't we all grab a bite to eat? I'm sure Asher's starving after that game." We are saved by Clara's quick thinking.

Asher responds this time. "That sounds perfect, Mom. My treat."

Although I don't know her well, I can tell that Clara is about to tell Asher that he doesn't have to pay, but I speak before she can get the words out. "It might take a bit, but I can see if my parents would like to come too?" I offer without giving it too much thought.

"That's a great idea! I've met your father several times, but haven't been introduced to your mother," says Clara.

That needs to be rectified. I pull out my phone to contact my mom. "We can try to fix that tonight."

"I should probably get to the locker room," Asher interrupts us.

"Oh yes, go, go! I'll bring your family down to the tunnel, where we can meet up with you," I reply.

Asher gives me a quick kiss and waves goodbye to Clara and Avery before he makes his way back to the ice.

I text my mom, hoping she and Dad are available to join us. Moments later, my phone buzzes with a response from Mom. "She said they'd love to come," I announce.

It takes a little while for Asher and Dad to wrap up their duties, but once we are at the Riverstone Grill, dinner goes well. Everyone chats with one another in an effort to get to know each other. I wish Grace could have been here, but she's back in California, dealing with something she won't tell me about. I swear she's gone through all the stages of grief, but I wish she would let us in so that we can better help her. We'll have to see if we can schedule some time for everyone to get together around the holidays or something.

I can't believe I'm already thinking of that.

Once dinner is over, Asher and I drive back to his house, where we already know the guys are throwing another banger. The main floor of the home is mostly silent, but when I think he is going to hit the stairs to head up to his room, Asher seems to have another plan up his sleeve.

"There's something I need to grab from the kitchen. I'll meet you upstairs, and I want you completely naked, lying on my bed, waiting for me," he says.

I'm left stunned, trying to process his words. Did he just say what I think he just said? Did that kiss we shared at the arena affect him as much as it had me ready to melt into a puddle on the floor?

Shit.

It is only going to take him a second to come back, I assume, so I dart up the stairs, enter his room, and slam the door shut a little louder than I intended due to my excitement. I quickly toe off my sneakers and remove my Crestwood hoodie and jeans. I still my movements for a second to see if I can hear Asher on the stairs. When I don't hear anything that resembles footsteps, I remove my underwear and ungracefully plop down on the bed. I'm grateful he isn't in the room to witness that because I would be embarrassed by how eager I am.

How did he want me to lay? Did he want me to—

The door opens, forcing any thoughts from my mind. Asher steps into the room, his eyes immediately finding mine. He makes sure to close and lock the door behind him. That's when I notice he's holding his hand behind his back. It's clear that he's hiding something. But what it is, I have no idea, though I assume I will find out shortly.

"You followed my instructions perfectly," he says. His voice is lower than normal as he drinks all of me in.

I feel exposed under his scrutiny, but there's a thrill there as well. He moves closer, and with every step he takes, I swear the pounding in my ears gets louder. When he reaches the edge of the bed, he reveals what he's been hiding: a can of Reddi-Whip.

"I wanted to have a little fun with two of my favorite things," Asher says. He tosses the container on the bed, and it's followed by a condom before he begins getting undressed.

"Two of your favorite things?" I whisper.

"You and dessert, of course."

"Not gonna lie, I expected you to say hockey."

He chuckles as he kneels on the bed, completely naked. The mattress dips under his weight and I can tell he knows exactly the effect he is having on me when he slowly and deliberately shakes the can of whipped cream.

"Now, Isla, I'm going to trace every line of your body. And then..." He pauses for a second, leaving me hanging off of his every word. "I'm going to savor every last bit."

The nozzle of the can hovers over my collarbone, and goosebumps appear along my skin in anticipation. The first touch of the cold cream against my body makes me gasp. Asher's steady hand moves lower, leaving a delicate trail of white across my chest, paying special attention to my breasts.

I close my eyes because all of this feels like too much. The coldness from the whipped cream, the heat radiating from my body and from Asher, plus the tension in the room.

"Open your eyes, sunshine," Asher commands softly. "I want you to watch me."

I obey, meeting his gaze. The intensity in his eyes makes me shiver, but I don't close my eyes. I'm too entranced now by the scene in front of me. Asher lowers his head and his tongue darts out, tasting the sweetness on my collarbone.

"Delicious," he murmurs against my skin, the vibration of his voice sending tremors through my body.

I fight to keep my eyes open as he slowly works his way down my body. Each lick and nibble stokes the fire within me. My hands clench the comforter under my fingertips; every sensation leaving me more desperate for something to hold onto.

His lips move lower, and I arch my back involuntarily. The room feels impossibly hot now, contrasting against the coolness of the cream on my skin. Asher's mouth has made its way to my stomach, and I shudder because I know where he's going next.

He looks up at me and says, "Patience, baby. We're just getting started."

I swear, before he even finishes his sentence, he's pressing the nozzle, squirting cream along my hip bone. His tongue soon follows, and I'm struggling to keep up with all of the sensations coursing through my body. When he moves down toward my pussy, I freeze. The feel of his stubble on my inner thighs is almost too much to bear.

"Please," I let out. The word falls out almost involuntarily.

Asher looks up at me with a wicked grin. "Please what, sunshine?"

I bite my lip, torn between desire and embarrassment. Do I really want to say what I want him to do with me out loud? But the hunger in his gaze makes me feel as if I can take over the world. "Please taste me. Eat me, fuck me. I don't care; I just need more of you."

"Those are the sweetest words you've ever said to me."

Without breaking eye contact, he lowers his head and drags his tongue along my folds. The sensation is electric. I cry out, and before I know it, my hands are in Asher's hair, anchoring him to me. He hooks his arms under my thighs and pulls me closer. That gives him more of an opportunity to devour me, and I'm not complaining.

Waves of pleasure crash over me as he works me with his mouth. The room fills with the sounds of my breathless moans and gasps. I hear a few groans from him too, as if what he's doing to me is bringing him just as much pleasure. My hips begin to move all on their own, grinding against his face as he continues his relentless assault on my senses.

The tension within my body grows, and I'm dancing on the edge. I'm so close to falling apart completely. Asher must sense it because he doubles down, focusing his attention on my clit with quick, firm strokes of his tongue.

"Oh, fucking fuck. Asher," I moan, my voice barely recognizable to my own ears. "I'm so close."

He hums against me in response, and the vibrations send shockwaves through my entire body. My back arches off the bed as the first waves of my orgasm hit. Asher doesn't let up, making sure to work me through every tremor and the aftershocks.

Holy. Hell.

When he finally pulls away, his chin is glistening. My eyes finally shut as I try to recover. I can feel him crawl back up my body, leaving a trail of kisses in his wake.

"You taste so good, sunshine," he murmurs against my neck, his breath dancing along my skin. His voice is rough with desire, and it does something to me. Something I can't quite describe.

I reach for him, running my hands down his muscled back. "Now it's my turn, hot-shot."

With his help, I flip us over and position myself so I'm straddling his hips. His eyes darken as he takes me in, using the opportunity to put his hands on my thighs. I reach over and grab the can of whipped cream. Asher's eyes follow my every move, and I notice that his chest begins rising and falling rapidly.

I trace a creamy line down his chest, all the way to his cock. I lean over and use my tongue to lick up every last bit of the treat before me. Asher's breathing grows more rapid as I work my way lower. I love the feel of his muscles tensing under my touch. When I reach his cock, I stop to watch him, looking up at him from where I am. His eyes meet mine as his hips twitch, obviously wanting more contact.

"Isla," he groans.

I put him out of his misery when I lick his dick. Asher's head falls back against the pillow as a strangled moan escapes his lips. I can tell it's taking everything for him to maintain control and it's only a matter of time before he'll snap.

Encouraged, I take him into my mouth, and a rush of air leaves his body. His hands find their way into my hair as I set a steady rhythm. I decide to alternate between long, languid strokes and quick, teasing flicks of my tongue.

"Fuck, Isla," he pants.

His words urge me to do more, so I double my efforts, taking him deeper, hollowing my cheeks as I suck. A couple of minutes later, he's finally able to form more words.

"If you keep that up, I'm not going to last."

When I need to take a quick breath, I move my mouth and his cock falls past my lips with a wet pop. "That's kind of the point, Bennett."

In one fluid motion, he sits up and pulls me to him just before he crushes his lips against mine. The kiss is all heat and desperation, which suits us right now.

When we break apart, both gasping for air, Asher reaches for the condom he threw on the bed earlier. "I need to be inside you," he growls, fumbling with the wrapper.

I take the condom from his trembling hands and tear it open with my teeth. Our eyes lock as I roll it onto his length. As I position myself above him, his hands grip my hips as if he wants to throw me down on his cock. Part of me wishes he would.

Slowly, I lower myself onto him. My eyes slam shut, and I can't help the moan that escapes my lips. The way he stretches me is the best feeling I've ever experienced. I pause as I take in the way we fit together, not to mention the pressure of Asher's fingers digging into my hips.

"Isla," he whispers. "You feel incredible."

And I feel incredible, especially being the one in control this time. My eyes open and my gaze meets his. I begin to move, setting a slow, torturous pace. I watch as the man underneath me clenches his jaw as he fights for control.

"Is this what you want?" I say, rolling my hips in a way that makes us both gasp.

His response is a groan that sounds as if it comes from deep within his soul, and it's music to my ears. His hands leave my hips and slide up my sides. When they reach my breasts, he cups them gently as his thumbs brush over my nipples.

I increase my pace because I know it's what we both want. The room is filled with the sounds of our heavy breathing and our bodies coming together. Sweat starts to form on Asher's forehead, and I wonder if it's from the workout I'm giving him or because he's doing everything in his power to let me control our movements.

"Isla," he says, sounding breathless. "You're driving me crazy."

I smile. "Good," I whisper against his ear before nipping at the lobe.

Suddenly, Asher's hands are on my hips again, and he's thrusting up to meet me. The change in angle has me seeing stars, and I cry out.

"That's it, baby," he growls. "Let me hear you."

I'm close, so close, and from the way Asher's movements are becoming erratic, I know he is too.

"Asher," I moan, "I'm going to—"

"Me too," he grits out. "Come for me, sunshine. Let go."

His words push me over the edge. My body shudders as I reach my climax. I scream out Asher's name, and I know for a fact the rest of the guys in the house have heard me, but I truly don't care. All that matters is that I'm riding out my release on my boyfriend's cock. He follows right behind me, and I collapse onto his chest. As a result, he slips out of me, and I immediately miss the connection. He must sense this because he closes his arms around me, and for a moment, we're both still. It's hard trying to come back to reality after that.

I nuzzle into the crook of Asher's neck, breathing him in. His skin is damp and salty against my lips.

"That was..." Asher trails off as if he can't figure out what he's trying to say.

"Yeah," I agree, unable to find the right words myself.

His fingers trace lazy patterns on my back, sending pleasant shivers down my spine. I feel completely at peace in his embrace. The world outside this room seems distant and unimportant. But I do know that we have a party we need to get ready for and that we both are sticky.

"We need to shower after all of... this." I somewhat gesture to our bodies, but it's half-assed.

Asher laughs at me. "You're right. You left some clothes over here that I washed, so hopefully they are comfortable enough for you to wear to the party. Unless you want to run back to your room really quick?"

I rise up so that I could look him in the eye. "You did my laundry? A man after my own heart. I'm sure whatever I left here is fine."

It takes a few more minutes, but we manage to gather the clothes we want to wear tonight, and once Asher confirms the hallway is clear, we sprint into the bathroom to take a shower. It takes a little longer for us to get out of the shower because of... the sex we just had, but once we are both clean, dry, and dressed, I open the door. As I walk out of the bathroom with Asher following behind me, I hear another door creak open down the hallway.

I glance to my left and my mouth almost drops to the floor. I see Selene sneaking out of what I'm assuming is another bedroom, and I think it's Knox's. Her cheeks are bright pink, her hair slightly disheveled, and she's wearing a Crestwood Red Wolves hoodie that's clearly not hers. My eyes widen as everything about the scene in front of me clicks into place.

Selene freezes when she sees me, but I can tell she's trying to mask her anger. "Oh, um... Isla! Asher!" she stammers, clearly flustered. "How are you? How was the game?"

"Fine...but what are you doing here?"

"I was just... helping Knox... with something. But I'm leaving now."

I raise an eyebrow. "Right. Helping. But why do you look pissed?"

Asher places an arm around my waist, and when I look over at him, his expression mirrors mine. We are obviously on the same page and know what this is about.

Before she can respond to my comment, Knox's voice calls from inside, "Selene, did you forget something?"

Selene's face turns a deeper shade of red. "Fuck you," she mumbles before she waves at us awkwardly and practically runs down the hallway.

"Wait—"

She cuts me off. "I need to calm down. I'll call you later, okay?"

I slowly nod my head as I watch her disappear. This is bonkers, and I'm completely thrown by what I just witnessed. Part of me wants to chase after Selene to find out what's up, but if she truly wanted to talk to me right now, she would have stayed or tried to find some place where we could talk alone without Asher or Knox.

Instead, I turn to my boyfriend and say, "I'm going to let her cool off, but I need to text her later because what the hell was that?"

Asher shrugs. "Your guess is as good as mine."

EPILOGUE
ISLA

Four Years Later

The bright California sun beats down on me as I leave our new house with my camera. I snap a couple of photos before I begin walking across our property. How is this my life right now?

Moving to San Diego was a leap of faith, but somehow, everything has fallen into place. Asher's with the Sharks, and I've found my stride in my photography career. It's funny how life has brought us here. We have gone from dating and breaking up when I was a senior in high school to getting back together after I transferred to Crestwood University. Then, we survived being long-distance while he chased his hockey dreams, and I focused on finishing school and building my portfolio.

We've come a long way. And now, here we are,

surrounded by the beauty of the coast, with everything we dreamed of becoming reality.

I reach my brand-new studio, but don't step inside. Instead, I pause for a moment to take in this space that we've built. This building is my protective space. The enormous windows let in all the sunlight, and I have lined some of the walls with memories I've captured over the years. Every photo has a story, each frame a chapter in the book that is our lives. And to think, there are so many more pages that need to be filled.

"Isla! Are you here yet?"

Asher's voice cuts through my thoughts, and I can't help but laugh. It is finally time for me to join him inside.

As I step across the threshold, Asher wraps his arms around me, pulling me back into his chest. I'll never get tired of this feeling of being loved and the passion that we share with one another. I lean back into his chest, and we stand there in silence for a couple of minutes.

"Just admiring the view," I whisper, looking into his green eyes.

"The view is pretty spectacular," he agrees, but his eyes never leave my face. "But it pales in comparison to you."

I allow a giggle to fall from my lips, and I know a blush is coming right behind it. Even after all this time, Asher's compliments still have the power to make my heart race. He makes me feel cherished, like the most precious thing in his world.

And deep down, I know that's because I am.

Gently, he turns me around in his arms so we're facing each other. His hands come up to cradle my face, his thumbs brushing softly over my cheekbones. I close my eyes, leaning into his touch. This brings me back to my junior year at Crestwood when he kissed me in front of an arena full of people after he helped the Red Wolves secure a tremendous victory.

The memory of that kiss and that moment makes me shiver from the thrill of it all. It was another moment that was a stepping stone in the journey that led us here. And now we can enjoy this life we've built together.

"Welcome home, sunshine."

I smile up at him. "What do you mean? You are my home."

Asher puts his index finger under my chin to tilt my head up. "Now who's saying all the sweet nothings?"

"You've inspired me greatly, I guess."

A knowing grin spreads across his face as he leans in. The moment his lips touch mine, I forget about everything else. His kiss is soft at first, but gradually, the intensity builds. I find myself clinging to him as I pull him closer, needing to feel every inch of him pressed against me.

When we finally break apart, we are both breathing heavily. I rest my forehead against his chest. The steady rhythm of his heartbeat is just another source of comfort for me, but there's a question I've been dying to ask him.

"Why did you want me to meet you out here?"

He gives me a playful smile as he points to something behind me. "I thought we'd celebrate your new studio by hanging this up. It deserves a spot."

I turn to look at where he's directing my attention and shake my head. "Asher, that's a picture of you. You just want to see your face on the wall."

He winks just before he walks over to grab the frame and come back toward me. "That's what makes it fun, Mrs. Bennett. Besides, it's my favorite. Remember that day? You made me run back and forth on the beach just to get the perfect shot."

I roll my eyes but take the frame, the memory bringing a smile to my face. "You were such a good sport about it. Not to mention that you looked pretty great in those shots, if I do say so myself."

Asher laughs. "Pretty sure you just like bossing me around."

He's not wrong there. I find a spot on the wall where the photo would fit perfectly. "Maybe a little," I tease. "But I love that you are always willing to help me, even back then. Remember when I wanted some shots that weren't sports-related, and you convinced half the Red Wolves to model for me?"

He chuckles, stepping behind me to help hang the frame. "How could I forget? None of them knew what they were doing, but you made us all look good. Even Coach joined in."

I shake my head at the memory. "I think that was more him helping out because he's my dad versus my photography skills."

"Nah, it was all about your talent and skills."

I let him have the last word because the photo frame is in place. I shift my body so that I'm facing Asher once more. My hands come up to rest on his chest as his arms find their way to my waist. "Well, whatever the reason, I'm grateful for all the support. From you, from the Red Wolves alumni, from my family. It means everything to me."

"You deserve it, Isla. You've worked so hard for this." His voice is soft enough that his just tone is bringing a tear to my eye. "I'm so proud of you."

I tilt my head back to meet his gaze. "And I couldn't have done it without you, Bennett. You've been my rock through everything."

"And you've been mine, sunshine." I chuckle when he kisses me again before he continues, "We make a pretty good team, you and me."

"The absolute best."

IF YOU WOULD LIKE to read a bonus scene featuring Isla and Asher, you can grab it here.

Selene and Knox's story will be the next book in this series.

ACKNOWLEDGMENTS

To say that this entire experience has been a whirlwind is an understatement. I didn't expect this book to take almost eight months to complete, but life hit me hard. While I could focus on how bad things were, I wouldn't because this dream of a book wouldn't have come to be.

TK and CB, I'm truly grateful for your friendship and thank you so much for holding my hand through not just writing this book, but in my personal life too.

Andra, you've hit it out of the park once again. Thank you for creating this because there's no other way I would have imagined Isla and Asher.

Ellie, thank you for not getting annoyed when I blew past deadlines because my life was a hot mess. Thank you for all the work you've done with promoting this book and I can't wait for our next project.

Chrisandra and Elizabeth, I can't thank you all enough for jumping on this project and for being so patient with me when things got rough over these last few months. Your hard work is immensely appreciated, thank you.

Kim, Sarah, and Samantha (and her boyfriend), thank

you so much for your thoughtful comments about the very ROUGH draft of this book. You all are rock stars and made this process so much easier.

And I can't not thank every single reader for picking up this book. You taking time out of your day to read my words means the world.

Thank you.

ABOUT THE AUTHOR

Emery Paige is a dreamer, a word crafter, and a wine lover. She has been a writer and reader for as long as she can remember. Being able to call herself a romance author is a dream come true.

When she's not pouring her soul into her next romance, Emery can be found indulging in her love for music or watching YouTube, where she enjoys everything from travel vlogs to fashion and cooking.

If you would like to keep in contact with her, please visit her website (www.emerypaigebooks.com) or sign up for her newsletter to receive the latest information about her and her books.

She's also on Instagram and TikTok.

Printed in Great Britain
by Amazon